The
Phoenix

The Phoenix

Ruth Sims

THE WRITERS' COLLECTIVE   Cranston, Rhode Island

Independent Books for Independent Readers

THE PHOENIX
© 2005 RUTH SIMS.

Cover Art and Design:Samantha Wall
Interior Design: MyLinda Butterworth

ISBN 1-932133-40-2
Printed in the United States of America
10 9 8 7 6 5 4 3 2 1

With the exception of Minnie and Harrison Fiske, Ellen Terry, Henry Irving, Oscar Wilde, Charles Frohman, Abraham Erlanger, W. T. Stead, and Ava Astor, all of whom play supporting or minor roles, all characters featured in this book are completely the product of the author's imagination and are not intended to representative any real person, living or dead. With the exceptions of the activities of the Theatre Trust, and stage appearances by Minnie Fiske, Ellen Terry, and Henry Irving, all events are completely the product of the author's imagination.

Library of Congress Cataloging-in-Publication Data

Sims, Ruth, 1939-
  The phoenix / Ruth Sims.
    p. cm.
  ISBN 1-932133-40-2 (TP : alk. paper)
  1. Americans—England—Fiction. 2. London (England)—Fiction.
3. Gay men—Fiction. I. Title.
  PS3619.I566 P48 203
  813'.6—dc21
                                    2002155413

THE WRITERS' COLLECTIVE ✦ Cranston, Rhode Island

Dedicated To

My Family
Who would prefer that I go into a more respectable line of
work like robbing banks or swindling the elderly.

My Friends
Tim and Dann, whose life together is an inspiration.

Ruth S. and Mary N. kindred spirits and fellow writers

Lisa Grant, Our Lady of Chutzpah, who dragged me kicking
and screaming into the 21st Century.

1

London, 1882

Michael turned anxious brown eyes to his twin, and said in an edgy voice, "He'll be here today."

Jack Rourke neither answered nor acknowledged his brother's spoken fear. He had no time to worry whether the old man was returning. He was too busy searching for an easy-to-pick pocket in the crowd boarding the Margate steamer.

Behind the thicket of curly blond hair, Jack's dark eyes were those of a man beset by devils, though he was not quite fourteen. Beyond and around the two boys, families and their baggage streamed toward the huffing steamer boats that would take them out of London on holiday. In front of Jack, a man's coat pocket gaped as he bent to pick up a caterwauling child. Jack expertly removed the man's purse and slipped it to his motionless brother. Then Jack bumped the man and ran.

The man shouted, "Thief! Thief! Stop him! Stop him! Thief!" A dozen men gave chase, but the fleet footed Jack ducked into alleys, jumped fences, ran through a dirty tavern, and left them behind. Michael passed unnoticed through the holiday crowd, the purse inside his shirt, heavy against his thin body. When he reached their hideaway, an abandoned bottle shop, Jack was already there.

Michael handed him the purse and sat down on one of the rickety upturned crates. Jack paused in opening the purse, and glanced at the smaller, frailer version of himself. Michael was paler than usual. "What's wrong?" he asked.

"I thought I saw him."

"Well, you was wrong," Jack said. "The old bastard wouldn't have been down there. He ain't supposed to come back for another week."

"I know. But he's coming today, Jack. I know he is."

Jack knew too, though he'd eat a rat before he'd admit it. He knew the same way Michael did. Whenever Mum got a letter saying he was coming home things got bad. She drank more gin, hit them with both her voice and her hands, and paced the floor. A dozen times a day she stepped outside to peer down the narrow, filthy cobbled street.

"Bugger the old man," Jack muttered, and shut him out of his mind. In a cracked brown jar hidden beneath a warped floorboard was every shilling they'd found, earned, or that Jack had stolen. When today's swag was added and the jar hidden again, Jack sat down beside Michael.

"We'll have enough money to leave here real soon, Michael. We ain't never gonna have to see that old sod again. God, I hate him!"

Michael's forehead wrinkled. "You oughtn't say that, Jack. The missionary man says we must forgive and turn the other cheek to our enemies."

"He likely says we oughtn't steal too, so what do you think he'd say if he saw you nip off with the money today, hey?" Seeing the hurt in his brother's eyes, Jack mumbled, "I didn't mean it."

"Jack, I don't like stealing," Michael said, not for the first time. "Can't we stop?"

"Not till we got all we need."

"Maybe...maybe things'll be better this time when he's home."

"Maybe I'll fly." Jack rubbed the crooked little finger on his right hand. The last time the old man was home he'd bent it backward until it broke with the sound of a stick cracking. It ached most all the time. There'd be new aches, and new bloody welts from the strap before the old sod left again.

Jack got up and rumpled the dirty blond hair that matched his own. "Are you rested? Let's race." It was an unequal contest. He was laughing and panting upon the sagging step of the sooty crumbling tenement that leaned against its neighbor when Michael ran up and flopped down beside him.

"Someday I'll be bigger and faster than you," said Michael, without much hope.

Jack grinned. "I'm twenty minutes older. You'll never catch up." Jack waved to his two friends, Toad and Spitter. Toad swung something as he walked. "What you got?" Jack asked.

"Dead cat. What's left of it. Gonna pitch it at the first copper I see." Toad chortled and held the sunken-eyed, maggoty object at arm's length. Jack laughed. Michael cringed. Toad said, "There's your old man. I ain't sticking around." He and Spitter disappeared into an alley.

Jack stiffened at the sight of a brawny man, well over six feet tall, who trudged toward them with a sailor's rolling gait, a seaman's bag over one shoulder, brass buttons glinting. Jack wasn't surprised when his friends ran away. Even grown men stayed out of Tom Rourke's way. And nobody interfered when he beat his wife and sons.

Jack scrambled to his feet. "I'm going away for a little while."

"Don't go, Jack," Michael begged, clutching his sleeve. "I don't want to be the only one here."

"Oh, you know he's always nice to start with."

"Then why go?"

"Because I don't want to have to look at him." He frowned and looked up, as if he could see over the roofs to another life. "Let's run away, Michael. Right this minute."

"We can't leave Mum alone with him."

Jack bit his lip to keep from saying what he knew, that she'd leave them quick enough if she had anyplace to go. Just yesterday he'd heard her say to her friend Lucy, "If I knew for sure who bred those brats on me, I'd leave Tom and go live with him." Then in answer to her friend's question, she said, "Take the boys? What would I do with them, I'd like to know. They can look out for themselves."

He hoped it was true they wasn't Rourke's boys. He'd rather be the bastard of that blood-hawking chimney sweep on the corner. Or maybe their old man was one of the nameless sailor boys who came home with her from time to time. They was usually young and drunk, and they laughed with her and told her how pretty she was with her yellow hair and dark eyes.

"I'll be back before he misses me," Jack said. "He don't ever remember which of us is which anyways." He patted his brother's shoulder and left.

Jack's quick and purposeful path wound through several neighborhoods of dingy shanties, tenements, gin shops, pubs and little shops with flyblown windows. He was going to the wonderful place he had found one night last year when he was running away from the old man's fists...

✿✿

He ducked through an open doorway that offered a hiding place, and stopped in confusion. Blood from his nose and mouth left red streaks on his hand.

People in strange clothes moved about on a platform; they spoke funny and waved their arms around. He saw a lot of benches, like a church he'd once stole from. He backed away, hoping to escape unseen, but one of the women left the platform and caught his arm.

"You poor baby," she said. "What happened to you? You're bleeding all over yourself."

He stared at her. He'd never seen anyone like her. She was soft and pretty and she smelled sweet. A large man bellowed that he had interrupted something called a dress rehearsal. The woman held Jack's arm and said, "Leave him alone. He's welcome to stay and I won't hear any more about it."

Lizbet Porter soon became his best friend second only to Michael. She was the owner of the small theatre, as well as its ingénue. She hired Jack to carry water and run errands and shine shoes and brush costumes. To Jack Rourke the Royal Lion, a run-down old alehouse that had been turned into a theatre, was a place of magic. He discovered that in the theatre you could become someone else altogether.

Jack loved everything about the theatre, from the actors like Lizbet and the juvenile lead, Roger, to the smells of makeup and old costumes and dust. One day he showed Lizbet a spider crawling on his hand. "It ain't really a spider," he said. "It's a mouse in costume and makeup."

When she discovered he had never been to school and did not even know his alphabet, she said in a no-argument voice, "You've got an excellent brain. I can't let you waste it."

"I ain't gonna go to school," he said.

"I didn't say you'd go to school. I'll teach you myself."

"Don't want to. I know enough."

"Enough to do what? End in prison, if you're lucky? Dead, if you're not? Learn, Jack. You can get away from here."

"Why should I? I got friends here."

She forced him to sit down. "I bought this for you," she said and put a slate into his hands. She gave him a piece of chalk, put her fingers over his and together they made a hook on the slate. "That's a 'J'" she said. "For Jack."

His reading primer was whatever script happened to be lying around at the time. The lessons came at rehearsals, between scenes, and at other odd times when he showed up. She refused to listen to anything he said that was not said properly. She insisted he say "Please" and "Thank you," "Yes, sir" and "Madam."

Starved for learning Jack devoured all that she taught him. She bragged about his quickness with as much delight as if he were her son. She trimmed his hair and found clothes to fit his rapidly growing body. She introduced him to soap and cleanliness. He liked the fresh, taut way his skin felt when it was clean.

Toad and Spitter hooted and called him a nob. He beat Toad up; they didn't say it again. He yearned to tell Michael about Lizbet and the theatre and his new friends, but Michael might let it slip to Mum and then the old man would find out.

One day as he sat on the floor under a window, struggling to read, he felt someone watching him. It was Lizbet; he smiled at her. "Jack," she said softly, "do you have any idea how beautiful you are?"

He shrugged, embarrassed. "Me and my brother look just the same," he said. He didn't realize that to the rest of the world Michael was frailer, smaller, clumsy, not as handsome. The only difference he'd seen was that Michael needed protecting, but he could protect both himself and his brother.

After leaving Michael on this night, Jack arrived at the theatre to find Lizbet and Roger deep in conversation. He heard his name mentioned and sidled closer to hear.

"I wish we could use Jack as Young Cedric," Lizbet was saying.

"I wish we could use anyone else for Young Cedric," groaned Roger. "Harry is terrible. He has ten lines and he gets half of them wrong. Not to mention he's grown too tall for the part." He saw Jack and paused. "Jack, be a good lad and run down to Frenchie's, fetch me a pint of the best."

Jack stifled the impulse to blurt out, "Why don't you just tell the director to put me on in place of Harry?" But he knew why: Harry was the Director's wife's nephew and they were stuck with him until the end of the run. He tugged at the bill of his soft cap and darted off. As his feet churned toward Frenchie's Pub, he thought about the too-tall Harry.

Harry Augustus: fifteen, and a head taller. They'd hated each other on sight. Jack knew that sooner or later he would have to fight Harry. Jack was a good fighter, a dirty fighter, but Harry was at least two stone heavier. By the time he returned from Frenchie's with the pint, he had hatched a plan to get rid of Harry without getting torn limb-from-limb.

Harry was behind the theatre, smoking a thick black cigar. Jack took a deep breath, swaggered up to him and snatched the cigar out of his mouth.

"Gimme that back," Harry said. "Pretty Girly-Boy."

"At least I ain't got a face what makes people puke."

"Oh, yeah?" Harry grabbed for the cigar and missed.

"Yeah." Jack opened his fingers; the cigar plummeted to the mud. He stepped on it.

For an instant Harry stared at him, open-mouthed. Then he clenched his fists. "I'm gonna pound the bloody snot out of you."

"You're gonna quit the play," said Jack.

"Sure I am." Harry had his fists up ready to pound.

"Let's bet. Winner goes on tonight. Loser gets lost."

Harry's fists lowered slightly. "Bet on what?"

"Winner's whoever stays in the yard with Wittenmeyer's bull-dog for five minutes."

"That dog's a killer!"

"Scared?"

"No, I ain't."

"If you wasn't you'd do it."

"Okay, Girly-Boy, come on. I'll show you." Harry led the way to the pen where the night watchman's dog was kept inside a stout, locked shed. They could hear the big dog snarl as it hurled itself against the door. People said the dog was mad, but since he had been the same for a long time Jack doubted it. He was just mean. Like Harry.

Jack went over his plan again. If his timing was off or if the dog did something unexpected, he would be chewed to ribbons while Harry laughed his head off. The boys went inside the pen. Jack, last in, left the gate ajar as Harry lifted the bar on the shed door. The dog hit the door and burst to freedom as Jack threw open the gate. While Harry stared at him, Jack shoved him into the shed and slammed the bar down.

From inside Harry pounded on the door and yelled, "Let me out! Let me out!" An impressive string of vile threats and filthy names spewed from inside the shed.

"Now ain't that fine talk for a gentleman!" Jack said with a grin. Still whistling, he went back to the theatre. With less than an hour before curtain, no one would go near the shed.

While the cast members got into costume and makeup, declaimed their lines, complained, cursed, worked themselves into the right state of mind for the performance, Jack was kept busy running here and there on errands. When would they ask him? They couldn't wait much longer. They'd better hurry. Or it would be too late.

The stage manager hurried past asking for the dozenth time, "Where's Harry? Anyone seen the little bugger?" Jack tried to get his attention, but he rushed away, and returned with the director in tow. "That bloody nephew of yours..."

"My wife's nephew, if you please. I don't claim the little devil."

"Sir," Jack said to the director and stage manager. "I know all of Harry's lines."

"You better be telling the truth," the stage manager said as he shoved Jack into the arms of the wardrobe mistress. "Fix him up as Cedric."

Jack's heart raced; his mouth became a desert. His first role! The wardrobe mistress, with large, loose stitches hastily took in Harry's costume and stuffed rags into the shoes. With a dab of makeup and a flick of a hairbrush, she pronounced him ready. He waited in the wings, jiggling with excitement, repeating the lines over and over to himself.

His cue came and he rushed on stage. "Mrs. Waring's coming and she's got—" He stopped, stricken, terrified of the vast black throng beyond the gas footlights. No words came to his mind or tongue.

"Blood in her eye," the prompter whispered.

Jack did not hear him. He knew he had to say something and do it quick. "And she's got steam out her ears!" he said.

The audience burst into howls of laughter. Jack was transfixed. It was supposed to be a funny scene but this was the first time anyone had ever laughed. The rest of his lines came flawlessly.

Afterward, when makeup and costumes were being taken off in two small, adjoining rooms, men in one and women in the other, the cast talked back and forth through the partly open door.

"Did anyone ever see Harry?" Lizbet asked.

"Not me, luv," said one of the actors. "Wherever the little fart is I hope he stays there."

Jack stripped off Harry's costume and shoes, biting his lip at the pain of the large blisters on his heels.

The actor who played the vicar, put his hand on Jack's shoulder. "Hey, kid, what are you doing in here? Women and children in the other room."

Jack slapped his hand away and glared. "I ain't a child. I'm an actor now."

Everyone laughed. The man drawled, "Well, listen to Mr. Irving."

Roger chuckled and rumpled Jack's hair. "That's right, Jack, You're an actor. Ignore him. You did a bang-up job for a new-comer. Saved that misbegotten scene."

Jack glowed. He wanted to run home and share it all with Michael. But he couldn't, not while the old man was there. His jaw squared. B'god, he'd tell Michael and the old sod be damned. He'd been on the stage. He would be on the stage again and again and again until he was an old, old man. 'Listen to Mr. Irving' was supposed to be a joke. Jack meant it to come true. He'd never set eyes on Mr. Irving, but he'd heard much about him. Well, some-day he'd be better than Mr. Irving, than all of the Mr. Irvings in the whole world. Kings and queens and dukes would come see Jack Rourke! Mr. Irving could then go hang!

It was well past midnight when he arrived home. As he reached for the door handle he heard Rourke's loud, gruff laugh from in-side, and his mother's giggle. He didn't have to see them. He knew they'd be guzzling gin and her clothes would be half off and her hair all a-tumble while the old goat slobbered and pawed at her.

"Jack." Michael emerged from the shadows. He held a small box that shone in the moonlight. "I didn't think you'd be away so long."

"Michael, I got something to tell you. It's important."

As if he either did not hear or did not care, Michael held out the small box. "Look, Jack." The box was enameled and contained candy. "It come all the way from America."

"You have it, Michael. All of it. I don't want nothing he brung."

Michael shrugged and bit into a piece of dark chocolate. "Where've you been?" he asked with his mouth full. "What's so important?"

"Keep a secret?"

Michael spit in his hand and crossed his heart. Jack's eyes shone and his words fell over each other as he told Michael everything. Michael listened with fear. "What if he finds out?" he asked when Jack paused for a breath.

"What if he does? I'll do it anyway."

"You'll get beat, Jack. You know you will."

"He'll beat me anyway so I might as well get beat for something important." His defiant words hid fear as great as Michael's. He knew his brother was right. "Anything to eat?"

Michael's hand disappeared into his coat pocket, and surfaced with a wedge of cheese and a thick slice of bread wrapped together in a dirty rag. "I saved 'em for you."

Jack wolfed the food taken from Michael's grimy hands, then the brothers perched on the warped stoop and talked quietly. Jack leaped to his feet as the door flew open. Tom Rourke filled the doorway.

"Where you been, boy?" Rourke demanded.

Jack was surprised to realize he now came up to the old man's broad shoulders. The last time Rourke had been home Jack had stood only as high as his massive chest. Jack's eyes glinted. Soon the old man would hit Michael and him and Mum once too often and he'd give it back to him, double.

"I said where you been, boy? You go deaf while I was gone?"

Jack drew out the coins Lizbet had given him for the night's performance. "Working," he said. The coins disappeared into Rourke's pocket.

That night Jack lay awake on the old mattress he shared with Michael. On the other side of the blanket that divided the room,

Mum and the old man were having at it. He heard the bed bounce and he clenched his fists as Mum cried from time to time, "Tommy, Tom, you're hurtin' me. Don't, Tom!" The old man never answered except to gasp, "Shut up," and the noise continued. Then her protests changed to grunts and groans to match his. In a few minutes it was quiet and Jack could hear her cooing to the old man. The old man laughed low and called her his baby.

Jack lay awake. His arms and fists were rigid with anger long after his parents fell silent and the old man snored in great, gulping snores. He hated when mum and the old man were at it. The old man always hurt her. Once Jack had gone raging to their side of the room. He'd kicked and screamed at the old man to leave her alone. The old man had knocked him about and thrown him out into the street. Mum told him the next morning that she wasn't really hurt, it was just what men and women did. She told him to leave it be. She said the words painfully, with a split lip and a bruise on her face. Finally Jack went to sleep, one arm over Michael, his lips against Michael's hair, just as they had slept since infancy.

Before two days were up Rourke was again cursing and beating his sons. Every time Jack saw the terror in Michael's eyes he hated the old sod even more. One night Rourke raised his fist to strike Michael, and Jack roared, "Leave him be, you old bucket of shit!" He rammed his head into Rourke's belly.

Rourke staggered back. He recovered his balance, knocked Jack to the floor, and seized the long, cracked leather strap. The doubled-over strap rained a torrent of pain on the boy as he curled up and shielded his face with his arms. As if from far away, over his own howls of anguish, he heard Michael beg the old man to stop, heard their mother say, "Tom, come on, Tom, don't lay on so hard." The old man shouted, "Stay out of it, woman!" She fell silent.

Jack lay all the next day in too much pain to move. He gritted his teeth and thought of the old gun Toad had shown him a few days earlier. "Ain't it a beauty?" Toad had said, waving it around. "And layin' right there in the pawn shop, just waiting to be pinched." Before Jack could get the gun from Toad and put a bullet between the old man's eyes, Rourke went to sea.

The old man haunted Jack's dreams. Big body, hands like clubs, brass buttons gleaming on his dark coat, thick black beard hiding the yellow teeth. Blood was often in the dreams. Sometimes it

was his; sometimes it was the old man's. When awake he fanta-
sized about sharks eating the old man, brass buttons and all; of
pirates running him through; of the old fool dancing at the end of
a rope.

When Jack returned to the theatre following Rourke's departure, Lizbet's heart ached at the sight of his shadowed eyes and
bruised face, but she did not pry. Instead, she scolded him with a
laugh for locking Harry in the shed. Then she asked, "How would
you like to play Young Cedric again, Jack? For the final two
performances?"

"Would I! But what about Harry? He's stupid, but he wouldn't
let me get rid of him again and I'd get the worst of it this time."

"Harry isn't with us any more. And neither are the proceeds of
the ticket box from last night, unfortunately. So, will you?"

"Yes, ma'am!"

"Our next play is *The Bridge Crossing*. You've read some of it.
Do you think you could play Christopher Brown, the crippled
boy?" At his vigorous nod, she smiled. "I think so too. I think you
would have the audience swimming in tears."

"I could, I know I could."

"But you'll have to work much harder on your reading."

He knew the story: Poor Crippled Christopher saves his home
from the Villainous Banker, rescues his mother, the Virtuous
Widow, from the clutches of the Villainous Riverboat Captain,
then takes a fever and dies in his mother's arms. But hark! A Heavenly Angel appears and says, 'Because you have been virtuous and
brave, I say to you: Arise, Christopher, live and walk.' Where-
upon Christopher arises, walks, and dances a hornpipe.

The hornpipe did not exist until opening night. Jack was seized
with the notion of doing it and did it without permission of the
director. It brought down the house. "I can't work with such a
boy!" the director bellowed. "I must have someone who follows
directions."

"The audience loved it," Lizbet said. "It stays. But it wants
music." The Poor But Honest Shoemaker Who Loves the Virtuous
Widow From Afar was pressed into service playing a mouth organ
in the last act.

His success in the play gave Jack an idea. "Michael!" he said a
day or so later, "We'll work together, you and me. We'll make lots
of money." The next day, for a ha'penny Jack bought a tattered

coat from the rag picker. Then he and Michael begged a ride from a river man who was sweet on Mum.

"Where we goin', Jack?" Michael asked.

"You'll see. You just do what I say and we'll be rich in no time."

By early afternoon they found themselves in a part of town where the streets were straight and the shop windows clean. The children they saw wore no rags, and they looked scrubbed to the point of pain. Men with hats, long coats, and side-whiskers, strode past absorbed in their own affairs. Ladies in bustles and fancy hats moved more leisurely, often in pairs, chattering and laughing softly.

Jack and Michael stood outside a toyshop where some toys bobbed or spun as if they were alive. Michael loved a mechanical clownish figure in tights and bells and a funny hat with points. The boys watched, hands and noses against the shining glass, until a man burst from the doorway and grabbed their collars. "On your way, you two! It's bad for my business to have the likes of you hanging about."

Jack squirmed free of the man and the fellow let Michael go. With a final, "Run along!" The man wiped his glass free of the marks from their fingers and noses, then stood with arms akimbo and watched as they left.

"We'll show him," said Jack. He led the way to a less high-toned part of the street, reasoning that the constables didn't watch them places as much. He draped the coat over Michael's shoulders, arms inside, and buttoned it, leaving the sleeves dangling. "Now, all you have to do is sit there and look unhappy. I'll do the rest."

Michael huddled at Jack's feet, his face averted as Jack called up the Cockney accent he worked so hard to discard. "Please," he said, as he held out his cap to passing women, his eyes filled with tears, his lips a-quiver. "Me brother ain't got no arms and he can't talk neither. And our Papa died of fever and Mum and the new babe just was called to Heaven and we ain't got no home no more. Help us, won't yer? God'll reward yer, mum."

Almost always, the ladies looked first at Jack and then at Michael and back at Jack. Jack gave forth a brave smile that called up the deep dimple in his left cheek. The power of that dimple was a mystery to him, but he knew it worked on women, and most of them gave him money. Whenever Jack spied a copper, he and

Michael melted into the crowd or a nearby alley, the ragged coat rolled up and tucked beneath Jack's arm.

At the end of the day they had enough money to go back to the toy store. Jack slapped the money down on the counter, and left with the mechanical clown. They had enough left for a shared kidney-pie and ale, with two shillings left to add to the treasure in the hidden jar.

Michael cradled the toy in his arms and worshipped his brother with his eyes. "You're a wonder, Jack," he said.

Jack's face turned red and he punched Michael's arm. "Ain't I?" he said.

2

One night near the end of the play's run, Lizbet kept Jack behind, and to his surprise gave him a brown paper parcel containing a suit of fancy clothes for a young gentleman, complete with waistcoat and stiff collar. "These are for you, Jack," she said.

He trailed his fingers down the fine wool of the coat and the silk of the waistcoat and regretfully returned them to her. "I don't have no use for such as this."

"Oh, but you do. You're my escort to the Lyceum Theatre Saturday next." She touched the end of his nose. "You, my lad, will see Ellen Terry and Henry Irving in *Romeo and Juliet*. And you'll meet them afterward. And you'll also meet a gentleman who is a great patron of the theatre."

"What's a patron?"

"Someone very rich and very generous. He helps me keep my little theatre open, and has made it possible for other struggling actors and actresses to continue their careers without starving to death."

He hugged the parcel to him. "I can't take them home. Mum would sell them."

"I'll keep them until that night. You can meet me here and change in the dressing room."

※ ※

"The bloody collar's going to choke me to death," he complained as he stood for her inspection that night.

"Oh, bosh," Lizbet said. "Women suffer much more than men in order to look splendid. And you look splendid."

He wanted to tell Lizbet she was beautiful, but he didn't know how. Her hair was drawn up in loops and curls with sparkles in them, and she had more sparkles at her ears and throat. He was amazed when a few minutes later a carriage pulled up in front of The Royal Lion, and a man jumped down and held the door open for him and Lizbet. Inside the carriage a silver-haired gentleman waited.

"Xavier," Lizbet said to the gentleman, "this is Jack Rourke, the young actor I spoke of. Jack, this is my cousin and my friend, Xavier St. Denys. The theatre patron."

Jack was so excited at riding in an actual carriage he barely glanced at the gentleman. The splendor of the theatre, both inside and out, amazed him. And the people were all dressed up like Lizbet and her cousin. The three of them sat in a box, which was like a small room, and Jack watched the people below and across in other boxes as they took their seats. Jewelry flashed like tiny flashes of lightning; opera glasses reflected the light.

Then he forgot himself and everything around him as the great drama swept away his soul. He understood almost none of the Elizabethan speech, but the acting of Mr. Irving and Miss Terry told him the story. He was starry-eyed when Lizbet took him backstage later. Miss Terry embraced Lizbet and her cousin as old friends. Mr. Irving kissed Lizbet's cheek. Lizbet introduced Jack to them as a budding actor. Mr. Irving said brusquely, "The only way to learn to act is by acting, young man." Jack was surprised how old Mr. Irving looked close up.

Miss Terry, who was almost as tall as Mr. Irving, laid one warm hand against Jack's cheek and said with a smile, "He's right, you know," she said. "Lizbet is giving you a good background. Come back to see us again, won't you, Jack?"

Dumbly, he nodded. Lizbet laughed and whispered, "I've never seen you so quiet." And then the magic world of the Lyceum was gone. He was home again, lying beside his sleeping brother, wondering if it really happened. For days afterward he relived Mr. Irving's and Miss Terry's movements, gestures, manner of speaking. For the first time he realized he had a lot to learn.

When he told Michael about it he grew more excited with each word. "I'll be a great actor. Then I'll be famous and we'll go to America." He put one arm around his brother's shoulders. He could feel Michael's bones through his clothing, and he could now see the top of Michael's head. It was as if he was growing and Michael wasn't.

❧ ❧

Rourke returned. He was drunk when he walked in shouting for the boys. "They ain't here," his wife said. Minutes later they had a fight that broke a table and several dishes and left her right eye swollen and purple. Then he collapsed into a snoring coma. Rourke's sons came home to find their mother bathing her face in cold river water.

Rourke was still asleep when it came time for Jack to leave for the theatre, but he was beginning to make the groaning sounds that meant he was waking. "Come with me, Michael," Jack pleaded. "You oughtn't be here without me, and I daren't miss a performance."

"You go, Jack. I'll be all right. He'll sleep for a while."

Jack listened. It did sound as if the old fool had gone back to sleep. "Are you sure you won't come?" he asked Michael again.

"Go on," said Michael. "You'll be back before he's about."

Jack came home to find the old man gone, Michael trembling in terror, and Mum crying like a crazy woman. He soothed Michael as best he could and cursed himself for leaving. Long after Michael was asleep the door creaked, and Jack sat up, fearing it was the old man. Instead he saw his mother silhouetted in the open door. She wore her hat with the single drooping feather, and carried a battered valise as she slipped outside and pulled the door shut behind her. He pulled on his pants and followed her. "Mum," he called, "where you going?"

She stiffened but did not turn. "I can't be wife to that man anymore. He ain't human, he ain't."

"Away? Ain't we going too, me and Michael?"

"I got no money to take care of two boys. But you're fourteen, Jack. Near a man grown." She turned slightly and he saw her profile. "Look after your brother, Jack. He ain't as strong as you." She started away.

"Mum!" he cried. "Damn you! You ain't much of a mum but you're all we got. You can't leave us here. Mum!" In seconds she was swallowed by the night. His hands curled into fists. "I never really believed she'd do it." He angrily dragged the back of one hand across his eyes. "I'll take care of Michael, and she can go to hell." Just him and Michael. And the old man. He shivered. The only hope he had was that the old man was on a ship bound for someplace so far away he'd never come back.

As he dragged himself back inside, Michael stirred. "I heard talkin'," he said.

"Mum's gone," Jack said. Michael started to cry. "We got each other. That's all we ever had. We don't need nobody else."

Rourke did not return the following morning. Michael sat with big scared eyes, expecting Jack to do something. Jack fixed breakfast. The coffee was thin and bitter but the thick slices of hard bread dipped in it filled them up.

Rourke did not come back that night or the next morning. "He must've shipped out again," Jack said. "Michael, come to the theatre with me. I want you to meet my friends."

"I'll go tomorrow. I'm awful tired today."

Jack hesitated. "Are you sure? I might be gone a long time."

"I'm sure."

"I'll be home quick as I can."

The old man had come back while he was gone; the dark room reeked of whiskey. Careful not to slam the door or step on the creaky floorboard, Jack went in. Rourke was not there.

"Michael?" he called, and lit a lamp. Michael was curled up on the mattress, shivering, with only his forehead and hair visible above the blanket. "Michael? You sick? You need a doctor?" He didn't know where to find one, but if Michael needed a doctor, he'd have one.

"No," whispered Michael.

"You're sick. I'll get Lizbet. She'll know what to do."

"No, Jack, don't get nobody. I'll be all right."

Jack yanked back the blanket and gasped. Michael's thin arms, face, and body were covered with bruises. Jack slammed his fist against the wall. "God damn him! He ain't gonna do this no more. Not to you, not to me. Toad's got a gun. He'll let me have it. I'll blow that devil's head clean off his shoulders, I will."

"Don't, Jack. Don't make things worse," Michael cried. "He said he'd kill me. You, too. Don't make him mad. Promise me you won't. Don't make him mad!"

"I'll try." It was said through clenched teeth.

"Promise!"

"I promise."

At the sound of drunken singing, the boys went rigid and stared at each other. The door flew open and Tom Rourke stood in the doorway. He lurched forward and grabbed Jack's shirt. "Where is she?"

"She's gone is all I know." Jack pushed at Rourke's hand.

"Oh, aye. You don't know! I asked you where'd she go?"

Jack's gut tied itself into knots. He wouldn't show the old bastard how scared he was, not if he had to turn himself inside out.

Rourke's voice rose; whiskey breath blasted into Jack's face. "I asked you where she is, you son of a whore!"

"If I knew I'd tell you. Then you'd go find her and leave us the bloody hell alone." Jack braced himself for the fist he knew was coming. He was shocked when the old man released him so suddenly he fell backward on the bed.

Rourke wiped his mouth with the back of his hand. "It's growing up, is it? Does it think it's becoming quite a man? Eh?" His lips curled back in a semblance of a grin. "Jack, my boy, you and me got things to talk about. Sit."

Jack edged around him and perched on the edge of a scarred chair. Rourke towered over him and held out a full gin bottle. "Drink it down, Jack. That's how real men do. Right outta the bottle."

Keeping his eyes fixed on Rourke, Jack took the bottle and downed the first swallow. He'd had beer and ale aplenty, but the gin sent red-hot razors all the way down. He choked and shoved the bottle toward Rourke. "I don't want it."

"Drink it like a man," Rourke demanded.

"No."

Rourke leaned nose to nose with his son; his spit sprayed Jack's face. "I said drink it like a man. All of it."

"Go to hell." Again he braced himself for a blow that never came.

Rourke straightened, dragged Michael to his feet by one spindly arm and stood him between himself and Jack, his bearish paws clamped to either side of the Michael's head. "Drink it down, boy. Or I'll snap his neck. And it'll be your fault."

Jack tilted the bottle up and gulped swallow after swallow. Sickness rose in his throat and he lowered the bottle. Rourke twisted Michael's head toward his shoulder and Michael whimpered. "Like a twig, Jack," Rourke said, his feral grin widening. "Snap!"

Dizzy, his gut ready to burst, Jack swallowed more. The bottle was still half-full.

"Drink it! Every drop!" Rourke increased the angle of Michael's head and the boy wailed, "Jack! Jack!"

Jack forced another swallow down. And another. And then it all came back up. He leaned forward, splattering Rourke's shoes.

"Damn you!" Rourke threw Michael aside and lunged toward Jack. "You bloody-damned pig! Okay, pig, wallow in your mess!" He knocked Jack from his chair; he sprawled belly down in the gin-reeking vomit. Rourke grabbed the boy's thick hair and ground his face into the foul stuff.

Jack clawed at Rourke's hand. Michael scrambled to his feet and held on to Rourke's arm, but Rourke shook him loose. He kicked Jack, rolling him over in the stinking puddle. "Clean up this mess, pig! Get this place ship-shape or I'll break every bone in his worthless hide." He picked up the gin bottle and stalked to the other side of the blanket partition. Soon raucous snoring told them he was asleep.

Michael grabbed a rag and feverishly started sopping up the mess. "Don't," said Jack. "I'll do it. You're sick. Go back to bed." Swaying on his feet, Michael did as told; Jack tucked the threadbare blanket around him. As he scrubbed the floor he choked, "I'll kill the old bastard. I will. I'll kill him. I'll kill him."

When he was finished he took his other clothes and a sliver of soap and ran through fog-heavy air to the river, not even hearing the familiar sounds of the night people. Not until he felt clean from head to heels did he leave the cold water and go home. He crawled into bed with Michael, and reached out to him for warmth as he always did. But Michael did not turn in his sleep and put his arms around Jack's neck. He did not murmur. He did not move.

The hair rose on the back of Jack's neck. "Michael?" he whispered. "Michael, are you all right?"

He touched his brother's face. It was no longer hot with fever; now it was cool. As if he, too, had just come from the river. No breath moved the bony chest. Jack put his arms around his brother and held him throughout the night, too grief-stricken to cry. As soon as day came he'd get Lizbet. She'd know what to do.

⚜

Jack and his friends from the theatre stood in a circle around the plain box in the pauper's cemetery as Michael's Methodist missionary held a brief, nervous ceremony. Lizbet had one arm around Jack's shoulders. He still couldn't cry. The service ended; Jack had heard not a word.

Lizbet said, "Jack, come home with me. There's no need to return to that place."

"Michael's things are still there," he said.

Later that night he sat at the table. In his hands was the toy he'd bought his brother. When the old man came in, he kept his eyes lowered to hide the blaze of hatred.

Rourke belched, and said, "Ain't much of a loss, you know. He was nothing, that brother of yours. A bloody molly-coddle. Now he'll rot and the worms'll eat him."

Jack's head lowered even more. Behind grief-blinded eyes he saw the cat, the maggot-eaten cat. He clutched the toy until pain shot up his hands and arms.

"Ever seen worms on a dead man, boy? They crawl in and out everywhere, inside, outside. And worms –"

"Shut up!"

"The worms ain't all. The eyes fall in and there's worms in the eyeholes, and the guts pop open and there's worms there, too, big tangled up messes of pink and slimy worms."

"Shut up!"

Jack threw the toy down and hurled himself at Rourke, beat with his fists at the big bearded face. Rourke slammed him backward against the wall. Jack scrambled to his feet and again and again flung himself against that unmovable wall of flesh and that grinning face. Then his fist struck one of Rourke's eyes.

Rourke's grin disappeared. He seized Jack's wrists in one huge hand and hit him back and forth across the face until red rivulets streamed from his nose and mouth. Jack's knees buckled; the only thing that kept him upright was the hand on his wrists. "You killed him! You killed my brother!" he screamed. Then the world went black.

Jack's eyes could not open all the way. He lay on the floor. The room was dark. He touched his chin and his fingers came away sticky. He stifled a whimper of pain as he clutched the edge of the table and pulled himself to his feet. A lantern left burning on the table cast a blurred circle of light.

Objects moved around him. Nothing was clear but the image of Michael's body covered in writhing worms. Scarcely able to see from his swollen eyes, he felt around until his fingers closed around the handle of his mother's long-bladed, razor sharp fish knife.

He staggered to where Rourke lay sprawled, his shirt unbuttoned. With both hands, he lifted the knife above his head and plunged it into the broad, black-furred chest. Blood shot out around the blade. Rourke's eyes flew open. Jack yanked the knife out and plunged it in again. Rourke tried to rise, then fell back and did not move.

Jack left the shack and crept through the misty shadows, hiding from the world, holding the one thing he had taken with him: Michael's windup clown. He made his way to the theatre and collapsed in the dressing room, moaning and hugging the toy to him.

Someone grabbed him; someone carried him to the hangman's rope. He struggled, and woke to find Lizbet kneeling beside him. "Jack, my poor darling, what happened? What did that monster do to you?"

"He killed Michael and I killed him and what am I going to do?" His teeth clicked together; he shook until it seemed he would shake apart.

She helped him to his feet. "Come home with me. It isn't far." In her small parlor Lizbet treated his wounds, and listened, her face ashen. "I should have made you come here."

"They'll catch me. They'll hang me!"

She held his icy hands in hers. "No, dear. They won't. No one knows you're here. You're safe." She brought a pillow and a warm blanket and fixed him a bed on her settee. "Drink this. It will help you sleep." She gave him a cup of tea laced with laudanum.

He lay down and Lizbet drew a blanket over him. "Don't leave me," he begged.

"I'll be right here. I won't leave you," she said, and made herself as comfortable as possible in the chair beside the fire. A hoarse scream jarred her awake. Jack's head was thrown back, his throat and jaw rigid, his limbs shaking uncontrollably. Lizbet wrapped her arms around him and rocked him. "Hush, hush, hush."

"He ain't dead! He's coming after me. He was there! Right there by the door. I seen his eyes. I seen the buttons on his coat."

"No, now, Jack. Hush. You're safe here. Safe. Hush now." Was Rourke dead? Uneasily she looked about, but saw no sign of an intruder. Gradually Jack stopped raving and, worn out, laid his head on her shoulder. She soothed him back to sleep and silently cursed the soul of Tom Rourke, hoping he was stone cold dead and burning in Hell.

Jack slept for almost forty-eight hours, tightly clutching the toy clown, and when he moved from the settee it was with slow, painful steps. His face was swollen and bruised. Dark finger bruises showed on his neck. Looking into the haggard, half-crazed young face, Lizbet said, "Jack, I think you need to go away. We don't want the police to find you."

His eyes filled. "My brother and me was going to run away together. I was going to take care of him. I waited too long. It's my fault he's dead."

"You're a child yourself. You did the best you could."

"If I'd done the best I could, Michael and me would be far away. The old man said worms are eating Michael." He shuddered. "I seen a dead cat that was rotten and that's the way he said Michael's eyes would be. I don't want him to be like that."

"Michael is in your heart and your mind and there he will always be young. He can't be harmed anymore, ever. Think of that, not the other. Hold him in your heart." After a moment she stood up. "Now, then. While you slept, I sent a wire to my cousin. He's agreed to take you in for a few days. No one would think to look there. That will give us time to think."

He said nothing. She handed him some clothes. "I brought you some clothes from wardrobe. I'll wash and cut your hair, and I think I can hide the marks on your face with makeup." He heard nothing she said. He needed Michael. But Michael was dead. Slowly he curled over the grinning clown.

3

Jack crowded closer to Lizbet as they boarded the railroad
train. Choking clouds of steam and head-splitting noises
spewed from the iron monster. People crowded around them
and stared, faces dark with suspicion. Any moment someone would
point at him and scream "Killer! Killer!" and the policeman nearby
would drag him away.

"See that copper," he whispered to Lizbet, "He knows what I
did! See him?"

For an instant Lizbet thought the policeman was, indeed, studying Jack. Then he turned away to speak to an elderly woman. "No,
he's not. No one is. They have their own affairs to worry about."
She glanced sideways at him. She had her fingers crossed he would
not rub the stage makeup off before they reached their destina-
tion.

Inside the coach, his eyes darted about; attack threatened from
every quarter. The train groaned several times, whistled, and
jerked forward. Jack clutched the arms of the seat until his knuc-
les were white. Gradually the rhythm of the train's wheels, the
sway of the coach, the heat of the close-packed bodies, the smells

of food, pipes, and cigars produced a stupor that let him block out everything outside himself. Later, he wondered whether they traveled for hours, days, or weeks.

He did not see the green beauty of the wooded hills or the valleys where cattle and sheep grazed. He was unaware of villages with ancient names passing by the grimy windows. Not even when they left the train to board another, and then finished the journey in a carriage, did he notice anything around him. From time to time he shuddered. Swinging across his mind was a black shadow of himself dangling limp and dead from a hangman's noose.

Lizbet felt the tremors and put her hand over his. "It will be all right, Jack. I promise. You're miles from the City."

For the first time her words roused him from the icy land of his mind and he raised his head. "Truly, Lizbet?"

"Truly, pet. I have never lied to you."

His voice quivered as he said, "I lie a lot. I steal too. My brother never lied. He was good. I ain't. So why did he die instead of me?"

Unable to speak past the ache in her throat, Lizbet just shook her head and tightened her hand on his.

He fell asleep with his head against her shoulder. When he woke again, the sun was bright. His interest was stirred a little as the carriage approached a narrow, clear river bordered by ancient trees. They clattered across a bridge, and stopped while a man opened ornate iron gates beneath an arched gateway. Then they proceeded into a wide courtyard toward a building so grand his mind could not take it in. And there, the carriage stopped.

A man dressed in knee breeches assisted Lizbet to the ground. She turned and smiled into the carriage. "Come along, Jack. We're here."

Jack ignored the footman and jumped to the ground. As he took in his surroundings the horror of the recent days was pushed to the back of his mind for a few moments. "Blimey! Who lives here, then?" he asked. "The Queen?"

"No, not the Queen, although queens have stayed here. This is my cousin's home." Lizbet spoke to a white-gloved man in black. He bowed and stood aside as they entered a room bigger than the church from which Jack had once nicked the poor box and a crucifix.

He followed her down a corridor and into another room that made him stop, overwhelmed by the length of it, and by the ceiling far overhead, painted with time-darkened figures he could not see clearly. Each end of the room had a massive fireplace taller than he was.

He saw things for which he had no words: the floor of veined marble, the immense marble table in the center of the room, suits of armor, statues, tapestries, large portraits and landscapes. He followed Lizbet from the room up a wide staircase worn with generations of passing feet, with smooth handrails darkened from the oils of gliding hands.

She took Jack to a room where hundreds of books on shelves lined the room from floor to ceiling. Small tables and shelves displayed vases, small paintings, and statues. Almost of their own volition Jack's hands slipped a small statue into his coat. He froze with the statue in his hand as the tall double doors opened and St. Denys strolled in.

Panicked, he knew he better run for it. He tried to slip the little figure back where it was. St. Denys looked square at him. Certain St. Denys would have him dragged away to prison, Jack tensed. He was ready to fight or flee. "I was just looking at it," he said defiantly.

"Quite all right. That's their purpose."

To Jack's amazement, St. Denys seemed to mean what he had said. Slowly he put the statue back where it had stood.

St. Denys and Lizbet walked a little way from him and spoke out of his hearing. St. Denys nodded several times, his expression grim. When they approached Jack together, St. Denys put a gentle hand on Jack's shoulder. "Elizabeth told me of the loss of your brother. I am most sorry."

Jack tried to swallow the sudden lump in his throat. "We was twins, you know. It was like he was part of me."

"I never had a brother, so I won't tell you I understand how you feel. Elizabeth also told me you are in some trouble in the City." A shiver ran down Jack's spine, but he said nothing. "Jack, I want to offer you sanctuary here."

"Don't know what that is."

"Shelter. A safe place to hide. This place is large enough for a hundred like you. I would be your guardian until other arrangements can be made."

Jack stiffened, his chin lifted. "I ain't charity. If I stay I'll earn my keep. I'll muck out the stables or..." He paused. He was good at nothing except picking pockets, fighting, and playacting. He was stuck with the stables.

"You'll earn your keep by learning as much as you can. For whatever time you are here you will have a tutor."

"Yes, sir," he mumbled because he knew Lizbet wanted him to agree. But his dark eyes were lowered and his jaw was set.

"Xavier," Lizbet said, "should he not take a different name for safety's sake? Even though the city is far away, is it not possible that he could be arrested here?"

"It's possible. A change might be prudent. But it's not a decision either you or I can make. Jack, it's up to you."

He looked up, eyes wide. "Change my name! No. The missionary said there's a heaven and Michael's in it. I don't believe it, but Michael did. And if there is, he's there. If I change my name maybe he can't find me."

"You could choose a name Michael would recognize. A character from a play, perhaps," Lizbet said.

"No."

"You need to take a new identity for your safety," St. Denys said.

"You said it was up to me but you won't listen to me!" Jack protested.

St. Denys and Lizbet exchanged glances. "You know what could happen if the police find you. You wouldn't be the first boy to go to prison, or worse," St. Denys said. "Please consider it, Jack."

"Isn't there some character Michael would know?" Lizbet asked. "You could take that name."

Jack wavered. "I don't know. Maybe. Christopher Brown. I told him about it."

"Perfect!" Lizbet said. "Be Christopher Brown until it's safe to be Jack Rourke again. It will be no different than using the name when you were on stage."

Jack once again looked from one to the other, feeling helpless. They were his friends. They wanted him to be safe. Maybe they knew best. He was frightened. He needed friends. He needed a safe place. Miserably, he nodded in agreement.

Lizbet hugged him. "Christopher. I always thought the name suited you."

St. Denys said, "Now, then, young fellow, Elizabeth and I have things to discuss. Brady will show you your room and then you're free to do as you please. If you're hungry, tell Brady." He pulled a velvet rope in the corner.

Jack heard nothing, but to his amazement, the white-gloved man appeared as if by magic. "I ain't goin' with him. I don't know him," he said.

"Brady's my butler, Jack," St. Denys said. "I trust him. You may, also."

Jack looked at Lizbet. She nodded. He followed the butler, his steps dragging. How would he find Lizbet in this big place?

"This is your room, sir." The butler opened the door to a room far larger than the place he had lived in with his brother. A young man, little older than he was, and dressed like Brady, was laying out clothing on the bed. "Tomkins will be your valet during your visit," Brady said. "He'll see to your requirements." He pulled the door closed behind him.

Jack eyed the valet. "What do you want?"

"Do you want me to have tea sent up, sir?"

"Go away," he said. When he was alone, he sat on the edge of the bed and looked all around this strange place. He wanted to be home, with Michael. Michael! He'd forgot; maybe it was for just a few minutes, but he shouldn't have forgot for even a second.

Loss wrenched him. He took the clown from inside his coat, curled up on the bed, mindless of his shoes muddying the silk coverlet, and fought the flood of grief that threatened. Crying was for kids; he wasn't a kid anymore. He wasn't even Jack any more.

"Christopher." He whispered it, his throat thick. "Christopher." It felt foreign on his tongue. His chin quivered. He pulled a soft pillow over his head so no one would hear.

Lizbet sipped sweet, creamy tea from the fragile old china cup and smiled at her cousin. "I can't thank you enough for taking him in."

"Your message was a masterpiece of cryptography, my dear. You said it was an emergency and I know you're no hysteric. If only he and his brother had been taken away from that animal years ago."

"I've thought that a thousand times in the last two days. I should have known, Xavier! The first time I set eyes on him he was bloody. I saw him often with bruises. I should have asked, but I didn't want to pry. I feel responsible."

"Nonsense. How strange life is, sometimes. Here I am, the last of my family, with more property, more money, more … everything than I can use in a lifetime, no son to inherit it, and no possibility of ever having one. And there's Rourke, every inch a devil from what you've told me. He had two fine sons and he brutalized them. No wonder I don't believe in God. If He existed such things wouldn't happen."

She said, "At least for a little while you can pretend you have a son."

"And I will," he said with a slight smile. "Even if it's only a week or a month. He seems like a good boy."

"I believe he is, though he doesn't seem to think so."

"Lizbet, did you see his face during *Romeo and Juliet?* He was transfigured. I've been meaning to see him perform at the Lion, but time got away from me."

"I've thought for a long time he should study at your theatre. He has a future, Xavier. I feel it as strongly as I've ever felt anything and I've taught him all I can."

"But first we have to keep him safe."

"First we have to keep him safe," she echoed with a decisive nod.

The weeks passed, then the month, and the year. Other years passed and still the boy fugitive stayed at St. Denys Hill. Bit by bit the name Jack Rourke receded in his memory. He became, even in his own mind, Christopher.

He'd never met anyone like St. Denys. Elegant, educated, intellectual, he was also a superb horseman and fencer. He told Christopher stories of going to America and hunting wildcats in the hills. "They're a worthy prey," he said. "Cunning. Courageous. Someday I'll take you there and you can see for yourself."

Lizbet visited often and between her, St. Denys, and the butler, Christopher gradually learned how to handle a bewildering array of tableware, finger bowls, stemware, and napkins, and became adept at society's required turns of phrase that charmed or amused but said little.

Each of the Hill's three libraries was packed with books, but Christopher's favorite remained the first one he had seen. One day he dared ask St. Denys about the statues there, each one of a man, perfect in every detail. "They're all naked," he said in an embarrassed croak. "Why?"

"For many reasons, the most important of which is that they represent ideals of physical beauty. Do you not like them?"

Christopher ignored the question, reluctant to admit how much he liked them. "But why didn't the sculptors put clothes on them?"

"Because an artist is allowed license other people are not. And because fashions grow dated and boring. Why preserve them in stone, when the human body is such a wonder?" That was just one of those fancy sayings Christopher did not understand right away. He filed it away for later thought.

As he had promised, St. Denys provided tutors. Christopher took to everything except geography and mathematics, which he ignored as much as possible. His Latin, Composition, Literature, and History tutor caroled, "Sir, the lad is a genius blessed with great imagination." The geography and mathematics tutor declared, "Sir, he cannot learn. I cannot teach him to border the countries of Europe and Asia, name the most important products of Turkey or any other place, or do simple equations. Sir, I fear the boy is perhaps an idiot."

St. Denys did not limit Christopher's education to the mind. When Christopher's voice settled, St. Denys hired a voice and elocution master who was enthused by the quality and depth in one so young. He hired the best French fencing master in the country. The first lessons unnerved the master, since the boy's immediate reaction to the master's precise, mannered attack was to throw the foil aside and swing his fists. Soon, however, he took to fencing the way he had taken to every other new kind of learning that didn't involve geography and mathematics.

St. Denys was widely read and widely traveled, and he instilled in the boy a curiosity about other peoples and cultures. But more important than all else in Christopher's eyes, St. Denys loved the theatre. He often took Christopher to the Xavier Theatre in London and the boy was enchanted. As time passed and it appeared the police had no interest in Jack Rourke, they spent more time in London, and took up residence in a palatial hotel suite. Certain no one would recognize tough, rough Jack as his tall, fashionably outfitted and cultured foster son, St. Denys bit by bit introduced him to London society.

Lest the boy become a *dilettante* fit only for attending operas and spending money, he put him to work in the Xavier Theatre. "I want you to learn the theatre from the ground up," he said.

"Anything," Christopher said, "so long as I don't have to tell you what bloody thing they export from bloody Russia." He painted flats, and got as much paint on himself as on the flats. He developed strong shoulders and arms as he worked with the fly men hauling scenery into place. And, once the pain and swelling went away, he was proud of the thumb he smashed with a hammer while driving nails into vignettes. His natural agility, refined by fencing, was apparent to anyone as he clambered around high up in the fly loft. He learned to make *papier-mâché* rocks and fruit and other stage properties, and thereby discovered he had no artistic ability at all. Sometimes he worked as the callboy, who made certain the actors were ready for their entrances.

Then, when he was sixteen, he disappeared for two days. St. Denys was terrified the police had somehow learned the boy's identity and had taken him in charge. Lizbet dismissed that fear: why would the law be still interested in the killer of a worthless specimen like Rourke? Her fear was equally frightening: he had been kidnapped for ransom. And then Christopher swaggered in. "Are you all right? Where have you been? Don't you know how worried we were?" Lizbet scolded while hugging him. St. Denys almost wilted with relief.

"I don't know why you worried." Christopher grinned. "I'm an apprentice now. To Henry Irving. And I did it without anybody's help. He let me sleep at the Lyceum."

"Irving? But I meant for you to study at my theater with Mr. Walsh when you were ready, " St. Denys protested.

"Mr. Walsh would have to take me even if he didn't want me." His eyes sparkled. "And I'll get to work with Miss Terry, too."

"If you ever disappear like that again you'll be severely punished. But this time, I am impressed. And proud." He laughed and slapped the boy's back.

Henry Irving was a brilliant tyrant. He taught by casting apprentices in plays. Script readings lasted hours, often without rest, food or drink. No one dared question his methods or interpretations. Christopher changed a tiny bit of business once, during rehearsal. Irving raged at him in front of the cast for thirty minutes. Several times during the tirade Irving bellowed, "Do not forget, any of you, that I am the table. The rest of you are nothing but legs to that table. You, boy, try that again, and you are out."

Christopher meekly returned to his place and recited his five-word line as directed. He resented Irving's high-handed ways, and yet learned much just watching the man famous for turning the simple act of tying a shoe into a masterpiece of performance.

He learned just as much from watching tall, willowy, beautiful Miss Terry, who became his ideal of an actress. Even more than Irving, she believed in and practiced the natural style of acting.

When Christopher performed his small role in *The Bells,* he was gratified to have Mr. Irving say later, "You have promise." And a moment later Ellen Terry hugged Christopher and said, "Take his words and multiply them."

❧❧

The lifelong wanderlust of Xavier St. Denys was as strong as ever. Every so often, he stopped all lessons for a few weeks, and he and the boy traveled. "There is so much of life you have never seen," he said. "If you are to be an actor, you have to watch people, and learn from them. You have to learn from history, too, because history is people."

They went to Welsh mining towns and the Liverpool docks. They visited the Midlands, the Shires and the Scottish Highlands, crossed over to Ireland and to Skye. Christopher loved the forests of Germany, the culture of France, the sun-washed ruins of ancient Greece and Rome. Wherever they went, St. Denys told him stories of blue-painted warriors and armoured knights. He told him about the Caesars, and about Alexander and Hadrian, and the gods of Greece and Rome. They visited Spain; Christopher was enthralled by the sound of guitars. St. Denys hired a Spanish guitarist to teach him how to play.

St. Denys was delighted when his ward showed an aptitude for foreign languages. He learned Spanish, French and German with ease. They went to California, where Christopher discovered a hundred dialects, all called American.

Throughout their travels, unseen by anyone but himself, Christopher carried the windup clown buried in a reticule.

❧❧

St. Denys fell into the habit of calling the boy by the pet name of Kit. One night at dinner Christopher asked, "Why do you do that?"

"I beg your pardon?" St. Denys paused, with a glass in his hand. "Why do I do what?"

"Call me Kit. You've called me that for quite a long while. So long I even think of myself that way half the time."

"I didn't know I was. Well, if there is a reason, it's because it fits you. Kit Carson. Kit Marlowe. Bright, audacious, a little reckless... If you don't like it, I'll stop."

"I do like it. It's mine, not just the name of a character in a play. I wondered the reason for it, that's all."

So without effort, Jack who had become Christopher now became Kit. Though not quite four years had passed, his life had become as nearly perfect as it could be, given the empty place in his life that belonged to Michael. But Kit harbored two dark secrets: peculiar needs that grew stronger day by day; and hideous nightmares that grew worse night by night.

Though St. Denys gave out that the handsome young man now at St. Denys Hill was a long-lost distant cousin, those in certain circles believed he was St. Denys' love child. Far from casting a shadow upon the boy, it made him a romantic figure, and one certain someday to be extremely rich. At parties, balls, masquerades, the daughters and nieces of ambitious matrons danced and decorously flirted with Kit from behind fans, daring their chaperones to see them. Kit flirted back because they expected it.

Kit was much made over by ladies of all ages, and he had to admit he liked being their darling. He played to them as if they were an audience and he the young hero of the drama. He was pleased to discover he could make a lady, young or old, ply her fan quite vigorously if he looked into her eyes and smiled.

On the first Friday of each month, St. Denys hosted a social event to which Kit was not invited. Curious, he spied, and was more puzzled. He saw no ladies, only varying numbers of men about his guardian's age. The nearness of all those men, the rumble of their voices undiluted by the shriller female notes, intoxicated his senses. He schemed to get into the gathering, even though he knew he would be in trouble if he did.

The next Friday evening, his valet helped him dress in his best evening clothes and after all the others were there, he walked into the Lesser Hall as if he belonged there. A string quartet played Mozart. The air was heady with male laughter, the smell of their pipes, the scents of their shaving soaps and colognes. His guardian was talking to a handsome black-haired man. Their heads were close together, and St. Denys laughed at something the man said.

Nearer the enormous fireplace a tall, large-faced man with long brown hair, regaled the small group around him. This man was the first to see Kit. He stopped talking and stared. When he did so, those around him looked to see what he was staring at. And then St. Denys and the black-haired man looked at him. He thought he must look a right fool for them to gawk like that. His cheeks grew hot.

The man with the long brown hair drifted to him and took Kit's hand in his, which was strong but unpleasantly damp. "What a lovely lad you are! A dainty blossom among us old withered weeds. You must be the ... cousin ... I've heard of. What a pity to keep you hidden away here."

Kit's mouth dropped open. He had never heard a man talk like this. 'Lovely? Dainty blossom?' Was the fool talking about him? He extricated his hand from the damp grasp.

"I cast my heart at your feet," the strange man said, spreading his fingers over his shirt bosom; "I lave my soul in the cool depths of your eyes..."

"Oscar," St. Denys said, shouldering between them, "my butler could produce better poetry than that."

Oscar laughed and inclined his head in a mock bow. "I but try, my friend. Once in a lifetime one encounters beauty so remarkable it fairly knocks the poetry out of one."

St. Denys put his hand on Kit's shoulder. "Gentlemen," he said, "I've told you about Kit, my cousin, now my ward. So far as I am concerned, he is my son, under my care and my protection. Do you take my meaning, gentlemen?"

The longhaired man smiled, showing discolored teeth, which he self-consciously covered with the tips of his fingers. "Oh, Xavier. We're not simpletons, you know. Of course we take your meaning." He winked at Kit, and Kit was more than ever convinced the man was a fool. He drifted away, leaving Kit with his guardian.

St. Denys said in a low voice, "Why didn't you ask for permission to come? Why did you think you had to sneak in? I trust you, Kit. I don't trust sneaks. Please don't do anything like this again."

And then Kit was alone. He left the room feeling like a kicked puppy, and went to the small library to read. He took a book and sat down to read, but his eyelids kept lowering. Nightmares had interrupted his sleep the night before, and the day had been spent in numb hours of geography and mathematics, followed by an hour of strenuous work with the fencing master, and several hours riding about the estate. He fell asleep holding the book, his right leg curled under him, his head tilted sideways against a wing of the chair. He dreamed, a nightmare of brass buttons and snarled curses and hard fists

The sound of a door shutting brought him awake with terror. *The old man!* He gasped and leaped to his feet, almost falling as his numbed right leg buckled. The book tumbled to the floor. He was caught before he fell and he found himself in the arms of the black-haired man who had been talking to St. Denys.

"I'm sorry," the man said. "The door was ajar and I saw you here." He smiled down at Kit and something leapt inside him. "Oscar was right. You're really quite extraordinary."

Kit managed an unsteady smile. "At least you didn't tell me I looked like a lovely blossom."

The gentleman laughed. "That's not my style."

Kit tried to regain his dignity and ignore his racing heart. "Do you always enter rooms uninvited?" Icy needles of returning sensation stabbed his foot and leg. Kit could not help noticing that the man's eyes were almost black, his lips were moist, and his teeth were white.

"No. But I've been hoping to meet you, and Xavier guards you as if you were his virgin daughter."

"Well, I'm not," Kit said quickly, his mouth so dry he could scarcely speak.

"Oh?" The question was asked with another laugh. "You're obviously not his daughter. Am I to infer that you're not a virgin either?"

"Think what you like."

"Ah..."

At that moment Kit realized that the gentleman had closed the door when he came in. He stopped breathing as the man touched his cheek and kissed him. Kit murmured deep in his throat and leaned into the kiss; his whole system exploded with the peculiar need.

The man drew back. "Xavier would horsewhip me if he knew I'd done that. And God knows I want more than that. Well, I'm not of a mind to be horsewhipped today. Good-bye, Kit." He turned toward the door.

"Wait. Who are you?"

"My name is Rawdon McPherson." He took a step away, and then turned. "It would be best if he did not find out about this."

"Mightn't we meet again? Somewhere else?"

"I don't know. You're very young."

"I'm past seventeen, Mr. McPherson, and I've never been young."

"Yes," McPherson said, "our friend has told me a little of your history." He held out a calling card. "Put this in a safe place. When you're older, we may indeed get better acquainted away from our friend when you're in the City alone."

Impulsively, Kit kissed him. Until tonight he'd never before kissed anyone; he was shocked again by the explosion of fire in the pit of his stomach, his brain, his entire body.

McPherson drew back with a quizzical smile. His face was red, his pupils wide. "Do you have any idea what you're doing?"

"Yes." Kit did not know, exactly, but whatever it was, he wanted to do it. To prove it, he pressed his palm hard against McPherson. The heat in his own body burst into a wildfire.

McPherson stared at him, then seized Kit's face between his hands and kissed him with hot, open-mouthed urgency. Kit pushed against McPherson in response. McPherson again broke away. "My God, but you're a randy little fool," he said. "I can't play this game. You're too young. And Xavier would kill me." He left Kit there, wondering what he'd done wrong. And wondering what would have followed. And what he had to do to make it happen.

Kit's sleep was troubled that night. He dreamt of Rawdon McPherson and, half-awake, he turned over on his belly while he dreamed. The dream ended with the inner melting that obliterated everything but itself. When he slept again, he dreamed, and it was not of McPherson.

The old man's face floated about him pulsing with hatred, covered with blood. Hands came out of nowhere to strike him again and again and again. Shiny brass buttons winked like malevolent eyes—

Kit jerked upright. "You're dead!" he cried. "Why won't you stay dead? Oh God, Oh God." He drew his knees up, desperate for someone warm and alive to be with him to keep the phantom away.

"Michael," he moaned. If only Michael was there, as he had been since the beginning of their life. But Michael was dead. He was alone. Wrapped in a blanket, he sat up the rest of the night in a chair, coming sharply awake every time his head nodded.

He was surprised when Rawdon McPherson entered the library a few nights later. "Hello," Kit said. "I don't know where he is."

"Quite all right. I've just left him." McPherson glanced at the title of the book. "What are you reading? Plays. I ought to have known. Our friend brags endlessly on your talent. He thinks you are another Edwin Booth or Henry Irving."

"Perhaps I am."

"Perhaps you are. Our friend will be away for a little while. Did you know?"

"I know he has to leave tomorrow for Edinburgh for a month."

"I'm to stay here and look after some things for him."

Kit's insides lurched together to form a quivering lump of nerves. "Really," he said indifferently.

"I've decided to stay at the Dower House. I thought it would be best."

Kit shrugged and returned to his book. McPherson waited as if he expected an answer. A moment later he took the book out of Kit's hands, and snapped, "You've disrupted my life, damn you. I can't get you out of my mind. I'm only human. I'll be at the Dower House. Come there if you want to. Tomorrow night." He tossed the book down and strode away.

Kit picked up the book and laughed softly. He did not sleep that night. He was racked by guilt, knowing how much St. Denys trusted him. But he was tormented by the determination to meet McPherson. Before dawn the next morning his guardian bade him farewell and left. At midnight he went to the Dower House.

His hand shook; he could hardly turn the heavy old key in the front-door lock of the Dower House. The candles in the wall sconces were still lit though the candles were burning down. McPherson was in none of the downstairs rooms. Kit noiselessly went upstairs to the bedrooms. Candlelight came from one of them. He stood in the doorway for a moment looking at the man sleeping beneath the sheet. As he threw aside his clothes, he could scarcely breathe. Never, in all the giggling toss-offs with Toad and Spitter, had he been as nervous or as excited. McPherson wakened and turned toward him.

He gave himself entirely over to McPherson's experienced teaching. Every inch of his body came alive with sensation. He wanted more and more and more. He knew pleasure, and unexpected pain that took his breath away. And then the pain was drowned in pleasure that drained both his body and soul.

When it was ended, McPherson sat on the edge of the bed and took a drink directly from a wine bottle. "Why didn't you tell me you'd never done this before? Had I known, I would not have let you come here."

"That's why," Kit said. "Now what? Again?"

McPherson laughed, and lay down. "Go to sleep. I need to recuperate, even if you don't."

The old man wrestled with him. Seized his hand. Forced it down upon his brother's face. Michael's rotting flesh gave way. His hand sank into soft eyes, into putrefying brain. From the old man's red mouth spewed words like worms.

Kit woke disoriented, slick with cold sweat, and he recoiled as his hand encountered the form beside him. But this was no decaying body; this was live, solid flesh and blood. In his nightmare-dazed state he could not remember the man's name. He didn't care what his name was. Whoever he was he would stand between Kit and Tom Rourke. He got as close as he could. The man, still asleep, roused enough to put his arms around him. Kit's eyes closed. Rourke would not dare come back now. He slept without dreaming again.

Over the next few days Kit discovered that his body remembered everything McPherson had done, with the same clarity with which his brain remembered words. During St. Denys' absence, Kit wondered how McPherson could sit at the dining table, cut his meat, drink his wine, and talk of commonplace things knowing that in a few hours they would be wild at the Dower House again. He himself, hot with anticipation, could hardly eat, drink, or sit still. And then one night in bed McPherson said, "You know it's all over now, do you not?"

Kit felt as if McPherson had dashed a bucket of cold water in his face. "What are you talking about?"

"I mean all good things come to an end. We won't be together like this again. He'll be home tomorrow."

"There must be a way."

McPherson's voice was pleasant, matter-of-fact. "I'm fond of you, Kit. But not enough that I want to lose Xavier's friendship because of you. If this goes on, that's inevitable. Do you understand?"

Hurt, furious, Kit said, "I'll tell him everything."

"No, you won't. Good God, boy, I didn't drag you here. You came here of you own free will and I took advantage of it as any man of my sort would. If that makes me a cad, so be it." He looked slowly up and down the length of Kit's body. "And you enjoyed every minute of it. As," he said with a lazy smile, "did I."

For several weeks Kit replayed every word, trying to learn what went wrong. One night, out for a late ride in a light mist, Kit stopped to walk his horse in the lush grass. McPherson's rejection still rankled.

"Power," he said aloud, as he stroked Jezebel's soft muzzle. "It all comes down to that, doesn't it. The old man had power over me. And so do Lizbet and my guardian. And McPherson." He walked in silence for a few more minutes and then said aloud, "Everyone has some kind of power over me except myself. Someday I'll have it. And when I get it I'll never let it go."

⧉

With McPherson's departure, Kit's nightmares came again, more often than before. He had long ago found that calling up images of strong-looking men would sometimes keep the nightmare at bay. But now that he had slept with a real man the images did not work.

St. Denys and Kit stayed in London during the winter, but St. Denys was called away to Edinburgh on business more often as the months passed. Whenever he was gone Kit prowled the City alone. There he found men more than eager to give his young body what it craved and his spirit what it needed, men who could help him sleep in peace.

For a while there was a stagehand named Hudson. Then an understudy named Albert. For a few nights there was a young tough who drove an ale wagon. He was followed by a photographer with elegant hands, who was replaced by a melancholy tenor. St. Denys knew nothing of it; Kit learned to live at ease with the deception.

4

A t eighteen Kit was a little past six feet tall. Hard work in the theatre, and training with the fencing master had given him an athlete's build and a dancer's grace. Most people thought he was at least twenty-one. He chafed under Irving's tutelage; he was tired of being the legs to Irving's table.

When the actor playing Mercutio at the Xavier Theatre choked to death on a bite of apple, the director approached St. Denys about letting Kit audition for it.

"Do you want to have a go at it?" St. Denys asked, knowing the answer before he heard it.

"I'd kill for it," Kit said.

"He's heard about you from Miss Terry. And others. It was Miss Terry's suggestion. And it is just an audition. Someone else may get the part."

"No," Kit said with grim determination. "He won't."

Kit was the last to audition, and the least experienced as well as the youngest. The director was a man named Coatsworth, with a round, creased face. As Kit stood on stage, waiting to be told to begin, Coatsworth said, "You have much to live up to, young man. Miss Terry sang your praises quite eloquently. She believes you can do the part."

"So do I."

"Very well. Audition for me."

When he was finished, Coatsworth said, "Report for rehearsal tomorrow at eleven o'clock. Oh, and you'll have to fill in as a guard and a strolling player."

As Kit left the stage, for the first time in his life he knew complete happiness. In the suite that evening, St. Denys handed him a folded paper and said, "I was so sure of your success, I had the programs already printed."

Kit opened the program and looked up, puzzled. "The printer made a mistake," he said. "This has my name as Kit St. Denys not Christopher Brown."

"There's no mistake. Kit, I've petitioned the Court to let me adopt you. It means falsifying certain records and paying a bribe, but it's worth it. Your name shall be legally St. Denys. But only if you approve. And even if you don't wish to be my son, I'd be honored if you would use St. Denys as your stage name."

Kit had to try twice before he could speak. "How could I not want to be your son?" He swallowed hard. "You will be my father? For real?"

"For real, Kit. And forever."

"Why are you so good to me? How can I ever repay you for everything you've already done for me?"

"It's my privilege, Kit. Repay me by never being false to your talent. Promise me."

"I promise." He didn't like to make promises. He could never keep them. He'd promised Michael not to make the old man mad, but he had. He'd promised Michael to take him away to safety, but he had not. "Father," he said aloud. "We never had a real one." He looked down to hide his surge of emotion.

"What is it?" St. Denys asked. "Kit, things can stay as they are if you would rather."

"Oh, no!" He hesitated. "Can we take Michael home to the Hill? Bury him in a special place in the woods? He never saw any place like that. He'd like it there."

St. Denys said gently, "Of course. I intended to do so if you became my son because then Michael would be also."

That night as he lay wide-eyed and unable to sleep, staring up at the moonlit ceiling, Kit whispered "You're going to be someplace nice, Michael, just like I promised."

The critics cautiously approved of young St. Denys in his first role, but none-too-subtly suggested he learn to be more forceful in his actions. "What do they mean by that?" he asked St. Denys. "I can't speak for them," St. Denys said with a shrug, "but in the case of at least two of them, they think you should chew the scenery more. Pay them no heed."

Kit preferred the natural technique of Irving and Terry, but he also knew he was inexperienced. In his next performance he tried to please those critics; he made grand theatrical gestures and exaggerated every speech. Instead of ignoring him, one critic devoted a column to the "delusion of competence the young man projected in his first performance." The other stated, "Young St. Denys was cast because he is the son of the theatre owner, who more than likely bought the part for him."

The director completed Kit's humiliation. "I am the director. You are not. Directors direct. Actors act. You perform it the way I said or you will be replaced. I don't care whose son you are. Is that clear?"

One more example of power. Kit faced Coatsworth without flinching. "Yes, sir," he said. "It's clear. I apologize."

The director was surprised; he had expected sullen rebellion. "Well," he said. "See that it doesn't happen again."

Kit was next cast in a comedy as a young curate. Though the part was small, the critics pounced. The consensus was that young St. Denys, son of the theatre owner, had seemed full of promise but with his inept performance in *Miss Lovejoy's Revenge* that promise seemed to be dead; he was stilted and unfunny.

As before, Kit felt the sharp sting of their printed words. The play did not run long. Next was a tragedy, *The Stone*. He played first lead as Paul, a young man who commits a crime out of desperation and takes his life rather than face the law. It was difficult to separate himself from the boy fugitive inside his skin. This time the critics veered in the other direction. "Superb." "The promise he demonstrated as Mercutio has returned with the brilliance of shining gold."

The play that followed *The Stone* was a drawing-room comedy. He knew he did not do as well in it. But the critics were even more complimentary than the last time. He decided critics were fools and he would never again let them influence anything he did in the theatre.

※ ※

Kit found ways to explore the secret side of his nature. Each liaison with a man confirmed his belief that this was what he wanted, that this was what he was. He did not understand it, but saw no reason to fight it. In Kit's nineteenth year Rawdon McPherson briefly figured once more as a lover, but this time it was Kit who ended it, over McPherson's protests. It felt good to be the one with the power.

During the day his intellect and talent gave him confidence. A night alone gave him only fear, and as time passed the nightmares grew worse. Nothing but the presence of another man could keep them away.

This was on Kit's mind as he rode about the estate during one of his father's absences. He wanted to get back to London. Suddenly a doe darted from the woods. Jezebel reared, threw him and galloped off in fright. Kit's right foot was caught in the stirrup. She dragged him across the rough ground, her hooves slamming into the earth inches from his head. When she regained her senses and came to a stop, he lay bruised and hurting, stunned by the realization of how close he had come to death. The left side of his face was scraped and bloody; his shoulders and back and head screamed with pain. He clambered up with difficulty and limped home, leading the nervous mare. That night, because of the pain of the accident, Rourke was more real than ever.

> *"Ye son of a whore!" Big feet kicked. Big hands closed around his throat and squeezed, squeezed. Blood poured from his eyes. His head was ripped from his shoulders. "Join your brother an' rot." His head cartwheeled through blackness. His empty eye sockets could still see Michael's peeling flesh, writhing with white worms. The worms, the worms—the worms were everywhere.*

Afraid to go back to sleep, he dressed, and started to the library. As he passed his father's suite he was surprised to see the door open and a bright fire burning in the grate. He was even more surprised when St. Denys appeared in the doorway and said in a strange voice, "Come here." He stood waiting, hands behind his back. He looked cold and harsh, unlike himself.

"Hello. I didn't know you had returned," Kit said, smiling.

"Obviously." St. Denys stared at Kit, then picked up a lamp and held it close to Kit. "How did you get those marks?"

"Jezebel threw me and dragged me a short distance."

"Really? You look more as if you'd been ridden hard and put away wet. Who did it? Your valet? Some groom? The gardener? A cowherd? You obviously have a taste for the lower class."

The vulgar sneer and the expression on the normally kind face shocked Kit. Bewildered, he said, "Why do you say that? Have I done something wrong?"

"You know what you've done! You've endangered yourself and played me for a fool."

"I still don't know what you're talking about!"

St. Denys thrust a small piece of paper at him. "This is what I'm talking about."

The paper was an obscenely graphic note from the stagehand, Hudson, to his father. In it was spelled out Kit's brief affair with him. In it were described places they'd never been and things they'd never done, and ended with a demand for a small fortune to keep him quiet.

"Do you deny it?" St. Denys asked.

"Would it do me any good?" Kit's smile was grim.

"How could you be such a fool? He was a common renter!"

"You sleep with men," Kit snapped.

St. Denys drew in a sharp breath. "You can't know that."

"I've known for years."

"We're not talking about me. Kit, don't you know you could be sent to prison if these accusations could be proved? And even if they couldn't, don't you know your life would be ruined just by the charges?"

"I'll pay him. There won't be any charges."

"I paid him," St. Denys said.

He held the paper to a candle and watched it burn to ash. When he looked at Kit again, the harshness was gone from his face. "Kit, if this is what you are, you must learn to be careful. Renters such as Hudson are everywhere, waiting to bleed you dry. Whatever their other talents, they're often accomplished liars. Not all that long ago, men such as I—and you, if what you say is true—could have been hanged or burnt at the stake. Now we're lucky. It could just mean life in prison, at hard labor."

Kit stammered as he said, "Thank you for taking care of it."

"I'd protect you with my life. I hope it's not my fault you're drawn to men. If it is, I'll never forgive myself."

"I've been 'drawn to men,' as you put it, long before I came here to live."

For a moment St. Denys said nothing. Then he laid his hand on Kit's shoulder. "Just be careful, my boy. I couldn't bear it if anything happened to you."

☙❧

Very little changed after that. He continued his liaisons, but with more caution, and was careful not to let St. Denys know. Resigned, St. Denys knew but did not acknowledge that he did.

Three months later, following another journey to Edinburgh, St. Denys came into Kit's room. Kit was propped up on the bed, reading a new script by the sunlight that flooded the room. He looked up, smiled, and put aside the book.

St. Denys sat down across from him and for several minutes said nothing. Then, gently, he said, "Kit, I have never told you how much I love you."

"Of course you have. More ways than I can count."

"I could not be prouder of you or love you more if I had sired you." His father's voice had a strange, ghostly timbre that alarmed Kit. St. Denys made a small, helpless gesture. "I'm dying," he said. "I won't live to see you become a man. I'll never see you become the great actor you are destined to be."

Kit threw aside the book and knelt beside the chair. "No. Someone's made a mistake."

"I have a cancer in my head, Kit. The times I was in Edinburgh were not business. I was consulting an old friend who is a physician. He has suspected for some time but is now certain. I have perhaps six months to live. Perhaps less. I am in constant pain. Death will be a relief."

Guilt and grief racked Kit. Why had he not seen how thin his father was? Why had he not seen the deeper groves in his face, and the shallow bulge beneath the skin just above his left cheekbone?

"No," he said when he could speak. "Let's go to America. Or Germany. France. Canada. Anywhere. Someplace there is a doctor who will cure you."

"I don't have time left to pursue hopeless dreams, Kit. I've too much to teach you. We must make the most of every day now." With his thumb he gently wiped away the tear that slid down Kit's cheek. "Don't cry for me. I've had a good life, and you've been the best part of it." He sighed. "But I worry about you, Kit. You're an intense, passionate young man. Those are good attributes for an actor or an author or a painter—to a point. Beyond that point they can cause great harm. Promise me you'll harness them."

"How can I promise such a thing?" Kit cried. "I don't know what the future holds. Without you here—"

"Then promise me this: as long as I still live, honor me and yourself by disowning the vice we seem to share. I'm seeking peace with God. If I knew you had done the same I could die with less regret."

Now, knowing what would soon happen, St. Denys spent hours each day teaching Kit about the business of the theatre. It was only a negligible source of his income, but it was the thing other than Kit that he loved most. He taught Kit everything about being an owner and manager. Kit insisted he wanted to stop performing in order to spend more time with him. St. Denys would not hear of it. "Don't cheat me of the joy of watching you perform," he said.

Kit was stunned by the ungodly rapid progress of the disease. Soon St. Denys was unable to go to the theatre. His face became more and more grotesque. The right side was wrinkled and skeletal while the left side was pulled smooth and unlined over the tumor, which grew like an obscene bubble beneath the skin. Kit had horrible dreams in which the thing exploded in a ghastly spewing of indescribable matter. Soon his father wore an eye patch, for he could not close his left eyelid and his eye was dry and painful.

"Why?" Kit asked Lizbet, who had come to stay for a while at the Hill. "Why can't he just die? Why does anyone have to suffer like this? It makes no sense. It's like Michael's death. The good die, the bad live."

Lizbet could only look helplessly at him. She had no answer.

Kit arranged for the cast of *Rose's Heart* to do a performance at St. Denys Hill while his father sat propped up on pillows to cushion his fleshless bones. Soon afterward St. Denys stopped coming to the dining room for meals. Kit himself took the tray to the bedroom suite and dined with him there, often joined by Lizbet. Little food was eaten. Soon St. Denys could not eat at all. Every moment of every day his moans could be heard. Laudanum in ever-increasing doses did not help. Kit stayed beside the bed hour after hour, both frantic to leave and unwilling to leave.

To his surprise, Rawdon McPherson also came every day, the only one of the dying man's friends to do so. McPherson spent many hours talking quietly or just sitting beside the bed with a silent calm that, to Kit, was the epitome of callousness. And yet, his father appeared comforted by McPherson's presence.

One day when Kit went into the bedroom and spoke to St. Denys, his father started. He was blind. "This is cruel, too cruel. If only I could still see you..." Kit's hand was gentle upon his father's shoulder. Before day's end his father could neither hear nor speak. He died the following day.

Kit was bitterly surprised at the small number of mourners who came to the services and to the family cemetery at St. Denys Hill. His father had helped many people, had been a patron of all the arts, yet few bothered to stand in the rain beside his grave.

When the funeral was over, and the few mourners had gone, Kit took a bottle of Irish whiskey into the small library, intending to lock the room and drink his grief away. He froze when he realized Rawdon McPherson was in there.

"What are you doing here?" Kit asked in a hard voice. The answer astonished him.

"Kit, I loved him. I know you don't believe that. But I did. Xavier and I were lovers for many years. If we could have lived together without scandal, we would have."

"You're right. I don't believe you. You seduced me, knowing how he would feel about it if he knew."

McPherson's eyebrows lifted. "Which of us seduced the other is a matter of opinion. And that has nothing to do with what I felt for Xavier."

The long weeks had taken their toll. Kit was thin and haggard. McPherson said, "Kit, Xavier wanted you to devote yourself to acting. You will never have to worry about money since all he possessed goes to you when you reach your majority. Until then, his will provides that I act as your trustee."

For an instant Kit's past swirled around him like autumn leaves in a sudden breeze. Filthy streets and alleys. Rats large as scrawny cats. Throats cut in alleys or whorehouses for a few coins or a pair of shoes. Jack Rourke, a thief as soon as he could walk. Stolen money in the cracked brown jar that held treasure and hope of escape. He, promising Michael he would take care of him. Mum whoring and the old man drunk and raging. Michael dead in his arms. He and the old man fighting. The old man's blood and his own, on his face and clothes.

A chill shook him. Michael. Papa St. Denys. Lizbet. He had loved three people and now two were gone.

꘎꘎

At twenty, Kit St. Denys played Hamlet to the cheers and applause of full houses in the Xavier. The critics sniffed because his portrayal was not traditional. The purists scowled over his ending the play with Horatio's grieving lament, and they were disturbed by his prowling Hamlet who simmered with violence just below the surface.

Kit smiled, shrugged, and threw away the reviews. When asked about them, he laughed. "The people come, don't they?" he answered. "What other critics do I have to concern myself over?"

The people loved it. And loved him. They waited in long queues for the cheap seats. When the seats were filled they stood in the aisles. Each curtain call brought a mixture of elation and sadness to Kit because his father was not there to see them. *Hamlet* played sixteen weeks, and always to a full house.

At twenty-one Kit came into his full inheritance. The dream that had been growing over the past few years could now be made to come true: the formation of The St. Denys Repertory Company. Advertisements in English, Canadian, and American trade papers brought him talented people. He handpicked the costume and set designers, the general manager, the stage manager. Given a free hand and told to spare no expense in creating striking sets and costumes and encouraged to be innovative, they outdid themselves.

Many actors auditioned; few were chosen. His leading lady was Rama Weisberg, a tall woman with wild copper curls who could portray a virago or a virgin with equal ability. One of the actors hired was Francis Mulholland, a rangy man with a plain but engaging face. His kind, easy-going personality appealed to Kit. Francis was enthralled by him. Kit thought perhaps it would be nice for a change, to have a real lover.

Francis became a unique part of Kit's life; he brought loving gentleness to Kit's life. But before long, Kit realized he had no grand passion for Francis and Francis became a fast friend, a competent actor in small roles, and a sometime bed partner. Francis accepted the situation as better than never being with him at all.

By the time Kit was twenty-five he was one of the most famous men in England. People recognized him in the streets. Women wrote love letters to him, offering to leave their husbands or fiancés for him. They begged for a lock of his hair. They begged for pictures. They begged for him. He gave the letters to his secretary to answer. When he wanted sport it was not with a woman. And it would never be with anyone who begged.

One gloomy afternoon he chanced upon a small, forlorn London gallery tucked away on a narrow, cobbled street. Kit half expected Charles Dickens himself to be there. Most of the artists whose works were displayed were untalented and the works forgettable. As Kit turned to go, he saw an unframed painting that took his breath away.

Kit looked so long at the painting that the artist coughed and ventured to speak. "Do you like it, sir? It's called 'Phoenix.'" Kit did not answer, but continued to stare at the bird rising on wings of red-and-gold flames from a flaming pyre. The artist persisted, "Do you know the legend? The phoenix destroys itself in fire of its own making, then gives birth to itself again, endlessly."

Without counting it, he shoved all the money he had with him into the artist's hands. "Is that enough?" he asked, seizing the picture. "If it isn't, come to the Xavier Theatre." The artist gaped after him, mouth open and his hands full of more money than he had ever seen.

In the carriage, Kit propped the painting up before him, mesmerized by it. "It's my soul," he whispered. "My very soul."

5

Four years before Jack Rourke was brought howling in protest into his squalid world, a boy was born to a self-taught physician and his wife, in a village lying on a slope of the Cotswolds. The village overlooked lush, sheep-dotted grazing meadows created by the Almighty with help from frequent flooding of the River Severn. The boy born to the physician was a late blessing of God, coming twelve years after his sister Agnes, the presumed last of the brood.

William Stuart delivered the child, though his wife neither wanted nor needed his help. "I've already had six, Mr. Stuart," she had reminded him. "If I don't know how to do this by now, I never will."

He inspected the infant for any missing or deformed parts. "A perfect boy child," he announced. The baby mewled, his rosebud mouth opened and shut like that of a little fish as William Stuart swaddled him and laid him in his mother's arms. She pressed her cheek to the downy little head. "Aye, he is the handsomest of the litter," she said, the Irish brogue of her youth still much in evidence.

"He is not a puppy, a kitten, or a pig, Mrs. Stuart," said William Stuart, in sharp rebuke. "He is my child. My son. I will thank you to remember that."

"Your son? And would ye be tellin' me, Mr. Stuart, when you started to feel the pangs of labor? We'll name him Patrick," Bridgett Stuart said, looking down at the baby. "After the Patron Saint of Ireland."

"Indeed, Mrs. Stuart, we shall not! That Papist superstition is not fit for a God-fearing Baptist family. We'll name him Nicholas after my father." He smiled proudly. "And he'll take over my practice when the good God calls me home."

"Perhaps the lad will have another future in mind, Mr. Stuart."

Her husband's face darkened. "We gave the other boy choices and lived to regret it. This boy will be a doctor and there's an end to it."

※※

The Stuart household began each day at 4:30. As the family filed into the small parlor, the children yawned and sometimes stumbled over one another. There they knelt, beside an open window in good weather, beside the bright hearth in bad. Mr. Stuart first, his wife beside him. At her side or in her arms was the youngest child, the rest arranged around their parents. As the years passed, son John took a wife and left home. Then Elspeth, Deborah, Elizabeth and Mary became wives and left. Only Agnes and little Nick remained, and their mother, reminded every day of Agnes' sour disposition, was resigned to having her at home forever. Even though the family dwindled, the tradition and the prayer never changed.

"Oh, Mighty God and Heavenly Father, Ruler and Judge of All, hear my prayers and those of my family." William Stuart exhorted God to bless them and to forgive Mrs. Stuart her sharp tongue, Agnes her quick temper, Nicholas his sauciness and teasing of his sister... The sins of each child, both home and away, and the sins of their spouses and children were laid before the Almighty and promptly forgiven. The prayer ended when the old clock chimed five.

If Nick's eyes drooped, Agnes jabbed his ear with her elbow. If he jabbed her in retaliation, his father's eye fell hard upon him and he sniffled into silence. After the morning prayer came thirty minutes of reading from the Bible as they wended their way through it from Genesis to Revelation once a year. Evening prayers preceded bedtime.

The three-hour church services on Sunday morning were torture. Nick's eyes glazed. In his head he was somewhere else. He ran barefoot in the thick green grass, or pranced with abandon in the rain, his head thrown back to catch raindrops on his tongue. Sometimes he rolled down hills in the snow, or lay spread-eagled in the sun, and baked like bread.

As sermons droned, he opened his eyes wide to keep them from falling shut. When that failed he rolled his eyeballs in circles, first one way and then another; that made him dizzy. He counted the cracks in the wood floor. He pressed his lips tightly together to capture errant yawns, and then wondered how he could yawn inside but not outside. If a yawn escaped Nick or he nodded off or looked about, Agnes dug her elbow into his ribs. Nick was convinced Agnes sharpened her elbows the way his mother sharpened kitchen knives.

Sometimes something caught his small-boy interest. One Sunday during the sermon, a fat fly landed on Mr. Duckett's hairless head. It stomped about, stopping every now and then to rub its front feet together in obvious glee. It trooped up and down and around the double pink hillocks above the starched collar where Mr. Duckett couldn't reach it without drawing attention.

After church Agnes always recited to their father the long list of her brother's wrongdoing. Their father listened, frowning, and asked Nicholas if the accusations were true. Knowing that Hell awaited liars, he always admitted his guilt, fetched the birch switch, and bent over.

Once he asked indignantly, "If she has her eyes closed during prayer, Father, how does she know what I'm doing?"

"God sees," said his father.

"Agnes is not God." Chin high, without another word, Nick brought the switch, dropped his trousers, and bent over his father's knee.

Once in a while he got revenge. Several times he tied Agnes' high-buttoned boots together. Once he dumped a fruit jar full of worms in her bed. Her screams were worth the birching his father gave him.

Nick was four when he fell in love with a ten-year-old girl named Angelica. She had hair like sunshine. She carried him around, teased him, played games with him, and helped him with his lessons. When she became a young lady he was jealous of the boys who courted her. Except for Martin, Mr. Somers' farmhand, who fascinated him. Stripped to the waist in the hot sun, Martin's body shone with sweat as he forked hay higher and faster than anyone else.

On Nick's sixth birthday his father announced, "Nicholas, today you begin your training. I'm going to geld Farmer Tucker's pigs and I want you to observe." He placed a proud hand on Nick's unruly dark hair. "I started my medical training the same way, watching my father."

Nick stared in fascinated horror as Farmer Tucker seized each struggling little pig by his front trotters, held him suspended, snout forward, while William Stuart made two quick cuts with his razor-edged scalpel. Shrill squeals of pain shattered the air and ribbons of blood ran down the pink little bodies. Nicholas gulped down nausea. Returning home in the old buggy, he asked, "Why do you geld them? It's awful cruel."

"It is done," his father answered, "so they have no desire to fornicate." He looked at Nick as if to add that the same should be done with little boys. Nick didn't know what 'fornicating' was. Like 'circumcision,' it was a word read aloud in scripture but never explained. Was he guilty of it? How could he be guilty when he didn't know what it was? But just because you didn't know something was a sin, didn't mean you weren't guilty of sin if you did it. The Scriptures were clear about that. He was confused and frightened.

After the pig gelding, he went regularly with his father. He made up his schoolwork with Mr. Spencer, the village schoolmaster, whenever he could. He and his father rode in silence from village to village, from farm to farm, in the valley. He stood at his father's side, helping wherever his father directed, handing him instruments or water or clean cloths. By the time he was seven, he was no longer dismayed when his father had to thrust his entire arm into a cow's body to help a calf get born. He often knew the joy of helping a new lamb, a wobbly foal, or a tiny pig stand for the first time.

When he was nine he assisted at the birth of a farm wife's baby. His father had intended to keep him well away from human birth for some years, but the woman had no female relatives, her husband was recently dead and the only midwife in the valley was ill. His son would have to do.

He gave Nick a basin of water, a small ewer of oil, several towels and cloths and directed him to sit beside the fireplace and keep them warm. Nick sat beside the fireplace and listened to the cries and grunts of pain that came from the birthing room. Finally he heard his father call, "Nicholas, bring the water and warm towels."

In the doorway, Nick blanched at the birthing smells. It was no worse than when a cow calved, he told himself, or when a mare had a foal. It was only the small, hot room that made the difference.

"Well," said his father impatiently, "will you bring those towels over here today or wait for Christmas?"

He kept his eyes averted from the woman, but need not have bothered. His father had her decently covered. His father took the baby, slimy with blood and mucus, wrapped it in the warm towel and placed the precious bundle into his son's arms. "Take him and wash him gently. Scarcely touch him. Be careful not to get water on the cord. Oil his skin and wrap him well. Then keep him warm until I call you again."

As he carefully carried out his assignment, Nick was almost overcome by the incredible helplessness of the tiny creature. It was the most wonderful thing he had ever seen. As he waited for the summons, he held the baby and gazed in wonder at the bruised, swollen eyelids, at the skin softer than any cobweb. When he was called again, he carried the newborn into the birthing room. Eyes shining, he smiled as he handed the infant to his mother.

The woman later told her neighbors, "The little Stuart lad is such a love. He helped bring my baby into the world, and when he smiled at me, it was like the sun coming out over the hills. I named the baby for him, you know."

William Stuart was thunderstruck when the story got to him a few weeks later that his young son had single-handedly delivered Mrs. Oliver's baby. Nick laughed in delight. His father did not.

֎

When he was fourteen, Nick's unquestioning faith was both shaken and reinforced. From his seat in the family pew, Nick listened, bewildered and angry, as his beloved Angelica and her sweetheart, Martin, were called before the congregation for discipline.

"These young sinners," the pastor declared, his voice quivering with grief and rage, "threw away the purity given them by God. They betrayed the trust placed in them by their families and by this congregation. Look at them. Two young people of good family. Two young people who know the Law of God. Two young people lured by the devil into carnal sin. Oh, my brethren, when fornication teases and torments, only those who put their trust in the Almighty God can withstand. These two before us did not listen to the Spirit. They listened to the devil."

Nick had seen other official disciplines, but none he had ever cared about. He heard Angelica's widowed mother stifling her sobs. Angelica's head was lowered, her face tear-stained and red. She flinched whenever the pastor thundered the word "fornication." Nick could hardly bear it when Angelica's shoulders shook.

The pastor sat down. Nick's father as elder took his place and further harangued them about their sins. He, too, used the word fornication many times. Nick wanted to scream, "Stop it! Let them go!" but the pastor and his father spoke for God and God's Law was bigger than the wishes of one fourteen-year-old boy. William Stuart finally said, "Angelica, Martin, you will kneel and face the congregation and ask their forgiveness as well as God's."

The two young sinners did as they were ordered. Many long prayers followed, and Nick lifted his head and stared. Martin's head was not bowed; the tendons of his neck stood out like cords, and his stony face was full of hatred. Nick was terrified: the Wrath of God would burst through the roof at any moment. He lowered his head again and squeezed his eyes shut. "Please, Almighty God," he prayed over and over, "Martin doesn't mean it. Please forgive him and don't send a bolt of lightning upon him. Please."

The prayer worked; lightning did not descend. When the service of discipline was over, Martin and Angelica walked separately from the church, forbidden ever to speak to each other again. The next day the village woke to the news that Angelica and Martin had run off together in the night.

Nick frowned often after that. New, unpleasant thoughts nudged at him. How could God have let Angelica be treated that way? How could God be so unfair? Nick missed Angelica's laugh and the way she pinched his nose when she teased him. And underneath the anger at the church was a current of curiosity that would not go away: what was fornication? He'd heard at least a million sermons about with it. And it was the reason baby pigs, young horses, roosters, and bulls were cut. It was a great sin when people did it. But what was it?

One day it occurred to him Agnes might know. She'd just turned twenty-seven; surely by the time one was that old one knew everything. He waited until he and Agnes were alone as he helped her weed the vegetable patch. "Agnes," he said, "may I ask you something?"

"I suppose," she said. She did not look at him. She seldom did. His birth had ruined her life and her prospects, and she had told him so.

"Well, it's a word. I don't know what it means. I thought you might." A little flattery couldn't hurt. "You know such a lot of things," he added.

"What word?"

"Fornication."

Agnes stared at her younger brother. "What did you say?"

"I just asked if you knew what fornication was. Ow!" He scrambled back out of reach, his face branded with a stinging red mark of her hand.

"You vile little beast! How dare you say a thing like that to me! Father! Father!" She got to her feet, burst into tears and disappeared into the house. Nick could hear her hysterical voice and his father's rumbling reply. He edged toward the garden gate; it might be a good time to be gone.

"Nicholas!" his father thundered from the doorway. "Stay where you are, sir! Come here."

Nick wondered how he could do both, and then reluctantly went toward his father.

"Apologize to your sister, sir," his father demanded.

"I didn't mean to make her cry. I just asked her what fornication meant."

Agnes, at their father's shoulder, shrieked and covered her face. William Stuart's face mottled. He grabbed his son's shoulders in a painful grip and shook him twice, hard. "Let me not hear that word from you again until you are grown! And never, never around a decent woman. Do you understand?"

"But Father, you said it in church and Mother was there, and Agnes was too."

"The words used in Scripture are not the same when they're said by nasty, wicked boys," his father thundered. A few minutes later the birch was applied with great vigor to the bare buttocks of the nasty, wicked boy.

The birching did nothing to end his quest to find out what the terrible word meant. Summer passed as was usual, in Scripture readings, prayers, church services, and helping his father throughout the valley. None of these things dulled his curiosity about the sin of Martin and Angelica.

One afternoon his father was called out and did not take Nick with him. Knowing this might not happen again for a long time,

Nick knew he had to "carpy dum: seize the day" as he'd heard the schoolmaster say, and find the one person who would tell him what he wanted to know.

Nick approached his mother as she bent over the kettle in the hearth. "Mother," he said, "I want to go out in the hills today since I didn't have to go with Father."

She straightened, the ladle dripping thick, savory soup back into the kettle. "Alone?"

He hesitated. His mother knew about his friendship with Hugh Prater and had not objected, other than to sometimes remark that Hugh was extremely messy. "I thought I'd find Hugh."

She pushed his dark hair back to kiss his forehead. "You go right ahead. The saints know you get little chance to be anything other than Mr. Stuart's unpaid helper." She put fresh bread, cheese, and apples enough for two into a burlap bag. "Run along now. Be back before your father comes home."

Nick gave her a quick hug and ran from the cottage to Hugh's place a little farther up the hill. Nick's friendship with Hugh, the son of the village drunkard, was the only secret he had from his father.

Two years older than Nick, Hugh was marked by the righteous of the village to be headed down the same path as his father. Nick liked Hugh because he was vulgar and funny and carefree. And with the mature wisdom of those two additional years, Hugh knew a lot of stuff. On the rare occasions when Nick could escape his father's keen eye and his sister's tale telling, he and Hugh roamed the countryside having what Nick thought of as Adventures. One memorable day Hugh gave him his first (and last) cigar; he coughed and hacked as he picked bits of tobacco from his tongue while Hugh leaned against a tree and regally blew great smelly clouds of smoke. Hugh showed him how to spit between his teeth with great accuracy. Hugh gave him his first taste of whiskey, and while he vomited his breakfast, Hugh observed, "You ain't good at much."

Today, Hugh was slopping the pigs when Nick approached the pen. Old bottles and buckets, insect-riddled wood posts, rusty nails, horseshoes, rakes, everything lay where it was tossed. Finished, Hugh took off the heavy boots, caked ankle deep with many layers of mud and manure.

"Little Stuart," he said, using the nickname he had given Nick long ago. "I didn't think I'd see you for a long time. I figured your old man would sit you down and make you stay to home so you wouldn't land in trouble like your two chums."

"My father was called out before dawn and didn't take me with him. He won't be home until tonight, possibly tomorrow."

"You don't say!" Hugh grinned. "The old tomcat's away so the little blue-eyed mousie will play."

Nick giggled; his voice broke into a deeper laugh. "My mother gave me cheese and bread and apples."

"She know you're with me?"

"Aye. But she won't tell my father or my sister."

"Your sister's a cold one."

"She's just old."

"Yeah. Wait." Hugh disappeared into the cottage and emerged with a whiskey bottle. Seeing Nick's expression, Hugh chuckled. "Don't worry. I won't give you any of it. It's a man's drink, not for little boys."

"I'm not so little anymore," Nick said in protest.

"No, you ain't, at that. Say, Little Stuart, did you notice I got a beard now?"

Nick looked more closely and was surprised to see reddish fuzz on the freckled cheeks and upper lip. "Doesn't it itch like fury?" he asked.

"Sometimes. But we only got one razor and the old man won't let me touch it. Says he might use it someday. I wonder how long I ought to let it grow?"

" 'Till you get two owls and a wren, four larks and a hen to nest in it."

Hugh chortled and punched Nick's arm. Nick took off his shoes, tied the laces together, and slung them over his shoulder. As they crossed narrow little creeks, Nick didn't know which he loved best, warm grass beneath his feet or the warm mud oozing between his toes.

Finding what Nick declared to be the perfect place, a sun-dappled meadow surrounded by trees, they devoured Nick's food. Hugh took several swallows of whiskey and held out the bottle. Nick took a small gulp and choked; it wasn't any better than it had been the first time he tried. Feeling like a lazy cat, Nick lay on his back, his hands beneath his head. Hugh did likewise.

After a while, Hugh produced a long, creative belch. Nick's laugh seesawed between soprano giggles and baritone guffaws. He tried to imitate the belch, but it took a half dozen efforts before he produced even a small one. "How do you do it so easy?" he asked in envy. "I have to try like thunder."

"I got talent," Hugh said, and did it again, an impressive three times in a row.

They watched the clouds form into odd shapes. Nick was struck by how different their perceptions were. The cloud he thought looked like a castle, Hugh insisted looked like a gunboat.

"I'm gonna be a sailor," Hugh declared. I'm gonna join Queen Vic's navy. Maybe this year."

Nick sighed. "I suppose I'll never leave. I'll be an old man here and die and be buried in the churchyard." Then he pushed himself up on one elbow and peered down at his friend. "I say, Hugh, what's fornication?"

Hugh choked on his grass stem. "What's your old man say it is?"

"Well, I asked Agnes first and she slapped me and then Father said I wasn't old enough to know and he thrashed me."

"God, Little Stuart, you've seen bulls do it to cows, and stallions do it to mares, and dogs do it to bitches. And what do you think the puss and the tomcats are screeching about in the night?"

"They're breeding. That doesn't answer my question."

"So where do you think babies come from? Trees?"

"Don't be an idiot. I've seen lots of babies born. I know where they come from."

"So how do you think they got in there?"

Nick's forehead furrowed as he peered down at Hugh. "You mean my mother and my father did—that?" He squeezed his eyes shut to banish the horrible image.

"You really are stupid!" Hugh rolled on the ground and howled with glee. When he could talk, he sat up and said, "You honest didn't know?"

Nick could not look away from his friend's eyes, which were fixed upon him with an odd expression. "It ain't always a husband and wife, you know," Hugh continued. "That's why them old goats in your church hung Angelica and Martin out to dry. They done it and they wasn't married. And sometimes it ain't even a man and a woman." His voice dropped to a raspy whisper. "I been to Liverpool, Little Stuart. I learned stuff there."

Nick's heart pounded in his ears. His body tingled from head to heels with the certainty he was about to find out answers to all his questions. Laughing, Hugh grabbed him, toppled him off balance, and pulled him down to lie on him, between his spread legs. Their noses bumped.

Nick's organ sprang into hardness, something that had never happened without his evil acts beneath the covers late at night, acts which would send him to Hell if God and his father found out. He gasped when he felt against his own erection something as hard but much larger in Hugh's trousers.

Hugh shoved him aside and scrambled to his feet, tugging at his own trousers. "Get your drawers down! Hurry!" Nick was struck dumb by the sight of Hugh with his trousers down around his ankles. When he did not move, Hugh fell to his knees, yanked at Nick's trousers, and fell upon him, gasping and rubbing against him, hard hot flesh against hard hot flesh.

Nick shut his eyes tight as the fiery pressure in his groin built up until he thought he would explode. And explode he did. He let out a raw moan just as Hugh yelled, "Oh, St. Peter-in-the-pocket!" Thick wetness that was not his spewed over Nick's belly; Hugh collapsed on top of him.

The wicked pleasure disappeared. Hugh's weight was squeezing the breath from him. Panic struck. They would be found there, dead. He'd be squashed like a bug beneath Hugh. What would his father say? Would he even be buried in the churchyard? What would they put on the tombstone, if there even was one? 'Nicholas Stuart Squashed To Death Whilst Sinning?'

Into Nick's ear Hugh said in an unsteady voice, "Now you know what fornication is. Sort of."

Directly over Hugh's head was a cloud that looked like an eye. The Eye of God. "Hugh, that was a mortal sin." Nick gasped. God was making a special pit for him in Hell.

"It felt good, didn't it?" Hugh pushed himself away from Nick and again lay flat on the grass, his arms out-flung, legs splayed, his sex at half-mast, bouncing as he laughed.

"All sin feels good," Nick said. "That's why it's sin. That doesn't make it any less wrong." Embarrassment set in, stronger than the pleasure, almost as strong as the fear that God was watching. He got to his feet, pulled up his trousers and with what dignity he could recover, hurried to a nearby creek. There he removed his clothes and waded into the water.

"There's a good idea!" Hugh joined him in the creek. Nick vigorously used a handful of grass to wash from his flat, hairless belly the evidence of his sin and tried to ignore Hugh. Hugh refused to be ignored. With a hoot of laughter, he grabbed Nick and ducked his head underwater. Nick surfaced spluttering. Hugh said, "That sailor I met in Liverpool, he showed me how to do lots of things. I'll teach you more next time." He ducked Nick again and slipped his free hand between Nick's legs. "Or maybe, right now."

Nick fought free and scrambled to the bank, his face burning. "There won't be a next time, Hugh! We're lucky God didn't strike us dead already!" Clumsy with haste, he pulled his clothing on over his wet skin. "I'm never going to do that again. It was disgusting." Some small voice in Nick's head told him he didn't believe what he was saying.

Hugh climbed out on the bank. "Oh, bollocks, Nick. The apple's off the tree now. You can't put it back. The sailor told me that when they're out at sea and there ain't no girls they do stuff with each other." He snickered. "And he said some fellows like other fellows the way some fellows like girls and no one knows why."

"I know why. It's sin."

"If you say that word again, I'll smash you in the face," Hugh said with a scowl. "You liked it, Little Nick. Might as well admit it."

With shaking fingers, Nick buttoned his shirt and pants and put on his shoes and stockings. All the while he looked at the ground to keep from looking at Hugh's body. He wanted to look and he knew it. "Hugh, we won't be friends after today. I won't ever talk to you again." As he trudged away Hugh's voice continued behind him.

"Oh, yes, you will. Ain't nobody else in the village who'll fuck you and that's what you want. You just don't know it yet. Maybe I should tell your old man what you just did with me. What'd he do, huh? Beat the shit out of you? Sure he would! And then you'd have to stand up in front of him and all them other holy men and confess, just like Martin and Angelica only worse! And they'd pray over you and tell you you'll go to hell."

Nick yelped as something hard caught him in the middle of his back. He turned and another rock whacked him on the shoulder. "Hugh, what are you doing? Stop it."

"You think I'm nothing, don't you!" A third rock hit Nick's chest and made him stagger. "My old man's a stew bum and I will be too. You think I ain't good enough for the likes of you even if I'm the only one."

"I don't think that at all," Nick said, afraid of his naked, wild-eyed friend. "I'll go home and pray for both of us."

Hugh's face was twisted. "Aye, you do that!" This time his seeking fingers found a large, hard clod of dirt and he hurled it with all his might. It caught Nick in the belly and bent him double. "You don't understand, you stupid little bugger," Hugh screamed. "I could've left here a long time ago but I was waiting for you to grow up. I always knew what you were. I wanted us to go away together like Martin and Angelica."

Nick retreated backward, shaken. What did Hugh mean 'always knew what you were?' He stammered, "I-I'll pray for you. I'll pray for both of us." The memory of their sin and the things Hugh was saying made him sick. He ran as fast as he could toward the safety of home.

For days he lived in dread that Hugh would tell. Any punishment given him by the church or God Himself would be mild compared to his father's punishment. He spent hours on his knees, in terrified prayer. He prayed for forgiveness. He prayed Hugh would either leave or be struck dumb. For the second time Nick had proof that prayer worked. Hugh left.

A fortnight after his terrible sin, secure in the knowledge that God had forgiven him, he stood before the congregation and his father and made an emotional promise. With a Bible held tightly in his hands he said, in a voice that several times cracked into the deeper register, "I pledge my soul to purity, my body to chastity, and my industry to mankind." Only the last would be easy.

6

illiam Stuart stared up at his youngest child who, at eighteen, stood almost a head taller than his father. "What are you saying?"

Nick said it again. "I want to study medicine at university, Father. I've been reading in the journals about such amazing new things. So many new discoveries and techniques! I want to learn how to transfuse blood, and how to use anesthetics. Don't you realize how much suffering, especially by women in labor, could be eased with the use of ether or chloroform?"

"Because something's new doesn't mean it's a good thing." William Stuart wished he had never allowed his son to read selected articles in the medical journals. He had forbidden him to explore them on his own, but obviously, the boy had done it on the sly, and picked up many wrong-headed ideas.

"If women were meant to have their children without pain God would have arranged it that way. And don't speak to me of putting one man's blood into another man's body. Blasphemy! And even if it weren't against the Will of God, would you want the blood of some Hottentot or Frenchman or even a woman in your veins? The idea of transfusing is obscene. And all university is good for is ruining young men. No son of mine will be exposed to that kind of corruption." His smile was crafty. "In any event, you don't have the educational background for it. You would never be admitted."

Nick took a deep breath. "Mr. Spencer says otherwise, Father. I did very well on my O Levels; you know I did. He says if I can study at a larger school for even a year I will do as well on my A Levels."

"He says! He says! I wish you had never set eyes on him. He's turned you against your family and destroyed your values. He says!"

"He's helped me more than anyone except you. He's a good man, a good teacher."

"And I'm not?"

"Father, it's not a contest between you." Nick looked at his shoes, feeling an unaccountable shame that made him angry with both his father and himself. One would think he was guilty of some terrible sin. Unbidden, unwanted, and unexpected, there sprang into his mind that moment of hideous ecstasy with Hugh; the memory was gone in a moment. He hoped it never came back.

He took a deep breath and returned to the issue at hand. "Mr. Spencer says within the year I should be able to pass my A levels if I can go to a better school and I continue to apply myself." When he looked up, his eyes pleaded with his father to be proud of him. "He's certain I'll be accepted at university. I've saved my money for a long, long time, every shilling I've earned, and I'll work. It will cost you nothing."

"Disgrace me. Reject me and all I've taught you. But of course he says that is acceptable."

"Father..."

"To practice medicine here, you can learn all you need to know from me."

Nick's jaw set. "Father, you're superb at what you do. But I don't want to treat cattle one hour and a man the next, a sick cat thirty minutes later and then deliver a baby. That's not wrong for you; it's what you want. I want to treat people, nothing else. And I don't know if I want to stay here forever."

"You are meant to stay here, to walk in my shoes. It's what we have planned your entire life."

Nick raked his fingers through his thick dark hair. "It's what you planned. I was never consulted. I want to go to university, study medicine and surgery. I've learned all I can from you and I thank you for it. Now I have to go my own way."

"You will do as I say until you reach your majority. You will start by ending your association with Spencer and you will ask my forgiveness."

"I'm going to university if it takes twenty years to get there."

"Against my wishes?"

"If I must."

"Follow this path and you will no longer be welcome in my house. I will not tolerate a rebellious child under my roof."

Nick had never known his father to make an idle threat. This small village was the only world he had ever known, its people the only people he had ever known. "Is that your last word?" he asked, his voice low.

"It is."

Nick had to try twice before he could speak. "Then I'll leave now."

"If you do, your name will be struck from the family Bible. Your mother will not be allowed to communicate with you."

They glared at each other across the chasm of their differences; the aging fanatic who was a good physician and the young man to whom good was not good enough.

When Nick left that night, his mother followed him to the door. "Aye, my Nickie, my baby, must you go?"

"I must, Mother. If I give in to him…"

"Nickie, he doesn't really want you to go. He's afraid if you leave, you won't come back, that's all. He thinks he can cow you into staying. Can't you wait another year or two? Can't you apologize to him?"

"He needs to apologize to me. I'm sorry." From her seat beside the fire, Agnes gave him a malicious grin. He glared back at her.

His mother wiped her eyes with the corner of her apron. "The Holy Mother be with you, my Nickie," she said, not caring that Agnes would report her Papist blessing.

All of Nick's possessions fit into two worn valises that had been his mother's. In a heavy rain, he walked to the schoolmaster's shabby two-room house on a hill overlooking the small school. When Mr. Spencer answered his knock, Nick said, "My father has expelled me, sir. Have you room for me for a few days, until I find somewhere to stay?"

Charles Spencer was not surprised. Nick had often bared his worry about his father's reaction. He gestured toward the hearth in the front room, which served as dining room, kitchen, and parlor. "You'll have to sleep there," he said. "There's only one bedroom and it's scarcely large enough to turn around in. I have a pallet you may have, and some blankets. It won't be very comfortable."

Nick smiled. "It will be more than adequate, sir. My father didn't coddle us." He looked around the room, furnished with odds and ends. Mr. Spencer, he knew, was paid little, but he was a happy man as long as he could afford to buy books. Mounds of books heaped up and spilled over from bookshelves and tables; others were piled on the mantelpiece and still others in the corner, and the air was pleasant with the dry mustiness of old books.

From time to time over the next few months he saw his mother, but never in the house where he had been born and never with his father's knowledge. Her color was off, but she denied being ill except from Mrs. Lofton's mince pie. "Mrs. Lofton," she declared, "never could cook any better than a shoat." Another time it was Mrs. Wink's mutton that made her sick. She had a different reason every time her son asked.

"Don't you think, Nicholas, that if something was wrong with me, your father would do something about it?" Would he? Nick wondered sourly. His mother saw it in his face. "Here now," she said softly. "None of that. Your father's a good man. Just set in his ways."

On a blustery November morning, his mother called at the schoolmaster's house. Nicholas asked her in, and fixed her a cup of tea. Her cheeks were redder, which he thought was a good sign, and her eyes were brighter. Spencer went for his daily walk so they might have privacy.

"Nicholas," she said, "I want you to leave here."

He stared at her, unsure he had heard correctly. "Mother, what—"

"Mr. Spencer tells me he has taught you as much as he can. He says you must go to a better school or you will never leave this village." She removed a small, fat purse from her coat pocket and pressed it into his hand. "This is yours. Every shilling. I want you to go at once."

"I can't take this."

"You can and you will. It's my inheritance from your grandfather in Ireland. My brother sent it me a fortnight ago. Your father knows nothing about it." The thin lines of her mouth turned up in a pleased smile as she repeated, "He knows nothing about it. Nor does Agnes."

"Mother, it's your money. I can't take it."

"Yes, you can. It's a great deal of money. My father was not wealthy, but he invested wisely, you know."

"I didn't know." His father had never allowed the children to meet or hear about their papist kin. He held the purse out to her. "All the same, I can't take it."

"All the same, you will. And you will study medicine at university, and you will become a great doctor, and you will find cures for all manner of diseases."

He looked keenly at her. Yes, her color was definitely off. But he knew it was pointless to ask about her health. It would just be Mrs. Lofton's mince pies again. "All right, Mother," he said softly. "I'll take it."

Charles Spencer arranged for Nicholas to enter St. Thomas Aquinas, a school with a fine reputation. He went as a private student and was tutored by one of Spencer's friends in exchange for tutoring smaller boys and doing menial work. When he was accepted at University, Nick wrote an ecstatic letter to his parents, sure his father had relented by now. No reply came from the stony man in the house of pink Cotswold stone. From his mother came a letter of joy.

꧁꧂

No one studied harder than the provincial boy with the frayed cuffs, too-short trousers, and empty pockets. He kept to himself, lived to study, and had few friends. He knew he was laughed at behind his back and tried not to care. With few exceptions, the few who tried to befriend him were courteously rebuffed. In those years his vow of chastity was stained only twice, when he ached with loneliness and a fellow student smiled at him in a certain way.

Despite his frugality, his mother's inheritance ran low, and he turned again to tutoring to make ends meet. He worked in a

London hospital until licensed to practice on his own. Then he opened a little surgery in the slums. It was not unusual for him to hear gunshots in the middle of the night. Not unusual to have stabbing victims brought to his door. The hours were long; he was often hungry. Prayer did nothing to fill a growling stomach. One foggy Saturday morning, as he walked along lost in thought, someone seized his arm.

"Stuart! It is you, isn't it?"

He glanced up and smiled. "Grainger," he said. "It's been a long time." Aubrey Grainger had been one of the few friends he had had at university.

"'Deed it has. I say, Stuart, Cummings and I were just talking about you the other day. We wondered what had become of you. Nosed about. Found out where you were. Always admired your pluck, Stuart. Such a high-minded chap, unlike us mercenary devils." Grainger laughed, and Nick felt the back of his neck grow hot. He was sure his threadbare condition was not lost upon his old friend. Grainger studied him. "Join us tomorrow night, won't you? We have an extra seat to *Hamlet.* This would be a jolly good opportunity to catch up."

Nick hesitated. Go to a theatre? Playacting was as great a sin as dancing. But he didn't remember the last time he'd done something just for fun. "I'd like awfully much to go," he said. He hoped moths had not eaten his one good suit of clothes. Later, Nick was aghast at what he had done. He had read *Hamlet* at St. Thomas. It contained not only fornication but also incest and murder. He had taken leave of his senses!

He shifted in his seat through Act One, Scene One, wishing he were not sitting in the center of the row; he could not leave without creating a stir and stepping on toes. And then Scene Two began.

There came onto the stage an entourage, at its head a king and queen. Near them and yet apart was a golden-haired figure in plain dark clothing, in contrast to the peacock robes and jewels of the others. The king was blithely grieving his dead brother while at the same time speaking with equal blitheness about his recent marriage to his dead brother's wife. But the other... the other... Nick leaned forward, unaware that most other people in the audience did the same.

The long-legged figure in black spoke. "A little more than kin but less than kind..." It was an aside, spoken so that the king could not be sure what was said. Even so, the voice that spoke was resonant and the words of simmering wrath reached the farthest seats of the balcony.

Throughout the play Nick remained as he was, transfixed by that lean youth who prowled the stage, whose every motion was spare and fraught with barely-leashed violence. At the end he heard women in the audience weeping, and truth to tell, his own eyes stung a bit as the dying Hamlet's head fell back against Horatio's arm.

"Good night, sweet prince," Horatio said, his voice breaking. "And flights of angels sing thee to thy rest."

As the curtains swept together, and the dead prince was shut from sight, the audience erupted into applause. Nick could not applaud. His emotions had been drained. He had never felt like this. In front and all around him people stood and applauded and called out, "Kit! Kit! Kit! Kit!" He had to stand to see the bows of the entire cast, then only the principal players, and finally only St. Denys alone, bowing to them over and over until he finally quit the stage and did not return.

Nick's friends teased him, and poked one another with their elbows. "Look at Stuart, will you? He's fairly dazzled!" "It's the girl who played the queen that's done it, I wager!" "No, no, Ophelia! It had to be Ophelia." "It's the queen, I tell you. Ophelia? That wasted, consumptive child?" "Come along, Stuart. Tell the truth. Is it Ophelia or the queen who has you looking like a moon-struck calf?"

"How did you like your first play?"

Nick, still a little dazed, said, "I think it was wonderful."

"The saint has been corrupted at last!" They clapped him on the back as if he had accomplished something amazing. "First the Theatre and now he is enamored of a loose woman! Oh, how the mighty are fallen."

Every night that week he returned to the theatre, sitting in the cheapest seats, paying for admittance with money that ought to have gone for food. It was more important to be there in the dark and absorb the beauty and power of Kit St. Denys. Every night he thrilled to the same lines delivered by the same voice but always with some slight difference in inflection or emotion. He watched no one else on the stage. If Hamlet were offstage Nick was impatient until he returned.

The theatre might well be an abomination. He no longer cared. He sat there in the dark and spun fantasies. Without knowing he was doing it, he prayed for a miracle: that he might speak to St. Denys. On closing night the miracle happened.

The last act this time was more lifelike than ever when something red splattered the stage each time Hamlet thrust or parried. Then, when the last curtain call had been made, and red continued to drip, St. Denys said calmly, "Ladies and gentlemen, we achieved an usual level of realism tonight. I have need of a physician."

While the chattering crowd streamed toward the doors, Nick pushed against the flow to find his way backstage, praying he got there before any other doctor who had been in the audience. He was guided to a dressing room where St. Denys sat, pale even through the grease paint. A wizened little man held a red-soaked folded cloth against his wrist. Nick heard the man say, "The doctor is here, Mr. Kit."

As Nick examined the injured wrist, he felt St. Denys watching him. He concentrated on the injured arm itself, seeing it as a disembodied entity and not as a limb attached to this extraordinary creature. Briskly, he said, "I need to send for my medical bag. This wants a stitch or two."

"No time," St. Denys said. "I've a wrap party to attend. I had the wardrobe mistress bring needles and thread."

"Mr. St. Denys, with all due respect that's asking for infection."

"Sew it."

Nick hesitated, and then stitched the wound. Throughout the procedure St. Denys uttered not one sound. As he finished bandaging, Nick looked up into dark eyes that saw into his soul. Something stopped in that instant. Time? His heartbeat? He didn't know. He knew only that something stopped and something began.

St. Denys' gaze held Nick's. His lips parted as if to say something important, and then he asked, "How much money is owed you, Mr...?"

"Stuart. I ask nothing, Mr. St. Denys. It was an honor, to do it."

"A workman is worthy of his hire, so I've been told."

"Please. Not a shilling." He prayed St. Denys did not notice his cuffs were frayed and his collar turned.

"Proud and stubborn as well as skilled, I see. Then you must join our party."

"I couldn't. Thank you. I begin work early." But wouldn't it be worth losing sleep to spend another hour or two in this man's presence?

"I wish you would. I must speak with the theatre manager before he leaves. Stay here and give some thought to the party. Otherwise I'll pay you in money." St. Denys left the room without waiting for an answer.

'Such arrogance!' Nick thought. He wasn't going to that party. And he wasn't going to take money, either. And he wasn't going to sit there like a smitten milkmaid and wait for St. Denys to return. He could leave. He wasn't nailed to the chair.

He glanced down and noticed a blond hair lying curled on his black sleeve. Slowly he pulled it off. It had a life of its own. He straightened it out. Released, it sprang back to its former shape. A single thread of gold in the form of a question mark.

Hugh's voice from long ago spoke in his mind. "The apple's off the tree, Little Stuart. You can't put it back." And the terrible thing was, he didn't want to.

7

large bathtub dominated one corner of the dressing room. The old man filled it with hot water and ignored Nick.

How, Nick wondered, could he have let himself come to such a place? A theatre, a place of actresses no better than painted harlots and actors who likely did not know the meaning of the word morals. Safety lay beyond that door. Just as he reached it, the door flew open.

A tall young woman swept into the room, her red hair flying in all directions. "Kit, are you all right?" She stopped. "Who are you?"

"I'm the doctor."

"You took care of his arm? I almost fainted when I saw real blood. Will he be all right? Our company doctor was drunk again; Kit's going to kill the worthless sot." She smiled and stuck out her hand like a man. "Thank God you were here. I'm Rama Weisberg. I played the queen." When he did not take her hand she withdrew it. "Didn't you like the production? Or was it just me you didn't like?"

"Nothing of the kind. It's just that my friends accused me of being in love with you."

"'Accused' you? It's hardly the same as being in love with a piece of three-day-old mutton! Some men find it quite pleasant." She flounced from the room and disappeared into the hallway.

St. Denys returned a moment later. "What did you say to my leading lady?" he asked. "She's positively spluttering."

"I'm not really sure. She seems to think I called her a mutton, but I didn't."

"Ah, well," Kit said, laughing. "She has a redhead's temper."

"Your bath is ready, Mr. Kit," the old man said, and helped him remove the jerkin and the full-sleeved bloodstained white blouse.

"Thank you, Nathaniel. Stuart, have you decided about the party? You will go, won't you?" As St. Denys talked, he sat down at the makeup table with its boxes and bottles, and removed the sweat-streaked makeup. The tips of his sweat-darkened fair mane lay in waves against the nape of his neck and hid his ears; the downward curve of his jaw was strong. Nick was near enough to notice the light brown freckles on his shoulders.

The words "No, I don't think so" died unspoken. Nick gazed at the actor's naked back and muscular arms. How would they feel beneath his hands? Was his skin coarse or fine? Nick shoved his hands into his coat pockets, lest he reach out and touch him. He wished he could put his eyes in his pockets as well.

A peculiar lattice of faded, jagged white lines marred the actor's skin. They looked like scars, but how could that be? A small dark mole resided on his lower back, just above the waist of the black trunk hose and tights. Just then Nick realized St. Denys, with a slight smile, was watching him in the mirror. Even the tops of Nick's ears turned crimson.

"If your wife is with you, she is more than welcome to join us," St. Denys said, as the last trace of makeup vanished.

"I don't have a wife," Nick croaked. He did not realize that the way he said it told Kit St. Denys a great deal. "Mr. St. Denys," he started to say.

"Please. Call me Kit; everyone does."

"Mr. St. Denys, I wouldn't fit in at your party. I don't enjoy that sort of thing."

"I assure you, Mr. Stuart, it's but a late dinner, a bit of the grape, laughter, and song. It is not a bacchanalian orgy."

"I didn't mean that."

"Then you will come." Kit turned toward him. Nick's good resolves sank out of sight. Nick had hoped that the glamour and sensuality were all an illusion. He could go home and forget he had ever spoken to the man. But no, the Devil himself had conspired to make St. Denys younger and more handsome than he had been with the makeup.

With complete unconcern, St. Denys stood up and let the old man help him finish undressing. Nick tried not to notice the authentic costume's codpiece. He broke into a sweat and clenched his fists tighter in his pockets. How would it feel to spread his hands on that firm arse? Or see him erect and ready? Oh, dear God, he had to leave there! But the Devil who had made St. Denys beautiful had also nailed Nick's feet to the floor.

St. Denys stepped into the high-backed tub of hot water and, careful to keep his injured arm dry, he exhaled a gusty sigh of pleasure as the old man fussed over him with scented soap and a sea sponge. "What is your given name, Stuart?"

"Nicholas."

"And what do your friends call you?"

"I have no time for friends."

"We must do something about that. Tell me, are you particularly interested in Shakespeare?"

"Uh... yes. Very interested. In Shakespeare. Yes."

"And your favorite of his plays is...?"

"Well, um, *Hamlet*, of course."

"Of course."

It annoyed Nick to know St. Denys was having fun at his expense. "Well, it is." Then it didn't matter because like a young Neptune rising from the sea St. Denys stood up in his tub and stepped out. He grinned as if he knew the evil in Nick's mind. Nick's eyes sought a fascinating blank corner on the ceiling.

"Only a few more minutes, Mr. Stuart. Then we can leave." The old man helped him into his clothing. As he started to do up the buttons on the shirt, St. Denys said, "I can manage from here, Nathaniel. Thank you. You go freshen up for the party."

"Very good, Mr. Kit." Nathaniel favored Nick with one more disapproving glare and was gone.

"I'm surprised," Nick said, still looking at the corner. "You socialize with your servants?"

"Nathaniel is not a servant. He's my dresser and has been for a long time. That I always have the right costume for any given scene is due to Nathaniel."

Nick wondered how any man who had just been nude in front of a stranger could answer with such dignity. He was surprised when

St. Denys said, "You'll have to learn the ways of the theatre if you're to be around us."

"I didn't know I was."

"But you are."

The actor's dark eyes seemed to pull secrets from Nick's soul. Nick was dazed by the ferocity of his desire; he had a forlorn hope St. Denys had not noticed the obvious.

"I knew the moment I looked into your eyes you that you were one of my kind. I'm never wrong."

Fear replaced lust. 'One of my kind.' Hugh had said the same thing. If St. Denys and Hugh could recognize his demon so did God. Then his fear was forgotten when St. Denys' sultry expression gave way to one of guileless charm.

"Devil of a time with the buttons. Ought to have kept Nathaniel in here. It's a bloody inconsiderate thing to ask of a guest, but could you help me?"

Nick's fingertips brushed the damp, smooth skin of St. Denys' chest and abdomen, and he was helpless against the sexual imagery in his mind as each button slid into its buttonhole. Then as he fastened the right sleeve button he saw the twisted little finger. Scars. A broken finger. What mysteries did they represent? He glanced up once more into St. Denys' eyes.

"After the party," St. Denys said softly, "you will go with me to my hotel." It was not a question.

"Yes."

"You'll stay the night." Still not a question.

"Yes." With those two yeses he accepted everything and questioned nothing, and the knowledge made him afraid.

"Then let us be off, Nicholas."

He was relieved that St. Denys made no effort to draw him into the festivities. Instead, Nick stood about with an alcoholic drink of some kind in his hand, not tasting it, free to watch St. Denys move, dance, talk, and laugh. Whenever another guest tossed a curious glance in Nick's direction, he studied one of the dozens of paintings and photographs that lined the walls. Four of the photographs were of Kit, in different costumes. Several were of different women in costume. A photograph of the queen looked down with disapproval.

The band played into the early morning. St. Denys was never off the dance floor. He danced with one girl and then another, laughing, tossing his unruly forelock out of his eyes. Obviously he had forgotten Nick Stuart's existence. The red-haired actress monopolized a great deal of Kit's time. He danced with her frequently, and held her closer than he needed to. As the hours passed, they were all dancing so plastered to their partners they might as well be in bed!

With disgust, Nick recognized his own hypocrisy. While he condemned the dancers, he was trying not to remember St. Denys naked, trying without success not to imagine what was going to happen when they were together later.

He left the ballroom, and discovered a side room filled with elaborate, massive dark furniture and enough potted plants for an arboretum. He poured his drink into the soil of a plant and sat down. Should he stay or should he go? If he stayed and St. Denys really had forgotten him, he would never get over the humiliation. But he wanted Kit St. Denys even if it damned his immortal soul.

Just as he convinced himself to leave, St. Denys breezed in. "Here you are," he said. "I was wondering where you had got to. You didn't have a good time, did you? I shouldn't have insisted you come. I'm sorry."

"No," Nick said, as he struggled against the quicksand of the soft couch. "I had a wonderful evening."

St. Denys laughed. "You're the worst liar I've ever seen. Your wonderful evening, Mr. Stuart, has not yet begun." Nick's eyes widened in disbelief when St. Denys leaned over and kissed him.

"St. Denys," he gasped, when Kit straightened up. "What are you doing? With all of these people about!"

"It's all right. Many of them have gone. And they're my people. They know all about me."

"Well, they don't know about me!"

The answering smile was enigmatic. "They will. And the name, as I have said, is Kit."

~❧~

For the first time in his life, Nick Stuart slept until late morning. He yawned and sat up, crossing his arms upon his drawn-up knees as he looked down at the man asleep beside him. The time with Hugh, and the two furtive gropings at university had not prepared him for the night before.

He was a doctor; he knew a great deal about the human body. But last night he'd found out how little he knew about what his body wanted and what it was capable of doing and experiencing. He had sinned and sinned and sinned again, and had done it with complete joy. His face reddened at a sudden memory: he had shouted something inarticulate, and Kit had laughed and bit him. He rubbed the spot on the back of his neck; there was a welt. Last night had been a delicious madness.

Kit in sleep looked vulnerable and very young, with his long dark lashes, slightly parted lips, and one hand loosely curled on the pillow. Nick wanted to run his hand the length of Kit's shoulder and arm. He wanted to again feel with his hands and taste with his mouth the fine skin and all the places where the pulse of life beat. He wanted to know the sensuality of hot skin against hot skin, of bodies joined, of knife-edged senses he hadn't even known he had. He leaned to kiss the sultry mouth that had started it all.

Kit stirred in his sleep. Behind his closed lids his eyes moved with frantic motion. A strangled cry of terror shattered the stillness of the room. His eyes flew open; he looked through Nick to something behind him and cried out something Nick could not understand.

"Kit," Nick said, shaking him. "Kit, you're having a nightmare. Wake up."

Kit flung his hands off. Before Nick could react, he'd been knocked flat. Kit's lips were curled back in a feral snarl. His forearm bore down against Nick's throat. Nick broke free, forced him back and cried, "Kit! Wake up!" The violence of the struggle intensified. "Kit!"

The glassy look faded from Kit's eyes, though his breath was a choking gasp. "Forgive me. Forgive me. Did I hurt you?"

"No." Nick sat up again. "You must have had a terrible dream. Do you want me to leave?"

"Oh, please, no." Kit reached up to put his shaking hands on either side of Nick's face and with a sense of awe Nick saw the devils leave the shadowed eyes. "Stay with me. No one else has ever made him go away so quickly."

"Who? What are you talking about? No one's here but you and I."

Kit's eyes were again hagridden. "I can't explain. Don't leave me, Nico." He drew Nick down to lie beside him, their heads on the same pillow. "He's devouring my soul, Nico," he said, his voice hollow. "Sometimes I don't know which I am."

"I don't understand."

"I can't tell you. I can't tell anyone. You have to take me on trust." They lay without moving until eventually Kit went to sleep again.

I should go, Nick told himself. *It's midday. Patients will be waiting.* But he could not move without waking Kit. Kit's arm remained across him. His breath was warm on Nick's neck.

Nick's musing turned from the surgery to the mystery thrust upon him. 'Made him go away.' Who? Kit was young and strong and rich. Who could possibly have the power to turn him into a terrified child? He was unnerved by the tenderness he felt. After all, this meant nothing. When Kit awakened they would resume their separate and very different lives. But there was no harm in pretending for a few minutes that it was something more.

He dozed, and was awakened by Kit's tongue teasing his lips. He blinked at the sight of Kit already dressed in white, his face damp with sweat.

"Come on," Kit said. "Everything's ready."

Nick sat up, disoriented, and rubbed his eyes. "What's ready?"

Kit laughed, pulled him from the bed and led him into the bathroom that adjoined the luxurious bedroom. Encased in mahogany was a large bathtub with fragrant steam wafting from it.

"Get in, you lazy creature." Kit said. "I always start the day with fencing practice and then a bath. The bath, at least, I'm willing to share with you. Breakfast will be brought up to our dining room in an hour."

"Breakfast? It's the middle of the day. I'm starving!"

"Bathe first. Breakfast later."

Nick sniffed. "What's that smell?"

"French scented oil. I borrowed it from my leading lady."

"Scented oil?" Nick said with ill-concealed disdain. "That isn't very manly, is it?" At Kit's lewd grin, Nick blushed again.

"I recall no complaint about my lack of manliness last night," Kit said.

Nick got in the tub without any further protest. To his shock Kit got into the water also. "There isn't room," Nick protested.

"Depends upon what you need room for." Kit slid his soapy hands over Nick's shoulders and downward. The effect was instantaneous. Nick had never been so close to fainting in his entire life.

In the days and nights that followed, Nick tried to convince both himself and God that he was sorry for the night of sin. But each time his prayer would be cut short by the fervent wish it would happen again. Soon. A month went by; he did not hear from Kit. Hope faded. What had he expected? He'd known it was nothing but two bodies meeting in mutual heat. He'd been a fool to believe that Kit's plea for him to stay meant anything.

Nick had set up his surgery in an old brick building on the border of the tough neighborhood some called the Rookery. During the day, when he was busy with the endless parade of sick and injured people, he could put Kit out of his thoughts. Then, alone on his cot in the back room, he relived the night they had spent together and admitted how much he wanted it again.

One night he had locked the door and was washing his instruments and setting up the sterilization tray when someone knocked at the door. "Oh, bother!" he muttered. "The sign says 'Closed,' doesn't it?" The knock came again. Sighing, he answered the summons.

Almost glowing with good health and vitality, money and privilege, Kit St. Denys stood there, one arm leaning against the doorjamb. "Hello, physician. I've had a devil of a time finding you. You didn't tell me where your house of mercy was." His smile hid the truth: he had known for days, but had been unable to make himself face the slums again. "Are you not going to ask me in?"

Nick was embarrassed by the shabbiness of his surgery, and thought that was why Kit looked ill at ease. He stepped aside with a mute gesture of invitation.

"Don't your patients pay you?" Kit asked, as he took the few steps required for a tour of the surgery.

"That is none of your concern."

"If you starve you're no good to me or to yourself. Do they?"

"When they can."

"I need a Company doctor. The one I had was incompetent and drunk when I needed him. I'll pay you well." He made a vague gesture. "You don't need these people."

"They need me. There's no other doctor nearby."

"Do you think they appreciate your sacrifice? You could lay down your life for them and most of them would step over your corpse without a backward glance."

"You don't know anything about these people or their lives! You come from a different world altogether. You'll have to find another doctor."

"I know more than you think." Kit stopped his restless pacing and said, "And I don't want another doctor. I want you. For my people. For myself. Please." And softer, "You helped me in a way no one else has done. I've spent a month trying to convince myself I didn't need you."

Nick did not look at him; the man was too good at reading thoughts. "I can't leave here."

"At least let me buy you dinner. You don't look as if you've had a decent meal for a year."

"I do quite well, thank you."

"Dinner. I insist."

Nick wanted to go and yet, there had been little conversation the other time. What would there be for them to talk about? "I can't go until I finish here."

"I'll watch. Perhaps I'll find myself playing a physician someday."

As he cleaned and sterilized instruments and then locked the powders, pills, and medicines in a cabinet, he answered Kit's questions about the method and reason for what he did. Kit was interested in the wrinkled, unstylish white coat he wore instead of the customary black wool. Nick's answers were clumsy at first, but became easier as he warmed to the idea of explaining.

He could not have said where Kit took him in the fine carriage, but knew his thrifty mother and father would have been horrified at the place and its silky-voiced, silent-footed waiters and gleaming crystal, wine list and potted palms. The menu was in French; he didn't know what any of the food was. Embarrassed, he told Kit to order for him. While they waited for their food, a constant stream of admirers and friends drifted by the table and talked to Kit for a few minutes. With each visitor Nick's discomfiture increased.

Kit saw it and said, "I'll have our dinner sent to a private room. There is too much traffic here." He summoned the majestic *maître d'* and spoke a few words in French. The *maître d'* bowed, and led them toward the back, up a short flight of carpeted stairs to a tiny, dimly lit room just large enough for a table and two chairs. Through an elaborate grille one could watch the diners below. Nick relaxed as he sat down.

Kit stood a moment at the grille, and then joined him at the table. "I'm sorry. It seems to be my lot in life to put you in situations where you're uncomfortable. We need never dine in public, you know. We can take our meals in the dining room of my suite if you like."

There it was again: that assumption they would be together often. Nick was silent; he didn't know what to say.

Kit finally said, "I think you do not like me."

"How could anyone not like you?" Nick asked, astonished.

"Many people do it without effort. I'm arrogant. I annoy them."

"I don't think so."

"You don't know me. But no one really does."

The dinner arrived just then. Nick kept a cautious eye on Kit's expert use of the extra cutlery. He supposed people like Kit who were born with a silver spoon in their mouths were also born knowing how to use it. His mother had placed a spoon, a knife, and a fork beside each solid, thick plate. And on the plate went boiled beef or mutton bought from valley farmers; thick-crusted bread with home-churned butter melting in little pools; potatoes, beets, and whatever vegetables the garden was producing. Certainly the Stuarts had never seen food that was set afire at the table. Never had slender, delicate glasses with wine been set before them. Gingerly, as if sampling poison, Nick took a sip. It wasn't as bad as he had expected.

As the evening went on, Nick's apprehension of a silent dinner disappeared. Kit carried the burden of conversation with charm and humor, and through the courses and afterward, entertained him with stories of the theatre.

"And there I was," Kit said, finishing a story, "with the bladeless hilt of a sword, going through all of the motions and feeling like a fool, especially when it came time to deliver the death blow."

"But why didn't you just stop the play?" Nick asked, laughing, "and get another sword?"

"Theatre is the realm of the imagination. Had I stopped, it would have destroyed the illusion even further. As it was, people realized I had no blade while they were watching, but the image they remembered afterward was of a complete sword."

"I envy you. You have imagination. I have none."

"I'm sure you do."

"If I ever had it, which I doubt, I've lost it. I see what I see."

"We each have our place, my friend," Kit said with a smile. "People like me tend to soar around in our own little world. You realists bring us back to earth. We're in the same business, you know."

"I don't follow."

"You heal the body with potions and pills. A jester heals the heart with laughter; a tragedian, with tears." His smile was crooked. "It's a tragedy we can't heal ourselves."

Nick gazed in wonder at him. Nothing about this man was ordinary. Not his person, not his language, not his thoughts.

Kit threw off the serious mood. "We've talked enough about me. Though wonderful and fascinating creature that I am, I could keep you enthralled several more hours. Where is your birthplace, Nico?"

The nickname was odd, like a new suit. But Nick decided he liked it. "A village in the Cotswolds, not far from Gloucester."

"A country lad, eh?"

Nick made a deprecating gesture. "Doesn't it show? I come from plain people. My grandfather was a doctor. My father is a doctor and an elder in the Particular Baptist church. From the time I was a small boy, I helped birth lambs and calves and babies. I helped him pull teeth, lance boils, stitch wounds and geld livestock."

"Ouch," Kit murmured.

Nick looked blankly at him an instant, and then laughed. "I have one brother and five sisters, all much older than I. Do you have brothers or sisters?"

"I had a twin brother. He died years ago. We were very close. Do you plan to return home to practice?"

"No. My father and I love each other, but we don't get on. I doubt if the entire County would be large enough for us both. I do miss the countryside, and I detest much about the City. But I believe this is where I can do the most good."

"And that's important to you, isn't it."

"It is. Laugh if you like, but I made a vow to God to be of service to mankind." He didn't add that Kit had led him into flagrant violation of another vow made at the same time, and that given the chance, he'd violate it again.

"Why would I laugh?" Kit touched his napkin to his lips. "My friend, the hour is late. Shall we go?"

Nick's mouth went dry. As they entered the carriage, Nick tried to justify going to bed with St. Denys again. He couldn't. But Kit took him straight to the surgery and bade him goodnight, leaving him bewildered.

A fortnight later Kit reappeared, unannounced, and again insisted upon Nick's dining with him, this time in the elegant dining room of his suite at the Warshaw. Nick had paid no attention to his surroundings the other time, and he was impressed by the amount of rich wood, velvet, and gold leaf.

"It must be expensive," he said.

"I suppose it is. The Prince of Wales maintains a suite here, as well as assorted dukes and at least one German baron and a brace of French chevaliers. Anyone who cares for titles can have his fill of them here."

"Do you have a title?"

"No. Merely disgustingly rich."

Nick ordered food familiar to him, and thoroughly enjoyed the beef. It was even better than his mother's. This time when dinner was finished, Kit said, "Tell me what it's like in your little Cotswolds village."

"It's beautiful," Nick answered. In a wave of nostalgia he painted verbal pictures of the rolling green hills where sheep and cattle grazed and drank from clear streams. He described the rosy-stone cottage and his mother's gardens, one for the bounty of vegetables, the other for the bounty of flowers that put forth a blaze of colored blossoms from spring until autumn. He told Kit about his mother and the sacrifice she made to send him to university. His voice was rough as he said, "I haven't seen her or my home for almost six years."

"Why not?"

"My father refuses to let her see me."

"Your father sounds like a bit of an ass."

"He's a good man. He's just set in his ways."

Kit cocked one eyebrow. "I'd say he's not the only one."

Determined to change the subject, Nick cleared his throat and said, "What social life there is in the village and roundabout revolves around the church. Prayer every day. Sundays and mid-week we went to church twice."

"So you are religious?"

Nick's forehead puckered. "I suppose I am. I believe in the Grace of God."

"And in the goodness of mankind?"

"I don't believe there is any inherent goodness, only what's given by the Grace of God to those who repent." Nick was amazed that he said these things. He had not thought them for many years and he had seldom gone to church since he had left home. Why did they now come from his lips as though he were a missionary?

Kit leaned his chin on his hand. "Repent of what?"

"Sin, of course. Whatever Satan has led them into."

"I don't believe in Satan."

"You don't believe in Evil?" Nick was horrified, and years of sermons clamored in his brain.

Kit's smile slipped. "Oh, my blue-eyed Puritan, I believe in evil. I've seen it. I lived with it. But I also believe that a man can achieve goodness through his own efforts. It's not a pat on the head from Jehovah because you're such a good boy." He shrugged. "It doesn't matter to me in any event. I'm a pagan; I live for life. I have no hope of ever achieving Christian perfection nor do I wish to."

Nick did not move for a moment, wondering again what he had gotten himself into. He had met many sinners but they knew they were sinners and some cared and some didn't. But not to believe at all in sin and redemption was unthinkable. He should run from this man and never look back. His hand lay on the tabletop, and his struggle showed in the way his fingers slowly clenched. Kit's hand descended upon it.

"Will you stay the night with me again?" His voice was quiet. "Since that first night, I've fought a quite insane attraction to you. I don't understand it. I don't want it, but there it is. You're not my sort at all. I wanted you that night because you're handsome and because I wondered if you were as innocent as you seemed. Now I want you because I..." He shrugged again. *"Je ne sais quoi?"*

Nick looked down at the strong hand upon his. A man's hand. Large knuckles. Prominent blue veins. Long fingers. His gaze rested for a moment on the crooked little finger. The strange tenderness swept over him again. "You must have many lovers," he said with difficulty.

"But none like you." Kit's smile was ingenuous. "I've never before had to share a lover with God."

Nick blanched at the blasphemy. But he did not return to the surgery that night. Or the next. Nor for many nights to come.

Days he spent with his patients and their endless problems. Between patients he convinced himself he had to tell Kit goodbye and find the proper wife for a young physician. But when the day was over, the surgery was locked and Kit appeared at the door, the proper wife was forgotten along with any notion of sin.

8

ama Weisberg crossed her arms over her bosom, and said, "I don't like it." The opinion was that of Kit's entire circle of close friends. Rama was in silhouette, her back to the window of the parlor in Kit's hotel suite. Her untamable hair had escaped from its neat coil and rose in a nimbus of tendrils all about her head.

Kit looked from her to Francis Mulholland, a quiet man not given to harsh words about anyone. Kit poured himself a brandy and eyed the two of them. Then he looked at the third person whose opinion he valued and whose affection he treasured. "And you, Lizbet?"

Lizbet picked up her glass of sherry from the small Queen Anne table beside the couch. "I don't care for him. But you do, and that is all that matters. I want you to be happy, my dear. If Mr. Stuart will accomplish that, then he has my blessing."

"Lizbet!" Rama cried, betrayed.

Lizbet patted Rama's hand. "It's not your life, pet. And the Company needs a doctor."

Rama glared at Kit. "Let him be the Company doctor, I don't care. Just let him keep to his medicine and stay out of your life."

"Out of my bed, you mean."

"Very well," she flung back at him, her face crimson. "Out of your bed."

"Now that, my dear, is where the trouble comes. I asked you three here to see how you felt about his being our company doctor, not to get your opinion about my bed partners."

Lizbet put down her glass and stood up. "And I, for one, don't want to know anything about it." Standing on tiptoe, she kissed Kit's cheek.

"Of course not," Rama snapped. "Your dear Kit could cut throats in public, and as long as you didn't see him do it, it would be quite all right with you."

"Rama," Lizbet said, "jealousy is dreadfully bad for the complexion." To Francis she said, "Goodbye, Frank. Kit, I expect you for dinner tomorrow."

"I won't be alone."

The fleetest of frowns tugged at Lizbet's eyebrows and was gone. "I didn't suppose you would be," she said. Rama crammed her hat on, skewered it with a lethal hatpin, and sailed from the room on Lizbet's heels.

"What about you?" Kit asked Francis, who still sat studying his hands. "If anyone has a right to an opinion, it's you."

"I don't like it either," he said after a moment. "I don't like him. He's not one of us." Then he looked up with a quizzical smile. "Why Stuart, Kit?"

"I don't bloody well know, Frank," Kit said with a sigh. "I've been with him every night for two months and I still don't know. I should be tired of him by now. God knows he can be tiresome! He's handsome, but I've had handsomer. He's intelligent, but he's no intellectual. He disapproves of everything that's fun. Well, almost everything. He doesn't know a thing about the theatre, though he is trying to learn. He insists upon maintaining that absurd surgery instead of working for me."

"In other words, he's as stubborn as you?" Francis asked with a laugh.

"No one's that stubborn." Kit gave Francis' shoulder an affectionate squeeze. "Frank, I wish…" He didn't finish. He wished he could feel for this devoted friend what he felt for Nick Stuart. He was in love with the Puritan, and he didn't want to be. Nonetheless it had happened.

Little by little each deepened the roots he had sent into the other's life. The one irresolvable conflict was Nick's refusal to exchange his surgery for the easier, more profitable work of being doctor to the Company. Finally, with no grace and little good humor, Kit surrendered the point.

For his part, Nick surrendered his refusal to let Kit outfit him in expensive clothes and drag him to social events. "I feel like a trained monkey," he grumbled.

"Not at all a bad idea." Eyes glinting with mischief, he walked around Nick as if appraising him. "I'll put a little red hat and waistcoat on you." Then with a grin he said, "You're a kept man and just don't want to admit it." He howled with laughter at Nick's outraged splutters.

The social evenings were slow death. Nick didn't know how to make small talk with common people, let alone how to talk to people with titles and money and elegance. The only pleasures for him at these events was to listen to people praise his lover and to watch Kit charm everyone. Every female in the room sooner or later attached herself to Kit's arm. Then he talked to her, smiled, and for a few minutes she glowed as if she were the most important woman in the world.

"How can you lie to them that way?" Nick asked as he unbuttoned his starched white shirt one night.

"Lie? To whom? God, but I'm tired." Kit yawned and climbed into bed naked, as always.

Nick looked at the pitcher on the bureau instead of Kit; he didn't want to be distracted. "The ladies. You make them think they're important to you."

"They are." Kit looked surprised at the question.

"But you don't like women."

"Correction, *mon cher*, I love women. I simply don't sleep with them. And those particular women are staunch supporters of the theatre in general, and of my Company in particular. They buy entire blocks of seats for the season and never miss a performance."

Nick pulled off his shirt, still looking thoughtful. "And what would these women do if they knew what you and I are to each other?"

"Turn on me like rats on a carcass, more than likely. As would the rest of the public. Except for Mrs. Campbell, of course. She doesn't care what anyone does as long it's not done in the street and frightens the horses. But they'll never know. Good God, but you're in a strange temper tonight."

Nick looked at him and was surprised at how distressed he appeared, like a child waiting for something bad to happen. He was sorry he had asked the stupid question. "It's too bad you're so tired," he said. "I think we should go straightaway to sleep and not frighten the horses." He laughed and caught the pillow Kit threw at him.

꿰 ꟼ

Nick attended rehearsals whenever he could, intrigued by Kit's ability to both direct and star. Even so, he could not understand how—or why— Kit could work patiently with one actor on the interpretation of a single line or the nuance in pronunciation of a single word or phrase, the turn of a head or an unimportant motion of an arm. When he asked, Kit had answered a bit snappishly, "There is no such thing as an unimportant motion on stage."

Some mornings he stayed to watch Kit practice with the fencing master in the hotel's ballroom, before breakfast. The clash of sabers, which Kit preferred to foils or *épées*, the controlled and gentlemanly violence, Kit's square-jawed, narrow-eyed focus and lithe movements, his pleased grin when the master yielded to a skillful *touché*. Those mornings Nick remained for the after-fencing bath. A thousand times he wondered how he had tolerated his dull life before Kit.

Nick remained baffled by Kit's friends. Rama Weisberg looked at him as if she would like to peel the eyes from his head. Francis Mulholland was polite but never smiled. The others, from the elderly dresser to the fencing master, pretended he didn't exist. Lizbet Porter was kind, as she would be to a stray cat. He wouldn't have been surprised if she offered him a saucer of milk. She was the only one he cared about winning over.

Kit bought a new toy from America, a Kodak camera. He drove them all to distraction for a while, dragging them outside whenever the sun shone in order to aim his wonderful box and take pictures. He made Nick take pictures of him. He had to send the camera back to America to get the results, but when they came back, Nick was delighted with the pictures he had taken of Kit. Kit let him keep them.

Most of Kit's time was taken up with auditions, rehearsals, performances, cast parties, business meetings, appearances, and a thousand other things Nick did not understand. Uninterrupted evenings in Kit's suite were rare but precious, and passed often in simple companionship while Nick read medical journals and Kit pored over scripts or theatre publications. Some nights Nick threw aside the *Lancet* and said, "Recite one of the sonnets, won't you? I'm bored."

"Some people actually *pay* me to entertain them," Kit said, and continued reading.

"If you don't, I'll sing."

"Oh, God help us, anything but that. You hang about only for the free entertainment, don't you."

Then, as often as not, Kit would imprison him in his arms and speak the honeyed words low into his ear or with hot breath against his throat. "'For thy sweet love remember'd such wealth brings that then I scorn to change my state with kings...'" "'If I could write the beauty of your eyes...'" Other times Kit would protest, "No Shakespeare! He's a dead, stuffy old goat and I'm sick of him." He would then launch into street ballads and limericks that became funnier and dirtier with each verse until Nick was laughing so hard he was helpless. Often the impromptu concert ended with the glow from the fireplace casting a golden sheen upon their naked bodies, with little piles of cast-off clothing attesting to their haste.

Kit told Nick about the tour later that year that would take them all over Europe. "I'll show you such wonderful places," he promised. "Splendid cities and forests, art and ruins that will stagger your imagination." Nick didn't want to leave his practice for months on end, and yet the idea of being separated from Kit was unbearable.

Nick was both amazed and frightened by the intensity of the emotions Kit aroused in him. And along with them came another emotion that rose like bile whenever anyone else touched Kit. And people who spoke to him always touched him—Lizbet, Mulholland, Rama, his troupe, his public. And Kit always responded with a warm smile and often an embrace. Nick made himself look the other way.

They were together every night through the chill, wet winter and the wet but promising spring to the wet and emerald May, when flowers sprang up everywhere, even in the City. Hotels and restaurants boasted large containers of growing flowers in front, and every tidy yard had almost more color than one could take in. Kit bought bouquets from every Cockney flower girl he saw, and gave them to amazed and delighted women he passed on the street.

"Rama and Lizbet are planning a surprise party for my birthday tomorrow night," he announced one day.

"If it's a surprise, how do you know about it?"

Kit laughed. "It's impossible to surprise me. Don't you know that by now? Twenty-five! I'm getting old. You will come, won't you? Give me your word."

"Your friends hate me. Everyone would be happier if I stayed away."

"I wouldn't be, and I'm the guest of honor. Anyway, they don't hate you. They just don't know you yet."

"They're not trying very hard."

"I won't force you, Nico. But I want you there. Please. It's important to me." Nick could no more refuse than he could grow wings.

The next evening the surgery door flew open as Nick was getting ready to leave for the party. A ragged little boy stood panting in the doorway. "Come fast! Sister's having the baby!"

Nick wrote a hurried note to Kit, grabbed his valise, and shut the note between the door and the frame. Kit's driver would see it and give it to him. The boy's sister was sixteen and carrying twins; the babies were not due for another fortnight. He hurried through the foggy night behind Freddie. Together they rushed up the dark, dank stairs to the cold, dank room where the family of five lived. The mother had shooed her husband and two older sons away, then crouched beside her daughter's pallet and looked up at Nick. "Can you help?" she whispered. "Can you help my Jane?"

"I'll do everything I can." As he removed his coat and rolled up his sleeves, he knew without looking that they had no water for washing. He gave Freddie some money, sent him for coal and ordered him to carry water up when he returned. He turned his attention to the girl, small and thin except for the enormous mound of her belly.

"Now then, Jane. Let's get this little matter over with, eh?" He smiled at her and patted her hand. Her pulse was thready, and her moaning never stopped. The hours passed into early morning. The first twin was delivered. It squeaked and died. The grandmother took it while Nick said, "One more, Jane. We're halfway finished, sweetheart."

"I can't," she tried to say, though no sound came from her lips.

"Why, of course you can." He poured a few drops of chloroform onto a cloth. "Breathe deep, Jane. Then push as hard as you can." By God, he refused to lose the second one.

At last he held in his hands the unmoving, wet fruition of twenty hours of weariness for him, and unbearable agony for the young mother. Quickly he cleaned the baby's mouth and nose and breathed a light puff of air into its lungs. A second light puff and a third. The tiny creature sucked in its first air and a moment later gave a little mew of protest followed by a wizened cry. Nick handed the infant to Jane's mother. He thought the baby would live, but he was not optimistic about Jane's chances.

He stayed all the next day and when he dragged himself back to the surgery, he did not see the note he had left for Kit lying unnoticed on the threshold. He stumbled to the narrow iron bed and lay down without undressing. His last conscious thought before drifting to sleep was that he'd make it up to Kit later for missing the party.

Across the City, while Nick slept, Kit paced the floor, alone and in terror, just as he had done the night before. Every gaslight was lit. A rapidly emptying bottle of whiskey was in his unsteady hand. He had made it through the first night knowing Nick would be there before morning. He had made it through the next day, protected by the sun and knowing Nick would be there soon.

Now it was night again. Nick was not there. But the old man was. He scratched on the window, tapped on the door. "Jack! I know you're in there, Jack. Let me in, boy. Let me in. Jack! Do it now!"

"Go away!" The whiskey bottle crashed against the door. "You're dead. You're dead! I killed you. Nico, Nico, God damn your bloody soul, where are you?" The door swung open; the breath stopped in his throat and he sank to his knees, unable to stand. The old man filled the doorway. "Stay dead," Kit cried, "why don't you stay dead?"

"Kit?" Francis Mulholland came in. "I heard something break. Why didn't you answer my knock? Kit?" Francis knelt beside him. "Kit, what is it? The dreams again?"

Kit stared at the old man whose lips were pulled back in a wolfish grin, his teeth glinting in the black beard and his brass buttons shining. He scrambled to his feet, ready to fight the demon.

Nick did not arrive until late the next morning. He had called upon the girl and her baby; both were as well as could be expected. He unlocked the door with the key Kit had given him and stopped in shock.

A vase lay in shards in front of the fireplace; its pathetic broken flowers lay on the stain of water. Two small tables were overturned. His foot clinked against something and he picked up the empty whiskey bottle. A tall clock lay stunned on its side. Draperies hung by one end of a rod. The room gave every sign of a violent struggle. The place stank of stale whiskey and vomit.

He ran to the bedroom, flung open the closed door, and sagged in relief. Kit had not been murdered. Whatever had happened, he was all right. Nick went to the bed and reached out to wake him, then looked up in disbelief as Francis Mulholland came out of the bathroom, wearing Kit's dressing gown. At the same moment Nick realized the bed had hosted more than one person. The actor stopped short, obviously flustered at the sight of Nick.

"What are you doing here?" Nick said.

His voice roused Kit, who raised halfway up on one elbow, a rumpled, absurd caricature of himself. "It's all right, Frank," he said in a hoarse, unsteady voice. "I'm fine now. You needn't stay."

Francis cast a resentful glare at Nick, who strode out into the parlor, where he grew more furious with each passing minute.

In the bedroom, Francis dressed. Kit sat on the edge of the bed, and leaned his cheek against Francis' chest, his eyes closed as Francis put his arms around him. "You're a good friend," Kit mumbled. "You didn't even hit me back when I punched you last night."

"I'm a good friend. But you want him." Francis' voice was sad.

"I wish I could say you're wrong," Kit said, his voice muffled against his friend's coat. "But you're not and we both know it. And I can't even explain it. Oh, God, I feel sick. Help me into my dressing gown, will you? I must maintain some shred of dignity."

Francis pulled the dressing gown up Kit's fumbling arms and tied the sash. "You look bloody awful," he said, using his handkerchief to wipe dried saliva from the corner of Kit's mouth. "Ring me if you need me." He left the suite without looking at Nick or speaking to him. Unable to bring himself to go into the bedroom, Nick waited.

Kit came out of the bedroom, groping and dizzy. "Nico," he said, as he shambled to the couch and collapsed upon it.

"You slept with Mulholland, didn't you. I am gone one night in nearly a year and you go to bed with someone else. I was told you were like that but I didn't believe it."

Kit leaned his head back and put one hand over his burning eyes. "I needed someone. You weren't here. You promised you would be. And it was two nights, not one. Two endless nights."

"I was delivering twins. One of them died, and the mother could have died. I thought that was a little more important than a party."

Kit lowered his hand and looked at him. "Twins? You're right, of course. I'm sorry about the baby that died."

"What was Mulholland doing here?"

Kit covered his eyes again. "Don't beat a dead horse, Nico. It wasn't what you think."

"You went to bed with him. What else could it be?"

"I don't see that it's any of your bloody business."

"I think it is." Nick looked around at the destruction in the room. "What happened in here? Did you and Mulholland get carried away?"

A humorless grimace touched Kit's lips. "Yes," he said. "That's what happened. Frank and I fucked on every piece of furniture in here and finished up in there."

"You have the morals of an alley cat!"

"That's better than no morals at all."

"You were drunk last night."

"As a lord. Frank and I sat here and downed a fifth of whiskey before we commenced our wild activities."

Nick slammed the door as he left. Outside the hotel, he hailed the first down-at-heels cab he saw and jolted along in unhappy thought until he had the driver let him out at a small, rundown church. He didn't realize until he was inside that it was a Roman Catholic church.

Behind closed eyes, he tried to find God. In the cold, echoing sanctuary, he tried to pray as he had done long ago, when he had a sure and certain belief that God was there. He prayed for God to forgive him for the sins he had committed with Kit.

The words, "I am most heartily sorry for what I've done," stuck in his throat. He wasn't sorry; he was only sorry it was over. He'd never tried to put a name to what he felt for Kit, but here in the chill of this place, with the blank plaster eyes of the statues accusing him, he knew. He loved Kit in the way God meant him to love a woman. It was as simple and as soul damning as that.

Kit was where Nick had left him. He looked up as Nick came in.
"I suppose I jumped to a wrong conclusion," Nick said.

"You suppose."

"Kit, you just don't know how difficult all this is for me."

"All what?"

"You and I. It's wrong."

"You're unhappy with me?"

"No. That makes it worse. I should be."

"My poor Puritan," Kit said with a faint smile. "Torn between Jehovah and a pagan. How do you ever manage to forget that burden of guilt long enough to enjoy yourself?"

"You make me forget it. For a while. But sometimes in the middle of the night when you're asleep and I'm awake and everything seems to be so wonderful with us, I feel as if God is watching me."

"And He's angry you're enjoying the life and the body he gave you."

"He's angry because I'm sinning. Kit, I grew up knowing God was watching everything I did."

"A bit arrogant, don't you think?" He sighed. "Nico, if you want to end it, then do so. You're a doctor. You know an amputation must be done cleanly and all at once."

"No! Kit, I couldn't live anymore, without you. That's why I can't bear the thought that I'm not the only one."

"So that's it. You have proprietary rights because you're jeopardizing your eternal soul." He said it with such a flippant edge Nick did not know how to answer. Then Kit took him unawares by saying, "Nico, close your surgery for a fortnight."

"I can't leave my patients that long."

"Can't you just once? *The Tempest* has two more performances and I need a holiday. So do you. Come with me to St. Denys Hill. I want you to see it."

"But I have women due to deliver."

"There are other doctors. You look as tired as I do." Kit's puffy face had never looked less handsome.

"I am." Nick smiled. "Perhaps you're right. We do need a holiday together."

Kit's bloodshot eyes were wistful. "Think of it, Nico. Fourteen days without a care in the world. And I assure you; God is too busy to pay any attention to us. We'll do whatever we like. Ride horses, eat pheasant, sleep in a different room every night. Anything. I've three hundred acres, Nico. We'll bathe without a stitch on in a forest stream, and then make love among the trees and none but the birds will know. We'll picnic. 'A Jug of Wine, a

Loaf of Bread and Thou Beside me singing in the Wilderness.'"
Then he laughed, looking more lighthearted than he had looked
for weeks. "On second thought, I'll do the singing. You see to the
loaf and the jug."

Nick could see how much Kit wanted this. So did he. "When do
you want to leave?"

"Sunday next."

"But I can't go that soon! I must arrange for another doctor to
see to my patients."

"You have four days. Surely you can find someone. Offer him
whatever he wants. I'll pay it."

"I'll pay my own expenses, thank you."

"Isn't stiff-necked pride one of those sins you're so concerned
about?"

In the end, Nick had to accept Kit's offer. No doctor he asked
would do it for the amount of money he could afford. *The
Tempest* closed to a full house and a dozen curtain calls. Long
before dawn on Sunday, they were in Kit's fast, specially built
carriage, on their way to St. Denys Hill.

As they left the city behind them, Nick felt as if a burden had
been lifted. "I'm so glad you badgered me into coming with you,"
he said.

In the privacy of the closed carriage, Kit turned toward him, his
mouth and caressing hands hot with promise. "When we get to
the Hill," he whispered against Nick's lips, "you'll be even more
glad." Then, he laughed and sat back, as Nick groaned and
reminded him that he was skilled with a gelding knife.

Finally Kit said, "Look. We're on my property now. We're
almost home."

They passed a crumbling stone wall that Kit said had once been
a monastery. The sun was bright; Kit insisted they get out and use
the Kodak. They took pictures of one another on the moss-cov-
ered wall. They passed through a village that reminded Nick a
little of his own. The modest spire of a small church lifted a white
welcome in the sunlight. The land around the village was rich and
green and beyond it lay the rocky Pennine Chain. A little farther
on was a stretch of wild moorland bounded by forest.

Nick glanced at his lover's profile. Kit was leaned forward, smiling,
with an eager tenderness Nick had never seen before. "You love it
here, don't you."

"Whenever I come back I think I shall never leave. But then the stage calls me and I go. Look. There are the gates. The house is just beyond."

The carriage clattered across an arched bridge that crossed a narrow rushing stream, and approached a set of intricately designed wrought iron gates, with carved stone pillars at each side and a stone archway over them. Great ancient trees shielded the house from view.

"Welcome home, Mr. Kit," said the elderly gatekeeper.

Kit leaned out. "Thank you, Page. And how are your wife and all the grandchildren?"

"Quite well, thank you."

"Was there any excitement while I was away?"

"Quiet as always, Mr. Kit."

They passed through the gates and past the shielding trees, and the great house burst into view. Nick had known Kit was rich, but he had not imagined anything like the wide gray stone building with four floors, columns, and a dazzling array of windows.

As if he knew what Nick was thinking, Kit said, "When you see it with the sun shining full on the windows it looks like a glass house. Only Hardwick Hall has more."

Nick was too awed to say much, and his awe increased as the road passed through elaborately planned and maintained flower gardens, colorful with early flowers. Statues peeked out at them from the color and greenery. Vines grew from huge, ancient jars. "I wish my mother could see this. She loves flowers and would know the names of every one."

"Bring her here. Bring your whole family here. They could live their lives here and never set eyes on me."

"I can imagine my father and my sister Agnes here. My father would condemn us to hell, and Agnes would wither the flowers with one sour look."

"Then we'll have just your mother. She simply must see it in summer. Compared to summer, this is nothing."

A small knot of servants met the carriage and acted glad to see their employer. If they were curious about his friend, they were too well trained to let it show. Inside, Kit let Nick take his time and stare at the same things that had amazed him so long ago. Then he led the way upstairs to the bedroom that had been his own as a boy, and introduced him to the gatekeeper's nephew, also named Page, who was to be Nick's manservant.

"I can't have a servant." Nick protested. "I wouldn't know how to behave with one."

"Well, the poor lad has a job to do, Nico. He's just in training. Trust me. If you feel awkward, he does too." He took young Page aside and said something Nick could not overhear. Page nodded, gave Nick a little bow, and left the room.

"This room...it's so big, so elaborate."

"Everything in this house is big, Nico. It started out as a small castle in the days of the second Henry, but a fire gutted it more than three hundred years ago. The original part of this house was built with the same stones on the same foundation. You can still see where the fire blackened the stones. The front part, which everybody calls 'the glass house' is almost new. It was built about the time of the American rebellion, and improved about the time Queen Victoria took the throne." His pleasure in the old stories was obvious and made Nick smile.

Kit left him to rest from the journey, and went alone to another, larger, suite that he had taken a few years before. A portrait of Xavier St. Denys hung over the mantel in the sitting room, and, looking at it, Kit wondered if his father would like Nick. "I think you would," he said aloud, "though he can be a bit of a trial at times."

Kit showed him the newest part of the house, starting with the smallest of the three libraries. "This was the first room I ever saw in this house," he said, eyeing Nick to gauge his reaction.

"Weren't you were born here?" Nick asked, puzzled.

Kit put his fingers to his lips. "No questions yet."

Most of the nude statues Kit had seen as a boy were gone now, some given to his father's friends as mementos of him, others donated to museums. Kit had kept his favorites: the four-foot-tall replica of Michelangelo's David, which he and his father had acquired on an Italian holiday, and the Antinous.

Nick had never seen a nude statue and he stared, first at the unabashed genitals carved with such care and then at the expertly executed muscles and veins and facial features. "If this is what the ancient gods looked like, no wonder the Greeks and Romans worshipped idols."

Kit laughed. "Dear Puritan. You do have such a strange way of looking at things. They weren't gods. They were just men."

"How did the artists do this?" Nick touched the Antinous' raised arm, which was broken off at the wrist. "It looks as if it would be warm."

"Michelangelo said the figure was always in the stone. It was the sculptor's work to free it. Not too different from an actor. We're given words on paper and we have to make them live."

"Who is this supposed to be? Was he a real person?"

"As real as you and I. He was Emperor Hadrian's *amoroso*. He drowned himself when he was eighteen, supposedly so he wouldn't grow old. This is believed to have been done from life seventeen hundred years ago. I suspect it's an international crime that I have it."

Nick could not stop looking at the face of the boy who had been adored by an emperor. He glanced at Kit and then back at the statue. "You look like him."

Kit laughed. "I don't think so."

"But you do."

"You flatter me. Hadrian declared him a god, you know. I'm not quite ready for godhood. However, you're more than welcome to treat me like one."

As they slept together that night in Kit's room, surrounded by things given him by his father, the old windup clown watched over them. Its bright paint had faded over the years, and the wood had become dried and brittle. He left it at the Hill during the London theatre season, taking it with him only when the troupe traveled. No one but Lizbet knew of its existence and what it meant to him. When Nick saw it for the first time, he asked about it. Kit said, "He's from long ago and far away, Nico. Someday I'll tell you his story."

After breakfast in the morning, Kit took Nick out on horseback to see a small part of the land. Nick had never ridden anything but his father's easygoing old dray horse, and Kit had to show him how to handle the double reins and the velvet-mouthed sleek thoroughbred. Nick pitied his mount, which was restive under his clumsy hands, and envied Kit's grace on horseback; he had probably been born on the back of a thoroughbred. Kit drew rein at an ivy-covered stone house in a clearing.

"What a lovely place," Nick said.

"Isn't it? It's called the Dower House. Long ago, when the eldest St. Denys son took a wife, his mother was expected to come here and live. So far as anyone knows, none of them ever did. They stayed in the castle and made life miserable for their daughters-in-law. The St. Denys men found other uses for the house." They dismounted and led the horses into the nearby stable. "They brought their mistresses here. Perfect place for a tryst." He added softly, "Now I'm bringing my love."

The next day was a continued tour of the manor house. "Some of these rooms I've seen but once," Kit said. "Some I've never seen at all." He made an encompassing gesture that took in the mass of stone, wood, and glass that was St. Denys Hill. "Royalty stayed here at the Hill, St. Denys women were launched into society, and a few St. Denys men hatched plots that could have cost them their heads. But they always landed on their feet. I think over the centuries no more than a couple of St. Denys heads were separated from the owners' shoulders."

That night, Kit took him to a room in the old part of the house. The cold stone walls were covered with ancient faded tapestries. A white deer pierced by an arrow was Kit's favorite. "Mary Queen of Scots did it," he said. "Duncan St. Denys supported her and was one of the ancestors who lost his head." Their bed that night was an enormous four-poster. "Bonnie Prince Charlie slept in this bed. When he was here, the servants decorated each of the four posts with huge clusters of exotic plumes. Plumes of what, I don't know." He grinned. "The bed of a prince, where you will be allowed to treat me like a god."

"I treat you better now than you deserve," Nick remarked with a laugh.

In the morning, Nick groaned, "Now I know why the upper class did so much plotting and back-stabbing. The beds were uncomfortable. They woke with backaches and headaches and were in rotten moods."

"Why, Nico!" Kit said. "You've made a joke. See? I am a good influence on you after all." As he dressed, he said, "I'm going to let you entertain yourself for a while. I have some things that need doing. You know where the library is. Or feel free to wander about and explore this great pile of rocks. Or if you wish, take a horse and enjoy the countryside. My home is your home."

Nick went to the stables in a feathery rain. He felt almost like a boy again, as he walked in the clean country rain. The smells of horses and leather, feed and manure brought back memories of the countless stables he had gone to with his father.

To the accompaniment of snorts and whinnies and shod hooves striking stone and wood, he talked at length with the head groom and was delighted when the groom, learning of his background, invited him to examine a mare about ready to foal. He borrowed a pair of high boots and leather gloves and spent the afternoon happily helping the stable hands muck out stables. The head groom was horrified. Gentlemen didn't do such a things!

The rain had stopped by the time Nick left the stable. He rode without direction and realized he didn't know where he was. Not until he came to the Dower House did he get his bearings. He gazed at it a few minutes, thinking that it looked like what it was: a place for lovers to hide away. He hoped they would come back here before they went back to the City. He liked it so much more than the overpowering manor house.

Kit's yearly conference with the butler and housekeeper was a matter of form. They were professionals and he trusted them implicitly with the care of everything at the Hill. When everything was finished to mutual satisfaction, Kit left the spacious office where the mundane business matters of the Hill were conducted. In his study, he unwrapped a small parcel he had bought for Nick the day before they left London. It was an old and special book. Smiling, he wrote on the flyleaf and put it away for presentation at the perfect time. Then he left the house and rode away without looking for Nick.

Michael was buried in a copse not far from the house. Kit had chosen the place, and with his own hands had, alone, built a stone grotto to serve as both shelter and headstone. Wildflowers now grew profusely over the exterior of it, and piled within the grotto were toys Kit had brought back over the years.

He knelt beside the grave. "Well, Michael," he said, pulling unsightly weeds as he talked. "Should I tell Nico the truth? I've told no one else, not even Frank and I trust him with my life. But I've known Nick for only a year. Can I trust him? Dare I? I love him. Far more than he does me. If he does at all. God knows he won't say it."

Sometimes Michael seemed to speak to him; today he was silent. Kit sighed. "If I tell him the truth about the old man and what I did, he could destroy me. And perhaps he would. He's a

Puritan and Puritans are good at judging others. And yet, how can I even pretend to myself that I love him if I can't trust him with the truth?" Kit touched the ground that covered his brother. "Michael, at times you're not much help."

9

it lay awake beside Nick, still turning the question over and over in his mind. By the time he fell asleep hours later, he had decided to risk it all. As soon as an appropriate time came, he would lay his past bare for Nick and hope for the best.

But the next day was warm and perfect, with a sky as blue as Nick's eyes. No fit day for exposing violence and sorrow. They took enough food for a day and rode miles from the house, passing over hills and streams without ever leaving Kit's land.

They dined on a hill under the full moon. Nick looked up, his sandwich forgotten, at the silver-white sky-face that looked back benignly at them. "I'd forgotten how wonderful it is to be outdoors on a night such as this," he said. "In the City I could never see the moon for the chimneys and the smoke."

Kit said nothing, remembering. Until he came to the Hill he had never seen a moon that wasn't clouded by dirty smoke, dirty fog, the tops of dirty buildings, strings of laundry.

They slept under the stars and at dawn headed for a dense wood cut through by a shallow, narrow river. There they took the promised dip in the icy water. And not even last year's damp leaves, the roughness of the ground, or the twittering birds was a barrier to a wrestling match that led to laughter which soon dissolved into pleasure.

The week ended. No appropriate time for painful revelation presented itself.

Nick was out of sorts because Kit insisted upon having a special evening for his father's old friends. "You're being childish," Kit told him. "I promised him I would do this whenever I was in residence. I hate broken promises. I won't say you'll like my father's friends, because you won't. But Lizbet will be here. You can talk to her."

Kit's prediction was correct. Except for Lizbet Porter the guests were well-dressed and well-off men from all over England and to Nick's disgust three or four were effeminate. He wondered how Kit could tolerate their butterfly hands brushing at his lapels, touching his face and hair, pressing his hands while looking at him with calf eyes.

But the man who annoyed him more than all the others combined was not effeminate. He was a handsome gray-haired man who arrived late in the evening, and talked to Kit for far too long. Kit had drunk too much and had eaten little; his words slurred when he introduced the man to Nick.

"Nico, meet Rawdon McPherson. An old, old, old friend. Rawdon, Nick Stuart. My latest conquest." He laughed and leaned on McPherson.

McPherson gave Nick a curious glance and put one arm around Kit's shoulders. "My boy, you're already smashed and the evening is young." He inclined his head toward Nick. "A pleasure, Mr. Stuart. Come along, Kit." As if he owned Kit, he guided him back to their mutual friends.

"'Conquest!'" Nick muttered indignantly to himself. He left to wander the halls with their portraits of Kit's long-dead ancestors. He studied a dozen St. Denys portraits from the past hundred years. Odd. Not one of them bore even a slight resemblance to Kit. And neither did the portrait of his father. Nick searched the portraits of ladies in satin, lace, and jewels. He was sure he would recognize her by her blonde beauty, for Kit had remarked one time that he looked a good deal like his mother.

A soft voice spoke at his elbow. "Walk with me, Nicholas," Lizbet said. She tucked her small hand in his elbow. "A tuppence for your thoughts."

"I doubt they're worth even that much. I was just wondering why Kit doesn't look like anyone else in his family."

She smiled. "He's a changeling." Nick did not know Kit had pleaded with her to make Nick her friend. "He's isolated from all he knows, Lizbet," he had told her. "Rama hates him. Frank resents him. The rest want nothing to do with him unless they need a doctor." She promised she would, though truth to tell she didn't like him very much either.

"You're Kit's aunt, are you not?" Nick asked. "His father's sister?"

"No. Cousins."

"He said you were the only mother he ever knew."

Without hesitation, she said, "Yes, poor lad. His mother died when he was quite young."

"I hoped to see a picture of his mother. Aren't there any here?"

"She was impatient and didn't like to sit for portraitists." It was an explanation she and Kit had worked out, in the event Nick asked this question.

"That must be where Kit got his restless nature."

"Possibly. Although my cousin, his father, was the most restless man I've ever known. He took that boy all over the world."

Their heels echoed on the marble floors as they strolled. Then they came to a sitting room which, compared to the others, was small and intimate. The colors were muted, the furniture graceful. An arched alcove across from the fireplace provided a cozy niche. Nick could imagine Kit as a small child hiding out in there. Over the fireplace was a large painting in a simple but elegant frame.

"This is my favorite room at the Hill," Lizbet said. "The colors are so lovely, and one doesn't feel dwarfed by the room itself." She gestured at the painting. "That's what I brought you here to see."

He approached it and gazed in wonder at it. Unlike most of the other paintings and portraits, its colors were undarkened by time. The reds and golds and deep blues and greens were vibrant, almost alive. It was of a phoenix rising from a nest of flames, its beak open; its one visible eye pierced the viewer with a beam of light.

"It's beautiful," he said. "It's also disquieting."

"Kit found it in a seedy little place in a London alley. Several people have tried to buy it from him. Artists themselves, some of them. Beardsley. Whistler. Even Bernard Shaw, and he has no taste at all. They've offered Kit many times what he paid but he won't sell."

"The poor creature looks tortured."

"You know the story, don't you? The phoenix burns itself to death and rises from its own ashes." She covertly watched him. He didn't understand. That meant Kit had told him nothing. She took his arm again and they walked across the room, sat in the alcove and talked of pleasant, inconsequential things for a while.

"Lizbet," he said hesitantly, "may I ask you something?"

"Of course."

"Why did you say he was a changeling? Wasn't he born a St. Denys?"

Lizbet's expression became wary. "I don't know what you mean."

"I wondered if he had possibly been adopted."

"What has he told you of himself?"

"Very little. He told me the history of the house, stories of his ancestors, and about his father. He told me you had done more for him than anyone except his father. Nothing about himself."

"I'm not free to tell you anything he has not. It isn't my place. Whatever I did for him I did because I love him, and in his turn he's made certain I'll never want for anything. He's built me a little house near the village, exactly the way I want it, for the day I retire." She laughed softly. "He's asked me many times to live at the manor house. So did his father. But it's too opulent for me. I'd feel as if I were on stage all the time."

Nick stiffened at Kit's voice and that of another man. His mouth tightened when Kit came in with his "old friend," McPherson. Kit walked unsteadily and McPherson's arm was around him, holding him up. Kit stumbled, and fell on his back upon a damask couch, in sprawling, loose-limbed invitation. McPherson laughed and sat down at the foot of the couch.

"Feet're wolly," Kit mumbled.

"They're what?" McPherson said.

"Wolly... you know ... woll ... oh, bugger ... wob-uh-ly."

"Oh. Wobbly. Well, I've a cure for the wobblies."

Nick watched in shock as McPherson leaned over and gave Kit a long, deep kiss that seemed to last forever. Kit's arms went around McPherson's neck, prolonging it. "Meet me at the Dower House. After they've all left," McPherson said. His left hand groped downward. "And don't tell me you don't want to. I've found proof to the contrary."

Kit snickered. "Hang on 'nother minute, I won' need t' meet you."
Nick leapt up, ready to kill one or both of them. Lizbet clutched
his arm just as one of the effeminate guests fluttered into the parlor.

"Oh, my goodness! Look at this. Sweet Kit and naughty Rawdon
doing a little grab-and-tickle! Bad boys!"

"Harold," McPherson said, "your timing is impeccable."

Kit scrambled to his feet and seized Harold, whirling him around
in an inebriated waltz until they both tumbled down, howling with
laughter.

Nick's furious glare left the exhibition of Kit and Harold and
settled again on Rawdon McPherson, who looked bemused and
not at all drunk. For the first time in his life Nick knew what it
was to hate someone. McPherson took Kit's hands, and pulled
him to his feet. "You're drunk as a bricklayer, my dear. Don't forget.
The Dower House at midnight."

Kit fumbled with his clothes as McPherson left the room. "What
y'going t'do at the Dower House, Kit?" Harold asked. "Who's
invited?"

"Just me. Harold, have you seen Nick? I can't find him anywhere."

"Oh, he's prob'ly with th'others. C'mon." He tugged at Kit's
sleeve, pulling him from the room. As they disappeared Kit
declaimed Juliet's lines in a falsetto. "Roooo-me-o, Roooo-me-o!
Wherefore art thou Roooo-meeee-ooooo?" McPherson followed
them, laughing.

Nick was almost ill with anger. The Dower House! Kit was
going to meet McPherson at the Dower House! And he would lie
about it just as he had lied about Mulholland.

"Kit is as he is, Nicholas," Lizbet said quietly. "If you love him,
you must love him without condition or reservation. If you can't
do that you have no place in his life."

Staring at her in disbelief Nick said, "You want me to excuse
what he just did? Accept it without a word?"

"If that's what it takes. Now I believe I'll join the others. Are
you coming?" Reluctantly Nick let her take his arm and walked
with her back to the Tudor Parlor.

The evening had degenerated into a game of charades at which
Kit, even drunk, was undisputed master. Nick did not take part;
he was not asked to. Glowering, he watched the faces of the men.
Look at them! All old enough to be Kit's father. But obviously
that made no difference to him! How many of them had he gone

to bed with? McPherson, surely. Was he the only one? Was that the tie that bound them all together? They'd all had Kit at one time or another? Damn them all.

Nick sought out Kit's flushed, laughing face. And then Kit had to pay a forfeit to McPherson in the silly game. The forfeit was another endless open-mouthed kiss that had the others applauding and whistling. Nick's hands curled into fists as he silently pleaded, 'Kit, stop this. I love you. You must know it. Stop making a fool of me!'

By midnight the guests were gone. McPherson was the last to leave and Nick was certain he saw a significant look pass between McPherson and Kit. And then he and Kit were alone in the echoing old house. Kit had stopped drinking hours earlier and was slowly sobering.

"It was fun, wasn't it, Nico?" he said with a bleary, contented smile.

"For you, I suppose. Not for me."

Kit squinted at him. "You don't like this; you don't like that; you don't approve of this; you don't approve of that. I'd wager a year's box office you and your sister Agnes are just alike! I'd better have the gardener make certain you haven't withered the flowers."

"At least I don't act like a whore."

Kit turned away. "I don't know what you mean and I'm not going to ask. You're being tiresome. Come to bed." As he walked away, Nick caught his arm. Kit stared at him a moment and jerked his arm free.

"Don't turn your back on me!" Nick said. "I saw you and McPherson tonight."

"Whatever are you talking about?"

"You. McPherson. He had his hands all over you. I'm surprised he got his tongue out of your mouth without surgery. You can't deny it."

"Why would I? I don't even remember it. And if it happened, I didn't plan it."

"Didn't you?"

"No, I did not. He and I left the party to visit some places here that have special memories, that's all. Talked about my father. He and Rawdon were good friends."

"And you expect me to believe that? You acted like a mongrel bitch in heat. Whether you planned it or not, you liked it."

A muscle jumped in Kit's jaw, and with effort he kept his temper. "I won't stand here and defend myself against your stupidity. Are you coming to bed or not?"

"Why? Isn't it time for you to go?"

"Nico, I am too sleepy for conundrums and I have a headache. Argue with yourself. I'm going to bed." He walked away. Nick followed him.

"And as soon as I'm asleep you will be off to the Dower House to meet McPherson, won't you."

Kit stopped again. "Nico, I have no intention of meeting Rawdon at the Dower House or anywhere else."

"He's there waiting for you."

"You meet him then, if it concerns you so much." Kit went up the stairs, refusing to respond to Nick's accusations with anything other than an annoyed shake of his head. They reached Kit's door, and Kit said, "There are twenty or so other bedrooms. Find one. Or sleep in the stable if that suits you. God forbid you sleep with a sinner."

"Is that what you want me to do?"

"I want you to do whatever makes you happy, though I doubt there is such a thing."

Nick followed him into the bedroom. "Just tell the truth about you and McPherson. I don't want some pretty lie."

"Unvarnished truth? Bloody hell. You couldn't take it."

"I said I want the truth about you and McPherson."

Kit snarled, "Rawdon was the first man to fuck me, the one who taught me how to fuck. Is that truthful enough for you?"

"And others besides McPherson?"

The defiance went out of Kit. He took a deep breath and said with infinite patience, "Nico, there were many men. I don't know how many. I remember few faces and fewer names."

"And of those there tonight?" Nick felt as if a weight were crushing his chest. "How many of them?"

"Only Rawdon."

"Only Rawdon. Many men."

"I admitted it, did I not? You said you wanted the unvarnished truth. Would you prefer a lie? It wasn't just sexual. You know that. I needed them to keep—" He couldn't tell Nick about Rourke. Not now. Later, when this silly little quarrel was over and Nick could laugh at his jealousy, he would tell him everything. "I needed them to keep away the nightmares."

"You don't even know how many!" Nick shouted. "You really *are* a bloody whore!"

The twisted expression of torture on Nick's face stunned Kit as much as his words. "I would let no other man on earth speak to me as you have. Don't ever do it again."

"The truth, Kit! The truth, or don't you know what that is? How many men have had you in the last year? Tell me!"

"Since we've been together there has been no one else. I give you my word."

"Your word! I've watched you with your friends. Touching, always touching each other. And Mulholland? He was in your bed a few days ago. But I'm supposed to believe you've changed."

Kit lowered his head like a bull about to charge. "I wouldn't expect you to believe that. You're perfect. You don't have flaws. You can't understand anyone who does." In an effort to give peace one last try, Kit said, "Nico, I need you. We need each other. Don't do this to us."

"I'm doing nothing. You did the harm. I defied God for you. And you repay me by playing the whore with half the men in England."

A bubble of unamused laughter rose in Kit's chest. "*Half*, Nico? Only *half?* My God, how did that happen?"

"You bypassed the ugly, the insane, and the dead!"

Kit swung from his heels and knocked Nick flat on his back. He stood over him, fists cocked. "I need you more than I've ever needed anyone. But by God I won't tolerate this. I've been faithful to you. I can't make you believe me so to hell with you. Sleep elsewhere. We'll talk tomorrow when your hot head has cooled off and you can see what a fool you've been tonight."

Nick got up, wiping blood from his chin with the back of his hand. He walked out without a backward glance. Kit slammed the door behind him and kicked it, then kicked it again.

Nick lay down in his clothes, but could not sleep. At the first light of day he set out on foot. He was to the village long before Kit awakened, and was in a coach on his way to London before Kit knew he was gone.

Lizbet arrived for dinner and went to the Petite Dining Room that had long ago been a lady's boudoir. There, she was surprised to see the table unset, and Kit sitting alone in the twilight dimness.

"Kit?" she asked, "why are the candles not lit?"

He roused himself from his stupor, and lighted the two nearest candles. "Lizbet. Forgive me. I forgot to send my man to tell you there would be no dinner this evening. You have come for naught."

A glass and an almost empty whisky bottle sat in front of him. He reached for them and she moved them out of his reach as she sat down beside him. "What happened? Where's your friend?"

"He's no friend. He's an ass. And he's gone. He left during the night." Kit retrieved his glass and tossed down the whiskey in it. "The bloody fool is gone!" He hurled the glass at the wall. Lizbet jumped when it struck and shattered.

"I don't understand," she said.

"Do you think I do?" Kit raked his hands through his hair. "What will I do without him, Lizbet?"

"But what happened?"

"He saw Rawdon kiss me."

"So did I. Somewhat more than a kiss, my dearest."

His face reddened. "He's an imbecile. He put more importance to it than it had. He said unforgivable things and I let him get away with it. I should have stopped him with the first word."

"Perhaps this quarrel is providential, Kit. Forget him. I knew from the first moment I saw him, he was not good for you."

The eyes that burned into hers had a maniacal gleam. "Forget him? Oh, no, Lizbet. I'll make him sorry he insulted me. I'll make him sorry he was ever born."

She put her hand on his arm. "Don't think like that. No good can come of it. Please, Kit. Forget him. You have a good friend in Francis and he worships you. If you must love a man, love Francis."

Kit looked away. She wanted only his happiness and she hated anyone who, in her eyes, wronged him. She knew him as well as anyone could and yet even she did not understand how deeply hurt he was by Nick's desertion. If he died in the attempt, he would make Nick Stuart sorry he had called Kit St. Denys a whore.

❧ ❧

Emotionally drained, Nick was unprepared for the letter he found waiting for him at his surgery. It had come from Agnes during his absence.

> Father is dying. He has made his peace with Our Heav-
> enly Father. He asks for you. No one else can comfort

him no matter how we try. He has the mistaken notion you care about him. Mother wants you to come home before it is too late.

As the railroad train hurtled from the City into the countryside Nick tried to strike a silent, desperate bargain with God. "Let my father live. I'm most heartily sorry for what I've done. I didn't honor my father. I went against his wishes. I let myself be drawn into mortal sin. But just let my father live and I'll forget Kit. There will never be another man. Never. I'll marry a good woman, have a dozen children if that's what You want. I know my father and I don't get on, but he is my father and I love him. I don't want him to die. Please, I am so sorry. Let my father live."

10

Nick went back in time, from the splendor of St. Denys Hill to the country village in the rich earth and lush uplands of his boyhood, His silent prayer continued unabated as the train huffed and screeched to a stop at the depot nearest the village but still thirty miles distant. Several buggies and wagons for hire clustered a few yards away, and Nick climbed into the nearest buggy. The team of horses looked as old and creaky as the vehicle.

Night had fallen when he arrived at the rosy-stone cottage. As he approached from the back, light shone through the two small, many-paned windows. He paused to inhale the heady scent of his mother's flower garden. In the light from the kitchen window he could see the silhouette of the water pump that stood near the door.

This had once been his home, his window, his pump. Why had he ever left the simple goodness of this life? Kit had called him a fool. For once, Kit had been right. He was a stranger in his own land. He lifted his hand to knock, then lowered it and stepped into the kitchen. His throat thickened at the sight of the hearth where his mother cooked, at the scarred thick table where she cut the meat and the long, plain table where the entire family had once gathered. His father's chair was at one end of the table, his mother's at the other, plain and substantial like everything in their close-to-God lives.

At that moment Agnes came in and stopped short when she saw him. She neither smiled nor welcomed him, but gave a curt nod of her head toward their parents' bedroom. Then she sat down at the table, put on reading glasses, and opened her Bible.

His mother sat unmoving beside her husband's bed. He said softly, "Mother," and bent to kiss her cheek.

Red-eyed, she looked up. "He wouldn't let me send for you sooner." She rose stiffly and leaned over the bed. "Our Nickie has come," she said, then with a heavy step left the room.

In spite of his experience it was hard to believe the frail stick of a man was his sturdy, strong-willed father. "I'm here, Father," he said.

His father's eyes slowly opened. "Nicholas." It was a dry, barely audible whisper. He attempted a faint smile. "Your mother believed you could cure me." His small store of energy was depleted.

"Agnes wrote me you were ill. She didn't say what sickness. Let me look at you. I can't cure you if I don't know what you have." He managed a smile. "How many times did I hear you tell someone that?"

As he spoke, he felt the cold, clammy forehead and took the small, fast pulse. His father was jaundiced, as well. From time to time, he would speak in a high-pitched nonsensical way, take a shallow breath and return to the real world. Nick knew even before he pulled back the blankets and saw the red streaks that extended death up his father's right arm from a red, partially healed wound on his father's thumb. Their eyes met. "Septicemia," Nick said.

"Foolish thing," William Stuart whispered. "Tiny cut. Thought healed. Was wrong." A moment later he was again speaking unknown words to unseen beings.

Nick's head lowered. He sensed his mother beside him and said, "I left him and went away to learn how to heal. And I can do nothing. If I'd been here as I should have been this wouldn't have happened." His breath caught in his throat. "All any of us can do is pray for a quick end."

"He thought it was healed, Nickie. He wouldn't let me send for you. And then the fevers began. Up and down they were, for days."

"Nicholas." His father returned once more from the fevered land of shadows, his voice weak as the cry of a new kitten.

"I'm here," Nick said. He held his father's hand between his own. "I should have taken time to thank you for all you taught me. You made me love healing and medicine. And I never told you."

His father's sunken, yellowed eyes fixed on his son. "Both should have said things. Proud of you. Never said." He drew a shallow breath. "Nicholas, the church?"

Nick tried to swallow the boulder-sized lump and wanted to lie. "I fell away, Father." He saw fear for him on the dying man's face. "I'll return to the church. I promise. I never should have left."

Slowly, slowly, his father's lips moved almost without sound, but Nick knew he had said, "Pray with me." A minute later, Nick gently closed eyes that would never see again.

William Stuart's body lay in his plain casket in the church all the next day. Nick saw again the strangers who were his sisters and brother, and saw nephews and nieces he hadn't known existed. Friends and patients came from farms and villages for miles around to pay their respects. Nick was moved by the affection with which his father was remembered. More than one neighbor grasped Nick's hand and said, "We'll miss your father somethin' dreadful, but it's good you're home to take his place."

Throughout the ordeal, his mother was silent, dry-eyed. He wondered if she and his father had ever loved each other. How terrible to live without love. The days and nights with Kit rushed into his mind. Hadn't that been love? Hadn't he thought he would be with Kit forever?

With the thought, his face became grim and cold. Love? No. He'd been bewitched; sin-crazed. He should thank God every day that he'd come to his senses in time before he was irrevocably lost. The casket shimmered before his eyes. He hoped Kit was all right. He hoped the nightmares had not returned.

His father had been gone a fortnight when his mother said, "Nickie, when are you off again for the City?" She poured tea into his thick cup, then sat down and took up her own.

"I don't know, Mother. I don't want to leave you here alone."

"I have Agnes." She said it without enthusiasm. Agnes had not been sweetened by passing years.

"When I go back to London, you must come with me," he said. He thought again, as he had several times since his return, that she did not look well.

She was silent for a moment, and then said, "Nicholas, I want to see a priest. I haven't made confession for ... since I married your father, fifty-one years gone."

Agnes overheard. "Mother! You mustn't even think of such a thing!"

"If she wants a priest, I'll find one," Nick said.

"Well, what else could I expect from you," Agnes retorted. "You were never like the rest of us. Wait until the others hear of this."

He stood up. "Mother, pack whatever you need for a vacation. You're going to London."

"Indeed, she is not! She's old, Nicholas. Father wouldn't hear of it!"

"Agnes, shut up. Father is not here, and it's her decision to make."

Their mother looked from one child to the other. "I've never been to London," she said. "Is there a priest there, Nicholas?"

"Yes, Mother. And beautiful churches. And statues. And parks. And the Queen. Perhaps you will even see the Queen go by, and I'll take you to see the changing of the guard at the palace, and you'll hear Big Ben, and the Bow bells." He had not thought before of taking her there, but now the idea was in his mind full-blown, he thought it was grand. London was large enough he was unlikely to see Kit as long as he avoided the theatre. And he had no intention of ever going close to one.

His mother's faded eyes were bright with longing. "Oh, Nicholas, to make confession, to see a statue of the Blessed Mother again, to hear the Latin... It's been so long." Something fell from her hands. Nicholas and Agnes both bent to retrieve it. Nick reached it first.

"What is that thing?" Agnes demanded, when Nick had straightened, holding it. "A necklace? Mother has no necklaces."

"No," he said, "it's a rosary." The beads were black and worn. The tiny crucifix was of wood, darkened from years of handling. How incredible. All those years, in secret. Nick pressed the rosary into her hands and closed her fingers around it.

"The congregation must be told of this," Agnes said, her voice as harsh that of any Grand High Inquisitor. "Mother, you will have to be disciplined before them."

"Agnes," Nick said, "go to hell. Mother and I are going to London."

"You can't leave," his sister said, her face red with anger. "Father's estate hasn't been settled yet."

"Then as soon as it has been, we are going to London. And you will say nothing to the congregation. Nothing."

"It's all right if she does," his mother said with spirit. "I don't care what they think now."

Nick stayed with his mother in the family home, in part to help his mother settle his father's estate and in part to save his mother from his sister's constant harping. Sometimes his mother walked with him out among the green hills, and sometimes he walked alone. He preferred to go with her; when he was alone Kit invaded his solitude.

In some ways the village had changed not at all while he was gone. In other ways it had changed completely. The schoolhouse had burned down and a brick building stood in its place, with separate privies for boys and girls. The vicar had died of pneumonia last year. Nick's beloved Angelica, now plump and bitter, had returned to the village alone and no one knew what had become of her partner in sin. While he was there, news came that Hugh Prater was dead, stabbed to death in a tavern in Bristol. The other boys and girls Nick had known were now sober, grown, parents many times over. He was invited to dinner many times at homes with marriageable young daughters.

He treated some of his father's patients, and for a while he mulled over the idea of taking his mother to London for the promised visit, then returning to take over his father's practice.

In the settlement of his father's estate Nick received the practice and the house, but the month of treating gout and grippe in people, hairballs in cats, and ulcerated udders on dairy cows, gelding pigs and young stallions, and delivering calves, lambs, and puppies as well as one baby, proved to him he did not want to remain. He sold the house to Agnes for a shilling, and the practice for a good sum of money to an enthusiastic young Scottish doctor.

He felt the lash of guilt when Agnes denounced him as an Esau selling his birthright. She turned her back on him then, and he knew he would never see his sister again.

❧

In the City, Nick once more lived in the surgery, and planned for his mother to stay with him until he could find suitable rooms. His mother astonished him when she announced the first day that she had found her own place, in a respectable rooming house owned by another Irish widow, Mrs. O'Bannon. It was only a short walk from the surgery, though in a much better neighborhood, and a five-minute walk from Our Lady of Sorrows.

The two Irishwomen instantly struck up a close friendship. "We talk and laugh enough to make up for lost time," she told him with a sparkle in her eyes. "We go to Mass every morning and then come home to gossip for hours over coffee." She helped Mrs. O'Bannon cook for the boarders and clean the rooms in return for free room and board, allowing her to save her widow's inheritance and the money from the sale of the practice.

"You don't need to clean rooms!" Nick had protested. "I have enough money to pay for your lodging."

"I don't want a man decidin' what I can do anymore," she said. "Not even you. I'll make me own way and that is that." When she told him she did laundry for the boarders in exchange for money, he sighed and said nothing.

Within a fortnight of returning to the City he hired a hack to drive him past the Xavier Theatre. It was like picking at a scab. He was startled to see no playbills. The theatre was padlocked. "Why is the Xavier closed, do you know?" he asked with fear as he descended from the cab a little later, back at the surgery. Something had happened to Kit!

"I hear that actor chap took off for them foreign countries. Hurt me bloody business, he did," the driver said. He slapped the reins against his horse's rump and moved off.

"Of course," Nick said to himself, weak with relief. "How could I have forgotten?" Kit had talked of the European tour for months. Belgium, Germany, Italy, France, Denmark, Norway, Russia, and Austria-Hungary. He had hoped he never set eyes on Kit again, yet it was unbearably sad to know he was so far away. "You are such a fool," he said aloud. "Good riddance to him."

One month to the day after his return to London, Nick was escorting a feeble gray-haired woman into the examination room when the bell on the door jingled. It had been a long day, the waiting room was still full, and he wanted to shout "Go away." But the young woman was clearly out of place and looked healthy. Her clothes were trim, clean, sensible, and, for all he knew, fashionable. She wore gloves; a small hat with a plain blue feather tilted forward on dark hair that was drawn back in a bun at the nape of her neck. In the crook of her right arm was a dainty bag, and in her other hand was a small leather grip. Nick stared at her as blatantly as did the roomful of patients. She seemed to be unperturbed by the scrutiny.

"Dr. Stuart?" she said in an American accent.

"Well, yes, though you shouldn't call me doctor."

She laughed. "I keep forgetting it's different here." She extended a note toward him. "I'm Miss King. I'm a trained nurse. Mr. Grainger gave me your name. He said you might need a nurse, and I need experience. It's all in the letter." Her speech was quick, her manner confident.

"Well, yes, I could use the help. But I can't afford to pay much and it would hardly be fair to you."

"It would only be for a short while, you understand. I'm here to study British nursing methods and I want practical experience and the other doctor didn't want me so he sent me to you and I shall be in England three more months." She said it all in one breath. Her smile was a little less certain now.

"Hey, now, doc," said a rough man with a black eye, "if ye don't hire the pretty little thing you need t'see a doctor!"

"You may be right, Mr. Jones." To her he said, "If you don't mind waiting until I'm finished for the day, I'll be glad to talk to you about it."

"Of course." She hung her coat on a peg without waiting for him to help her with it. When Nick emerged again from the examination room, she held a soiled-looking baby on her lap, cradled him close with one arm and rubbed his belly with her free, now ungloved, hand. And though his face was streaked with recent tears, he had quit crying. His mother stared in awe at her. "He ain't quit bawlin' since he woke up," she said.

"It may be a touch of colic," said Nurse King. She returned to baby to his mother and showed her how to rub her hands together to warm them and then massage the baby's abdomen. "Doctor will tell you what to do, and perhaps give you medicine. But rubbing his tummy and keeping him warm may bring some comfort for a little while." Just then she realized Nick was watching her. "I hope you don't mind," she said to him.

He spoke to the mother. "Jane, take him into the examining room. I'll be right there." To Nurse King he said, "Thank you. The poor little fellow had a difficult start in life and his digestion is faulty. I hope..." he paused, then said, "I hope we can find a way for you to work with me."

"So do I," she said. "If you like, I can start right now. I'll talk to the rest of the patients and find out their symptoms and complaints and perhaps save you a little time. I can also take their temperature and blood pressure for you."

Nick smiled. "That would be excellent if I had more than one stethoscope and thermometer."

She opened the clasp on the small leather grip. "I carry my own. If you have something to sterilize the thermometer with between patients I'll set right to work."

Nick laughed in delight. "Are you always this prepared?"

"Yes," she said, and he didn't doubt it. "I wanted to prove from the first minute that you needed me."

Nick did not have time to read the note she had given him until the end of the day. His old friend, Aubrey Grainger, wrote:

> I wish to most highly recommend Miss B. King, a trained nurse from America. The young lady has worked with me at hospital and I found her to be a well-qualified nurse with excellent skills. She desires a few weeks' experience working with charity patients. A strange ambition, to me, but I thought immediately of you and your clinic of mercy...

Nick chuckled at the thought of charity patients in Aubrey Grainger's genteel Mayfair practice, where the waiting room was like a lady's parlor, complete with silver tea service and a maid to serve the tea.

> People like Miss King. She has a natural way with those who are ill and those who are very young or very old. Please take her. She has quite talked my ear off with her eternal questioning. You won't be sorry, though you may be earless before she leaves.

She waited expectantly while he read the note, and said after a moment, "I read it. It's true that I talk too much except when I'm with patients. Then I'm the soul of brevity and tact. Tact, anyway."

"He didn't say you talk too much. He said you asked many questions. That's good, Nurse King. How will you learn if you don't question? Quite frankly, I think doctors should be questioned more than we are." He hesitated, and wondered if he were about to commit a social error. "If I may take you to dinner," he said, "we can talk there. I'm much more on my game when I'm not hungry. And right now I'm starving."

"So am I," she confessed. "I was too nervous to eat before I came."

"I haven't a private vehicle. Do you mind walking? There's a place not far from here, but the food is decent and the atmosphere is pleasant though a bit smoky."

"I don't mind a bit," she said. "I walk a lot at home."

"And where is that?" He took her coat from the peg and held it for her.

"New York. I'm a city girl. I was born in Chicago. Have you ever been there?"

"No. I'm not much of a traveler. I'm rather a stodgy old goat."

She looked up at him, laughed, and took his arm. "You're far from being either stodgy or old."

He was inordinately pleased. He had felt both stodgy and old since he left Kit. He glanced down at her and wondered why he had not noticed earlier that her eyes were the same rich brown as Kit's.

The restaurant was not crowded, and the owner showed them to a table as far away from the kitchen as it was possible to get in the small establishment. He beamed at Nurse King. "Excuse me for saying so Miss, but it's about time he brought a saucy young girl in. He needs to get married. My wife says so."

Nick's face turned bright red. When the man had left, Nick said, "I'm sorry you were embarrassed. I treated his wife and they've adopted me."

"I wasn't at all embarrassed. It's been a while since anyone called me a saucy young girl," she said with a laugh. She had an enchanting laugh.

"I hope we can come to a mutual agreement," Nick said, steering the conversation to business, "though I know I shan't want you to leave at the end of your time here."

She smiled. "I like it here, but I'm needed at home. I'm a little homesick."

"I know that feeling well. May I ask why you want to work with charity patients?"

She sipped her strong coffee and frowned a little. "I came from poor people. Pop was a brewery worker in Chicago. He made good wages and he was thrifty, but he was injured at work and the union had been beaten down. Perhaps they couldn't have helped anyway. When my parents' savings were gone we survived on charity. I was young but I could have found work. They wouldn't hear of it. I had to go on to high school; it was their dream."

Just then their meal came, and she stopped talking to eat. He noticed with approval that she had a healthy appetite. While waiting for dessert she went on with her story. "They died the year I graduated high school, and I'll always believe they died because they couldn't afford medical care. That's not right, Mr. Stuart. Not right at all. I went to New York to become a nurse. I had to apply many places before I got in, and then it was in Boston at General. I graduated two years ago. And I know it's immodest to say so, but I graduated *Summa cum laude.*"

"I can see why." He leaned his chin on his hand. "And I don't think it's immodest at all. How did you come to be here?"

"My own doctor. I went to work for him, in his practice. He was so pleased he bullied a foundation he's associated with into paying for nine months' study in England. Dr. Baker's so old and crotchety they don't argue with him."

"No strings?"

She laughed. "Not quite. When I go home, I can't go into private nursing for a year. I have to work at the Women's and Children's Hospital in New York as a trained nurse, and teach English methods to two nursing classes a week. Lucky I don't need much sleep!"

"And how do you like it here?"

"I love it more every day. I truly do." Her dark eyes glowed. "I even met Florence Nightingale recently."

"Really!"

"She likes to welcome American nurses at her home, you know. She's still beautiful, but old and frail. She has been an invalid for so long I was almost afraid to breathe for fear a breath would wither her even more."

"She's a remarkable woman." His smile was shy. "I'm beginning to think you're a remarkable woman as well." His face grew hot and he wanted to hide. He sounded like such a fool!

"It's been a wonderful experience. Sometimes I've actually met doctors I could respect." Her smile was impish. "I mean no offense to your profession, sir, but some doctors, American doctors at least, are asses."

The term was unexpected, coming from this fresh-faced girl. "We have our share of that breed here as well."

"That's different. When an Englishman is an ass he sounds so elegant doing it!" She laughed again and he was struck by how good-natured she was. They talked a little longer about her working with him for the rest of her stay in the country. Then he hired a cab and saw her to the flat where she was living with an English nurse and her family.

The time passed too quickly. Soon it was time for Nurse King to return to New York. "I'll miss you," Nick said, knowing how inadequate those three words were. She had become his right arm. At one point she had told him her first name, but he had never used it. He said again, "I'll miss you, Bron— Miss King. I hope your journey home is uneventful." After a moment of awkward silence, he reached in his pocket. "This is a token of my appreciation." He held out a small box.

She still had not spoken. Then she opened the box and found a tiny silver angel.

He said, "An angel for an angel of mercy."

She stood on tiptoe and kissed his cheek. Her voice quivered as she said, "I'll never forget you and all I've learned from you." Her words tumbled out, faster and faster, as she handed him a folded note. "This is my address in New York. Please, I know I'm being horribly forward, and you'll think badly of me, but I would like awfully much to hear from you once in a while, and if you ever get to New York, you must call on me." When she finished her face was crimson.

"I will. I promise. My loss is American nursing's gain." He wondered afterward if he had seen tears in her eyes or if he had imagined it.

※※

On a sunny Sunday, while his mother knelt in church saying her beads in the shadow of the Blessed Virgin, her heart stopped. "She had such a sweet smile when she passed," Mrs. O'Bannon told him, dabbing at her eyes with a sodden handkerchief. "One minute she was there. The next minute she sighed, just a little, and Our Blessed Lady took her away."

Nick had a funeral Mass, attended by his brother and all his sisters except Agnes. Their mother was laid to rest in the churchyard, and Nick ordered a headstone with an angel and the simple words "Beloved Mother."

After his mother's death, Nick's need for Kit became almost overwhelming. He knew that if Kit came home immediately he would go to him and beg his forgiveness. But the *Times* said the

St. Denys Repertory Company was extending their triumphal world tour by two months. "I can't go back to him," Nick said, as he lay sleepless. "I can't. I know what he is. I must exorcise him, but how can I when he will be coming home to England soon? What am I to do?"

He prayed for strength to stay away from Kit when he returned. One night, after having prayed and felt no strength from God flowing into him, he found the letter he had received from Bronwyn King a few days earlier. Preoccupied with his tormenting desire for Kit, he had laid the letter aside. Now he ripped it open. If nothing else, it would provide diversion.

In the letter she told him her elderly physician, Dr. Baker, wanted to sell his practice and retire. Enclosed with her letter was a brief statement from the doctor, written with an unsteady hand. In it he tersely recited the statistics of his practice: the location, the number of patients, what he was including in the sale, and the amount of money he wanted. He mentioned at the end that he himself was a transplanted Englishman and desired that a countryman take his place. The price he named would take everything Nick had, but it would be worth it to save his soul. The Lord had sent his deliverance. With an ocean between them he would never see Kit again.

❦❦

In far-off New York City, Bronwyn King mended a small rip in her starched white apron, squinting in the yellow gas light. She was glad of the interruption when her best friend, Ida Barr, came in and handed her an envelope.

"This just came for you. It's from England." Without waiting for Bronwyn to open it, Ida called out into the dormitory hallway, "Bronnie's got a letter from that Englishman." Within moments four other young nurses crowded into the room, demanding to know what it said.

"Give me a chance to open it," Bronwyn said. She read it quickly, her eyes shining. "He's going to write to Dr. Baker about buying his practice!" She did a pirouette, her long hair swinging like a soft black cape behind her. "He's coming, he's coming, he's coming."

"Don't act like a giddy girl," Ida said, to a chorus of indignant protests. Ida was five years older than the others, and proud of being sensible. "He's coming to the United States. So what?"

Again the other young nurses chorused protest at this cold water so callously thrown. "So what?" cried out one of the girls. "Didn't you hear her say Dr. Baker is selling his practice to her Englishman?"

"I heard her say he's going to *ask* him. Dr. Baker could sell it to someone else."

"Oh, Ida, you're an old poop," one of the girls complained.

"I knew he'd come," Bronwyn said. "And I know something else. He's going to marry me. He doesn't know it, but he is."

"And what about Dr. Galvin, Bronnie," piped up one of the nurses. "If you don't want him I do."

"Yes, Bronnie. It's not fair that you have *two* handsome doctors chasing you."

Bronwyn blushed and laughed. She liked David Galvin, who had brought her flowers once. And he was handsome. And he adored her. But she was heels over buttonhooks in love with "her English doctor."

※※

Nick never forgot his first sight of Lady Liberty in the harbor of New York. He'd been told her torch stood for the light of freedom. No other passenger on the ship was gaining the sort of freedom he was. As a last act of emancipation, he threw his only remaining mementos of Kit into the water: the pictures he had taken with the magical Kodak a lifetime ago.

※※

"He's not in England, Mr. St. Denys," said the nondescript little man, one of the most reputable detectives in the country. "I have found no close friends, and his colleagues know as little as we do. His parents have both died. None of his sisters claim to know where he is, nor does his brother. If anyone knows his whereabouts they are not disclosing them."

Kit, dark smudges of weariness beneath his eyes, stared at the man. He had hired him the week he left for the Continent. The fool had had ten months to find Nick and here he was, saying he could not find him.

"Royster, it is your business, for which you have charged me a great deal, to find him."

The man cleared his throat. "It may be a long undertaking, sir."

"I don't care how long it takes."

"I may have to travel extensively."

"I don't care where you have to go."

"I can't do it alone. I'll have to hire additional detectives."

"Hire them."

"It'll be very expensive."

"I don't care what it costs."

"We'll find him."

"Yes," Kit said. "You will."

For several minutes after Royster left, Kit stared fixedly at the spot where he had been, his fists clenched. "As God is my witness, Stuart," he said, "I'll make you face me if it takes the rest of my life."

11

Bronwyn King met Nick the day he arrived in New York, and after seeing that he had a good meal in a good restaurant, she took him immediately across the river to Brooklyn, to meet Dr. Baker. She was prettier than he remembered, and the warm but high wind mussed her hair and reddened her cheeks. Her voice was sweeter than he remembered, and he didn't remember detecting a subtle perfume before. It was like meeting her for the first time.

Dr. Baker was as crotchety as she had said he was. The practice was in three spacious rooms of Baker's two-story house. Nick fell in love with the house, though he couldn't imagine what he would do with six extra rooms. The place even had a widow's walk, reached through a peculiar cramped stairway off the kitchen. The widow's walk made up for the bad state of the exterior paint, which peeled in green scabs.

"Knew I was going to retire," said the old doctor. "Couldn't see spending money to paint it." His laugh sounded rusty. "That was fifteen years ago. There's indoor plumbing, upstairs and down. Some things even a skinflint like me can't be cheap about. And

there's electric. And a telephone, though damned if I don't sometimes think it's an instrument of the devil." He took Nick to the
well-maintained stable, which also served as carriage house for
the Stanhope buggy. "You'll have to get your own horse," he said,
stroking the soft muzzle of the old mare in the stall. "This old girl
will spend her days eating clover."

Bronwyn was patiently waiting in Dr. Baker's office when they
returned. "You should have come with us, Miss King," Nick said.
"I would have liked your opinion." He wouldn't know for a long
time that while they were gone she had inspected all the rooms
and made a long mental list of needed improvements.

Within a week he had moved into the house, and a week beyond
that saw him welcoming patients. He was delighted when Miss
King offered to work for him. "My contract is nearly up," she said.
"And you know we work well together."

"I can't pay nearly what the hospital does," he said.

"Believe me, they don't pay that well." She arrived every day, as
trim and soldierly and competent as she had been that first day in
London. The patients loved her.

Within a month he started to see her socially. Little things, such
as long walks after the office was closed. Buggy rides in the country
or across the Brooklyn Bridge, a wonder of engineering made
beautiful. They went to lectures and magic lantern shows. She
coaxed him to a roller-skating rink and, laughing, held him up as
he tried not to break every bone in his body.

Several times they went to parties at the homes of her friends,
all fellow nurses. He noticed a young colleague, David Galvin, at
these parties, never with the same girl twice. And Dr. Galvin
seemed to spend a great deal of time looking at Miss King with
the expression of a dying hound.

Nick wasn't sure when he dared to call her Bronwyn; they just
slipped into it naturally. During nice weather they drove around
New York City and she introduced him to his new home.

She pointed out the gilt-domed Pulitzer Building, the Tower
Building, and Madison Square Garden with the tower topped by
the Goddess Diana. One day she showed him the mansions of the
Astors, Vanderbilts, and Rockefellers. "People call it Millionaire's
Row," she said, then added in a harsh voice that took him off
guard, "I hate people like that."

He was as shocked by the intensity of her expression as by her
words. "What people?"

"Rich people. Do you know how most of them got rich? They exploited people like my Pop." She glanced up at him. "Now you think I'm a terrible person."

"Of course I don't think you're a terrible person. I liked you before you said it, I like you just as much now."

They went to free concerts in Central Park. At little sidewalk tables in front of the many cafés in the city, she drank coffee and he drank tea. Eventually she won and he began to tolerate coffee. They went to libraries and museums. Whenever he had a few cents left, he bought flowers from sidewalk vendors for her. And of course, she talked. He enjoyed listening to her.

If she had shocked him with her hostility toward the rich, he shocked her with his gentlemanly but vehement refusal to attend a Broadway play when a friend gave her two tickets. He had no intention of ever setting foot in a theatre again, as long as he lived. He did, however, let her drag him to Brooklyn to a circus and he discovered they both had a liking for the gaudy spectacles presented by Mr. Barnum and Mr. Bailey.

Eight months after he set foot in America, he married Bronwyn King in the visiting parlor of the Nurse's Residence. His bride was beautiful in a simple dress of such a pale blue it appeared silvery, with white artificial flowers in her hair.

He went to their marriage bed fearful he could not do what she expected. He could diagram a woman's body inside and out; often he could heal it. He knew nothing about a woman's emotions or needs.

Bronwyn, demurely covered by blankets and a maidenly but lavishly laced nightdress, held her hands out for him. Covered in a nightshirt as demurely as she was, he lay down with her and gingerly embraced her. She was so little, so soft and delicate, so … foreign. Though it was absurd, he felt as if he might break her small bones.

Then, in a way that seemed miraculous to him, her arms and body were open and eager, and he was ready. She was a virgin but received him with abandon, as she arched against him and uttered little cries. When it was over her eyes were luminous. "I love you," she whispered, going soft and clinging in his arms. He buried his face in her long, loose hair and said, "I love you, too."

He did love her. And with her he had known release, if not the mind-numbing pleasure he'd known with Kit. Savagely he put that hateful memory out of his mind. Bronwyn, sleeping, murmured his name and cuddled closer. He held her, and went to sleep, pleased with himself.

༜ༀ༝

"And is the wonderful English doctor still wonderful?" Ida asked, as she put sugar into her coffee. She had met Bronwyn at their favorite place, "Rose's Ladies Tea Shop" which had mediocre tea but marvelous confections.

"Marriage is fabulous," Bronwyn said. "You should try it."

"No thank you. I have no intention of expelling a baby every eighteen months to keep some man happy." Ida looked at her over the rim of her cup. "Dr. David was asking about you yesterday. You broke his poor, boyish heart when you married."

"I didn't break his heart. I didn't even know him that well."

"Well, I'm the one who told him you'd gotten married and his face fell about a mile."

"Don't tease like that, Ida." It was such a silly notion, but she had to admit it was a pleasant silly notion. And flattering.

"So tell me all about married life," said Ida.

"Oh, where shall I begin?" Bronwyn said. "He's perfect. What more can I say? The house is a different matter. The wallpaper is impossible, the kitchen is appalling, and the floors haven't been waxed since the American Revolution. It will take elbow grease and money to get it the way I want it, but a year from now it will be a paradise."

Young Mrs. McWorth was indignant. "Palpitations, doctor! I have palpitations." She panted heavily to prove it. "How can you say there is nothing wrong with me? I think you ought to listen to my heart again. Where did you say your dear little bride is today?"

"I didn't say." Nick stifled his impatience, touched the bell of the stethoscope to her chest and listened to the healthy pumping of her heart. With a little sigh she straightened her spine, thrusting her ample bosom at him.

Mrs. McWorth had been one of Dr. Baker's patients, one of the old man's many patients who remained with Nick. There seemed to be a puzzling esteem attached to being a patient of "the English doctor" and now, at the end of his first four months he had almost more patients than he could see. Several of them were women like Mrs. McWorth, who had nothing much wrong with them other than an excess of fashion and overbearing husbands.

He folded his stethoscope and said, "Mrs. McWorth, I still find nothing wrong physically."

"It is unusual, Dr. Stuart," she said, "for someone with hair as dark as yours to have such blue, blue eyes. Violet, actually. Your eyes are violet, did you know that?" She giggled. "Why, a man with eyes like yours could just about have his way with any girl. Even if she were married."

"The color of my eyes has nothing to do with your health."

"My health? You just said there's nothing wrong." She rebuttoned her bodice.

"It's nothing that can't be made better if you will just loosen your corset lacing. If you must wear that foolish thing, at least be sensible."

"One cannot be both sensible and fashionable, Dr. Stuart."

"Then don't listen to me. Have fainting spells and palpitations. I can't see what good it is to wear a fashionable frock if you're lying on the floor, blue from lack of oxygen. Now if you don't mind, I do have other patients waiting and you aren't going to listen to me in any event."

"That's unkind!"

"But it's true."

When Bronwyn came in, Nick was at the old table that served as an office desk. She leaned over him for a kiss, and peeked at the appointment book. "Oh, dear," she said with a smirk, "I forgot Mrs. McWorth was coming in today. Did she ravish you, my darling?"

"She tried. Don't ever leave me again. See here? We've actually made a few pounds, I mean dollars, profit this week. At this rate, in one-hundred-seventy-five years we can afford to buy a new kitchen range."

"I'll settle for the old range and someone to cook on it. You must admit I'm a terrible cook."

"Someday soon you can stop working and learn to cook."

She wondered if he had the peculiar notion that cooking was like a vacation. To get the subject away from cooking, she tilted her head and looked critically at his white cotton coat. "It's all over wrinkles," she said. "The laundress says you won't let her iron them."

He shrugged. "I can't pay extra. Anyway, they're not for show. They suit my purpose. Surely you don't prefer that I wear one of those vile black wool surgical coats some of the doctors still wear. Dr. Baker left me a whole moth-eaten wardrobe of them."

"Heavens no! But what harm would a touch with the iron do?"

He looked down at the one he wore. "Well, I suppose they are a little wrinkled. I suppose we can afford it."

"And a little starch?"

"You needn't get carried away."

Each day after the last patient left, Bronwyn replaced her gray uniform dress and starched snowy apron, with a sturdy cotton frock covered with a Mother Hubbard, put an old-fashioned cap on her hair, grabbed mop, broom, and cloths, and sometimes a paint brush, and helped Nick in the refurbishing of the house. When the weather was especially nice, however, she deserted him and the house for the garden.

"We will have fresh vegetables this year if it kills me," she declared. "That was one of the things my mom hated about Chicago. A tiny garden and nothing would grow but sickly things no one wanted to eat." As the house improved room by room, and the vegetables were planted, she turned her energy to the neglected flowerbeds and empty urns.

"My mother would have loved you," he said, and put his arms around her. "The flowers, the vegetable garden, the fact you never stop working. She was like that."

She dropped her trowel, pulled off her gloves and put her arms around his neck. Her eyes were lambent, and he kissed the little vein throbbing in her temple. "I stop working every once in a while, dear husband. And now seems like such a good time."

As his first year in America neared its end, Nick knew peace such as he had never imagined. His reputation grew as fast as his practice. He was accepted as a surgeon by St. Vincent's. Twice a week he lectured students at the Nurses' Training School, which added several courses and a second year of study. He seldom missed church on Sunday and spent much time in prayer trying to rid himself of thoughts of Kit. But it seemed Kit was his cross to bear.

On the day of their first anniversary, a Saturday, Bronwyn shooed him from the house, and ordered him not to return until evening. After her gift to him was delivered, she luxuriated in a bath and stroked jasmine-scented oil onto her skin. Her new dress revealed a great deal of bosom. Eyes twinkling, she tugged the bodice down a bit and pushed her breasts up a bit, until she showed even more bosom. Looking in the mirror, she chuckled low. "You look like a shameless hussy," she said to her reflection. "Perfect." It had been several nights since he had come to her. She was determined that would not happen tonight.

She waited for him outside the closed office door. When he came in, he called her name. "In here," she said. "At the office." As his footsteps neared, she pinched her cheeks and bit her lips, then struck a seductive pose.

He approached her, a small jewelry box in hand. When he saw her, he whistled and walked around her. "Aren't you a beautiful wench! What have you done with my wife? Bronwyn, Bronwyn, you are a vision."

"I should think so! It was a lot of work."

"Nonsense. You're beautiful by nature. How could it be work?" He held out the little box. "For my favorite wife."

In the box was a ring with a small sapphire stone in an elaborate setting. "It's so beautiful," she whispered and slipped it on.

"Someday," he said, "I'll get you a big diamond."

"Goose. I don't want a big stone. They're vulgar. I love this one." She threw her arms around him and kissed him. Then she seized his hands, ordered him to close his eyes, and opened the office door. "Now you can look."

He gazed in astonishment at the massive roll top desk that stood where the old table had been. "Bronwyn! Where did it come from? How did you get it?" Like a child with a new toy he rolled the top up and down. "It's splendid! And it locks, too. Where did you find it?"

"It belonged to a lawyer's widow. She sold it to me for a song. And a few dollars I had saved."

He opened each of the dozen small drawers, inspected the dozen slots, and practiced locking and unlocking the top. He pictured his meticulous records, his pens and papers, the journal he had been keeping since his arrival in America, all safely locked away in this desk. Grinning in delight, he discovered a hidden secret drawer underneath, with its own little brass key.

He folded her in his arms. "You're a wonderful woman, Bronwyn Stuart. I don't deserve you." Unexpected desire surged through him. He scooped her up in his arms. "Let's celebrate, Mrs. Stuart." Bronwyn whispered his name, dizzy with her need for him.

A few weeks afterward, he confirmed what Bronwyn already knew. "I'm going to be a father," he said with a grin. Bronwyn's smile was a little uncertain, though she said the words expected of her. "I'm so happy..." In a way she was. But she loved nursing and knew Nicholas disapproved of mothers working unless there was no other way to put food on the table. Unconsciously she rested her hand on her belly. She would talk him around; she always did.

🙚🙛

London.

"It took you long enough," Kit snapped, glaring at the detective.

"I told you it would take a long while. You said you didn't care."

Kit turned away and gazed down into the London street without seeing any of the dozens of cabs or people walking or the many kinds of carts and wagons or the occasional motorcar. "You're certain?"

"Yes, Mr. St. Denys. I have a photograph of the house. Here."

"A house," Kit mumbled, staring at the picture. "A *wife*, of all things! My God. Nick Stuart building a nest. Lying to himself as usual."

"Sir?"

"Nothing."

"Do you want me to do anything further?"

"No." Kit gave the detective a bank draught. "This covers everything, does it not?"

"More than sufficient, sir. I hope I can be of service to you another time, sir."

"I'm sure you do."

When Kit was alone with the knowledge for which he had waited so long, he didn't know what was he going to do with it. Every scene of confrontation he'd rehearsed in his mind had been crafted in the belief he would never actually see Nick again.

Since Nick's desertion Kit had frantically hunted for a replacement in pubs and nightclubs, theatres and opera houses, backstage and on stage, among performers and hangers-on. His nightmares had worsened and he had twice been frightened by waking hallucinations of Tom Rourke following him in the streets of London.

He slept little. If he were alone, the old man invaded his mind as he slept. The mirror told him it was all taking its toll. His work was not suffering yet, but that was only a matter of time. He was a sick man. The only cure was to find Nick and tell him to go to hell.

After a few minutes, he roused himself from his morbid thoughts and went to the office of his booking agent. Flannery stood and shook the hand of his most profitable client. "Kit, good to see you. We should begin planning your next tour."

"I've got it planned."

"Really? Europe, I presume. I have letters here from Copenhagen and Paris asking you back."

"They can wait. I want to go to America. "

"America! Kit, there is a situation there now that makes American bookings almost impossible."

"Get us into as many cities as you can, ending with an extended run in New York."

"Kit, it's unwise, perhaps not even possible, to book in American houses just now. And New York City may as well be on the moon."

"America, Flannery. Ending in New York. I want to be there within three months."

"Three months! That's impossible and you know it."

"Anything's possible."

"Kit, listen to me. Even if the best theatres weren't already booked, there are difficulties. Extreme difficulties."

"America in three months. Any theatre anywhere, as long as we finish in New York. If you can't do it, I'll find someone who can."

"I'll do it, I'll do it." With a shake of his head, he said, "You're the most unpredictable man."

Kit's smile was tight. "Oh, no. I'm in all likelihood the most predictable. I have a goal in mind for everything I do. Nothing is random." What a half-truth that was! He should have said, 'Nothing I do in the theatre is random.' God knew his private life was out of control.

※※

Other than medical journals, Nick read little. He brought a newspaper home from the city every night for his wife and trusted her to keep him informed. He was far more interested in the discovery of the malaria bacillus than he was in the doings of President McKinley; far more interested in a new technique for doing a cesarean section delivery than he was in another of the endless wars, this time between Spain and the United States. The only bit of news that caught his attention was that of Queen Victoria's Diamond Jubilee.

Bronwyn put the paper down in front of him at breakfast, folded with the photograph of the Queen on the front. "She must be as old as the hills," she said.

"She is the Queen of England, the ruler of the British Empire. She has been Queen for three-quarters of a century and she is a great lady."

She cocked her head to one side and studied him. "Are you homesick for England?"

"I suppose I am, a little."

"Then why don't you go home for a visit? See your family and your friends." She crossed her fingers beneath the table. She didn't want him to go and leave her alone and pregnant.

"Go home?" he said. *Kit. His sisters and brother. Lush green hills. His parents' graves. Kit.* It lasted but an instant and was brushed aside. "Perhaps someday." He enclosed her small hand in his. "Everything I want is here, with you."

Nick pushed the paper aside and drank another cup of tea. Had he picked the newspaper up and turned to the theatre section he would have seen a column headed:

St.Denys Repertory Company
Arriving For First American Tour

༜༜༜

Rama, Francis, Lizbet and several other friends gathered in Kit's London suite to toast the new American tour. None of them knew the American tour had been put together in haste, nor did they know that a second European tour was delayed for two years. All they knew was that they were going to America. They would end in New York City, which was becoming the theatre capital of the world. One and all, they were excited, eager to show the Americans how good theatre was done. Lizbet left first to make the long journey home to her cottage near St. Denys Hill. One by one the others left, until only Francis, Rama, and Kit were left.

A roughly dressed young man arrived shortly afterward and stood shifting from one foot to the other. He was good-looking in a brutish sort of way. His dark hair was rough and his light eyes showed both boldness and uncertainty. "I was told to come here and ask for a Mr. St. Denys," he said, crumpling a soft cap in his hands.

A spasm of distaste crossed Rama's face and she said to Francis, "Frank, I don't think we're needed here any longer." With a wistful glance at Kit, Francis followed Rama.

Kit appraised the young man. Then he said, "You'll do. Behind that door are the bathroom and toilet articles. Bathe. Shave. Clean your nails and wash your hair. Clean your teeth while you're about it. Have you eaten dinner? No? While you're doing that I'll order you up a meal, and breakfast in the morning." As an afterthought he asked the young man's name and at once forgot it. He never remembered their names.

12

The girl with the sailor hat elbowed her seatmate on the train. "Look there, Maddie. That man. I seen his pitcher in the Chicago paper when I was visiting my sis. That's Kit St. Denys, the actor."

"I know. Ain't he the prettiest man you ever seen? Wouldn't I just love t'run my fingers through them curls!"

"I'd love t'do more than that."

Kit could hear the whispers over the clackety-clacking of the wheels of the New-York bound train and knew he was meant to hear. He smiled at the girls across the aisle. "Thank you, ladies," he stage-whispered. "The feeling is mutual." They answered with red-faced giggles. Several people ahead of him in the car turned to see what was happening, and he knew people behind were craning their necks. Publicity. One couldn't have too much of it. That damned Wilde was right: the only thing worse than being talked about, was not being talked about.

In time with the monotonous racketing of the wheels, Kit ticked off in his mind all the cities they had covered in their grueling eight-month tour. Montreal. Toronto. Chicago. Albany. Buffalo. Boston. Philadelphia. Boston again. Washington, DC. Small towns throughout the South that were still visibly scarred from the War Between the States. New Orleans, where the scent of flowers battled with the reek of open sewer ditches. Northward again through Missouri and Kentucky, to Cincinnati. A second visit to Chicago, where winter forced a long, unscheduled stay and the thaw found them ankle-deep in mud. He had decided the mud and stink in Chicago were worse than anywhere in the British Empire. Chicago to Cleveland. Then New England again, where hillsides were buttered with daffodils and jonquils.

Now they were on their way to New York and their final six-week engagement of Rostand's new play, *Cyrano de Bergerac.* Flannery had succeeded in booking a private performance for Ava Astor, "The American version of lesser Royalty."

He was dead tired and wondered how he would find the strength to perform. Raspy voices and sore throats had plagued the cast for weeks. One performance had been canceled when both he and Rama developed laryngitis.

If they'd had a good doctor traveling with them it might not have happened. Now that they would be in New York for several weeks, he'd have the opportunity to hunt down Nick Stuart and say what he had crossed an ocean to say.

"Kit?" Rama said, joining him. She tilted her head to one side to show off a startling hat of turquoise, folds and knots of black and white, finished with bows and a pair of tortured dead birds. The height of the decorations added several inches to Rama's height, making her almost as tall as he. "What do you think of it?"

"Words fail me," he said. "I've never seen anything quite like it." They were both aware of the hostile glares from the girls across the aisle. "I was just thinking of you," he said.

"No, you weren't," she retorted, her voice still hoarse. "You were thinking about *Cyrano.*"

"So I was."

As she settled in the seat across from him, she said, "Cyrano's a wonderful part for you, all that romance and swashbuckling and that wonderful death scene. But—really!—Roxanne is such a muttonhead, mooning about in a convent for years and years, grieving for some simpleton with a pretty face."

"The way you do for me?"

She kicked his shin and mouthed, "You're an ass. Oh it will be heaven to stay in one place for six entire weeks."

Kit's thoughts returned to the upcoming performance. Ava Astor, from what he had read and heard, was beautiful and rich, the wife of John Jacob Astor the Fourth. She lived to spend money, gamble, and annoy her mother-in-law, who called herself *the* Mrs. Astor. The mother-in law considered herself the queen of New York Society.

This American tour had cost him an ungodly amount of brass. He needed backers. He wondered how he could get both Astor women in his camp if they hated each other as much as gossip said. He could've had money from Diamond Jim Brady, the enormous and unpleasant gambler he'd met in Chicago. But to get it he'd have to replace Rama with Lillian Russell. He refused; Brady shrugged his shoulders and dismissed him. *Dismissed* him! The memory rankled. He was still mulling over the problem of backers when the train huffed into the terminal.

Staff and guests of the Marlborough Hotel stared and nudged each other as the tall, handsome young man and the striking woman with the enormous hat came into the rococo, electrically lit lobby. Rama held her head high in her most haughty fashion, and bestowed regal smiles.

He left Rama in her room, giving her a chaste kiss on her cheek. With a sigh, she tossed her hat on the bed and said, "Oh, Kit..." Critically she studied the woman who looked back at her from the cheval mirror beside the window. Good figure. Extraordinary hair; he said so himself. Clear-cut features. Most expressive eyes in the universe, according to him.

"I'm not beautiful," she muttered. "But I don't scare blind men, either. He could do worse. Much worse." And he was fond of her; that much she knew. *Fond!* What a mewly-pukey word that was. She wanted him to be in a frenzy of love for her. But no. He preferred Frank. And Stuart. And street corner sweepings. "Why?" she said aloud, not for the first time.

She was not naïve. She knew about men like Wilde and his ilk; she'd met many of them over the years. But Kit wasn't like them. He wasn't girly. He didn't do strange art like Beardsley. He didn't write poetry. He didn't prance or mince and he didn't lounge languidly like that twittering, diabolical Alfie Douglas. He didn't wear green carnation buttonholes. Oscar's limp wrists and hands held nothing weightier than a pen or a cigarette; Kit wielded a fencing saber. He was not like them in any way. But then, with a sigh she had to admit that neither were Frank or Stuart. She was back where she began, with the same question, and the same answer-that-was-not- an- answer that had tormented her for five years.

From the large window of his suite, the most luxurious place he'd been in since he'd arrived in America, Kit peered down at the busy street. A rainbow of ladies' hats and parasols flowed below him. The street was sludgy with every kind of horse-drawn vehicle, carts, bicycles and people on foot. Every now and then an automobile banged out a series of loud pops and fumes, terrified nearby horses, and brought shaken fists and curses from the drivers of the horses.

Automobiles. He loved the noisy, smoky, nasty things. Some day he'd own a stable of them, one of every kind manufactured. Well. No time to think of that. Business called. Because of the Chicago delays, they would have to rush stage setup and rehearsals to meet their opening date at the Barclay in only five days. The Barclay had been the first decent theatre they'd been lucky enough to get on this tour.

He paused outside Rama's door, thinking he should take her with him. But when he finished at the Barclay he intended to explore a few murky corners of the city. It would be awkward if she were with him when he met the inevitable attractive man with a certain gleam in his eye.

He entered a cab bearing the hotel crest, and as he rode through the busy streets, he thought again that getting the Barclay had been a stroke of luck. The scheduled performances by Minnie Maddern Fiske had been canceled because of her health. Kit had regretted that; the lady was a fine actress. But in the theatre world one actor's distress was often another actor's blessing.

When the cab stopped in front of the Barclay, Kit stared in disbelief at the playbills. Playing now and for five more weeks: Miss Maude Adams in *Midnight Belle.* Following Miss Adams: *Rip Van Winkle* with Joseph Jefferson. He looked up at the theatre's name, thinking the driver had made a mistake. He hadn't.

"There'd better be a bloody good explanation," he muttered. He charged into the theatre, across the columned foyer and without knocking burst into the manager's office.

A cherubic man looked up from a desk piled high with papers. His eyes rounded and he jumped to his feet. "Mr. St. Denys! I tried to reach you, I've tried for months."

Kit leaned in, his fingers spread upon the one clear spot on the man's desk. "Say that again."

"There's been a mistake. I tried to reach you."

"If you'd tried, you would have succeeded."

The man gulped. "It's not my fault. I didn't book you. This is the previous manager's fault. He booked you."

"I don't care if the rat in the wall did it. I have a contract."

"You don't understand. You aren't represented by The Theatre Trust."

"What the bloody hell are you talking about?"

The man scribbled on a piece of paper. "Talk to one of these gentlemen. They can explain it to you. I can't discuss it with you, sir." He mopped his gleaming face. "Please. Talk to one of them."

Kit snatched the paper from the man's sweaty hands. Not until he was getting into the cab did he realize his teeth were clenched so tightly pain shot from his ears down to his neck. When he strode into the Empire Theatre, his fury could be heard in the sound of his heels on the marble floor. In the nearest office, Kit stopped at the desk of a young man whose good looks gave him a moment's pause.

"Erlanger," he demanded. "Now."

"Do you have an appointment?"

"No. The name is St. Denys. I won't leave until I see him."

"Mr. Erlanger is not in," the secretary said with a sniff.

"You're a liar."

The secretary smiled at someone behind him. "Go right up, Mr. Frohman. Mr. Erlanger's expecting you."

Frohman. The other name on Grant's list. The man was a head shorter than Kit, and delicate in appearance. "Charles Frohman?" he said.

"Why, yes." The gentleman smiled. "I'd know your face anywhere, Mr. St. Denys. Welcome to my city."

"Stow it. I want to know what's going on at the Barclay."

The smile did not waver. "You didn't know?"

"Suppose you tell me."

Frohman put a manicured hand on Kit's shoulder. "Come with me. I'm certain we can come to an accommodation."

"We'd better," Kit said. His fury cooled a little under Frohman's pleasant demeanor. He followed Frohman into a lift.

When they reached the third-floor door with "A. L. Erlanger" etched upon it, Frohman peeked inside. "Abe, are you here?" he called. "It's Charles and a friend." He beckoned Kit to follow.

The man who emerged from an adjoining room was short and homely, and a fat black cigar wreathed his face in smoke. He removed the cigar and said with a grin, "The famous Kit St. Denys, I presume. I knew you'd show up."

"Abe, Mr. St. Denys was not notified of the cancellation at the Barclay," Frohman said.

Erlanger took out his cigar and widened his eyes in mock innocence. "I'm so sorry about that, Mr. St. Denys."

"Why don't we discuss this like gentlemen?" said Frohman, smoothing his waistcoat.

Kit ignored him. "I want to know what's going on," he said.

"You sound hostile," Erlanger said. "We formed the Trust solely for the protection of the artist." A mocking grin played on his mouth as he repeated, "Solely for the protection of the artist. Under the Trust the actor will always be assured of a quality house in which to perform. He will always be assured of receiving the monies due him."

"Horseshit. Why are Maude Adams and Joe Jefferson playing my dates?"

Erlanger shrugged, "They know which side of the bread the butter's on."

"What my colleague means, Mr. St. Denys," said Frohman, "is that far-seeing artists such as Mr. Jefferson and Miss Adams realized their careers would benefit more from working with the Trust than against it. You see, American booking was an inefficient hodgepodge, contracts were signed in the middle of the street, fine actors had to demean themselves to win roles, actors and playwrights were cheated out of their just earnings. No one benefited, least of all, the actors." Kit frowned. It sounded reasonable, and yet...

Frohman saw his hesitation and pressed on. "If you sign with us, Mr. St. Denys, a prime theatre will be available to you at once, along with the power of the Trust in promotion and advertising. Why don't we take care of that matter right now, and then adjourn for a friendly glass of wine." Smiling, Frohman retrieved a typewritten sheet and a pen. "Details can be filled in later," he said. "Not standard business practice, I admit, but we trust you. All we need is your signature. This time tomorrow you will have a first-class theatre at your disposal."

"You may trust me. I don't trust you." Kit took the contract and glanced at it. "Did Mrs. Fiske lose the Barclay because of poor health? Or was it that she didn't cooperate?"

Before Frohman could give a soothing answer, Erlanger's face became the color of old brick. "That redheaded hellcat," he spat. "She and her bastard husband! Before we're through she won't be allowed to perform in Kentucky barnyards!"

"Abe, Abe," Frohman said. "You're overwrought. Mr. St. Denys, if you'll just sign now and reserve your place as our client, we can settle the finer points tonight at dinner."

"On the surface it seems fair enough. But I suspect it's like a golden lid on a chamber pot and I don't like the stink." He tore the contract in half and dropped the pieces on Erlanger's desk.

As he reached the door, Erlanger barked, "You either work through us, or you don't work."

Kit turned. "My people and I *will* perform in this city. And I give you my word we'll outdraw any production you're backing." Sick with anger, he realized he had broken one of his own rules: Don't make threats or promises you can't carry out.

❧ ❧

"Kit, where's your mind? It's not here," Rama said. "You've missed three cues in a row." They were rehearsing the final scene for Ava Astor's private performance.

Kit hadn't realized how distracted he was by the situation with the Trust. He had not yet told anyone. "I'm sorry," he said. "You're right. My mind was elsewhere."

"Well, bring it back here. We need it. We have two days left, you know. And when are we going to get into the Barclay? Time's running out."

"Don't worry. There's been a delay." He'd made that excuse over and over since they'd been in the city. No one questioned him. He had only two days until the performance for Ava Astor. When it was over the Trust would again loom as formidable as the Dover cliffs, but until then he had to force them back under a rock in his mind and give himself to Cyrano. He straightened the plumed hat and gripped the sword, the only two props that would be used. "From the top," he said.

❧ ❧

One end of Ava Astor's ballroom became a stage for the evening and there the dying Cyrano fought his last battle against Falsehood, Prejudice, Compromise, Cowardice, and Vanity. The sword fell from his nerveless fingers. He swayed, and leaned upon Roxanne, who had just learned of his lifelong love for her. "One thing left me," he whispered. "*Mon panache!* My white plume..."

Even the sophisticated Ava had tears in her eyes as she joined the other wealthy ladies in enthusiastic applause. Afterward, she draped her hand in the crook of Kit's elbow and proudly introduced him to an array of gowned and jeweled women whose last names were a roll call of American society. Vanderbilt. Rockefeller. Palmer. Pullman. Morgan. Everyone who was anyone, except *the* Mrs. Astor.

"And where's your redoubtable mother-in-law?" he asked.

She laughed, wrinkling her delicate nose. "My mother-in-law would die before breathing the same air as a common actor."

"I'm a great many things, madam. Common is not one of them. And, " he said with a grin, "I will conquer *the* Mrs. Astor or die trying."

For three more weeks Kit searched for an available theatre. Actors to whom he spoke were evasive. The ones who would talk, were adamant: no Trust contract, no theatre. His people were alarmed when their opening date came and went with no entrance to the Barclay and no rehearsals. Rumors abounded. For the first time they looked on him with uneasy suspicion. He finally summoned them all to his suite.

When everyone was there, he said, "My friends, we will not perform *Cyrano* in this city." He waited until the shocked murmurs died down. "I have not been forthcoming with you, and I apologize. You know we do not have the Barclay. What you don't know is why." He told them of the stranglehold the Trust had on the theatre in America, and ended by saying, "My search for a theatre has produced nothing. We've been blacklisted."

"There must be somewhere!" Francis protested.

Someone else said. "We don't need this city or this country. Let's go home."

"You can. I can't," Kit said. "I promised Erlanger I would perform here and I will, even if it's a one man show in a beer hall."

He let their outbursts go on for a little while and then quieted them again. "Each of you must decide what's best for you. If you go, I'll pay your fare home, give you what is due you, and a little extra to help until you get settled once more. If you stay, I can promise you nothing. I don't know if or when I will find a theatre. And if I find one, I don't know if we can mount a successful production in the face of their opposition. They control the crews, advertising, everything."

"Break up the Company?" Rama cried.

"I have no choice. I can't keep you all here, drumming your heels for God knows how long. It would be unfair to all of us. We've survived other setbacks and come back better for it. When I've done what I vowed to do, I'll come home. Then the St. Denys Repertory Company will reassemble and triumph again." He made them believe it. He wished he could.

"What if we stay?" Rama asked.

"Anyone willing to sign with the Trust will work steadily." He drew a deep breath. "Friday next we'll meet in the dining room for a farewell dinner for those going home."

He turned away to the window so he did not have to watch them leave. Pulling back the draperies he looked at his reflection and behind it the darkness of what had become a hostile and foreign city. He leaned his forehead against the cool glass. He was thirty different kinds of fool. Bringing them all halfway around the world so he could find a man who despised him.

"Jack!"

He gave a violent start; cold sweat burst out on his body. The old man leered at him through the window. "Jack, ye cowardly little rat, let me in." Kit jerked the draperies shut. When he turned he saw Francis leaning against the door.

"How did you know?" he asked, trying to smile.

"I always know," Francis said. But tonight his presence made no difference.

All night Kit fought Tom Rourke, and the hideous apparition of his brother. He fought the noose that strangled him, and he fought the blood. He fought the decay and the worms, always the worms, and tried to shut out the old man's voice and his shards of laughter.

Francis tried to soothe him, but all he could do was listen helplessly while Kit babbled, and begged for Nick Stuart to come back and make the nameless terror go away.

Kit peered at the mirror as Francis rested an affectionate hand against his back and commented, "With those red eyes, you look a bit of a berk today, old boy."

"That bad?" Kit said, squinting. "It's just as well. I want to look as if I could and would chew someone up and spit him out in pieces."

"Really? Who, or what, are you going to attack?"

"A barricade," Kit said with a grim smile. He finished with his waistcoat, slipped into his coat, and said, "I'm away."

A little while later, Kit confronted the manager of the Barclay, who cringed before the threat of imminent murder he saw on Kit's face. "I told you," the manager sniveled, "The Trust controls everything. There's nothing I can do."

"Somewhere in this city there's a theatre. Give me a name or we'll picket the Barclay from now until there are icicles on the rafters in Hell."

The man gulped. "Well, um, you see, there might be one but it's not really available."

"The name. Now."

"The Flambeau. Off Broadway. Closed now. Owned by Judge Wescott."

The name sounded familiar. "Write down the particulars."

"For the love of God don't tell him I told you about it!" said the manager. "No one's supposed to know." Handing a folded paper to Kit, he said, "You won't picket the theatre now, will you?"

"No, Mr. Grant. No pickets. I'll just nail your bollocks to the wall with extremely dull nails." His grin was wolfish. Grant's right hand dropped to protect his endangered crotch. As Kit put the paper into his inside pocket, he saw the detective's directions to Nick Stuart's house. But he had no time to deal with him now. He had to send a note to Judge Wescott.

At two o'clock he was picking at his portion of a fine luncheon, while across from him sat a distinguished gray-haired gentleman whose age Kit surmised to be about fifty. Wescott was influential, wealthy, an American aristocrat. He had met Wescott when the Company played Boston, and he suspected he and the judge shared certain proclivities.

Judge Wescott looked at Kit over a glass of wine and said, "I can't believe you'd even remember an old fellow like me."

Kit smiled. "Hardly. You're less than forty, surely?"

"Fifty-one. Soon they'll be calling me Old Judge Wescott."

"Age is subjective, is it not? Michelangelo's 'David' is four hundred years old and it's still breathtaking." The judge's eyes kindled and Kit knew his suspicion was correct. "I'm in a desperate situation, Judge Wescott. You may be able to help me."

"Call me Philip. Please."

The look, the smile, were caresses given in the presence of dozens of other diners. Kit was attracted to the man but even if he weren't, he'd go to bed with him if that's what it took to get a theatre and save the Company at the last minute. Nick would say he was a whore. What of it? He didn't care what Nick would say or think.

"I need a theatre, Philip. I've run afoul of some cretins who call themselves the Theatre Trust."

"I heard."

"Then you know the situation in which I find myself. Can you help? I was told you own a theatre."

"Who told you that?" Displeasure crossed the judge's face.

"It doesn't matter. Do you, Philip?"

"Yes." He dropped his voice. "But it's questionable that I do, since I acquired it as a result of a bankruptcy. Not very ethical."

"I don't care about the ethics of it. I need a place to perform. Will you lease it to me?"

"Oh, no, Kit. It won't do at all."

"Why?"

"It's in deplorable condition. It hasn't been used for years."

"Then why did you take it?"

"The lot will someday be worth a great deal of money if I read my city development right."

Kit slumped, his expression mournful. "You were my last hope, Philip. The Trust has beaten me."

"Well, I suppose if the place can be made usable you could have it. But once you see it, you wouldn't have it as a gift, I'm sure. If you like, we can go there this afternoon."

The Flambeau huddled all alone on a short side street, separated from the bustling Broadway theatre district known as the Rialto, with its lights, theatres and hotels, restaurants and nightclubs. Obscenity-decorated boards covered the Flambeau's windows. The heavy padlock that secured the chipped and gouged door bore the marks of a saw blade.

Kit held the lantern while Wescott unlocked the padlock. "That's the third one I've had put on," the judge said. As he pushed the door open it groaned in protest. "When I was your age this was a nice little theatre."

The blackness inside was relieved by slivers of light that came between the boards on the windows and the lantern light. The air was thick with dust and fallen plaster and fetid with the stench of

human or animal waste. Seats had been ripped from the floor and
thrown about, and lay like shadowy gargoyles in the dark. Ragged
remnants of curtain hung like dark shrouds over the stage. Kit
sensed rather than saw the overhead bulk of a balcony.

"Now you know why Frohman and his gang weren't interested
in it," the judge said. "The ornate facades of the balcony and box
seats are cracked and broken or missing altogether. There's
scarcely a wall where the laths do not show through. The stage
floor is sound as far as I know. The orchestra pit has been used as
a privy. The dressing rooms and the orchestra rehearsal hall are
beneath the stage and only God knows what they're like. I've never
had nerve enough to go down and look." He made a vague gesture
toward a dimly seen door leading from the orchestra pit to the
below-stage area. "If you want to take a look..."

"No. I don't need to see any more. It would take a fortune to
make it usable," Kit said. Disappointment sliced through him. "I'd
have to get backers, millionaires. Even then... Damn."

"I'm sorry," said Wescott as they left. "I'll ask about, see what I
can find, but they control every theatre of quality. Not just in this
city but across the country. I'm surprised you didn't find yourself
locked out on your tour." He paused. "I don't suppose you'd want
to visit an elderly but spry judge this evening?" A tentative touch
of his hand on Kit's arm finished the incomplete question.

"I'm sorry, Philip. I'd be dreadful company tonight. I have to
think what to do now. I'll be bloody damned if I give in to them."

The corners of Wescott's mouth drooped but he said, "I understand."

"Philip, do you know Mrs. William Backhouse Astor, Jr.?"

"Of course. Caroline's a friend; not a close one, but we've known
each other for years. And she doesn't consider herself to be Mrs.
Anybody."

"Except as the one and only *The* Mrs. Astor, so I've been told.
Philip, if you could get me an invitation to meet her, my gratitude
would be boundless."

"My dear boy, the invitation is as good as in your hand."

A little later, as Kit passed the desk at the hotel, the clerk gave
him a note addressed in a dainty, feminine hand. He was tempted
to throw it away unread; he wasn't in the mood for another 'I love
you madly let us fly away together' letter. But good manners insisted he read it. He was glad he did.

Mr. St. Denys,

The theatrical grapevine has it that Erlanger & Co. have painted you into a corner. They did it to me, as well, and other of my colleagues. The others yielded to them. I shall not.

Perhaps you and I could find a way together to defy these evil creatures who would stifle us. I would be honored if you would meet with me tomorrow at 7:00 in the evening at the Brevoort dining room.

Yours in adversity,
Minnie Maddern Fiske

Mrs. Fiske! Erlanger's redheaded hellcat. Anyone who could irritate Erlanger that much had to be worth knowing.

But first, while he was still in as foul a mood as he had ever been in his life, he would take care of Nick. On a rented horse he rode across the Brooklyn Bridge, marveling at the mighty grace of the twisted steel cables of the "Eighth Wonder of the World."

Then he put everything else from his mind and rehearsed the confrontation with Nick. While the fool was reeling from that, he would tell the truth to Nick's bitch wife. Whatever she did to Nick after that would be no more than he deserved. Kit hoped she gelded him.

Once on the Brooklyn side, he proceeded through the city to the rural area beyond. With the city behind him, he rounded a curve in the road and came upon the house, a yellow monstrosity with lavender shutters and hideous scrollwork on every horizontal piece of wood in sight. The wide porch had comfortable wicker furniture; luxuriant green and flowering plants brightened each end. A low gray stone fence surrounded the house, and a lawn sign suspended from a wooden arm proclaimed, N. STUART, PHYSICIAN & SURGEON.

Kit hitched his horse to the iron post and went to the door. No one answered his knock. He knocked again, louder, as a pleasing image came to mind—Nick had seen him approach and cowered inside, afraid to answer the summons.

The door was opened by a girl in the plain dress, white apron and white cap of a maid. "Yes, sir?" she said, "Are you wanting to see Dr. Stuart?"

"Yes. It's personal. I'm not a patient."

"He's keeping office hours now, sir. Would you like to speak with Mrs. Stuart? She's in the garden?"

"Yes. Thank you." Slight change in plans; tell the wife first. The maid came out and beckoned to him to follow her. The brick walk was tidy and lined with flowers on either side.

In the center of the flower-lush garden was a gazebo and in the gazebo was a dark-haired lady fanning herself with her wide-brimmed hat. The maid said, "Wait here, sir. Let me speak to the mistress." Kit watched as the girl spoke to the woman and gestured toward him.

The lady smiled at him and motioned him closer. Even in the heat, she had a lap robe. No doubt trying to camouflage that she was stout. "I'm Mrs. Stuart, sir," she said. "My husband is occupied with his patients. May I help you?" Her manner was direct, her smile warm. She had splendid dark eyes. Nick was a fool for dark eyes.

He gave her a little bow, unsure what to say. He had expected to find a banshee, not a lady. "I'm an old friend of your husband, madam. I came to pay my respects. How is he?"

"He's doing very well. What's your name, sir? Perhaps he's mentioned you."

Kit doubted it. "Kit St. Denys. I'm an actor. "

"I've heard of you. You're famous," she said, smiling with every evidence of delight. "I can't imagine my husband knowing you. I've not been able to drag him into a theatre since I've known him. I wonder why he never mentioned you. But then, he doesn't talk much, as you know."

"There are times, Mrs. Stuart, when he talks entirely too much."

"You must know things about him I don't. Nicholas should be free from his patients in half an hour, if you'd care to wait. Would you dine with us?"

"I don't believe so, Mrs. Stuart, though it is kind of you to ask." How bloody ironic. She was offering him Nick on a silver platter and he was going to walk away. Temporarily. "Your husband and I had a severe difference of opinion when last I saw him. I'm not certain he'd welcome me. I'll return another day. "

"He has no patients on Friday afternoon."

"If you have no objection, I'll return then."

"Please do."

"And Mrs. Stuart, would you be so kind as to not tell him I was here? I want it to be a surprise."

"I understand." She smiled. "Until Friday, Mr. St. Denys. I insist you join us for dinner then."

"It would be a pleasure, Mrs. Stuart. Until Friday."

He took his leave of her and sat in the saddle for a moment looking at the house. Then, giving a short, sharp bark of self-mocking laughter he turned the horse's head and left.

~~~

Bronwyn's pregnancy was proving to be a difficult one; miscarriage threatened early on. Long before she and Nick planned, she had to stop working as his nurse. A little walking in the garden every day, light meals, and rest. That was her life now. He'd hired a maid and a cook. Bronwyn hated not working, but tried to make light of the situation. "At least now I have an excuse not to learn to cook," she said.

He had hired and fired three nurses in the nearly five months of Bronwyn's pregnancy. Then, as luck would have it, her friend Miss Barr lost her position at the hospital. Ida was quick and efficient, but she didn't have Bronwyn's bright smile and caring ways. The patients missed Bronwyn as much as Nick did.

By the time he was finished in the surgery on this day, Bronwyn had retired for the night. He was famished, and went to the office with the latest issue of *The Lancet* in one hand and a bread and cheese sandwich in the other and read until the tiny print blurred.

The downstairs parlor was now Bronwyn's bedroom until after the baby was born, and when he went in to wish her goodnight, she was propped up in bed, reading.

"You'll have a nice surprise Friday," she murmured as he leaned over to kiss her.

"You're going to bake an apple pie?"

"I said it would be *nice*. No apple pie of mine would be nice."

"That's true." Her one attempt was still a joke between them. "What's the surprise?"

"If I told you, it wouldn't be a surprise."

"You're a maddening wench, Mrs. Stuart. Goodnight."

As he reached the door she said, "I'll give you a hint. An old friend of yours from England is going to call on Friday."

He pivoted, suddenly afraid. "Who is it, Bronwyn? Bronwyn?" He returned to the bed. She laughed and refused to say anything else. He shivered. What he was thinking was impossible.

13

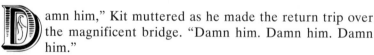amn him," Kit muttered as he made the return trip over the magnificent bridge. "Damn him. Damn him. Damn him."

What right did Nick have to drag a woman into this? Through her Nick had more power to hurt him than ever before. Unacceptable. Nick had to be punished. If the woman was hurt too, that was too bloody unfortunate. Why couldn't she have been what he had pictured: Medusa without the snakes?

Kit's mind ran around and around the questions until he was almost too numb to think. Back in his suite, he paced, more and more agitated, talking aloud. "I have to do what I came to do. It's not my fault he brought her into it."

The suite was too confining for his anger. Outside, he walked without direction, following the crowd and letting himself be carried along on its current. He didn't notice the passing of time until he realized the shadows were growing longer and bringing darkness on their heels. When he turned to hurry back to the hotel, he bumped into a man. His apology was choked off by horror. He looked into the black-bearded face of Tom Rourke. Kit fled, not hearing the protests of the people he shoved aside. At the hotel, Rama's room was empty. Frank's room was empty.

He locked himself into his suite. He was alone. And the old man was out there, waiting. He sat down and seized a pen. "Think," he mumbled. "Think of things to write. Write to Lizbet. Yes, that will help. That will be like a medicine. Write to Lizbet." The necessity of planning what to say calmed him.

He painted for Lizbet a bright picture of standing-room-only crowds at the Barclay. He wrote until his neck ached and his hand hurt, wrote until he could think of no more lies. Reading over the letter, he saw that he mentioned a dainty handkerchief he had bought for her. He did not remember writing that but it was a nice touch. Tomorrow he would find a fancy handkerchief for Lizbet.

The anxiety returned. From time to time he brushed clammy sweat from his forehead and glanced toward the windows, hidden behind the heavy drapes. "Get angry," he ordered. "Get angry. That will help, too. God knows you've plenty to be angry about."

He wrote to his booking agent, severing their connection. He wrote a venomous letter to Nick and one to his wife, and then tore both letters to shreds. He began to draw fast random lines of nothing in particular. Then he stopped and stared at the paper. They were not random after all. They had form. A stage. The stage of the Flambeau. Hesitantly at first and then as though his hand was possessed he added more lines, changed others.

A long time afterward, he looked at it again. It was the same stage but the curtains were whole, with a hint of a set. A stage waiting for a performance. His pen flew over fresh paper as he wrote to his London banker instructing him to forward a bank draught for a great deal of money. The second letter was to his solicitor authorizing a mortgage of the Xavier Theatre if it should prove necessary.

He put those letters aside and wrote one more, one addressed to the Trust, which in the morning he would take to the newspapers.

> I, Kit St. Denys, accuse you, Messrs. Erlanger and Frohman and your cohorts of the Theatre Trust, of strangling the theatre. I accuse you of extortion. I accuse you of dishonesty toward the public. I accuse you...

For a page he went on, read it over, tore it up, and rewrote it. He wrote it several times before he was satisfied. This time the letters were at an end. No more distraction was to be had. The suite was a chill cavern of malignant shadows, any one of which might be the old man. He got up and with unsteady hands turned on all the lights.

He drank the rest of the evening, then fell fully clothed upon the bed, staring at nothing. He remembered the good days he and Nick had had together, the laughter and the caring, the fun it had been to take that naive country boy and show him the world of theatre and teach him about love between men. He thought of the few happy days at St. Denys Hill before it all turned sour. He'd intended to tell Nick about Michael and Rourke. He couldn't remember why he hadn't.

"I trusted you, Nico, the way I trusted Michael and Lizbet and Papa St. Denys, but they didn't abandon me. You're so close. McPherson meant nothing to me. Tried to tell you. You wouldn't listen. Self-righteous tin saint. Hate you. God, but I hate you. Saw the old man tonight. Why aren't you here with me? God damn you. So close, Nico. Just across the bloody river. Need you. You know I'm here. You must know. She'd tell you. You should ... know ..."

He fell into a stuporous sleep that broke into splintering terror. He knew he had cried out; it hung silently in the air. Something moved behind the bedroom drapes. He leaped to his feet, staggering a little, and jerked the drapes open. Nothing was there except the faint tea-colored sun just rising in the foggy morning. Drained, he fell back on the bed and slept until noon.

He was pale that afternoon when he set out with his letter to the Trust, and blue shadows webbed the skin beneath his eyes. He went first to the offices of the *Sun*. The editor glanced at the letter and laughed. He was dismissed out-of-hand at the *American*.

The *Evening Post* editor read it, then handed it back. "Mr. St. Denys, I admire your work and empathize with your feelings. But I can't print that."

"Why? Nobody will give me a reason."

"My dear sir, you labor under the delusion that newspapers exist to print news. Newspapers exist to sell products. In order to do that we must have advertisers. In order to keep advertisers we must pander to them. We carry a lot of theatre advertisements. If

I printed that, the Trust would pull the ads of every theatre they control. We would lose thousands and thousands of dollars."

"And the moral justice of it means nothing?"

"Mr. St. Denys, moral justice is keeping food on the table and clothes on the backs of my family and my employees and their families. Good day, sir."

The publisher of the *World* asked Kit in with every show of respect, and read the letter twice before handing it back. "You're right about the Trust. I myself accused them of fraud for sending out second-rate road companies and advertising them as the original cast. I know full well what they are and what their methods are."

Kit leaned forward. "Then you'll print this?"

"No. I'm sorry."

"If you know, then...why?"

The editor looked at a point over Kit's head. "Cowardice, I suppose. At the time I wrote my editorial, an organization of well-known actors promised to back me. Richard Mansfield was its president. When the Trust bought him, the others melted away. The Trust represents all of them now, and they have burgeoning careers in Trust-controlled theaters. I couldn't defy the Trust alone. It wouldn't have been fair to the stockholders and the others who depend on us."

"I've heard that speech before. And they're not all acting under the Trust. Mrs. Fiske is not."

"And she hasn't played a decent house for the past year. "

Kit got up as he folded his letter. "The famous American free press is a farce."

"Try *The Dramatic Mirror*. It's just a theatre weekly, but he's enough of a fool to print it; no one else will."

A few minutes later, stepping down out of the cab, Kit wondered what kind of joke the *World* publisher was pulling. He was in front of the Empire Theatre, where the Trust offices were. Then he realized that the Empire wrapped like a U around a much smaller building. The impression was that of a python about to squeeze a mouse to death. A modest sign in the window of the mouse declared: "DRAMATIC MIRROR. Theater Weekly Dedicated to Freedom of the Arts And Independence of the Artist." He was suspicious. With the Trust offices and the *Mirror* in such proximity, how could they not be in league?

He stopped inside a large, jumbled room in chaos. The nimble fingers of a bespectacled girl flew over the keys of a typewriting machine, accompanied by the clack-clack-clack of the type bars hitting the paper. Magazines, books, and newspapers were stacked everywhere. Theatrical posters adorned the walls. One poster had a large cartoon of a gowned Frohman with a tiara, holding hands with a bestial Erlanger as they trampled small figures of actors and actresses beneath their feet. Kit chuckled at the caption: BEAUTY AND THE BEAST AND THEIR BEASTLY BUSINESS.

"I must speak to the editor," he said to the young man behind the desk.

"Harry?"

"Yes, if Harry's the editor."

"Editor. Publisher. Manager. Owner. Right this way." The young man beckoned to him to follow and talked over his shoulder. "Say, aren't you Kit St. Denys? Sure you are. I've seen your pictures. Never saw you on stage but I heard you're dynamite." He talked so fast, Kit was a little lost. The boy knocked on a door and opened it. "Man to see you, Harry." With a flourish he ushered Kit in and closed the door.

Behind a desk heaped with papers was a tall, slim man who looked to be in his thirties, with thinning hair and a luxurious mustache. The gentleman rose and extended his hand. "It's a pleasure, Mr. St. Denys! My wife has said she wished she could work with you."

"Your wife, sir?"

He chuckled and motioned toward a painted portrait of a delicate, plain-faced woman with red hair. "Mrs. Fiske, sir. Minnie Maddern Fiske. I'm Harrison Fiske; I have the honor of being her husband." He laughed. "Erlanger called me Mr. Minnie Maddern in public, thinking he was insulting me. Not a bit of it! My wife's a genius."

"As they say, it is a small world, Mr. Fiske. Your wife has invited me to call upon her this evening."

"I'm not surprised. Bunner is always a few steps ahead of the rest of the world."

"Bunner?"

"Did I call her that just now? She'd kill me. That's my pet name for her. She calls me Boy. And do you know what? Neither of us remembers where the names came from. Now, then, I assume you came here for a purpose."

Kit handed him the letter. When Fiske had read it he looked up, smiling. "I'd be delighted to print this, Mr. St. Denys. A *caveat*, however. We're a small circulation weekly. Actors, managers, playwrights who are with the Trust are forbidden to read the *Mirror*. Hotel newsstands that sell Trust theatre tickets are not allowed to sell the *Mirror*. In short, a small but select minority will read your letter. You'll be preaching to the choir."

"But it will be read."

"It will indeed be read."

They shook hands again. "Until this evening, then," said Fiske. "I look forward to it."

Kit felt good about events for the first time in several days. The Trust could be brought down; he would be the one to do it. He hoped Erlanger was looking out the window as he left.

His next stop was the Fifth Avenue home of Judge Wescott. The place reminded Kit of a dowager whose family has been around since Adam and Eve and therefore does not need to put on airs to impress anyone. The mansions around it were garish and overblown in comparison.

The butler conducted him to the library and left. Kit looked around, remembering the St. Denys library as he had first known it, with its the unabashed collection of rare nude statues. Here the statues and pictures were no different than one would see in any grand home on the Avenue. Such neutered and strangulating respectability.

His thoughts were interrupted by Philip's arrival. "What a pleasant surprise," Philip said. "I was sitting down to a late luncheon. Will you join me?"

"Another time, Philip. I'm sorry to have disturbed you."

"Another time. Is that all I'll ever hear from you, Kit? If not the pleasure of my company, what does bring you here?"

"I want the theatre. The Flambeau. At once."

"But you didn't even see all of it. If I allowed you to sink money into such a wreck, I couldn't sleep at night."

"Philip, I want to buy it. Have an engineer go over it for structural integrity, and if the walls will hold the roof and the floors will hold the audience, then I want it as soon as possible. I've already written to my people in London to send money. A lot of it."

"I think you're a little mad." An affectionate smile took the sting from the words.

"More than a little, I suspect. How soon can I have the place?"

"Within the month."

"Not good enough. I must have possession in a fortnight. "

"I'm afraid this is an impulse you'll regret."

Kit smiled. "I seldom act on impulse."

"I wish I had that kind of courage. There are many things I'd do if I didn't have to consider whether a certain thing is wise or acceptable." Wescott sighed, his eyes sad.

"Well, one of us is far more likely than the other to get his head split open or end his days in poverty. I leave it to you to guess which is which."

"If you say so. I'll start the property transfer process tomorrow, then. You should have the engineer's recommendation within a day or so." When they shook hands, the judge held Kit's hand a moment longer than was necessary. "Kit, if you're free Saturday night, Caroline Astor is having a small dinner party and she has expressed a desire to meet you. And there are many contacts to be made there, and any number of backers for a theatre with your name on it." He laughed. "Caroline's small dinner parties never have fewer than one hundred fifty people, by the way."

"What!" Kit was delighted. "Philip, you're a miracle worker. Of course, I'll be there."

"And afterward, if you like, we can go to my country home and, ah, talk the night away."

Kit lifted one eyebrow and smiled. He had done worse things than "talk" the night away with a handsome, influential man.

From Wescott's home, Kit went to the shopping district known as Ladies' Mile. Building after building displayed ready-made dresses, coats, hats, bonnets, and gloves, shoes and boots, scarves, trimmings of fur, feathers and jewels. Women passed him in chattering twos and threes. Sometimes they were accompanied by obviously suffering gentlemen.

Lord & Taylor's was a quiet, elegant store, where the air was overly sweet with perfume and the only sounds were the rustling of long skirts and soft murmuring voices. When he left, he had what he wanted. The salesgirl called it a handkerchief, but it consisted of about three square inches of silk and a six-inch-wide border of lace. Lizbet would declare it the most impractical thing she had ever seen and she would love it.

As he walked back to the Marlborough with his prize in hand, he was struck from behind and knocked off balance. An instant later his he saw his money clip disappearing down the street in the hands of a fleet-footed boy. He sprinted after the child. The pickpocket was younger but Kit's legs were longer. He closed on the zigzagging boy, seized his arm, spun him around and clamped the boy's skinny arms to his sides.

"Give me back my money, you little bastard," he snarled. Then he sucked in his breath. The years fell away as he looked down into the dirty small face.

"Getcha hands offa me," the boy cried, fighting like a ferret.

A passing officer stopped beside Kit and the struggling boy. "At it again, hey, Billy?" The boy spat at the policeman, who grinned and tapped his nightstick against his palm. "I'll take'm off your hands, sir. We know Billy down at the station, we do. Gonna wind up in prison, he is, if he lives that long. Reg'lar limb of Satan. Come down and press charges, sir. We'll get him off the streets."

Kit stared at the officer a moment. "No," he said. "There'll be no charges."

The officer muttered, "Damn fool Englishman!" He touched his cap with his club, and went on his way.

Kit dragged the boy into the nearest restaurant and shoved him into a seat near the window. He remained standing, blocking the boy's escape.

"Why didn't you turn me over to the copper?" the boy demanded, eyeing his captor. Kit knew he was gauging his chances of slipping under the table and out the door.

"I will unless you give me back what you took."

"Didn't take nuttin'."

"How old are you, Billy?"

"Fourteen, almost."

"Fourteen, my eye. You're not a day over nine, are you."

"Am so. I'm twelve. I just ain't very big. Can't all of us be big and rich like you."

"Cheeky cub, aren't you. When did you last have a decent meal?"

"None of your business."

"I think it is my business since it was my bloody money you stole." With a flourish he produced his money clip, grinning at the instant admiration in the boy's eyes.

"Je-suz, You're good. How'd you get that?"

"Kid, I could have your back teeth in my pocket before you could say ouch. Rule Number One: don't try to fox someone better at it than you."

"Well, how's I supposed t'know that? You look like any other old fart t'me."

Kit almost choked. *Kit St. Denys an old fart?* "Where do you live?"
"None o' your business." At Kit's warning glare, he mumbled
"Bow'ry."

Kit had little doubt the Bowery was not much different from
the London stews. He sat down across from the boy. The instant
he did the boy leaped up snatched the money clip from Kit's hand,
and ran for the door. "Wait, I want to help you!" Kit shouted,
chasing him again. He was closing in when he tripped over a small
stray dog. Pain shot up his right ankle. The boy vanished. Kit
limped back into the restaurant. Maybe the kid was right; he had
become an old fart at twenty-seven.

❧❧

Minnie Fiske was small and feminine, with a thin nose, golden-
red hair, a delicate chin and a mouth too wide for beauty. Intelligence blazed in her dark blue eyes.

"Mrs. Fiske," he said, bowing over her hand after Harry introduced them, "The portrait in your husband's office does not do
you justice."

She laughed. "You didn't tell me he would be such a shameless
flatterer, Boy. Please call me Minnie. I'll call you Kit, if you've no
objection."

"I'd be pleased."

Dinner conversation was pleasant, mostly about theatre, with
no mention of the Trust to spoil appetites. When the dessert had
been cleared away, Minnie said, "Kit, I have a proposition but it
would be better discussed in private. Have you time to join us in
our suite? I'll tell you what's on my mind while you and Boy
indulge in brandy and cigars."

And so a little later Kit found himself in their modest rooms, a
glass of brandy in one hand and in the other the script for *Tess of
the d'Urbervilles.*

"Everyone has told me not to do this play," Minnie said.
"Everyone. They say it's savage, and immoral, and depressing.
They predict failure on a grand scale. Well, I say better to fail on
a grand scale than succeed with safe, boring, and predictable plays.
I'm going to do it. But of course, I have no theatre and the actor I
wanted for Angel Clare decided to throw me over for the Trust. I
was ready to give up."

"You don't know how unusual that is!" Harry Fiske said.

Minnie ignored him. "Then I discovered you were in the city and my prayers were answered. Be my Angel Clare, Kit."

Kit had read the novel by his countryman, Thomas Hardy. The character of Angel Clare had interested him from the first. A handsome, pious hypocrite who turns on his bride when he finds out she was seduced and bore a child out of wedlock. A handsome, pious hypocrite just like that damned Stuart.

"Take the script," Minnie said. "Read it. I want you to do it, but I realize you may not want to take a supporting role."

"I'll do it."

"You haven't read the script yet."

"I've read the novel. I trust your judgment. And my instincts. As to being in a supporting role to Minnie Fiske, it will be an honor."

Her smile was rueful. "Even if we must play in a livery stable?"

"Even then. But it shan't come to that. I may be able to get some wealthy angels by the name of Astor," he said with a grin. "And though I can't give you the details tonight, when next we meet I'll have a theatre of my own."

"How extraordinary. Were you serious about the Astors?"

"Tomorrow evening I have an audience with *the* Mrs. Astor."

"Well, you're famous, rich, charming, and British. She'll welcome you with open arms."

"I don't know about the open arms part of it. I'll find out soon enough."

☙❧

Every inch of wall space in the Astor ballroom was taken up with ornately framed Masterworks. At one end, over the two sets of double doors was a filigreed balcony. In every corner was a piece of priceless sculpture; rare vases decorated the many small tables.

It was obvious *the* Mrs. Astor saw herself as Queen. Kit treated her as such, amused by the way she posed her plump little body beneath the life-sized portrait of herself and greeted her guests with regal aloofness. She was homely and without a shred of charm. Diamonds glittered in her too-black hair, her ears, around her neck, wrists, and fingers, and on the bodice of her gown. As he played courtier, Kit wondered if she had diamonds on her knickers as well.

"I can't tell you, Lady Astor, what a great privilege it is to be in your presence." The haughty eyes warmed just a bit. "I've dined with princesses and duchesses, Madam, but you could teach them how to be truly gracious." He was surprised he didn't gag. With one final bow he passed on to let the guest behind him pay his respects, freeing him to join her daughter-in-law.

Ava put a glass of champagne into his hand. "I can't believe you're here," she drawled. "Well, my dear Mr. St. Denys, you are amazing." Her eyes twinkled. "My mother-in-law is prepared to invest in your theatre, by the way. I told her I was, and when she found out how much she let it be known that she would invest half again as much."

"You are indeed an angel," Kit said. "How did you find out about the theatre?"

"A mutual friend." She winked. "I can't reveal the source of my information." The orchestra struck up a Strauss waltz. "Dance with me," she said.

"I wish I could, but I injured my ankle the other day and it's still a bit painful. Might we sit and talk instead? Or would that be considered gauche."

"Probably gauche. But I don't care. I want to talk to you." Her eyes narrowed and she leaned in toward him. "I have a list of backers for you in exchange for one little favor." Her hand rested lightly on his. "Be my lover and the list is yours. It's safe. My husband is in France. He's always in France."

Kit had not blushed for years, but he did now. Dear God, a list of millionaire backers, and all he had to do was the one thing he wouldn't do. He let her talk and tried to think his way out of this. He became aware that she had stopped talking, and was looking at him over the rim of a champagne glass. "Why so quiet?" she asked after a moment.

"I don't know what to say. In your presence what man can think of anything but you?"

Ava laughed. "You are more full of bullshit than a pasture."

"What an unladylike thing to say." He lifted his glass to her.

"Obviously I'm not a lady, just a pretend one. Did I frighten you with my naughty proposal?"

"Yes."

"I don't usually frighten men. Well." She made an encompassing gesture that took in the ballroom and its glittering inhabitants. "Now then. How did you get an invitation to this house?"

"Charm."

"A distinct probability if you were ever that close to her. But you weren't. No, there had to be another agent involved in this."

He caught sight of Judge Wescott talking with two other serious-faced gentlemen. The judge looked up and caught Kit's glance. He smiled and inclined his head.

Ava caught the look and the salute. Her face froze for an instant. "So that was it! Uncle Phil helped you."

"Uncle Phil?"

"A distant relative. I've known him since I was a little girl." She looked from Westcott, once again deep in conversation, and back at Kit. Her eyes widened slightly. "That's why you won't take me up on my offer, isn't it."

He rose to the challenge in her eyes. "What if I said yes?"

"I've known Uncle Phil's secret for years. I'm a woman of the world, you know." She smiled. "I'll send the list around to the Marlborough by messenger tomorrow."

"You're an extraordinary lady, Ava."

"No," she said with a rueful smile. "At least I'm not according to my mother-in-law. I'm a tramp, a gold-digger. Ask her. Never mind that my family's older and better than hers. It's always said of me that I can't keep a secret. Now I have two."

Philip Wescott approached, and kissed Ava's cheek. "Dear child, you are the most beautiful woman here, as usual."

"Of course I am."

"I wonder if I might borrow Mr. St. Denys for a few minutes?"

Ava patted his hand. "Oh, Uncle Phil, you may have him. I'm quite finished with him."

When she was out of earshot, Philip said in a low voice, "I'm leaving for the country house in a few minutes. Do you remember the directions?"

Kit nodded. Meeting Philip Wescott made him what Nick said he was. Nick could go to hell. He didn't care anymore what Nick might think.

The pleasant country retreat was isolated and inviting, with fresh flowers, a fire in the grate, cold delicacies and an abundance of wine. Kit ate little and downed a good deal of wine while Philip talked. After a while Kit put his glass aside, seized Wescott's face between his hands, and took his mouth in a bruising kiss. "Never had a judge before," he said, "What happens now? Does a bailiff come in and say all rise?" He chuckled at his own joke. "Where's the bedroom? A few more drinks and I won't be able to do anything."

For Kit, what followed was pleasant if forgettable. When it was over, it was over. His debt was paid. And he could sleep secure tonight, safe from the old man and the nightmares. Just as he was drifting to sleep, Philip spoke again.

"You're not going to sleep now, are you? I thought we would talk a while."

"For what reason?" Kit managed to say.

The judge got up, pulled on a dressing gown, and then sat beside the bed where he could look into Kit's face, touch his naked arm. "We've never really talked, you know."

"I passed the point of making sense some time ago."

"I listen to lawyers all day. What makes you think you have to make sense? This isn't all I want from you, Kit. I want so much more than just to bed you."

Through a haze of alcohol and sleepiness, Kit mumbled, *"Bed* me? Quaint."

"If that was all I wanted, I could've hired someone and sent him on his way, not even knowing who I was. You mean more than that to me."

Kit looked away from Wescott's yearning eyes. "Don't. I'm poison. Ask Nick."

"Who's Nick?"

"Nobody. I hate him. I want t'kill him. I want him back."

Philip Wescott did not want to hear about Nick, whoever Nick was. "I saw you perform in London when you were about nineteen," he said. "I fell in love with you then. And when I heard you were performing in Boston, I gave myself a holiday and went to every performance there. You see…"

Kit's hazy mind left the bedroom and the quiet, droning voice. Unpleasant shadows were trying to surge to the fore. If he waited too long before going to sleep he would dream. The judge was in mid-sentence when he realized Kit was asleep. With a sigh, he shed the dressing gown and got into bed. When he woke the next morning, Kit was gone.

14

At sixty, Lizbet had sold the Royal Lion and moved into the cottage at St. Denys Hill and, in the year since, had never looked back. Her life was simple: books, a garden, a few aging hens to which she had given names. She was learning the homey things she'd never had time to learn, and the next time Kit came home she planned to shock him with a loaf of homemade bread. She wore stout shoes and plain woolen dresses. In winter a heavy coachman's coat and scarf, bought from a coachman's widow, kept out the cold and boy's size Wellingtons kept her feet dry. Her fine clothes and dainty shoes were saved for visiting the Hill when Kit was there. For him she even made the supreme sacrifice and wore a corset.

'Miss Elizabeth' fascinated the villagers. They knew two facts: she was supposedly cousin to the late Xavier St. Denys and had been an actress. Embellishing Miss Elizabeth's story was a new pastime that helped while away the few idle minutes they had, and facts would have gotten in the way. She had been ruined many years ago, by none other than the man she *said* was her cousin. If he was, which they didn't believe for a minute, then the delicious tale involved incest! 'Poor thing. She was... well, you know." Young Mr. Kit was their love child, hidden away somewhere until he was half grown and then brought to the Hill to be raised to manhood. Now her son took care of his mother. It was a satisfying scenario that could be embroidered upon forever. No one really believed it.

The tales amused Lizbet, though when she went from her cottage to the village tavern once a week to pick up her post, she never let on that she knew of the gossip. She wondered how much further they would take it. It sounded like a naughty play to her. "Someday," she told herself, "I'll write a melodrama about it all. *The Ruination and Salvation of Elizabeth*."

The postmaster and tavern keeper greeted her as he always did. "Good morning to you Miss Elizabeth. Miserable foggy weather, ain't it." He squeezed and bent a thick envelope before handing it to her. "From Young Mr. Kit I see. Heavy for a letter. What do you suppose be in it, t'make it so fat?"

"I don't know." Their entertainment was in creating her past. Hers was in foiling their avid interest.

"He's in America now, is he?"

"Of course." She tucked the letter into the pocket of her coat. "Cheerio, Mr. Sand."

"Cheerio, Miss Elizabeth," he responded with a sigh of disappointment.

The tavern's only customer at that hour, a very tall and burly man seated at the back, had watched and listened to the exchange between Lizbet and Mr. Sand. He'd let the attic room several days before, sat himself down in the same chair every day at the same hour, and stayed there, watching everyone. Mr. Sand was afraid of him or he would have asked him to leave because he was scaring the regulars off. A few moments after the door closed behind Lizbet, the big man paid for his drink and also disappeared into the fog. Mr. Sand hoped he wasn't coming back.

Lizbet liked fog, liked the eerie mystery it lent to familiar things. After Xavier's death she and Kit had taken many long walks, often in the fog, with his arm around her shoulders. "Kit. My boy," she said softly. "You've been away far too long this time. Come home. I miss you. Oh!" She gave a start. A shape moved in the fog— Then with a breathy laugh she realized it was just the stunted, twisted old apple tree a few yards from her home. "Silly imagination," she muttered.

Inside the cottage, the handsome, nickel-trimmed coal stove Kit had sent from America welcomed her with warmth and soon removed the fog-chill from her bones. Not until she was seated beside the stove with a cup of tea on the small table beside her, did she open the envelope.

"Oh," she said in soft pleasure when the handkerchief, carefully folded and wrapped, came into view. "What a lovely thing." She treasured it because he had chosen and sent it. But really, he was a precious goose. She had no need for things such as the Dresden china teapot, which held the money she had not spent, or the linen shirtwaists, kid gloves, boots, fur muffs, and elegant hats. She put the handkerchief aside and unfolded the letter.

> Dearest Lizbet,
>
> I hope you find pleasure in the handkerchief. The young lady salesclerk in this very fancy shop assured me that the Mrs. Astor (who has tea with the Queen on Mondays and with God on Fridays) always buys this style. She, however, buys them by the dozen. At this price you get only one! I hope it makes you feel frightfully nobby.
>
> I wish you were here to see the Company in our latest triumph.

He went on for four pages with the latest news about the tour, about the marvelous reception they were receiving at the Barclay Theatre and in New York itself.

> Queues every night! I like it so much in this wonderful city I may buy my own theatre and remain for a few years. Of course I'll send for you. I need my Lizbet here to take the wind out of my sails once in a while.

She frowned and tapped the edges of the folded pages against her lower lip. "That," she said, "was a little too cheerful." His normally bold, decisive handwriting had a tentative look. He made no mention of the inevitable problems that plagued any touring company: illness, houses less than capacity, a poor review, miserable traveling conditions, bad tempers from tiredness. "Well, my darling,

I know where you are. I'll simply write you and ask. You know you can't pull the wool over my eyes."

From under the apple tree, the big man watched the cottage all day. Midmorning a boy with a pony cart arrived to deliver milk. A peddler stopped by. Then a vicar. The vicar stayed for an hour. After he left, the old bitch came out and fed a dozen chickens. He heard her talking to them as if they were pets. No one else came. Darkness fell; the cottage went dark.

He waited another hour. He suspected the old cunt was the kind who never locked her door, and he was right. Moving quietly, he went to the bedroom where Lizbet lay asleep. He clamped his hand down upon her nose and mouth. Her eyes flew open. She struggled, and was crushed against the intruder's chest. His buttons cut into her breasts.

"Now listen, slut. I'm gonna take me hand off your mouth. Ain't nobody gonna hear anyway but I can't stand a screamin' woman. Scream and I cut your throat. Understand?"

She nodded and gave a stifled cry of pain as he grabbed a handful of her white-streaked gray hair and made her look with uncomprehending fright into his swarthy, bearded face. "Where's me boy?" he demanded.

"I don't— I don't know what you're talk—" And then she did know. "Tom Rourke!" she cried.

He laughed and threw her flat on the bed. "The same. Now where is he?"

"I don't know." She squealed as he struck her.

"I been watchin' and I been askin' in the village. I was there today. I know you got a letter from him. Where is he?"

"Please," she begged, "don't bother him, Mr. Rourke. He's happy. He's got a good life. Don't bother him, I beg you. I have money. I'll give it to you, all of it, if you'll just leave him alone."

"A good life? I reckon he does have a good life! A smart 'un, me Jack. Got hisself adopted by that rich old fart. Inherited a lot o' brass, so I hear. Well, I figure he owes me."

"H-he thinks you're dead."

"Aye, he does. Why wouldn't he? He tried t'cut me heart out, the little bastard! That son of a whore! I bet he done old St. Denys in like he tried t' do me in. But I ain't dead. And I ain't of a mind to work no more, neither. He'll keep me in bloody good style the rest of me days."

"He has no reason to help you." She tried to sound defiant and sounded like a scared child.

"Oh, I think he does, lady. I think he'll pay plenty to keep his fancy friends from knowin' who he really is. The great Kit St. Denys, really Jack Rourke, river scum, dirty little thief, a filthy kid what tried t'kill his own lovin' papa. And I have me a suspicion there's other things he wouldn't want people t'know." He threw back his head and laughed.

Lizbet lunged for the heavy porcelain pitcher on the washstand beside the bed. She swung it with all her strength. He caught her hands in midair. The pitcher flew from her fingers and smashed to pieces on the floor. He flung her back on the bed and struck her repeatedly across the face. "Help!" she screamed. She fought with all the strength she had, using her nails, using her teeth, twisting and turning. "Kit—!"

Rourke laughed and closed his fingers around her throat, tighter and tighter. He gave her scrawny neck one last squeeze and demanded, "Now tell me where he is." He stared down at her and cursed his stupidity. He hadn't meant to kill her. Yet.

He ransacked the house, and found at least two hundred quid in paper and coin stuffed in a teapot, and filled his pockets with things to pawn. He dumped contents of every drawer. In one of them he found letters, but the damned things had no address on them.

He dragged her to the floor and tore apart the mattress. Nothing. On the shelf in the wardrobe he found a scrapbook of Jack. But 'Jack' wasn't good enough for the brat. 'Kit,' he called himself. The book was of nothing but 'Kit' this and 'Kit' that. What a bloody sissy name! Papers and more papers! Newspaper stories. Pictures. Programmes from the theatre. Old tickets. All autographed, 'With all my love to Lizbet, your Kit.' For several moments he stared at the most recent picture.

"Goddam," he growled, "if you ain't the spittin' image of that cunt mother of yours." He ripped the picture out and stuck it in his pocket. On the floor he saw a letter he'd missed. It took him a while to decipher it, but it brought a chuckle. Now he knew where Jack was, and the brat had told him himself.

With the letter was a lacy scrap of cloth. He put them both in his pocket with the money and the picture. That hanker was a fancy piece of work. It'd get him a whore for free. As he strode toward the door he paused and stared down at Lizbet, face down on the pieces of the broken pitcher, her nightdress twisted around her.

He put her on the bed, and then splashed lamp oil liberally on the bed and about the room. A Lucifer in his pocket produced a bright little flame. Tossed into the bed it instantly flared into fire that snatched the blankets and her nightdress. In seconds her bed was her funeral pyre, and the flames were spreading to curtains and furniture.

Before he reached the village, the torch that had been a cottage lighted the country sky. Rourke's plans were made: a few weeks of high living, then a ticket to New York City. There he would find Jack and would never have another care in the world. But first the high living!

Food, drink, and whores. Soon the money was gone. He pawned what remained of the old bitch's things. Soon that money, too, was gone and he still didn't have a ticket to America. He thought on the situation. He could ship out again. Or he could steal. Didn't want to ship out; it was too much work for too little money. He heard talk in a whorehouse that a certain customer was going to the Continent for an extended visit; his mansion was to be shut up. Great pickings. But it was too big for one man.

He hunted down an old friend, Blackie Stonebed and for fifty per cent of the swag, Blackie agreed to help him. Good old Blackie. If it hadn't been for Blackie, by god, he would've died when the brat stabbed him. He owed Blackie this chance to get rich. Rourke was good at picking locks and they got in without trouble. The burglary went without a hitch. And then, as they crept along a hallway carrying sacks of swag, Rourke blundered against a tall clock and sent it crashing to the floor. The butler charged into the hall, gun in hand. Blackie died on the spot, a hole where his left eye have been. Rourke surrendered.

At his sentencing Rourke laughed to himself to think that the Court believed they were sentencing a thief to five years at hard labor. If the rum-heads had known the truth they would have sentenced him to the gallows.

While he served his sentence he resigned himself to working his way to America. Since the brat bought a theatre he would still be there when his fond papa got off the boat. In the meantime, he scrubbed his cell, walked in the exercise circle, did his work, went to chapel, and was a model prisoner.

Of the Company, only Rama and Francis decided to remain in New York. Rama took work in an exclusive girls' school. Frank was still looking. None of the others could face the uncertainty of knowing when or if they would work again. Kit had told them nothing about the Flambeau because of the uncertainty. Neither he nor they could afford to idle for months. And they were all homesick.

Kit hired the private dining room of the hotel, brought in a Parisian chef, and threw a grand farewell dinner. Beside each plate was an envelope with a name, and in each envelope was the amount of wages owed, as well as a generous bonus to see them over the arrival home. Throughout the evening spirits were kept up with jokes, and laughter. Reminiscences cropped up and they cried. Everyone had an anecdote about a play or about Kit or about his or her own embarrassment on stage.

When the food was gone and the drink was running low and time was running out, they called for Kit to recite to them. They called out plays, scenes, characters, and lines and he did them, sometimes to laughter, sometimes to tears: Bottom, Lady Macbeth, Juliet, Romeo, Hamlet, Calaban, Shylock. And then it was over. Every one came to him to say goodbye with a hug and a few words. Some of them cried.

The fencing master embraced Kit and made him swear never to abandon his daily practice.

Kit returned to his suite, despondent and lonely. Even though his people would be there for one more night, he did not want to see them. He couldn't bear to say good-bye a second time.

He was sitting alone, staring into the fire in the grate, when his head jerked up. Someone had called him. It had been a call, a wail, of unbearable anguish. The voice of a terrified woman. Lizbet's voice. The hair stood on his arms and the back of his neck. The cry did not come again.

"Too much wine," he said. He must have fallen asleep sitting there and had a dream. Yet the very air in the suite had changed. It was disturbed. Heavy with malevolence. He spent the night with Frank. "What would I do if you'd decided to go back too?" he asked Francis.

"You'd find someone else. You'd forget me."

"I might find someone else," Kit admitted. "But I'd never forget you. You're too good a friend." He paused. "Frank, Nick Stuart is here, in New York."

"If he is I don't want to hear about it."

Kit pushed himself up on his elbow and looked down at him. "It's all right. I found out by accident."

"And you're going to find him, I suppose."

"I wouldn't spit on him if he was on fire." Kit waited for a response from Frank, but Frank said nothing. Kit lay awake until dawn. He did not feel safe from the nightmare tonight, even though Frank was there. The next morning, while shaving, Kit had an inspiration. "Frank!" he called.

Francis strolled into the lavatory, buttoning his shirt. "What?"

"Be on my payroll again."

"As what?" sniffed Francis, still smarting from the mention of Stuart's name. "Your gigolo?"

"Don't be an ass. I need someone at the theatre to watch over everything. There are carpenters and electrical workers and so on and so forth, and they all have their own supervisor but I want someone of mine there for them to answer to."

"I don't know anything about that sort of thing," Francis protested. "I'm an actor, not a builder."

"You know honesty, don't you? I can't be there to watch over it all. Please? You know you'd rather work for me than anyone else. Besides, I pay better wages."

"But if I find out I can't do what you want me to do, then where will I be?"

Kit grabbed him by the collar, and kissed him, deliberately smearing shaving soap on his face. "Then I'll hire you as my gigolo."

Francis swore good-naturedly as he shoved Kit away and wiped the soap from his face. Kit's confidence in him, and the teasing kiss, almost served to take away the sour taste caused by the name of Nick Stuart.

"I'm going to the theatre after I breakfast with Judge Wescott. Join us, why don't you, and then come to the theatre with me."

"I don't like him."

For a moment Kit wondered if Francis knew about the night at the country house, and asked cautiously, "Why? Because he wants me?"

Francis snorted. "If I were jealous of every man and woman who wants you, I'd be green as grass. No, I just don't like him. I'll breakfast alone, thank you, and join you at the theatre."

"As you wish. Frank, if it's any comfort, the judge holds no great attraction for me."

The answer was quiet. "He would if the night was dark enough and you were frightened enough."

"The theatre," Kit said, ignoring the comment. "In two hours."

Kit walked to the restaurant since the day was clear and beautiful, unusually warm for March. He strode along, dodging ladies' parasols, rowdy children, the traffic of wagons and carriages and an occasional motorcar without really seeing any of them. His thoughts were on Angel Clare. The more he dug into the character of Angel Clare the more he felt an uncomfortable similarity between his own flaws and those of Angel Clare, but that was a notion that he did not examine too closely.

Without warning, a sharp blow across his ear staggered him, and a voice bellowed, "You liar! You goddamned liar! I'll sue you for libel! I'll sue you for slander!"

He put up his hand to ward off a second blow, grabbed the walking stick that had delivered it. Abraham Lincoln Erlanger was at the other end. "Are you mad?" Kit glared down at the short, stocky man who danced around in a fury.

"No, but you are, you lying bastard!"

Kit released his end of the walking stick; Erlanger splatted ignominiously into a fresh pile of dog manure. Kit did not even try to stop his laughter. Erlanger scrambled to his feet, his face scarlet. "I'll show you! You can't accuse the Trust and me personally of criminal acts and then assault me in broad daylight and get away with it!" Erlanger grabbed Kit's arm as he walked away, spun him half around, and punched him on the jaw.

It was Jack Rourke who slammed a hard fist against Erlanger's nose. Blood spurted, and Erlanger staggered backward, his hand over his nose, blood streaming between his fingers.

A young policeman appeared from nowhere. "You're under arrest," he said to Kit.

"He attacked me. If you arrest anyone, arrest him."

"Well, since you're bigger than him and he's bloody and you ain't, I'd say the evidence says otherwise."

Kit started to retort, then realized he had been set up. "You came with this little cockroach, didn't you! Two can play that game. How much did he pay you? I'll double it."

The policeman started to splutter an indignant protest then gave Kit a conspiratorial grin. "Five dollars."

"Would ten do anything to soften your position?"

"If you take it I'll have your badge, Kelton," Erlanger screamed.

"Come work for me, Kelton," Kit said. "I need a watchman."

"How much?"

"Name it."

"Ten dollars a week."

"Done."

"Where?"

"The old Flambeau. Do you know where that is?"

"I'll find it. When do you want me?"

"Start tonight."

They shook hands. Erlanger watched them, his hand still on his streaming nose. His eyes darted from one man to the other. "St. Denys, you'll never open that rundown old relic. We'll break you. Run you out of town, you and that witch Minnie Fiske."

With exaggerated politeness Kit lifted his hat. "Good day. I'd change clothes before I went home, if I were you. Ladies tend to disapprove of dog shit on their settees."

Behind him the little man's voice rose to a shrill threat. "You've been warned, St. Denys! You've been warned!

By the time Kit arrived at the restaurant, he wished he had taken the little man by the throat and shaken his teeth out! The obsequious headwaiter showed him to the private room where Judge Wescott waited.

"Kit," Philip said with a warm smile. "I was beginning to think you weren't going to make it." Then the smile disappeared. "Good Lord, man, what happened? Your ear is bleeding."

"Is it?" Kit drew out his handkerchief and gingerly touched his swollen ear. The handkerchief came away red.

"Here. Let me do that. I can see it." Philip dipped his handkerchief into his water goblet and dabbed at Kit's ear. "I think you need a doctor."

With a self-mocking little smile, Kit said, "I do indeed need a doctor but the one I need is not available."

"Any one would do."

"Oh, no. I need a certain one."

"Are you going to tell me what happened?"

"I was attacked by a cockroach." When Philip looked at him as if he had lost his mind, Kit laughed. "The honorable A. L. Erlanger attacked me with a walking stick."

"Attacked you! What did you do?"

"I bloodied his nose and knocked him on his arse in a pile of shit. I wish it had been face first."

"Don't underestimate him, Kit, or the others. They're powerful. They have a great deal of money behind them. And scruples were something they left behind in grammar school. If they ever had any."

"They should not underestimate me. Enough of that. Any more talk of that vile little man and I'll lose my appetite. Did you bring the deed?"

Philip placed the deed in Kit's hand and closed his fingers over it. "The theatre is now yours. Lock, stock, and barrel, for better or worse."

"Sounds like a wedding," Kit said with a laugh.

"Kit, meet me in the country again. Soon."

"Now, Philip, you don't want to get too much of a good thing, do you?" He pretended not to see the hurt in Philip's eyes. He raised his glass. "To the St. Denys Theatre," he said.

"To the St. Denys Theatre," Philip echoed.

~ ❦ ~

It was a quiet Sunday afternoon at the Stuart house. Smokey-sweet-cinnamon smells of ham and sweet potatoes and apple pie curled throughout the house from the massive black range in the kitchen where the cook reigned supreme.

Just now Bronwyn reclined on the chaise in the formal parlor, and looked through the stereopticon Nick had brought her the day before. "It looks so real I feel I could reach out and get my hand wet," she said, and replaced Niagara Falls with a charging locomotive. "I know the scientific reason it works, but no matter how many times I see it, it's still magic."

Watching her, Nick felt the magic in the room was Bronwyn herself. His life, which had been a blur of never-ending motion and emotion with Kit, was now calm and predictable. Though Bronwyn could be unpredictable in her own way, it produced nothing like the chaos of being with Kit, that stage-treading, immoral lunatic. The thought brought him up short. Why was he even thinking of Kit? He had no intention of doing it, didn't want to, spent a great of time and energy not letting himself. But the instant his guard was down that bloody madman sneaked into his mind.

"You heard Reverend Lanston's sermon this morning, young lady," he said with mock severity to get his thoughts back where they should be. "Stereopticons and magic lanterns, not to mention electricity in the home, will send us all to Hell."

"He means well."

"I'm sure he does. But perhaps we should rid ourselves of our electrical before it softens our brains."

She made a face at him. "The electrical stays. You go. Anyway, I think my brain's already soft."

As she changed the next picture he said, "You look fatigued. Your doctor says you should lie down."

"I am," she admitted. "Perhaps you're right." She laid the stereopticon aside and with his arm around her shoulders and her arm across his waist, they walked to her bedroom.

"I'll call you for dinner," he said. "Rest until then."

"I hate being so tired all the time," she said, and brushed away a sudden tear. "I hate not working with you. I hate feeling like I want to cry every five seconds."

"Cry? Why? Are you afraid Mrs. McWorth will snatch me away?"

"I wouldn't put it past the old witch," she said.

"Bronwyn, you know as well as I what a precarious state you're in just now. You know how important light food and short walks in fresh air are for you. But most of all, rest and a great deal of it. I think I should hire someone to stay with you during the day. And see that you do what I say."

"Yes, sir, your worship, captain, sir, your honor, your doctorship, sir." She wrapped her arms around his neck. "I love you so much. All I want from life are you and our baby."

"We do have a good life, don't we," he said with a chuckle. "My word, but I've become complacent. I'll be fat and bald next."

She giggled. "Me too. Only not bald, I hope. I can see it now. On Sunday mornings Dr. Stuart, *paterfamilias,* will parade into the church followed by his stout but loving wife and their seventeen children."

"Seventeen! *Paterfamilias* is going to have to work much harder to support seventeen children! Now, you have a lie-down. I have to go to the stable. The boy there sent me a note that your mare was limping when he exercised her this morning. "

"Poor Cleopatra. I can hardly wait until I can ride again. Remember the rides we took at dawn when we first moved here? So romantic, with the mist from the river, and the silence."

He kissed her fingertips. "Once our child is here, we'll take many dawn rides. And we'll bicycle again and do whatever else you want to do. I promise. Perhaps before too long I'll take on an associate. Then I'll have more time to spend with you."

"That would be wonderful. Do you have anyone in mind?"

"Not really. I only know I don't want some old fogy who still wears a frock coat in the office."

"Well, I know the first thing I want to do when this associate of yours arrives on the scene. Go to Coney Island."

"Coney Island!"

"It's one thing we never did. I want to ride the Ferris wheel, and see the elephant and we can take the baby on the merry-go-round. You promised."

"And you'll hold me to it."

"I most certainly will."

"Coney Island!" he said again, laughing. He stuck out his hand. "Done. Coney Island it is. You're an underhanded baggage, Bronwyn Stuart."

Later, as he passed the gazebo on the way to the stable, he paused. Bronwyn had said the mystery man from his past had talked to her there. He still shuddered at the occasional and fantastic idea it might be Kit, but the fear was receding. The man, whoever he was, had not returned. He was a fool, jumping at shadows.

He had everything he could ever want, right there, with Bronwyn. If the mystery man turned out to be Kit, it didn't matter. Let Kit do his damnedest. He couldn't hurt them.

15

r. Stuart, sir, you have a visitor."

The day maid's voice interrupted Nick in the midst of adding new information to a patient's records, and he only half heard her. "I'm sorry," he said. "What did you say?"

"A visitor, sir. A man. He didn't give his name, sir."

Ice water. That was how the message felt. Ice water crashing into his face. Bronwyn's mystery man. Kit. What if it was Kit? He nodded and rose, and went to the small visitor's parlor across the hall, steeling himself for what he would see. He almost wilted in relief.

Smiling at him, hat in hand, was a lanky, thin man with a striped suit and vest, and an old-fashioned collar so high his chin looked imprisoned. "Dr. Stuart?" the man said. He had an Irish accent.

"Yes, but the office is closed for the day. Do you want an appointment? Is it an emergency?" The man looked the picture of health.

"No, sir. Nothin' like that. I want to see you." His thick brogue reminded Nick of his mother. "Me name's Kelly. I got a proposition," the man said.

Nick observed that the man's suit of clothes was threadbare, the collar had seen better days, the shoes were scuffed and worn-out, and he had no chain and fob stretching across his belly. "Please sit down, Mr. Kelly. What kind of proposition?"

Kelly lowered himself to the new couch and sighed. "That's nice, that is," he said in appreciation. "Well, Doc, it's a proposition that'd mean a lot o' hard work for little pay. And ye might be riskin' your neck."

"Why would you make such a proposal? And why to me, Mr. Kelly?"

"I asked other doctors and one gave me your name." He leaned toward Nick. "Sir, I live in the Bowery. We're packed like pickles in a barrel, families of eight-nine-ten or more all livin' in one or two rooms, new babies, gran'parents and all."

"I've heard conditions are appalling there, but I don't know what I could do."

"Nothin' about conditions, sir. That's just the way it is, at least for now. We ain't got a doctor to our name, sir, not one. A bunch of us got to thinkin' maybe folks wouldn't drop dead like summer flies if we had a doctor. We got plenty of females, sir, and they tend t'be lusty breeders. Too many of 'em die. Too many of the babies die. We'll take up collections to pay you. It wouldn't be much, but you'd be there to treat us Irish. You wouldn't have to dirty your hands with kikes or niggers or dagoes."

"Mr. Kelly, I'm sorry. But my practice here occupies me most of the time, I'm at the hospital several hours a week, I teach nursing students, and I'll be a father soon. I wouldn't have time."

The corners of Kelly's mouth turned down. "Should've known. Could've saved the ten cents it cost to come here. And I got me suit out of hock, too. And I had to borrow a collar from me brother."

"I wish I could help. I'll be glad to pay your fare home."

"I ain't one for charity."

Looking at him, Nick saw his long-ago surgery in London. He remembered the long, long hours and the hunger. No, he could not do that again, under any circumstances. And then he remembered frail little Jane and her twins, and other women worn out from bearing child after child and trying to survive with too little food.

"See here, Kelly, I might be able to be there in a surgery for a few hours a week and that would have to suffice. Let me think on it a day or so."

"Just a few hours, sir, would save some lives, give some ease."
He stood and held out his hand. "I'll be goin' now, sir. I'll see you
again, soon."

Nick jotted down Kelly's address, saying as he did so, "Mr. Kelly,
I haven't committed myself."

"I know, sir. But I can tell by lookin' at you that you're a caring
man and I know you'll do it."

Nick knew, just as sure as he knew the sun came up in the East,
that he would do as this man requested. He wondered how
Bronwyn would react. If not for the baby, he knew she would be
enthusiastic. Now, he couldn't even guess what she'd say. He also
knew he could not call himself a physician if he turned his back
on people in need.

"We got a place all picked out," Kelly said as they went to the
front door. "It used to be a kike business."

"Mr. Kelly, one thing must be understood at the start. I'll turn
no one away. If that's not acceptable then you'll have to look elsewhere."

For an instant Kelly's jaw became pugnacious. "But who'd want
ye to touch him if you'd just touched a kike or a nigger?"

"That cuts both ways, Mr. Kelly. They might not want me to
touch them after I'd treated a mick." Kelly's nostrils flared, but
before he could retort Nick said, "Nothing personal. I'm half mick
myself. My mother was from a village near Derry."

The hard jaw softened. "Well, sir, one Irishman to another, we'll
do whatever you say."

After Kelly had gone, Nick regretted the impetuous decision
he'd already made. Kit had laughed at him for not being adventurous enough. Well, committing himself to work in a dangerous
part of the city for a small stipend ought to be adventurous enough
to satisfy even Kit. Oh, why wouldn't that damned name stay out
of his head?

Two days later, Nick met Kelly at the hospital and hired a cab to
take them to the Lower East Side. The cabdriver balked at pen-
etrating clear to Oliver Street. "I'll take yez as far as is safe and
yez can walk from there."

Kelly looked at Nick and shrugged. "He's afraid we'll eat the
horse," he said.

"Would you?"

"Had worse."

They had to walk several blocks through neighborhoods that were increasingly bleak and ugly, and denser with people. The dinginess, the sullen and suspicious faces, the worn-out women and dirty-faced children could have been plucked from Whitechapel. "I see no Negroes," Nick said. "Nor Chinese nor Italians. I thought you were worried I might treat some of them."

"Just a bare chance one of 'em might stray down here, Doc. Someday they can have these dumps. We'll get out. They won't."

"Mr. Kelly, I meant what I said. No one will be refused treatment."

"Hey, Kelly, who's the swell?" someone called.

"The new doc I brought back," Kelly hollered, his hands around his mouth. Nick felt like a prize fish. A tail of noisy children followed along hooting and tugging at Nick's coattail until Kelly chased them away. Two of Kelly's friends joined them, and a few minutes later they were at the "old kike store," on the ground floor of a tenement. Heads poked out of windows as the occupants looked out to see what the fuss was about.

Kelly and two of his friends stood expectantly beside the door as Nick finished his brief tour. The place was filthy and infested with insects and vermin, but it would serve if cleaned up. It was larger than the one in London.

"Well?" Kelly asked, "What's the verdict, Doc?"

"Sure, Doc," said one of the friends, "it'll do fine, won't it? Get some brawny lasses down here with mop buckets and we got a surgery!"

"It will take more than that. You men have to take responsibility for getting it emptied out, cleaned up and painted."

"Painted?" someone squawked.

"Painted. Every inch. Twice. I won't treat people in a sty."

"That's a lot of work," said the third man, scratching his head.

"Ye sure a good scrubbin' won't..." The second man's voice trailed off as Nick stared at him.

"Doc wants it painted, we paint it," said Kelly.

"I'll need a cabinet with a stout lock and an examining table and some chairs. Get me someone to help, boy or girl, man or woman, doesn't matter, someone strong in case I need help with a patient. Put a door on that open doorway. Paint everything white but the floor. I'll need someone responsible for keeping it clean. And I do mean *clean*. I don't want any trouble from the landlord. And I don't want any trouble from whatever gang runs this neighborhood, either."

Kelly said in a no-nonsense tone of voice. "Landlord's already given the go-ahead. The gang won't bother you. You got my word on that."

Nick looked hard at the other two. "I'll come back in a week. If it doesn't meet my standards you'll do it again. Is that understood?"

"Yes," Kelly said firmly, answering for his friends.

"Good." Nick left the dirty shop and stepped out once more into the noisy street. Pushcarts lined both sides of the narrow street. Peddlers haggled with customers over sunken-eyed fish and shriveled vegetables. The street was frequently blocked by carts and wagons pulled by horses too decrepit to interest even a knacker. Voices of both sexes and all ages filled the air with a continuous shrill cacophony. Every doorway was peopled with groups of talking women or sullen men. A fight broke out between two men; other men gathered to watch. Broken glass littered the equally broken sidewalks. Excrement lay in smelly fresh flops in the streets. Large, vicious horseflies rose in swarms, almost as numerous as the people. At least, Nick thought, in the better parts of the city the government made an effort to clean the streets once in a while. A rat passed brazenly at his feet and paused long enough to give him a beady look.

Among the broken glass and the excrement, children ran and screamed, played and fought. Listless small children stayed with the women, many of whom were pregnant or holding an infant. Nick had read that more than a thousand people per acre lived here, and that tuberculosis, influenza, syphilis, gonorrhea, malnutrition, childbearing illnesses, violence, alcohol made from garbage, and every childhood disease known to man, were rampant. He wondered if he would be able to make even a tiny dent in the misery.

"Ready to go, Doc?" Kelly asked. "I'll see ye safe to the polite side of town. Ye don't want to be down here alone for a while and even then I'd be careful. Check your pockets ever once in a while. Some of these kids is slick. And if you're smart, you'll get a pistol and learn to use it."

By the time Nick got to the hospital he was an hour late to do his rounds. As he shrugged into his white coat, an older doctor in black wool, smirked. Nick gave him an overly polite bow, then realized to his chagrin he had unwittingly borrowed that sarcastic gesture from Kit. He went to the maternity ward first, to check the progress of a mother and her two-day-old infant. She was in high spirits and the infant could not have been better.

Most of his patients preferred to deliver at home and Nick encouraged them in that. Even a well-run hospital, he suspected, was a haven for bacteria and infection. Even in the short time he'd practiced in the city, he had become known as a doctor who seldom lost a mother or baby to infection. His patients were often amused by his rubber gloves and his no-nonsense insistence on hand washing, and by his rumpled white coats.

As he went into the mothers and babies ward to see a patient, Nick was pleased to see a young doctor wearing a crisp, new white coat. The fingers of a rubber glove made a comically obscene gesture from a pocket. He was new to the hospital, and it took Nick a moment to remember his name. Galvin. David Galvin. That was it.

Nick watched him a moment as he spoke with a girl who held a newborn. Dr. Galvin looked up and grinned. "My first caesarian, Doctor Stuart," he said. He looked as proud as if he had invented babies.

Nick nodded. "It looks as if mother and child are both doing well, Doctor Galvin. Congratulations are in order to all three of you."

Over the next few days he became more aware of young Dr. Galvin's presence in the hospital, and observed him with his patients. He had a soothing manner. His touch seemed gentle and sure. Perhaps Dr. Galvin's coming to this hospital just now was providential. One morning Nick asked him to lunch with him the next day at the Brevoort; he had an important matter to discuss with him.

The Brevoort dining room was more than he could afford, really, but if all went well this would turn out to be an auspicious occasion worth the expense.

During the excellent dinner, they talked about patients and recent medical news. A little gossip and mutual disgust with the mustard yellow walls in the hospital came in for their share of discussion. Both were keenly interested in the work of Roentgen in Germany.

"Isn't it strange," David said, "to think we'll be able to see into the body without cutting it open? I'd give anything to see it work."

"So would I. We should try to attend his next symposium. You know, don't you, his work is the work of Satan, according to some of the local churchmen."

"Someone should tell them the Middle Ages are over."

Over dessert, Nick came to the reason for the luncheon. "I have been thinking of taking in an associate, Dr. Galvin. My home practice has grown tremendously, not to mention the hospital, the nurses' school, and I've just agreed to open a clinic in the Bowery. And I'm going to be a father very soon. The truth is, I'm only one man and I'm feeling stretched too thin. I want time with my family, but I don't want to neglect my commitments. Would you consider working with me?"

"Would I! Is this a formal proposal? Are you interviewing other doctors? Are you—"

Nick laughed. "We'll have to work out the details. And there are no other candidates. I've been watching you work and I like what I see. But if you come in with me, I'll expect you to take my place in the clinic from time to time. I did the same kind of work in London, and I guarantee you'll learn more general medicine there than you would in a year anywhere else. The population is as volatile as it is overcrowded. Not the safest place to work. Can you agree to that?"

"Of course."

Just then Nick's attention was caught by a group of four being taken to their table by the headwaiter. A petite, red-haired woman followed by three men. One of the men had thinning hair and a luxurious mustache. The middle man was dark-haired and handsome, in early middle age. The other was younger. He was tall; his hair was fair. He bore an uncanny resemblance to Kit.

A sudden paralysis swept over Nick. Dear God. Kit. It *was* Kit. What was he doing in America? Was he the man who had come to the house? David spoke. Nick heard his voice but not his words. He could not take his eyes from Kit. He was too thin. Wasn't he taking proper care of himself? Every passionate and tender and laughing moment they had shared rushed through Nick's brain in a tangled skein of memories. He prayed Kit would not see him. Kit did not look in that direction and when he was seated, his back was to Nick.

Nick dragged his gaze back to David. "We'll talk more in a few days. But I—" Against his will he glanced again at the back of Kit's head. "I must go. My wife is waiting."

Over David's protests, he paid for both dinners and left. He had been so certain he would never see Kit again! And there he was, only a few feet away. He prayed Kit had not seen him.

Kit had seen Nick the moment he entered the dining room, and to his embarrassment, he stumbled, wrenching his injured ankle. After his party were seated, he risked a discreet look behind him. Nick was gone. So was his attractive young companion. It didn't take much imagination to put one and one together.

He forced himself to put aside his hateful vision of Stuart and his whore cavorting in a hotel room, and turned his full focus to the discussion at hand. Shortly after they met, Minnie had introduced him to Steele MacKaye, a theatrical engineering genius who had made and lost several fortunes. Kit had instantly recognized MacKaye as a kindred spirit, willing to gamble on new ideas. MacKaye had proudly shown Kit the innovations in his theatre, the Lyceum, and he had been generous with suggestions for Kit's theatre.

Thanks to MacKaye, the stage would be so well lit the actors would no longer have to come to the footlights to be seen by the audience. Velvet drapes would sweep in from the sides instead of rolling down from above. Patrons would have tickets showing the seat number and row, a small matter unless one had witnessed patrons coming to blows over seating. An asbestos curtain, Steele's invention, would protect the audience from the disastrous backstage fires that took lives every season.

Like MacKaye's Lyceum, Kit's theatre would be cooled in summer and warmed in winter. MacKaye took great pains to explain how the air could be fortified with ozone and circulated by fans in summer to blow over huge blocks of ice, and in winter to blow over radiators. These marvelous ideas added heavily to the cost, and Kit had mortgaged a large portion of land at St. Denys Hill.

Tonight, talk turned to Kit's favorite MacKaye invention: a system of two stages, one beneath the other. Complete sets could be put in place on each. Massive arrangements of gears and levers lifted one stage out of sight while the new one rose from below.

"You must come to London," Kit said, "and install those stages for me in the Xavier." MacKaye agreed. Kit's enthusiasm for the project put Nick out of his thoughts, at least until he was alone.

In his suite again, Kit drank and raged. He damned Nick Stuart to hell and back, and kicked everything he could kick. His ankle throbbed wildly by the time he dropped into an exhausted, half-drunk sleep.

The next morning he arrived at the theatre late and stopped in his tracks in the foyer, where painters were busily at work. "Francis!" he bellowed. "Come here. Now!" Francis, in the auditorium, was annoyed by the summons and took his time. "I didn't think you'd get here before the turn of the century," snapped Kit.

"I'm not a slave, in case you hadn't noticed," Francis said. "What's wrong?"

"Look at the color of this wall. Just look at it!"

"It's what you ordered."

"I didn't order paint that looks like dog piss."

"It's pale gold. You chose it. What do you want me to do?"

"Why should you do anything? Nobody cares about this place but me. Why don't you just go to England? See if I care."

Francis motioned the painters away. When he and Kit were alone, he said, "Talk. What's deviling you now?"

"Piss-colored paint."

"No, it's not. You're acting like a two-year-old who's had his favorite toy taken away. That means it's something to do with Stuart."

"No such thing." Kit bit his lip, then admitted, "I saw him last night. At the Brevoort. I was with MacKaye and the Fiskes and saw him making sheep-eyes at some cheap-looking, two-shilling-a-night rent-me-arse."

"Why do you care?"

"I don't." He jabbed the floor with his cane. "I don't—" (jab) "give a—" (jab) "double—" (jab, jab) "damn!"

"Kit?"

"What?"

"Why won't you admit you still care about him?"

Kit stared into Frank's honest eyes. Then he abruptly said, "Do you really think this color paint is acceptable?"

"Yes, I do. Come along, now. Let the painters do what you're paying them to do. You haven't made a complete inspection for a few days. Come see what miracles we have wrought, my man!"

With the boards gone and new glass in the windows, the auditorium was bright with sunlight. The old seats were gone, new seats ordered. The floor had been stripped and awaited refinishing and polishing. Beneath the stage, the four dressing rooms had been enlarged, and were waiting for fresh paint, new mirrors, electric lights, makeup tables, lavatories and running water. Large wardrobes would be installed in each room. Kit's dressing room, the largest of the four, would also have a custom-made, locking cabinet and a bathtub. The bathtub would have another innovation: a shower bath. There was even an indoor loo constructed at the end of the hall.

By this time, Kit's bad temper had dissipated. "I'll be at the hotel if you need me," he said. "I've an enormous pile of post waiting for me. I haven't opened an envelope for more than a week."

Every spare minute had been spent with MacKaye or Minnie, or trying to charm more money from an Astor here, a Vanderbilt there, a Lowell elsewhere. He wished Rama could have been with him, but she had found a well-paying job teaching Deportment and Elocution at the Squires Academy For Select Young Gentlewomen. He missed her.

He sorted through the letters, disappointed Lizbet had not written. She always wrote at once when she received a gift, telling him he should not have spent the money, scolding him for not delivering it in person, wishing him love. A letter from his solicitor enclosed the papers that mortgaged the Xavier and land from St. Denys Hill. He held them for a long time and promised his father he would not lose the land and theatre they both loved. Then with firm resolve he put the document into the small metal box with other important papers.

Three letters came from female admirers who made coy advances; one letter contained a key. Another, with interesting pornographic suggestions, was written in a heavy, masculine hand. That one, to his mild regret, included neither name nor key.

The envelope on the bottom was from the housekeeper at the Hill. Assuming it was her quarterly report of expenditures, he laid it aside to be dealt with later. Then he changed his mind and opened it; he had to look at the boring thing sooner or later. Instead, he took out a letter. Odd. She had never before written a letter.

> Dear Young Sir,
>   It is with grief I have to write to inform you of terrible loss to us and to yourself. Miss Elizabeth is dead

He sat bolt upright. An invisible fist slammed into his chest and closed tight around his heart. He could not breathe. His horror mounted with each word.

Dear Young Sir,

It is with grief I have to write to inform you of terrible loss to us and to yourself. Miss Elizabeth is dead taken by the Lord in a most terrible accident. Her little house was caught on fire in the middle of the night whilst she was asleep. Everything was burned up but the walls and the chimney. She was found in bed. We pray she died quick and didn't suffer.

We arranged for her to be buried here at the Hill with Mr. St. Denys and your family and we hope you approve of going ahead. We had a nice funeral service in the village church and the rector said she was a good woman. There is but a simple marker at her grave now as we thought you would want to see to a proper one on your return. All the staff here wants you to know we sympathize with your grief, Young Sir, because we know you and Miss Elizabeth were the best of friends.

He was unable to move, speak, or weep. Why did this happen? Dear God, dear God! Lizbet. Dead. How could it be? Lizbet was meant to live forever. Lizbet, who had taken worthless Jack Rourke and gave him a love of theatre, coached his first lines, washed blood from his face. Lizbet, who would have fought the Devil to protect him. The kindest, best woman who ever lived. Lizbet. Dead.

A sudden memory shook him. He had heard a woman cry out in his mind. The woman had sounded like Lizbet. From his frozen throat one brief, keening cry escaped. "Lizbet! No!"

16

ronwyn nervously rearranged the flowers on the new cherry wood dining table. Nicholas had not told her until the previous evening that the new associate who was coming to dinner was Dr. David Galvin. She wondered if the young doctor who had once brought her flowers would even remember her. Not that she cared. Still, she knew it would tickle her vanity if he did. She had been tempted to put on a corset, but had decided against it. Nicholas was adamant about it, believing them to be dangerous for pregnant women. Well, she would just have to stand very straight, suck in her middle, and not breathe.

She looked critically at the flowers, removed one and put it back. Just then Nicholas came in with their guest. She had forgotten how handsome Dr. Galvin was. He held a small bouquet.

"David, may I present my wife," Nick said proudly as Bronwyn smiled and held out her hand. "She tells me you met when she was at the nursing school."

David Galvin stared, seeming nonplussed for a moment before taking her hand and bowing over it. "Charmed." He handed her the bouquet. "For my gracious hostess. I didn't realize Mrs. Stuart was once Miss King."

She blushed and laughed softly. "Nor did I know until yesterday the name of my husband's new associate. Welcome to our home, Dr. Galvin."

"It was once my earnest hope," David said, still looking at her, "to win the hand of the best nurse and prettiest lady I ever met. But she never had time for me. She was hopelessly gone over some English doctor. My congratulations, Doctor. You're a lucky man."

"How well I know," Nick said, wondering why Bronwyn hadn't told him David had once courted her. Somehow he had never considered that Bronwyn had once had other suitors. He was glad of the previous acquaintance. It would make the transition to having him present in the surgery every day much easier.

❦

Years before, a novelist had told Kit, "Good or bad, everything that happens to an artist eventually comes out in the art." The man had been a fool in many ways, but Kit was coming to realize he had been right about that. Whenever he stopped working long enough to allow himself to think about Michael, St. Denys, and Lizbet, it was like losing them all over again. Nick's desertion was no small part of that sense of loss. And yet, his grief brought something out in him as an actor.

Minnie noticed it before he did. He brought to the role of Angel Clare a vulnerability that had not been there before. Angel Clare had always been easy to condemn, but now, as he begged Tess to forgive him when all was lost, one realized that he was damning himself far more than anyone else could. Should he not be pitied just a little for the foolishness that sent the woman he loved to the gallows?

One afternoon Minnie answered a knock and found Kit there with a small man, each holding one end of something covered with burlap. "Minnie, forgive my bad manners," Kit said, "but we have to come in before we drop it."

"Kit, you're up to no good. But come in. Whatever that thing is I don't want it all over the floor in front of my door."

"On the contrary, I'm up to a great deal of good. Be a dear and clear that table." Minnie removed a vase of flowers, a lamp, and two books, and then watched as they placed the strange object onto the table. Mr. Morris pulled off the burlap to expose a large square wooden cabinet with a handle on top.

"What in the world is it?" she asked, unable to wait any longer.

"The Twentieth Century, Minnie," Kit said, "right here in the parlor. A Graphophone Talking Machine."

With a showman's florid gestures, Morris removed the machine from the case, put on a wax cylinder, and positioned the reading horn. "The Twentieth Century, right here," he echoed, smiling like a proud parent.

Kit said, "We're going to make a record, Minnie. You and I. Some key dialogue with just Tess and Angel. We'll reproduce them and give them to stores that sell Graphophones. The stores will advertise that they have them; Mrs. A will listen to one and tell Mrs. B who will tell Mrs. C. The free publicity will be priceless. The Trust can stop us from advertising in the newspapers. They can't stop people from talking."

"I don't know," she said, a frown of doubt appearing. "I've never heard myself on one of these contraptions. "

"Contraption, Ma'am?" Morris cried. "This is a superb machine, the best there is, and the best there will ever be."

"My apologies, Mr. Morris. Well, then. Mr. St. Denys, your humble handmaid awaits."

Later, Minnie clutched Kit's hand and held her breath as they waited for Morris to work his magic. He removed the smaller horn into which they had spoken and replaced it with a longer horn with a much larger bell. As he repositioned the cylinder and cranked the machine, Minnie held her breath. For a moment only a slight scratching came from the machine. And then they heard it. Angel's first light and flirtatious words to dairymaid Tess, and her shy, confused reply. This was followed by Tess' confession of Alec D'Urbervilles seduction of her, and Angel's cruel repudiation of her following her confession.

"It's wonderful," Minnie said, applauding. "How amazing! And you're right. People will talk and there's nothing the Trust can do about it. But doesn't it give away too much of the plot?"

"Enough that the ladies will come with a half dozen handkerchiefs. Shall we do it?"

"Oh, yes!"

"I've made an appointment for photographs of you, me and Coghlan in costume." He hesitated. "You are still determined to use Coghlan, aren't you?"

Her answer was a firm, "Yes." Charles Coghlan had been the only disagreement between them. Coghlan was ideal in the part, but he had a history of walking out on productions. "I'll keep him in line," Minnie said. "What will we do with the pictures?"

"We'll put posters on every wall not controlled by the Trust. And if they're torn down, we'll put up more. We'll pass out broadsides on the street corners."

"We must begin reading with the rest of the cast at once," Minnie said with a decisive nod of her head. "We can work here in the small ballroom until your theatre is ready. When do you think that will be?"

"Within six weeks. The electrical is being installed this week and as soon as there is light I'll pay double the wages and work around the clock."

"Good. We'll begin blocking in the ballroom."

He nodded. "And what the scenic artist?"

"Hired. He's excellent; the best I've ever seen. And the electrical lighting artist?"

"I have him." With a grin, he added, "He was fired from a Trust theatre for calling them 'a bunch of damned hooligans.'"

"Kit, I have one role uncast. Did Miss Weisberg stay in New York? Would she consider playing Izz and understudying me? I've seen her perform. She's very good."

"Of course she will," he said, though he had no idea how to talk her into it. Facing the Devil would be easier.

"Now," Minnie said, "all I have to do is get the director under contract. He's dragging his heels."

⚜

Kit took a deep breath before he rang the bell beneath the tasteful sign: Squires Academy for Select Young Ladies. He was taking the coward's way out by seeing Rama at the academy instead of at her rooming house. At least here, with witnesses, she wouldn't be as likely to kill him. A light-skinned Negro maid admitted him to the formal parlor. Moments later a woman with a plump, fluffy body and flinty eyes came in: Miss Squires herself.

"Please," he said. "I need to speak to my cousin, Miss Weisberg."

In a crisp, precise tone, Miss Squires said, "Our ladies are not allowed to entertain gentlemen here."

"Miss Squires, it's terribly important." He put on a look of desperate pleading. She resisted a moment, then without comment, she tugged four times at the pull cord that rang the summons bell code in the upstairs classrooms.

The day he had gone to the school to tell Rama about Lizbet, he had been too distraught to notice her appearance. Now he looked down to hide his grin when she arrived wearing a plain black dress with a collar that went clear to her jaw, a gold watch on a gold bow hanging upon her oddly reduced bosom, and her rebellious hair drawn back into a severe bun.

Kit put an extra dollop of charm into his smile. "Miss Squires, I must speak with Miss Weisberg alone."

"That is out of the question. No spinster may entertain a male person unchaperoned. Ever. Our Academy's reputation is synonymous with the reputations of our staff." Over the woman's shoulder, Rama rolled her eyes in a silent plea for help.

He looked soulfully at the headmistress. "It's a serious and delicate family matter. Surely a lady of your refinement will understand."

"It's against the rules."

"Please. I beg you. Five minutes. Surely a school with the sterling reputation of this one can grant me five small minutes with my cousin." He repeated, "It's extremely serious."

The woman thawed a little. "Five minutes," she said. "Not one second longer." She stepped into the hall and pulled the door closed.

As soon as the door shut behind Miss Squires, Rama fell into his arms. "I'm dying here! And just look at these horrid clothes. The only hat I'm allowed here is small and plain. I'm surprised they haven't made me color my hair black! And I have to wear a binder because I have, as Miss Squires put it, too much bosom for a respectable spinster! I wish she didn't pay so well!" Kit spluttered with repressed laughter and she punched his shoulder, hard. "It isn't funny. Please, tell me your theatre is finished and we're ready to perform again!"

"I have a part for you."

"Wonderful! I don't even care what it is. Lady Macbeth? Kate?"

"Izz."

"What?" She looked blankly at him.

"The part of Izz in *Tess of the d'Urbervilles*. Mrs. Fiske thinks you're perfect and so do I."

"Mrs. Fiske!"

He flinched. If Wellington had made that kind of error they'd be speaking French. "Rama, hear me out."

"A small part?"

"Small but important."

She turned away from him. "I'm a leading lady, Kit. I am *your* leading lady. Something you've forgotten while I've slaved in this refined dungeon."

"It's just one play. Then you'll be my leading lady again. My theatre will be a success. You'll see. Do it for me. Mrs. Fiske wants you to understudy her."

"You're wheedling." Then, frowning, she asked, "She agreed to let me understudy?"

"It was her idea."

"Her idea? You didn't ask for me?"

Damn. Another battlefield error. "For a little while Izz thinks she's going to be Angel Clare's mistress," he coaxed, playing with the gold watch on her bosom. "I'm playing Angel Clare."

Rama snorted and slapped his hand away. "I hope she had a better chance than I have. What about money, Kit? Here I have a secure job and a regular income."

"You hate it. And what good is the money if you can't go out and buy a red frock and a hat the size of Buckingham Palace?"

"But once *Tess* is over, what then? I won't go on playing second fiddle to Mrs. Fiske."

"We'll rebuild the Company, divide our time between New York and London. I'll own a theatre both places."

"And you think the Trust will simply vanish?"

"The Trust will be dealt with." He trailed his thumb down her jaw to her chin. "You'll do it?"

"As if you doubted it. When do you want me?"

"Next week," he said, reaching into his inside pocket. "I accidentally have a script with me."

She took it and shook it at him. "Bloody sure of yourself, Mr. St. Denys! Bloody sure of yourself!"

He hugged her. "You're a trouper," he said.

"I'm a bloomin' idiot."

Kit arrived at the theatre, expecting to hear the orchestra of hammers, saws, and heavy feet accompanying a chorus of talking, cursing, joking men. Instead, silence. His heels echoed on the floors. A large fly droned past his ear. There were no other sounds in the auditorium. Francis, alone, sat on the top apron stair. "They're gone," he said, dejection in his voice. "Carpenters, painters, the entire lot."

A man spoke behind Kit. Kelton, the policeman he'd hired away from Erlanger. "Trust bought 'em," Kelton said. "They tried to buy me too."

"I paid more than anyone in the city. I made sure of that!"

"The Trust found out what you were paying," Francis said, "and gave each man a month's wages to walk out and sign an agreement not to work for you."

Kelton spoke up. "They say your theatre's dead, sir."

"They'd like to think so. I'll bring workmen from Canada if I must."

"Well, sir," Kelton said. He fidgeted, twisting his cap in his hands, "I'll need to find myself a new job."

"It would appear so, Mr. Kelton." Kit looked about, jaw tight, eyes unreadable. "What a cock-up. What a bloody-damned cock-up this is!"

"But maybe I could just hang around, sir?" Kelton asked. "I could sweep and things like that, or anything else you need done. I got me a wife and five children t'feed."

"All right. Stay. One loyal man out of the whole pack." To Francis he said, "I'm going back to the hotel. Come with me."

They left Kelton standing there. Outside, Francis said, "You should sack him. Somebody's been telling the Trust everything. I think it's Kelton."

"Don't you think I know an honest man when I see one?"

"I doubt it."

Annoyed, Kit said nothing else. As they crossed the lobby, the clerk called, "Mr. St. Denys. A word with you?" Francis continued on alone to the restaurant. "Mr. St. Denys, you have a visitor," the clerk said. "A gentleman, in the Smoking Room."

The Gentlemen's Smoking Room was a fashionable cave of dark carpet, dark paisley drapes, dark-toned floral wallpaper, several brass spittoons, and threatening potted palms. One of the ugliest rooms Kit had ever seen. He avoided it whenever possible. A solitary figure stood beside the fireplace. "Sir?" Kit asked. "Are you the— Nico?" His voice was harsh. "It isn't a gentleman. It's an ass. What is it doing here?"

"Please. I must talk with you."

"Go home to your wife."

"Please talk to me. Someplace private."

Kit shrugged. "My suite." Nick followed him to the lift. There, not a word was spoken and Kit refused to look at him. In the suite,

Nick sat in the chair Kit indicated. Kit remained standing, and leaned against the desk, one ankle crossed over the other in a show of unconcern.

"You came to my home," Nick said.

"I did."

"Why?"

"I intended to wreck that cozy parody of respectability you've built."

"What stopped you?"

"Your wife."

"What's that supposed to mean?"

"It means, had she been the shrew I expected I would have told her without turning a hair." His voice dropped. "She's a gracious lady. You don't deserve her."

"For once we agree."

The momentary silence was so complete they both jumped when the mantelpiece clock struck the hour. "You're like a damned disease!" Nick said. "I don't *want* to think about you. And sometimes I believe I'm cured of you and then, without warning, you're back in my mind. I promised God I'd never want you again." He looked so woebegone Kit almost felt sorry for him. "And here I am. Promise broken." He stood up. "It was a mistake to come here. Seeing you again... too many memories."

"All bad, Nico?"

"Don't call me that." Nick tried to say it as a warning, but it came out as a helpless plea.

"Before you go, I must have the answer to something. Did you ever love me?" Nick's look of astonishment was all the answer he needed. "Nico, are you happy?"

"I'm content."

Kit grimaced. "Contentment is for cows chewing their cud in a field and old cats asleep by a fire! I'm proud to say you were never content with me."

"I was a great many things with you. Angry, crazy, jealous, wicked."

A muscle knotted in Kit's jaw. "And you were happy as long as you allowed yourself to be. Admit it! I taught you how to be young and enjoy life. I taught you that your body was more than a piece of inconvenient baggage fit for nothing. I taught you how to love, damn you. You knew nothing until you met me."

"And you learned nothing from me?"

"Oh, yes. I learned how to tolerate a fool."

They glared at each other. "Fool?" Nick demanded. "You're call-ing me a fool?"

"You called me worse than that."

Nick reached for the door. Kit grabbed his arm and turned him half-around. "You're not going to leave here until you admit you were happy with me."

"You're right," Nick said, throwing Kit's hand off his arm. "I was. But you changed all that, not I. You opened my eyes to just how vile we were."

"You lie. It was you and your damned Puritan condemnation that ruined things." And then Kit saw himself and Rawdon McPherson as they must have looked through Nick's eyes that night. Rawdon had aroused him; he couldn't deny it. And Nick had been watching. "My God," he said, stricken.

Nick turned again toward the door. "This is just rubbing salt in a wound."

"Nick, wait. That night at the Hill, with Rawdon, it meant nothing."

"I don't want to hear about it."

"I was wrong. I should have shown at least a little common sense and decency."

"A little decency is all you ever showed."

"You damned me without giving me a chance to defend myself. Well, that's the way of your kind; I accept that. But you have to accept me as I am, too."

"I don't have to accept anything."

"You do. You know you do. Nico, like it or not we're bound together forever."

"What are you talking about?" The question was a feeble attempt to fend off the longing that had built in Nick since that first sight of him at the Brevoort. He gripped the door handle so tightly his fingers hurt, and he closed his eyes as Kit trailed his mouth across the back of his neck. Kit's teeth gently nipped the same spot he had bitten their first night together.

"Bound together, Nico," he repeated. "Hearts and minds." His breath was warm against Nick's ear. "Souls." He made Nick face him. "Bodies."

"Oh, God." Nick did not know if he uttered a prayer or blasphemy as Kit's mouth and tongue sought his. Kit slid his hands inside Nick's coat and downward to spread over his backside, forcing Nick's stubbornly resisting body against his. "I can't do this, Kit. I can't. I have a wife. We're going to have a baby. I've got to leave here." He turned once more toward the door.

"Give me an hour, Nico," Kit said. "For old time's sake. An hour. Is that so much to ask?"

Nick looked into his eyes and said in a strangled voice, "You are my private devil, do you know that?"

"No. I'm not," Kit said without a smile. "I'm your one true love. You simply don't know it yet." And then he kissed him savagely.

It was much more than an hour before they untangled their naked limbs on the bed. Nick lay back. The guilt would come. But not yet. "Whether you believe it or not, I did want to leave," he said.

"If that were true, you would never have come here in the first place."

"I thought the answer was to go away from England, away from the familiar places." Nick sighed. "Now I don't know what to do. Rather, I know what I should do. But I can't." He gave an inarticulate murmur as Kit lay down beside him, and gently cradled his sex.

"You can have it all, Nico. Your family. Your practice. And me. No strings, no demands. We'll be discreet, take whatever time we can have and be grateful for it. The one thing I won't do is share you with God again."

"I doubt if God would have me now." A feeble little voice in Nick's head urged him to fight the good fight again and keep on fighting. But that feeble little voice was lost in a soft moan as Kit's warm hands made the heat rise again. And then nothing mattered but this hour, this minute, and this man.

Escapes were neither easy nor common from Dartmoor Prison, but Tom Rourke, model prisoner, had stood prison life as long as he could. He worked out a plan with two others to flee from a work crew in the moors by jumping a stone wall. The day of the planned escape he was assigned to work inside. Damned lucky. Of the two would-be escapees, one had been killed outright and the other brought back and beaten to death by the warders. Every time he tried working in tandem with some other bloke it ended bad. From now on he'd go it alone. So he bided his time, planned, and watched.

Warder Peabody was about his size and build. On a chill, foggy night, when the time seemed right, he lured Peabody into his cell by pretending to be sick. With one well-placed and expert blow he broke the warder's neck, switched clothes, and walked out of the prison a free man.

The search for the escaped convict in the warder's uniform was pursued vigorously. His body was found a few days later, in a river, his face eaten away by fishes. Satisfied Rourke had been found, further search was abandoned. But this, like many things, was not what it seemed. A stroppy bloke on a dark road had made the fatal mistake of picking a fight with Tom Rourke. He finished the fight with a broken neck, a warder's uniform, and a watery grave.

A rust bucket of a steamer called the Dazzling Lady set out from Liverpool on a beautiful April day, bound for New York City. One of the stokers was a brawny man with a gray-streaked black beard and mean eyes that kept everyone at a distance.

With every shovel full of coal he fed the red maw of the boiler he told himself aloud, "Soon I ain't goin' t'have t'work no more. Live like a bloody gen'leman. The brat'll pay through the nose t'keep his secrets." He often broke into laughter.

"Loony old man," the other stokers called him behind his back. They could see that under the grime was the kind of pallor a man got only from a long stay in stir.

An American stoker claimed to know what made the crazy old man tick. "I used t'live with a Creole gal in N'Orleans. She taught me about voodoo. I tell you, that old man's got the evil eye. I'm keepin' away from him. Don't want him puttin' no hex on me!"

The others laughed, and one cackled, "I reckon you think he can change into a bat or somethin'."

"Wouldn't surprise me none," the American retorted, and made the sign to ward off the evil eye.

17

Nick kissed Bronwyn's cheek and gave her the silk shawl he had brought. "I'm sorry, dearest," he said, "There was an emergency at the hospital." He hoped he sounded convincing. He hated lying, but he was prepared to lie and lie again if he had to. He couldn't lose Kit again.

It still seemed strange. He and Kit had parted in anger, and met again with distrust. Yet now that the barrier was gone, they talked, and loved and laughed, as though they had never been apart. And Kit was right: he could have it all. Why not? He loved them both. What Bronwyn didn't know could not hurt her and he'd make sure she never knew. Because the burden of guilt had not fallen on him, Nick knew God had given up on him. He would have to make the best of it.

Bronwyn draped the shawl over her shoulders and busied herself arranging it, hoping he didn't notice her tear-stained face. He'd rung her on the telephone the night before and told her he had to stay in the city. She knew she was being foolish; a doctor's life was not his own. "It's beautiful," she said.

He lifted her face and seemed surprised. "You've been crying! Why?"

She shook her head and tried to laugh. "You know how emotional pregnant women can be. I was worried."

"But I talked to you on the telephone. I thought you didn't mind."

"Of course I mind." She kissed him, to make light of her worries. "My handsome husband alone in the big city with thousands of unattached women? But it's all right. I understand."

"I'm going to stay in the city on Wednesdays, " he said. "I'm too tired most of the time to make the trip home. But I'll hire a woman to stay with you. I don't want you alone."

"I'll ask Ida. She's a good friend, and a good nurse. And she's already here."

He hesitated only a moment. It would give Bronwyn ease. And he could be with Kit without worrying about Bronwyn. The perfect solution.

❦

Nick did not know what to say when Kit took him to the theatre for the first time a fortnight later. It looked like half-finished chaos.

"The Trust stole my entire work crew away except for that fellow." He made a vague gesture toward a broad-shouldered young man. "He's loyal, anyway. But there's not much he can do alone. I have to find workmen. I've advertised, but the only ones to answer were drunkards or too old to work. But I'll find a way if it takes every shilling I possess. I'll advertise in Canadian newspapers."

Nick looked about. Kit was capable of accomplishing anything, he thought. But this looked too big even for him.

The solution came to Nick in the middle of the night a week later and he shook Kit awake. "I know what to do," he said, excitement in his voice.

Kit yawned. "So do I, but I'm too tired. Go back to sleep."

"I know what to do about your theatre."

Kit looked up at him. "What? I've racked my brain and I have no solution yet."

"What kind of workmen do you need?"

"I'll take what I can get, as long as they're sober and strong."

"Come with me to my surgery next week. There are a lot of men there who either can't find work or can find nothing but menial work for starvation wages. Some of them, I'm sure, would prefer to steal, bash you over the head, cut your throat or sell you their sisters instead of work. But I'm just as certain there are those who want work."

"An inspired idea! I'll look them over. I wish I didn't have to wait a week."

"I know. But I can't get away oftener. " Nick hesitated. "I must warn you, though. It's a tough area. You've never seen that kind of overcrowded squalor, so be prepared." Kit's answering smile was ironic; he did not correct him.

〰〰

Kit had not told Minnie of the standstill at the theatre and continued to give her vague reports of progress. The rehearsals in the hotel ballroom were going well. Charles Coghlan was living up to his promise as Alec D'Urberville and, so far, had not shown signs of bolting. After a tense beginning Rama fit into the cast as if she had always been there.

Mrs. Fiske told Kit in private that she liked the young lady, and added, "Might there be a romance in your future? She's obviously in love with you."

"She and I are such good friends," he said, "I wouldn't ruin it by mixing in romance."

On Wednesday Nick advised Kit to dress a bit less nobby as they readied to go to the surgery. Kit fastened a gold watch and chain across his rust-colored waistcoat and said, "I'll have more luck hiring workers if I look as if I can pay them." He placed a black low-crowned hat at a rakish angle, shrugged on his severely elegant black coat and grinned. "My riverboat gambler look," he said.

"It's your 'I'm the most desirable man in the world' look."

"I can always take the clothes off, if you like." He tilted the hat over one eye and blew a kiss.

"I'd take advantage of the offer, but I don't have time," Nick said, laughing. "I've patients waiting." He gave a little tug at the watch chain. "You'll be lucky if you don't lose the watch and the hat."

"I'll be lucky if I can get good workers. I can always get another watch and hat."

Many of the neighborhood denizens stopped whatever they were doing to stare after the swell with their doctor. Several men and boys followed them, peppering Nick with questions as to his companion's identity. "All in good time," Nick said, and motioned for them to accompany them. By the time Nick and his companion had reached the surgery, they had collected a sizable following.

Kit's head was up, his stride easy and confident, but every step along the narrow, filthy street brought him closer to Jack Rourke. No one could know how near he was to sicking up. The voices, the sounds, the smells, the sights of poverty— different and yet the same. Not since the night he had forced himself to go to the slums in search of the elusive doctor, had he been near a place like this. How many Jack Rourkes were here? He saw a familiar sullen, dirty-faced boy who might have been himself.

"We're here." Nick's voice brought him out of his morbid thoughts. "I have some news for you," Nick called out. "This gentleman is in need of workmen." Kit looked into their faces. Some of the men were obviously thugs, brazenly assessing him as a potential target. He returned their looks in a way that told them he was on to them. A few of the thugs moved on. The grimy boy was in the forefront, scowling.

"Gentlemen," he said, "My name is St. Denys. I own a theatre. Just now the renovation work on the theatre is halted because of underhanded shenanigans by my rivals. I need two twelve-hour shifts of men." He told them what he needed, what he demanded, and what he would pay for workmen and foremen. He let them buzz about the princely wages for a moment before saying in a no-negotiation voice, "Because of the problems I have had with desertions, you will sign a contract with me if you are hired. There will be no payment until the work is completed. Anyone quitting before the work is finished will be paid nothing."

"You mean we could work for five weeks and not be paid at all?" one incredulous man blurted.

"Exactly." He stood quietly while they grumbled and talked among themselves. Several men gave a disgusted wave of their hands and walked away. To those who remained, he said, "The only exceptions will be someone provably ill or affected by other situations he cannot control. You will not drink spirits on my time. You will not come to work drunk. You will not come to work late. You will not shirk. I can't afford any more lost time."

Another handful walked away. "If the work is done well and done in less than six weeks there will be an additional twenty-five dollars bonus per man." He gazed around, taking the measure of the hard faces. To the pugnacious man in front he said, "You there. Do you have it in you to be a foreman?"

Kelly grinned. "For sure I do, Mr. St. Denys."

"Good. Then let's go to the nearest tavern and start talking. Mr. Kelly, you will assist me. I'll buy a drink for every man hired." As the men lumbered toward the tavern, Kit clamped his hand down on the shoulder of the sullen boy. "You," he said. "Billy. Do you want to work?"

The boy looked sideways as if looking for a quick escape route. "How'd you know my name?"

"Billy, you know damn well how I know it. Those blokes are going to work up heavy thirsts. They're going to need water and plenty of it carried to them. Do you want to do it?"

"I dunno."

"Let me put it another way. You stole something of mine." The boy tried to squirm free. Kit tightened his grip. "Work for me without wages for a week and we'll be even. After that you'll be on the payroll like the others."

"I dunno. Lemme go."

"Let me put it still another way, Billy. If you don't work off what you owe me, I'll take it out of your hide."

The boy's scowl deepened. "All right. I s'pose."

"Come to the tavern with us and sign up."

With the boy in tow, Kit met the waiting men at the Killarney tavern. Again Kit was almost overcome by a nauseating sense of *déjà vu* brought on by the fumes of cheap liquor and beer, dirt, vermin, chewing tobacco, cigars, unwashed bodies, unwashed clothes. The barman pointed him to a sticky table where he and Kelly could sign the men up. Some of those who had left came back and in less than an hour he had his thirty men hired, as well as an additional foreman and the boy. He then took Kelly aside.

"I expect trouble; I want to be prepared." He grinned. "I don't suppose any of your friends like to fight?"

Kelly feigned horror. "Never!"

"I'm sorry to hear that. I'd hoped to find eight tough lads to stand guard at night, armed and willing to crack heads if necessary."

"You'll have them."

"They'll be there to defend my theatre, not to start trouble. Is that understood? If any of them starts a fight, he will be sacked without pay. They have to be told that from the beginning. My hope is that all they need do to earn their pay will be to stand around and look tough. And Kelly, I'm serious about no drinking on the job. The minute they leave the theatre, they can drink themselves blind for all I care. I've been known to do the same. But not when I'm working."

"That'll make it a bit harder. But I'll get your lads, Mr. St. Denys." They shook on the agreement.

"Kelly, one more thing. How safe is Dr. Stuart in this neighborhood?"

Kelly's rough, red face was touched by a smile of genuine affection. "Safe as church. The word is out on the street. Any man who harms one hair on his head is a dead man. Ye can rest easy on his account."

"If that ever changes, Kelly, if he's ever in harm's way, will you get word to me?"

Kelly nodded decisively, and repeated, "But he's safe as in church."

Kit hoped Kelly was right. Nick was too sheltered to survive in a place like this, but any effort to pry him out of it would fail. He left his new crew downing their celebratory drinks and returned to the surgery. From a corner of the waiting room he observed the people, and watched Nick whenever he emerged from the examination room.

Kit had never seen this side of him. The arm around the elderly woman's shoulders, the gentle way he took the howling baby from its mother and quieted it. Was this how he was with his wife, how he would be with the soon-to-be-born infant? Until now, Nick as family man had never been quite real. Kit frowned and thoughtfully bit at his thumbnail.

⁊⫯ ⫯

Francis was delighted to learn that one of the new crew had been a stagehand in London. The fellow knew all about the grid, pin rails, the rope system that raised and lowered scenery, the difference between the working curtain, the drape, teasers and tormentors. He was, in short, a godsend. Francis hired him for permanent work. The rest of them were, for the most part, hardworking or at least adequate, and Kelly proved to be a good foreman.

Several times Kit went at night, unannounced. Menacing guards stood at each corner, one at the front door and one at the back, two more at the sides of the building. One moonlit night, as his hansom approached the theater, he saw thirty or more thugs striding from the opposite direction. Kelly was out front talking to one of the guards. He gave a shrill whistle between two fingers and yelled, "Dusters!" The other guards ran from behind the theatre. A moment later the inside night crew poured outside, yelling. The gang halted.

Someone bellowed, "At 'em!" The next instant the two groups merged. The writhing knot of men spread over the sidewalk and the street. Fists and clubs, heavy boots and lead pipes produced a cacophony of yells, grunts, groans and curses.

Kit jumped from the cab. His eyes were bright as he waded into the melee. He punched and was punched. He ducked a pair of brass knuckles and took the owner of them down with a well-aimed kick to the balls. A hard fist grazed his cheek.

Gunshots cracked in the night. Police whistles shrilled over the noise. Crew and gang members alike took to their heels. The officers arrested everyone they could lay a hand on. Kit stopped them, pointing out his own workers, who had been defending the theatre against attack. Reluctantly, the officers let his men go free and carted the others off in paddy wagons.

Someone slapped Kit on the back as he sucked his skinned knuckles. "You fight good for an Englishman," said Kelly. He had a black eye.

"Thanks. You're not bad, yourself." Kit glanced at one of the guards, who was stanching blood from a gash in his head. "Is he badly hurt?"

"Him? That's Ironhead Dirk. Ain't nothin' or nobody can do more than put a bit of a dent in his skull." Ironhead Dirk heard, and grinned.

"Do you know who they were?"

"Yeah. Dusters, from around Fourteenth Street. If the cops hadn't showed up we could've had a real nice little brawl. There'd been some blood. Them Dusters are mean bastards."

"I thought they were all mean bastards," Kit said with a wry laugh.

"Yeah, but some's meaner 'n others."

Kit handed Kelly some money. "Make sure the guards are fit to work. Then give this to their foreman, let him buy them a couple of rounds. They deserve it." At Kelly's woebegone look, Kit peeled off more money. "Lord God, you could put a hair shirt to shame. Here. Take everybody out. But not on my time."

"Let's hear it for the boss," bellowed Kelly. "He ain't afraid to use his mitts!"

"Can't cheer him yet; he ain't got a proper name," Ironhead Dirk said, and he proceeded to christen him. "Three cheers for the Fightin' Duke!" They cheered him. He laughed, waved, and went into the theatre. The fight had been incredibly invigorating. His pulse was still racing as he flexed his painful hand. Jack Rourke lived. And he wasn't that far under the skin.

Stories in the newspapers the next day were free publicity, worth the bruise on his cheekbone and a few skinned knuckles. Discovering that stories about the feisty young Brit sold newspapers, a few of the independent papers defied the Trust and ran a few more. The stories gradually moved from small type on the back page closer to the front page, carefully skirting the theatre news. Every time Kit read one, he grinned, picturing Erlanger's apoplectic face.

❦

Bronwyn, still determined to make her husband reconcile with his old friend, carefully cut out the stories and saved them. She was less enchanted with Mr. St. Denys when she learned from the stories that he was rich. Very rich, from inherited, unearned wealth. Still, he had been Nicholas' friend and he seemed like a nice man. They should be grownup enough to bury their grudges. She simply had to figure out how to bring it about.

❦

Francis was proud of the progress he could show Kit every day. If only that damned Stuart wasn't with him so bloody often. Francis was mollified a bit when Stuart said, "It looks wonderful. I wouldn't have believed it possible in such a short time." For a moment Francis almost liked Stuart.

The stage floor had been repaired and refinished; it gleamed with wax. The flies were ready for the delivery and hanging of the sandbags, lines, curtains, and scenery. Electric light would flood the stage when needed, from whatever direction was required. Auditorium seats were to be delivered within the week. The once pocked, gouged, and ugly walls were now a smooth pale blue.

Kit showed Nick the custom-made locking cabinet in his dressing room. Here he kept the daggers and jewelry he used in the roles of royalty. Some were paste, costume things. Others were antiques from St. Denys Hill, with precious and semiprecious stones. Nothing of enormous value, and they were kept too sharp to use as prop weapons, but Kit liked their air of authenticity as part of a costume. "Come upstairs," Kit said. "It's finally finished."

"What is?"

"The loft. I'll live there. When I first saw it, it was jumbled with old flats, pigeon droppings, and live pigeons, for that matter. And worse." He led the way to the outside stairway that led to a landing and a door. "Behold," he said, throwing open the door. "The New York branch of St. Denys Hill. By the end of the week I'll have furniture."

The walls were papered with something subtly floral. The tiles in the fireplace were darkened by the stain of past fires but other than that they were clean, lovely ceramic tiles. A rich, dark carpet hid the worn floor. Kit said, "Through that door—"

"I know," Nick said with a laugh. "The bathroom. It's a wonder you don't have barnacles."

"Actually, it's the bedroom. Where you're more than welcome to search for barnacles. The bathroom opens from it. I have a gift for you." Kit placed a key in Nick's hand. "If you need to stay the night in the city, even if I should not be here, I want you to use the flat."

Nick tried to kill an ugly, unwanted thought. What if he walked in and found Kit with somebody else?

With his uncanny way of reading Nick's mind, Kit said, "There's been no one else since you came back to me. Nor has there been one single nightmare since then. You cured them."

⁊〣

Two weeks later the cast of *Tess* were allowed for the first time into the St. Denys Theatre. They inspected every corner of the stage and dressing rooms and were universally delighted. Minnie, whose opinion was the one Kit wanted most to hear, stood alone on the stage and spoke to Kit, listening from the farthest corner of the balcony.

"It's splendid," she said without raising her voice. "Can you hear me?"

"Clearly," Kit replied. "Damn the Trust. Our show will go on. Can you hear me?"

"Loud and clear, dear boy. Soon all of New York is going to hear you." When he joined her on stage, she said, "Harry has the final advertising copy all ready. All we have to do is insert the date and to the printer it goes!"

"I've one more thing to show you."

"Something else? Good heavens."

Kit held a large umbrella over her as they dashed through a downpour to the large old brick building behind the theatre. He switched on the electric lights to expose a vast room filled with flats and props, "Is this yours as well?" she asked, wide-eyed.

"It is. Come along. Let's take the grand tour. There are the interior walls for the cottage. Still wet." Further on they came to a huge flat that was finished and standing up. "Stonehenge," she said, gazing at the mammoth upright stones with their equally mammoth lintels. "Breathtaking."

In an adjoining room carefully labeled costumes hung on racks. The walls of a third room were lined with shelves that held the hundreds of small items essential to believable sets, from the milk pails of the dairymaids to the wooden bowls used by the family. "I have room to add everything I'll ever need." He tried not to remember that more land at St. Denys Hill had been sold.

One by one and in pairs the rest of the cast found their way to the warehouse. When their curiosity was satisfied, everyone returned to the theatre and gathered on stage around Kit and Minnie.

Minnie said, "As all of you know, the Trust is also opening a production of *Tess*. We're moving our opening up by one week, which means we open four weeks from tonight. Rehearsals start at eight o'clock in the morning." She waited while the groans died away. "I know," she said, ruefully, "I don't like it either. But it's necessary. Expect to be here twelve hours a day, perhaps more. The wardrobe mistress and costume designer will be here every day for fitting. When you're not required on stage, report to wardrobe. We'll have the dress parade in one week, and we'll make any final changes in lighting and curtain cues."

"What curtains?" someone asked.

"They'll be here," Kit said. "We have an enormous amount of work, an enormous number of hours before us. Invite two guests to the dress rehearsal if you wish. Any questions?" No one had any. "Everyone get a good night's sleep. You'll need it."

A little later after everyone had left, he discovered he was not alone after all. Rama said softly, "The theatre's beautiful."

"But you wish you'd seen it before Mrs. Fiske."

"Yes. Don't you think I have a right to be disgruntled? I always assumed I would be part of whatever you did." She sighed again. "And Frank told me Stuart is back. I had hoped he was gone forever. He's nothing but trouble."

"Rama, you're one of my most loved friends, but I'll never again hear anything against him."

Defeated, she searched his face. "He's that important to you?"

"He is to me what you want to be," he said gently.

"Then I suppose all I can do is to say, be happy." But, she told herself, if he thought she was giving up, he was greatly mistaken.

The actors were impatient to begin rehearsal the next day, but the director had yet to appear. Kit was ready to send someone to drag him out of bed when a messenger arrived with a note for Minnie. She read it and turned white. Without a word she handed the note to Kit.

"Holy Jesus and all the Saints!" he exploded, after reading it. "I'll see him in court." The director had quit and gone over to the Trust.

"We've been beaten," Minnie said in a dull voice. "We can't get another director at this late date."

"Yes, we can," Kit said. "I've acted and directed at the same time in several productions. It's not easy, but I can do it."

Her chin firmed. "All right. Let's get started."

A few days later another messenger arrived and handed a note to Kit. Nick wrote:

> My wife is nearing her time; I can't leave her. I won't see you until my child is safely delivered and my wife is out of danger. I'm confident your enemies will be reduced to quivering rubble when Tess opens. My thoughts will be with you.
>
> Ever yours, N

"Not more bad news, is it?" Minnie asked.

"No." He slowly folded the note and put it in his pocket. "It's personal and disappointing. But not unexpected." And then he had no time to think about Nick.

The seats arrived late, as did the curtains. The stage manager followed the director into Trust employ. Francis stepped in as stage manager. Rehearsals stretched to eighteen and sometimes twenty hours a day. Fatigue caused short tempers, muffed lines, and missed cues.

Kit dragged himself upstairs after rehearsals, kicked off his shoes and fell on the bed fully dressed. "Doesn't matter," he mumbled as he teetered on the edge of sleep. "Doesn't matter if we all drop dead soon as it's finished. Nothing matters but beating the Cockroach and his friends."

One evening Kit discovered the water boy, Billy, hiding in the balcony, lost in the world of make-believe. Now Billy proudly carried a rake as a villager.

Opening night was sold out. Voices cascaded in comments about the soft beauty of the interior with its light colors and gold trim, the electric lights, the elegance of the proscenium arch with its gold-painted medallion in the center, embellished with the initials KSD in scarlet enamel.

Over the protests of his financial manager, Kit reserved a block of free seats for the workmen and their wives. They arrived dressed in the best clothes they owned or could borrow, some of the styles out-of-date but with shoes shined, collars high, and the women's hair piled into pompadours beneath feathered hats. The financial manager declared, "Free seats don't make money, Mr. St. Denys."

"If it hadn't been for those men this theatre would not be open. Some of them may never see another play."

"So what? People of that class couldn't possibly care."

Kit said coldly, "They'll be seated without charge. You're fired."

Triumph was in the air. Kit felt it as he, Angel Clare, knelt at the stone altar beside the waking Tess. He felt it as Tess saw the lawmen round about and said, "Have they come for me?" and looked at him with full knowledge that it was all over and that she would hang for murder. He felt it as the curtains closed and acclamation burst from the other side as the audience leaped to their feet.

He and Minnie hugged and Minnie cried, laughing, until the curtain parted for curtain call after curtain call. At the back and in the aisles, were other actors and actresses who had come to the theatre, some directly from their own performances, to see the end of the play.

Kit withdrew and let Mrs. Fiske take the last curtain calls alone. Only Nick's absence marred the otherwise perfect evening.

Exquisite Maude Adams came backstage and took Minnie's hands in hers. "Dear Minnie, you were heartrending tonight. And you, sir," she said to Kit, "were wonderful."

He lifted her fingers to his lips. He couldn't be angry with her, though he knew he should be. It was she who was playing his dates at the Barclay, acting under the auspices of the Trust. Maurice Barrymore had tears in his eyes. Lillian Russell escaped Jim Brady long enough to come backstage. "Even I could not have played Tess as well," she told Minnie.

The critics the next day could not praise *Tess* enough. It was described as "glorious," "Wagnerian," "breathtaking," "a victory," "intelligent and restrained," a "miracle of emotional expression, humanity, and genius," "perfect casting."

🦢🦢

On the night *Tess* and the St. Denys Theatre opened, Bronwyn went into labor. Nick knew it was going to be a long, harrowing labor and he sent for David Galvin to assist. James William Stuart dallied and delayed for ten hours before he took pity on his mother and decided to be born. "Is he all right?" Bronwyn whispered. "Nicholas, I don't hear anything. Is he all right?" Just then, James bellowed in protest.

Nick grinned. "He's perfect, except for a monumental stubborn streak. Everything's present and where it ought to be. Miss Barr will clean him up while we finish this little project, and then you can hold him."

A half hour later, Bronwyn held him in her arms and tears of happiness slipped down her cheeks as she touched her lips to the silky black hair. "He's so beautiful," she whispered. "He's going to look like you." She surrendered him to his father, and gratefully took the sleeping potion of warm milk and a few drops of laudanum.

Nick held his infant son in his arms and looked with wonder at the ruddy little face, squashed nose, puffy eyes, and rosebud mouth. He grinned at David and Ida. "He's a handsome baby, isn't he," he said. They agreed wholeheartedly. Ida volunteered to stay all night beside Bronwyn's bed.

A little later, with Bronwyn and Jamie asleep and Miss Barr immersed in a book, Nick and David went to the office for a drink of celebration and talk. David left as the first faint streaks of dawn appeared over the trees. Yawning, Nick walked out onto the porch and looked in the direction of New York. He hoped opening night had gone well.

※ ※

During her last curtain call following the sixth performance to a sold-out house, Minnie was handed a bouquet of roses so large she could scarcely hold it. As she had been every night, she was ankle deep in flowers that had been tossed onto the stage. Laughing, she called Kit out from the wings, to another storm of applause, to hold the gigantic bouquet.

When she read the card afterward in her dressing room, she hurried to Kit's dressing room and burst in without knocking. "Look at this, will you?" Laughing in glee, she handed him the card.

"I'll be bloody damned, if the lady will excuse the language," he said.

Flowers for the fair Tess and a courtier's bow to Angel Clare. A gentleman knows when to gracefully yield the point if not the game: Our production of *Tess* has been canceled.
C. Frohman

18

he desk clerk at the Marlborough glanced up at the big, uncouth man with dirty hands, nails with black crescents and a thick gray-streaked beard. "Back door," he said sternly.

The man slammed down a five-dollar gold piece on the desk and leaned forward. "Matey, I want information and you'll give it to me."

The clerk glanced around and pocketed the money. "What information?"

"St. Denys. What's his room number?"

"He's no longer here. He resides elsewhere."

"Where?"

"I can't give you that information." The desk clerk quailed as the man clenched his ham-sized fist. "Over the theatre he owns. The St. Denys Theatre. Or so I've been told."

"Directions," Rourke ordered, and took the hastily scribbled paper in his grimy hands. It was a long walk to the theatre, but the weeks of backbreaking work on the steamer had given him back the strength he had lost in prison. He didn't even feel the exertion, except in his feet. No more cracked, worn-out boots for him! He'd soon have the best.

He watched the theatre from across the street. An hour passed; no one went in or out. Then two men, arguing in belligerent voices, came toward the street from behind the theatre. Rourke crossed over to eavesdrop and get a closer look.

The taller and better-dressed of the men shouted with an English accent, "I said you are dismissed! If you set foot here again I'll have the law on you." Rourke eyed him, trying to see a resemblance between the Englishman and the picture he stole from the dead bitch. There wasn't none.

The other man, an American, made an angry gesture. "You can't fire me. Nobody can but him and he ain't here."

"Get out. I told him you weren't to be trusted! I told him you were telling the Trust everything we did. Don't come back, Kelton. Ever."

"You'll be sorry, Mulholland! I'll get even!" Kelton stalked away, pausing just long enough to lift his middle finger to Francis.

Francis Mulholland stood there a moment, rubbing the back of his neck, and gave a start when a big, bearded man spoke to him. "That bloke lost his job, did he?"

"What of it?"

"I'm lookin' for work. These Americans don't take kindly to hirin' somebody like me, big and rough-lookin'."

"Well, I am short a pair of hands now." Francis looked him over. "Are you as strong as you look?"

Rourke held up his big hands. "Been stokin' on a steamer, mister. That ain't work for a sissy."

"I need a stagehand to carry large, heavy pieces of props and scenery. They sometimes have to be moved fast. You have to follow directions to the letter." The man nodded agreement. "Come inside with me and I'll get your name for the payroll. I'm Mr. Mulholland. Come with me and we'll find my foreman, Kelly."

As Rourke followed Francis around to the back of the theatre, he noticed the stairway that must lead to the rooms over the theatre. Excitement shot through him. The brat lived up there. The brat with the answer to everything in his life! He had to get a glimpse of him. "Mr. Mulholland," he said, "Mr. St. Denys is so famous and all, when do I see him? I ain't never seen anyone real famous except I seen the Queen once."

"You'll see him at rehearsals and performances. Perhaps sooner."
They were behind the theatre and Francis motioned to a nearby
brick building. "There's the warehouse where we keep the flats,
the painted scenery, the props and the costumes. Everything has
its proper place there and you must become acquainted with it."
He lead the way into the theatre itself.

Rourke paused outside a closed door. "Where's that go?"

"Downstairs. That's where the orchestra practices. And the
dressing rooms are down there. You don't have any reason to go
down there."

A man came toward them, carrying a chair. "Mr. Mulholland,"
he said, "I'm taking this over to the warehouse to be fixed. If Mrs.
Fiske sat in it tonight, she'd land on her bustle for sure."

"Kelly, I just sacked Kelton. This is his replacement. What did
you say your name was?"

"Smith. John Smith."

"Kelly, take Smith with you to the warehouse and then finish
showing him about. I need to speak with Mr. St. Denys."

Rourke said, "Lemme carry the chair, Mr. Kelly. Believe in
gettin' in good with me bosses."

Kelly grinned. "You and me are goin' to get along fine, Smith."

Rourke walked beside Kelly, the chair under one arm. "What
kind of bloke is this St. Denys, anyway?"

Kelly shrugged. "Pays good money. And I like him. He's got
balls; ain't afraid of nothin'. Good man to work for. We work hard
but so does he. And he let us and our families come for free to the
first time they did *Tess.*"

"Pays good, you say? He's rich, then?"

"I'd reckon as he is. Some say he's got castles and the like back
in England. And he bought this old place and put in electricity,
fixed everything that was broke, bought new curtains and seats
and all, so he must be rich as they say." If he had looked at Smith
he would have seen a smile of immense satisfaction. They reached
the warehouse and Kelly said, "He might be here."

As they walked in Rourke's gaze swept the room, which was
filled with what looked to him like rubbish. Kelly took him around,
and pointed out the various pieces that would have to be moved
from warehouse to theatre and back again. A tall fair-haired young
man was talking with a woman who had pencils stuck in her hair,
a measuring tape in one hand and a pincushion in the other.
Rourke tensed.

"Mr. St. Denys," called Kelly.

Kit looked up and glanced at the two men. His eyes froze on Rourke's face and he paled. His breath caught in his chest.

"Mr. St. Denys, this is our new stagehand. Name of Smith."

Kit was nauseated, his thoughts chaotic as they approached him. Smith looked just like the old man. He forced himself to hold out his hand, aware it was clammy but hoping Smith would not notice. "Mr. Smith. Good to have you with us." Had Smith noticed the sweat on his upper lip? The cold hands? Had his voice quivered at all?

"Thanks for the job, Mr. St. Denys."

Sweet Lord, the voice, the voice! 'Drink it like a man. The worms crawl in the worms crawl out. You didn't lose much.' The voice! It was the same but the old bastard was dead! He saw his own hand plunge down twice, saw the blood pool out into the black fur on Rourke's chest. Insanity. This was madness. He dropped Smith's hand and took a step backward, his terrified eyes still on Smith's bearded face.

"Mr. St. Denys, Mr. Mulholland is lookin' for you," Kelly said.

Kit walked away from them and not until he was outside in the sunshine could he breathe. Frank had to fire Smith. He couldn't have him around. It would drive him mad. He broke into a run and did not slow down until he was halfway up the stairs to his flat. He heard Francis call to him.

"Kit, wait. I need to see you."

Kit did not stop. He rushed into his apartment and seized a whiskey bottle, not bothering with a glass. The bottle clacked against his teeth. He gulped the liquor, choking. Francis came in and jerked it away from him.

"Kit, what the bloody hell is wrong? You can't drink like that before a performance. What's the matter?"

"What's the matter? I'm going to end my days chained to a wall in a lunatic asylum, babbling to the rats."

Francis started to laugh, and realized Kit was serious. "You're tired, that's all. But you're not mad. Not even close to it. You need old St. Francis, that's what. Do you want me to stay with you tonight?

Almost, Kit said yes. But Nick had sent a note saying:

> If all is well with my wife and son I will be there for the performance tonight and afterward if you are of a mind to have me stay.

After all, Nick had said if. If Nick could not come, he would be alone and he knew the specter of the old man would drag him through hell tonight. But if Nick came and Francis were with him, it would be the end of everything.

He squeezed Francis' shoulder. "My dear friend, I think not tonight. I'm all right now. It was just a fit of some kind, I think. You're right; I'm tired."

"Will you ring me if you change your mind? I'd be here before you could put the receiver down. I want you to promise."

"I give you my word."

Francis looked searchingly at him, started to say something else, and then with a shake of his head, kept silent.

🙊🙊

The twelfth performance of *Tess* was the first Nick saw. The acting was restrained yet so powerful that he forgot he was watching Kit. The ovation, as it had been every night, was prolonged and overwhelming. On stage the stagehands and property master were returning everything back to Act One, Scene One for the next night as Nick started to Kit's dressing room.

A bear-like man came out from backstage carrying one of the stone altars from Stonehenge, the one upon which Tess had slept. Kit had shown them to Nick while they were being constructed, and told him that they were made of a combination of wood, papier-mâché, and thin pieces of stone. The big man carried it as if it weighed no more than a chair.

A few minutes later, as Nick knocked at Kit's door he was surprised to see the big bearded man again, empty-handed this time. He wondered why a stagehand was downstairs. The man stared at him a moment, and went on his way. Then the man was forgotten because Kit was at the door, smiling a welcome. Nick looked for Kit's elderly dresser, expecting to see the familiar sour look.

Kit said. "I gave him the evening away. I'm so glad you're here." Nick drew up a chair and sat close to Kit as he removed his makeup. "I was getting worried," Kit said. "I presume mother and child are doing well?"

"Perfect. I still can't believe I have a son." Nick caught sight of his foolish grin in the mirror. "There has never been an infant like him. Twelve days old—and today he recited the entire Old Testament. Backwards. In Latin."

"I'm impressed. But not surprised," Kit said with a laugh.

"I've read the reviews. They're going to run out of adjectives before long."

"I know. Isn't it grand? Erlanger and Company threw in the towel as far as putting on *Tess*, did you know? By the way, I received a most gracious note from your wife the other day thanking me for the gift."

"It's beautiful. I can't imagine your buying a pram."

"I didn't buy it, I just paid for it. Mrs. Fiske and Rama bought it. My inclination was toy soldiers or something wind-up." He looked with a fond smile at his brother's old windup toy that sat on his makeup table.

"Well, in another two weeks, Jamie will undoubtedly be walking. You can get him toy soldiers then."

"Of course."

"You look tired," Nick said. As Kit removed the sweat-streaked makeup, dark shadows appeared beneath his eyes.

"I can't imagine why." He uttered a little groan of pleasure as Nick kneaded the tension-knotted shoulders. "Over a little to the right. Oh, that's the place."

Nick bent and kissed the nape of Kit's neck, where his hair lay in thick waves. "I used to do this after every performance, remember?"

Kit turned his head slightly so that his cheek rested for an instant against Nick's arm. "How could I forget? Are you staying here tonight?"

"Oh, yes. It seems much longer than it has been."

Kit's left eyebrow quirked. "How much longer is it?"

"You are such a nasty, vulgar child." Nick thumped the top of Kit's head with his knuckles.

"Ouch!" Kit got up, locked the dressing room door and turned. "Nico," he said softly.

"The theatre's full of people!"

"So was the hotel, *mon cher*. Hundreds of people." He grinned. "Come along. I have something I want you to see."

"I'm sure you do," Nick murmured, and followed Kit into the bathroom. An ornate, claw-footed tub stood in pristine glory, with lions carved into its side and at one end the inglorious and dangerous but vital water heater. A strange-looking arrangement of curtains and pipes rose five feet or so above the edge of the bathtub.

"What in the world is that contraption?" Nick asked.

"What I wanted you to see. It's called a shower bath, and it's like standing in the rain. Most invigorating. For one. Or two."

"I'm not getting in there with you. Not this time."

"You don't know what you're missing." Kit stripped, almost destroying Nick's good intentions, then stepped into the tub, and fiddled with some knobs. Nick gave a start as hot water spouted from the overhead pipes.

"I've seen everything now," he said.

Kit pulled the curtains to keep water off the floor, leaving enough of an opening that Nick could watch and they could talk. After a moment, Nick said, "I've often wondered how you come by those scars on your back." Kit did not answer, but continued soaping his hair, face, and body, every movement ratcheting up Nick's desire. Kit turned off the water. "Is it something you don't want to talk about?" Nick wished he had not asked.

"It's nothing I can talk about. Suffice it to say that I received the scars from the same man who gave me this." He held up his right hand with its crooked little finger. "I'm not ready to talk about it. Perhaps I never will be."

Nick looked toward the closed bathroom door. "What was that?"

"What?"

"I thought I heard the dressing room door open." Nick went to the dressing room and was surprised to find the door unlocked and ajar. He locked it again and returned to the bathroom. "Someone must have come in looking for you."

"Impossible. I locked the door myself. Dry me."

Nick picked up the thick white towel folded over the brass stand, and said, "The night we met, I remember thinking you looked like a sea god when you stepped from the water."

The water dripped from Kit's hair, leaving silvery trails down his face and neck. Dozens of shiny trails slid over his broad shoulders and chest, narrow waist and flat belly. With wide-eyed wonder, Kit looked down at his rising sex and said with guileless innocence, "Now where did that come from, do you suppose?"

"I'm busy," Nick said. "I'm ignoring you. And it."

He toweled Kit's hair and face and got as far as his lips. With a sheepish grin of surrender, he dropped the towel and kissed him. From there his mouth and hands proceeded slowly down Kit's damp, slightly soapy-flavored skin.

"Oh, my dear Nico," Kit said, "you do learn your lessons well!"

Tom Rourke had managed to spy out the below-stage area and knew it like the back of his hand, knew who was there and when they were there, and how to get in and get out again without being noticed. Now, for the second time, he put his lock-picking skills to good use. He crossed soundlessly to the bathroom door, opening it far enough to see. What he saw filled him with hot disgust. Like he thought. The brat was a nelly-ann. And he'd almost missed the show. The little bugger would pay plenty to keep this quiet! He watched avidly as Jack twisted his fingers in his fancy-man's hair and gave a low cry.

Rourke's breathe quickened. There'd been a few times on board ship when him and some other bloke found a dark corner... He slipped from the room and hurried from the theatre, into the first tavern he could find. It took only two whiskeys to find a whore willing to go into the tavern's storeroom with him. He finished so quickly he threw only half the agreed-upon amount in her face. "Ye didn't earn the rest, ye dirty old screw," he barked.

❦

Razor-sharp knife and bloody hands—the old man stabbing him over and over in every part of his twisting, terrified, naked body while Michael's decayed eyeless face screamed—

A feral snarl burst from Kit's throat. He fell upon the old man, his strong hands about the old man's throat tightening, tightening. "No more! No more! Die, God damn you! Die and stay dead!"

Nick, brought to shocked wakefulness, choked and struggled. Lights danced behind his eyes. With a final effort, he broke Kit's hold, shoved him to his back and pinned him to the bed. Kit's teeth were bared, the muscles in his neck stood out in cords, his head thrashed like a thing alive by itself.

"Kit!" Nick shouted. "Kit! Kit! Wake up! Kit!" He called it over and over until the glazed look went out of Kit's eyes.

Dazed, he looked at his clenched fists and his arms being held immovable in Nick's white-knuckled hands. "Nico, what did I do?" His eyes were wide with fear.

"You tried to strangle me and damn near succeeded." He released Kit's arms and slowly moved away from him. "You said the nightmares were over. Kit, I want to know what this is all about. I deserve to know."

"Yes," Kit whispered. "You do. I should have told you long ago." He sat up, wrapped his arms around his knees, and sat there for a long, painful silence. When he spoke it was in a voice that sometimes broke, sometimes halted, sometimes fell silent for minutes at a time.

"I was born Jack Rourke. My father was a demon and my mother was a Whitechapel whore. I was a thief. I stole everything I could get my hands on. I was good at it. The scars on my back are from whippings my old man gave me just for existing. He broke my finger for no reason except that he could. My excuse for a mother did nothing to prevent any of it. I had a brother. A twin. My old man killed him and tried to kill me. I killed him instead. I was fourteen."

The ticking of the clock thundered in the silence. Nick pulled Kit down into his arms so that Kit's head was nestled between his chin and shoulder. "Why didn't you tell me this in England?" he said when he could speak. "If only I'd known. I would never have left you to face it alone. Tell me more about your brother."

"Michael was innocent and gentle. I don't know how he could be, living as we did, but he was. I made him steal with me, and he hated it. He even went to the Methodist Mission church there, and he believed in Heaven. He prayed, Nick. Every day he prayed. A lot of good it did him." He rubbed at his eyes with the back of his hand. "He was frail as a baby bird. I tried to look after him. If I hadn't failed, he'd still be alive. Sometimes I truly don't know where he ended and I began. Papa St. Denys had him reburied at the Hill, in the woods. I wanted you to see where he was, and tell you about all of it when you were there, but..." He sighed for opportunities lost. "The windup toy belonged to him. It's all I have left of him."

"Did no one else know?"

"Only Lizbet and Papa St. Denys, and even they didn't know the whole story."

"Dear Lord, your life has been like a play, a tragic play."

"Not all tragic. I had Papa St. Denys, and Lizbet, and the theatre and my friends. And you."

"But what triggered this dream tonight? Do you know?"

"This morning Frank hired a man named Smith. He's the image of the son-of-a-bitch who sired me. He even sounds like him. I know it's absurd and the man can't help how he looks. But I can't have him around here. Frank is going to have to sack him."

"No. Don't do that."

"I can't look at him every day!"

"But you have to, in order to overcome your fear. Listen. When I was a boy I was deathly afraid of heights. My father took me out into the country and forced me to climb the tallest tree he could find. I climbed it, bawling like a calf all the way up. And then he went home and left me to get down alone. I stayed there for hours, until after nightfall, terrified I'd fall out. Then I got so angry with him I forgot I was afraid. I inched my way down, hating him more with every minute that passed. But I've never again been afraid of heights."

"You think I should keep this man on?" Kit doubted the wisdom, and was afraid of the idea.

"I do. The only way you'll ever get over these nightmares is to convince yourself Smith is Smith and that Rourke is really dead. Face him. Face your fear. I'll be here; you won't be doing it alone this time."

❧ ❧

In a sordid room little different from the thousands of other sordid rooms he had stayed in all over the world, Tom Rourke stripped off his shirt. He stared into the cracked mirror on the wall, concentrating upon the two hairless ridges of scar tissue near his left nipple.

He would've died if that knife had been in the hands of a real man instead of a kid. He had come out of his faint and had found himself covered with his own blood and the brat gone. He had staggered out into the street, bleeding like a stuck pig. Lucky for him, Blackie Stonebed had been passing by, drunk but not too drunk to help a friend. Blackie had taken Tom Rourke back into his house and sent for the sot who served the neighborhood as undertaker, doctor, and dentist. He credited Rourke's recovery to his own medical skill and the fact that Tom Rourke was too mean to die young.

When Rourke recovered he began searching for the kid. He meant to smash his pretty face to pulp like he had his worthless brother, break every bone in his damn body. If it killed him too, so much the better. But Jack had vanished.

Years after he'd given up hope of finding the little bastard, he'd heard a down-and-outer named Harry Augustus, in a pub telling how a certain famous actor was nothin' more than a mud-lark who'd wormed his way into a lot of money. The bloke mentioned the name Lizbet Porter. Rourke's ears had sharpened. Wasn't that the name he'd beat out of Michael that last day?

He'd kept the man's glass filled and asked him questions. The description of the famous actor, Kit St. Denys, convinced Rourke. "And he's rich, you say?" he asked several times, to which the man replied, "Like bloody King Midas."

Now, as he looked in the mirror, Rourke rubbed the ugly scars, and his face tightened with hatred. He'd by god get the money like he planned, but first he'd get even for the stabbing. In the warehouse, Jack had looked like he knew who he was. He'd have to move fast, before Jack found some excuse to sack him or call the coppers. Too many delays already. Time to make the goddamned bugger pay for what he done.

19

 unlight through the stained glass windows cast rainbows upon James William Stuart, dressed in a lavishly laced christening gown bought by Bronwyn's friends at the nurses' school. Jamie frowned mightily at Reverend Lanston as water from the font touched his forehead, but he did not cry.

Nick stood beside Bronwyn in the front of the church, wistfully remembering the intense excitement that religious ceremonies had once held for him. Today, he knew he was chief among hypocrites, and he had always detested hypocrites.

After the ceremony, family and friends left the church to go to the yellow house to visit and enjoy the outdoor refreshments in the flower gardens, lush with their late spring blossoms.

Jamie cried for his dinner. Bronwyn took him from the gazebo to the upstairs bedroom and nursed him. Nick came in not long after and stood watching her. He said softly, "Madonna and child."

She blushed. "I didn't know you were there. And I'm far from being the Madonna."

"Not in my eyes."

A little later, in the gazebo, with Jamie asleep in the elaborate baby carriage that had arrived yesterday as a gift from Mr. St. Denys, Bronwyn chatted with friends. Nick was nearby, talking medicine with David, when he heard someone say with a touch of awe, "What do you suppose he's doing here?" Someone else remarked, "Have you seen the play? It's wonderful."

Nick stopped breathing as Kit approached from the gate, in riding clothes and boots, his guitar slung on his back. Bronwyn laughed at him. "I made up my mind you and your friend should make up," she said. "And today was the best day to do it. He, at least, wants to make amends or he wouldn't have sent that beautiful baby carriage. Now go on. Speak to him. I insist."

For an eternity he and Kit looked at each other across the chasm of a few feet. Was everyone watching them, avid to see the look on his face and hear the tone of his voice? His lover. His wife. Himself. Together. Bronwyn had no right to invite Kit. Kit should have had better sense than to come. He walked woodenly toward Kit and managed a smile. "It's good to see you after such a long time." He could feel Bronwyn's approving smile behind him.

"Your wife was most insistent in her letter this morning," Kit said. "I'm never able to resist a charming lady." He looked beyond Nick and smiled at Bronwyn. "And where's the object of all this celebration?"

She laughed and motioned him forward. "Right here. Come, sir! You are to adore him like everyone else."

Needing a moment to collect himself, Nick fetched two glasses of punch, one for Bronwyn and one for Kit. Turning, he collided with one of the churchwomen. He apologized profusely, rattled by what he thought was suspicion in her eyes. But he had done nothing to make anyone suspicious—had he?

He was amazed to see Kit in the gazebo, seated at ease beside Bronwyn, Jamie in his arms. He held Jamie awkwardly, to be sure, but Jamie didn't protest. Words passed between Bronwyn and Kit; both smiled. Kit returned Jamie to his mother, took his guitar, and tuned it.

As Nick stepped up into the gazebo, he heard Kit say, "I have a confession, Mrs. Stuart. I didn't even see the pram until today. When my friend Mrs. Fiske suggested one as a gift, I didn't even know what one was. I gave her *carte blanche* to find a suitable one and have it sent. But I do have a gift of my own choosing for the young gentleman."

Soft notes were plucked from the strings and Nick was stopped in his tracks by the sound of Kit's sweet singing, a centuries-old lullaby. He had been dreaming to think he could keep his two worlds separate. They had touched; the edges had blurred. His gaze moved from Bronwyn and Jamie to Kit and back again. God help him if he ever had to choose between them. The song ended. Little Jamie was fast asleep.

"My singing doesn't usually put people to sleep," Kit said, laughing. The guests applauded, and several ladies dabbed at their eyes with dainty handkerchiefs. Kit looked up at Nick. His smile was rueful, helpless, and devastating. He stood, bowed to Bronwyn, and once more slung his guitar on his back, looking like a traveling troubadour. "Mrs. Stuart, I regret that I must be going."

"So soon! But you just arrived."

"I have an appointment in the city that can't be delayed."

"Promise you'll come again when you can visit," she said, looking squarely at Nick and stressing the last word. "You promised once before and didn't come."

"I apologize for that. As soon as it's convenient for everyone concerned, I'll come back."

Nick put in, "If you must leave already, at least I'll be a good host and walk you to your horse." They fell into step beside one another and did not speak until out of earshot of the others.

"Are you angry that I came?" Kit asked.

"I was. Not now."

"Her letter was delivered by messenger this morning. I wondered how you would feel about it."

"It was difficult for me, seeing you together."

Kit glanced sideways at him. "I saw it in your face. You know you can hide nothing from me. Don't worry, Nico. I'll never put you in a position of having to decide between us. With her you can have a home, and you are such a domestic puppy you need a home. With me, what can you have? Desire. A flimsy reed to lean upon."

Nick's voice dropped as if the trees around them could hear. "It's more than that and you know it."

"Yes. I know. But you can't leave them. Nor would you."

"No."

"I rest my case." He reached into his inside pocket and removed a small, old leather-bound book and handed it to Nick. "I intended to give this to you at the Hill."

The printing date inside was 1725. On the fragile flyleaf were words written in Kit's fine hand:

> Without the sanction of Society
> Without the sanction of the Church
> Without the sanction of God
> I love you

"I can't accept this. "It's too old and valuable," Nick said, his voice rough.

"You must," Kit said. "I quite ruined the value by writing in it."

"You are a damn fool," Nick said past a lump in his throat.

"Aren't we both?" The gentle breeze fanned their faces. A cardinal called his mate somewhere in the trees. "'Alas! why, fearing of Time's tyranny, Might I not then say , NowI love you best,' I remember that was your favorite." In the sunlight Kit could see faint lines radiating from the outer corners of Nick's eyes and other faint lines across his forehead. He knew such faint lines were beginning to mark his face as well. They were no longer boys. Time's tyranny.

Nick said, "I couldn't live without you."

"Of course you could. You have. Had I not chased you here, you would have been...content... without me." Kit looked up at the achingly blue sky, accented with a few lazy clouds painted on. "I think I'll kiss you here and now, in front of God and everybody!" He burst into laughter at Nick's expression of dismay and swung up into the saddle. "Oh, Nico, you take me so literally. When will I see you again?"

"Wednesday will not be possible this week. But I'll find a way to be at Friday's performance. Kit, what about that workman, Smith?"

"I pretend he doesn't exist." With a jaunty wave, Kit rode away.

When Kit was out of sight, Nick put the book into his pocket and returned to his wife, his child, and his guests.

꽃

That night, someone knocked at Rama's door as she brushed her hair. She groaned, hoping whoever it was would leave her alone. She was tired, and with no performance tonight, she had looked forward to doing nothing. The knock came again. She clutched her wrapper closer around her and padded barefoot to the door. She didn't give a bloody damn if her unwelcome visitor was shocked by her state of undress. She was surprised to see Kit standing there with a bouquet of roses large enough to choke a dray horse.

"Kit? What in the world?" She took the roses and he thrust out a box of French chocolates. "This is for you, too."

"Have you lost your mind?" she asked with delight. "Or have you done something I need to forgive you for?" As she shifted the flowers to her other arm, her wrapper opened a little.

"When a Greek comes bearing gifts, the least a lady can do is invite him in. Although," he added, with a vaudeville leer and a twist of an invisible mustache, "ye be showing an uncommon amount of fair bosom, me pretty."

"I only wish you cared. Come in. And you're not Greek. And I think that line says something about looking in the Greek's mouth."

"That's gift horse. And you're not supposed to."

He sauntered in, helped himself to a chocolate, and sat down with his arms spread wide upon the top of the sofa. "Take your choice, wench. Either put on a fancy gown and we'll invade the first high society party we can find, or throw on something less swell and we'll find a low dive where we can kick up our heels."

Her eyes brightened. "Like we used to do at home? That was such fun!"

"Remember the £5 we won doing a polka?"

"How could I forget it? You let me buy a hat with it."

"The hat that looked like the Leaning Tower of Pisa."

"It did not! It was a lovely hat. Remember the names we used? Sebastian O'Toole and Pomegranita Snark. Oh, I'd much rather do that than go to some society thing." To her surprise, she was no longer tired.

They found exactly the kind of place they wanted: dim, noisy, and vulgar. A narrow stage filled one end of the dive, and on the stage a Negro quartet played waltzes, polkas, and fox trots. A dingy bar ran the length of one wall; a small dance floor was in front of the stage, while small tables crowded together took up the rest of the space. Several patrons and performers recognized them and egged them on until they stopped dancing, took the stage, and performed a burlesque of *Romeo and Juliet*, with Rama, as Romeo, wearing Kit's coat, and Kit wearing her feathers-and-flounces hat as Juliet. The people howled and applauded, whistling.

Bored with that, Kit remembered having heard of a new music called ragtime, from the American South. When he asked the band if they were familiar with it, they laughed and broke into strident, syncopated, wailing music unlike anything Kit had ever heard before. It got into his head like champagne and into his feet like the thrill of a standing ovation. What the steps were to ragtime, he didn't know. He and Rama made up their own. She lost her hat and her hair became a red whirlwind about her shining face. The other patrons stood back and watched them, applauding, then joining in one at a time or in couples to make up their own dances, too.

It was near dawn when Kit and Rama finally left to walk back to the hotel. They meandered with his arm over her shoulders, her arm around his waist.

"I must learn that music," he said. "What a marvelous sound. And that rhythm!"

She murmured agreement, and then said, "This is as good as the old days."

"Are you happy, Rama?"

"Happier than I've been for a long time. I wish this night would never end."

"Next time we'll go to Coney Island. I've heard it's 'Splendiferous' "

A shiver of anticipation chased through her. She'd heard all about Coney Island and the Elephant Hotel, with its exotic rooms in various parts of the elephant's anatomy. The Elephant had a raffish reputation for assignations. If she could inveigle him into the Elephant, by God, she'd have him. She tightened her arm around his waist and said wistfully, "Kit, won't you ever change? I mean, won't you ever want to marry and have children, a wife who looks after you and darns your socks and washes your clothes? Won't you ever love me the way I love you?"

"No, my dear. Does it really matter?"

"It matters to me. I want you to take me to bed, make love to me. Oh, Kit," she cried softly, "you could drive me out of my head if you just would."

"I've made love to you thousands of times before thousands of people."

"That's meaningless!"

He stopped and turned her to face him. "How can you say that? Rama, if I didn't feel a certain passion for you, it wouldn't work. Do you think when I am Romeo to your Juliet that it's a lie? Do you think my Macbeth is not besotted by his lady just because I don't leap into your bed when the curtain falls? I wouldn't expect anyone else to understand, but I thought you did."

She searched his face. He meant it. With a little sigh she turned, slipped her arm around his waist once more and they resumed walking. "I never thought of it that way," she said.

At her door he kissed her. Inside, she closed the door and leaned against it. Thinking of what might have been. What might still be, if she played her cards right. She knew beyond doubt that she could change him. All she had to do was get him to that Coney Island Elephant.

⁜

Friday at the theatre, Kelly was furious. "I told that bastard to be here at four o'clock and he isn't here yet." Some heavy pieces needed moving from the warehouse to the theatre and Smith was the strongest man in the crew. Kelly pulled two workers from another job and sent them to the warehouse.

Rourke, at that moment, was sleeping off last night's two bottles of whiskey. After tonight he'd never have to work again.

⁜

Before taking a brief rest prior to getting ready for the performance, Kit went to the office of the new business manager and asked how ticket sales were. The new man was proving his worth. He had discovered overpayments, and missing funds. "Sold out every night this week," the man said. "I've never seen such a long run of sold-out shows. There are a half dozen tickets left for Saturday's matinee." His grin became wider. "And one block of tickets for tonight's performance was bought by an agent for Caroline Astor."

"*The* Mrs. Astor? I'll be damned. I'm still waiting for her investment money. I'll give her a performance she won't forget."

"You'll be glad to know that if sales keep up as they have been, you may see a profit by the time the run is finished. A small one, understand, but a profit nonetheless."

"That is good news!" Kit was relieved. The first thing to do would be redeem the mortgage on the Xavier.

From there he went to his rooms over the theatre. As always, since the hiring of Smith, he looked edgily around for him. Thank God the gorilla was nowhere in sight. Perhaps Francis had fired him after all, for shirking or not following orders. It was a cheering thought. He put the man from his mind. First, the play. And afterward, Nick.

He took a shower bath, read the script of Ibsen's *A Doll's House*, which Minnie wanted him to direct and produce, and then went to sleep. His mental clock was set to wake him in an hour. He hated taking time to rest, but the performances and worry about money were taking their toll. He woke refreshed and joined Francis for dinner.

※ ※

By observation, Tom Rourke knew the theatre was deserted for two hours between the placing of the last prop and the return of cast and crew. He chose this time, at twilight, to go up the stairs to his son's rooms. He knocked on the door. No answer. The door was locked; a momentary delay. Within moments he was inside.

"Looks like a bloody female's place!" he thought in contempt. Pictures, fancy tables, la-de-da china gewgaws. He spat on the floor at the sight of a male nude statue. Silently he crossed the room and pushed the bedroom door open. Empty.

Just as he pulled out a drawer to rifle, he heard footsteps and then a key turned in the lock. A man's voice said, "Odd. I thought I locked it." Rourke hid behind the bedroom door, ready to attack. Someone walked around the parlor. A chair squeaked. Rourke cautiously peered out.

Jack was at a small desk, writing something. Rourke stepped forward, his right fist clenched for a sledgehammer blow to the back of the head. The brat would be helpless as a gutted dog. Someone knocked. Rourke ducked back into the bedroom, and watched through the crack between the door and the frame. A man came in with something wrapped in a cloth. The brat unwrapped the object and inspected it. Rourke saw small flashes, like light reflecting off jewels and licked his lips. Real jewels? Had to be. Jack was rich, wasn't he?

"Excellent," Jack said. "You do good work." Rourke saw him count out some money into the man's hand. The man bobbed his head and left. But Jack, instead of returning to the desk, left the flat.

A few minutes later Rourke followed, slipping into the empty theatre. The brat was not in the dressing room, but he soon would be. Rourke's plans had been laid for a long time: scare the bloody hell out of him, get the first of many large payments to keep his mouth shut, and get out. Then once he had enough money amassed that he wouldn't have to work, he'd get even.

Rourke looked in the dressing room's tall wooden cabinet. Gorblimey! Look at the swag in there! He grinned as he tucked a circlet of gold into one large pocket, and several rings into the other. His lip curled as he inspected the makeup pots. He picked up the windup toy. The sissy even had play toys. Then he hid behind a folding screen in the corner. He did not have to wait long.

Kit was whistling as he let himself into his dressing room, puzzled that the door was unlocked. "Epidemic of unlocked doors these days," he muttered. He would have locksmiths in, immediately. In his hand was the knife that had just been repaired and sharpened.

Some of the jewels in the hilt had come loose over the course of its two hundred year existence. On stage he never took it from the scabbard, but when a part called for armament he always wore it for the sense of pride it gave him. He laid it on the makeup table.

He decided not to wait for Nathaniel and started to costume himself. As he pulled on the loose, soft-collared shirt, coat, and trousers of Angel Clare as a student on holiday, he glanced at the clown.

"You know, my little wooden-headed friend, Nico is deviling me to do *Hamlet*. Perhaps I won't direct Minnie after all. Instead, I'll go back to what I love best to do. About time, don't you think? No argument, eh? That's what I like about you. You never hold a contrary opinion." He inspected his image in the full-length mirror and then seated himself at the makeup table.

"Jack," said a gravelly voice behind him. "Me own dear boy."

Kit's throat closed. The door lock snicked. The devil himself leered at him in the mirror.

"Jack. Don't ye want to give your old pappy a kiss? Or maybe you'd rather go down between me legs, hey, cocksucker?"

Kit leaped to his feet. The chair clattered over backward. Then Rourke was on him. His huge hands closed around Kit's throat as he toppled Kit backward onto the makeup table. Kit's head shattered the mirror. Containers of makeup flew off the dresser. The fragile old clown fell to the floor and splintered. Paralyzed by terror, all Kit could do was gape at the grinning face over him.

"Can't ye even fight, ye little bugger?" Rourke sneered. He seized a handful of Kit's hair. Their faces were almost touching.

Rourke ground his crotch hard against Kit. "I know what you are," he snarled. "I seen you and your fancy-man together. And if ye don't want everyone else t'know it, you'll pay me and pay me good and keep on payin' me as long as I want it. That ain't all they'll find out if you don't pay. They'll find out you ain't no St. Denys at all. They'll find out you tried t'kill your own old man."

His eyes blazed with hatred; he snatched up the jeweled dagger and pressed it against Kit's throat. "I'd slit your throat right now, but I don't want t'kill the goose with the golden egg."

"You're dead," Kit managed to gasp. "You're not real."

"Oh, I'm real, all right. You son of a whore! Stickin' a knife in me! I owe you a beatin'! I owe you worse than that." The sharp blade nicked Kit's skin and a drop of blood slid down his throat.

Kit's numb mind insisted that this wasn't real; it was just another nightmare. Nick would save him and he would wake up.

Rourke threw the dagger aside and it clattered on the floor. "Don't need that to take care of a pussy like you." He struck Kit with full force. "Won't even fight t'save your hide."

A thin stream of blood trickled from Kit's nose. His eyes focused on the bearded face. This was no nightmare. This pain was as real as it had been on the day they buried Michael. Rourke's big hand cracked his face again.

"You killed my brother!"

"So what? Didn't lose much when he croaked. I throttled that friend of yours too, that old bitch. Then I burned her up. And I ain't sure she was dead when I did. What do you think of that?"

Hatred shattered the terror. Kit slammed his knee into Rourke's balls. Rourke gasped and staggered back. Kit launched himself toward the old man and drove him backward into the cabinet. It tottered. The doors flew open, showering them with jewels as they fell to the floor. Rourke's fist smashed Kit's face once, twice. Something crunched. Blood burst from Kit's nose. He gagged on the blood in his throat. They grappled, bucking and rolling. Rourke hit him in the face again and opened a gash over his left eye. Kit faltered, blinded by blood. Rourke overpowered him, pinned him flat against the floor.

"Christ," Rourke panted, "ye look like your whore of a mother. By God, you do!" He forgot the millions that waited. He couldn't think of anything but making his slut of a son sorry he'd ever been born. His fist split Kit's lip.

Kit blindly flung his arm out. His fingers closed upon the ancient Italian stiletto. Repaired. Sharpened to razor keenness. With all the strength he possessed he drove the blade hilt-deep into Rourke's throat just under the bearded jaw. Rourke stiffened; his mouth opened in soundless shock. Kit yanked the knife free of its scabbard of flesh. Blood rained down upon his hands, his face, his clothes.

Clawing at the deadly wound, Rourke fell on him. Kit shoved the heavy body aside and got to his knees. Looked down into pleading eyes glazed with death. Raised the dagger in his slippery hand. Plunged it downward, through the dark coat, through hair, skin, and muscle, into the still-beating black heart. He tugged the blade free and drove it down again. "For Michael. For every beating, every scar. For Lizbet, and every—filthy—thing—you ever—did." Sobbing he plunged the knife downward again. And again. And again. And again.

🙚🙚

Nathaniel arrived to find the dressing room door locked. He'd suspected for a long time that Mr. Kit would like for him to retire and didn't know how to suggest it, but this was an unkind way to do it. He turned away and left the theatre. He had never gotten drunk in all his seventy years. It was time.

Before each performance, it was Kit's custom to go to the dressing rooms and speak to the performers, make a joke, ease some of the high-strung nerves. They wondered why he didn't come this night. Rama and Francis, meeting in the hallway, spoke of it. Rama had an instant answer.

"I suppose," she said in a tart, low voice, "that he's with Stuart upstairs."

Francis did not want to admit she was right, but she probably was. He went on his way, to make a last-minute check backstage.

Minnie Fiske was uneasy. She, Kit, and her husband always had a small glass of sherry together before the opening curtain. It wasn't like him not to be there. She drank her little glass of sherry with just her husband for company. She was more concerned not to see Kit backstage as it came time to start the performance, but said nothing. A play could be jinxed by the wrong words.

Nick had been delayed at the hospital and arrived just in time for the opening curtain, still wearing his workday suit of clothes. Impatient, he sat through ne'er-do-well Jack Durbeyfield's discovery that he was in reality Sir John d'Urberville. He fidgeted through the arrival of the young farm lasses and their dancing among the flowers, with each other for partners. He sat up in eager anticipation as the moment came for the three Clare brothers to appear, at which time Angel Clare would first set eyes on Tess, and the audience would first set eyes on Angel.

The action on stage faltered. Mrs. Fiske threw in lines that Nick knew were not in the script. He tensed. Kit never missed a cue or an entrance. Never. The actresses carried on, valiantly improvising. From his front row seat, he faintly heard hushed, distressed voices backstage. Two of the Clare brothers came on and they, too, improvised, waiting for Kit's arrival. Then the speeches and the acting floundered. Francis Mulholland, stage manager, stepped forward. "Ladies and gentlemen, there is a slight delay in the continuation of the play, a technical problem. We beg your indulgence for a few minutes and then we shall continue."

The new golden curtains swiftly slid closed. The audience sounded like a gigantic hive of bees.

Nick was out of his seat before the curtains met in the center, running backstage. He saw Mulholland rushing from the wings and seized his arm. "What is it? He's never missed a cue!"

"I know that better than you do," snapped Francis. "Come on. Perhaps he's taken ill."

They ran to the dressing room. "Kit! Kit!" called Francis. "You should be onstage!" There was the sound of a voice, but the door remained shut and locked. Francis fumbled with the key. The door opened only a little and would go no further. Nick and Francis put their shoulders to the door and managed to shove it far enough open to see that it was blocked by a man lying on the floor. Another shove let them slide past, into the room.

The floor was littered with fallen paste jewels, crowns, rings, and knives. None of the rubies were as red as the red that pooled out around the man on the floor. None of the rubies were as red as the red on Kit's face and hands and clothes as he lifted the knife and drove it downward.

The bearded man's eyes and mouth were open in eternal disbelief.

Nick knelt in the pool of blood. "Kit," he said softly, "Kit, it's over. Give the knife to me." Kit did not acknowledge him. He lifted the dagger and plunged it in again. The terrible movement of Kit's arm was sluggish, as if he had barely enough strength left to raise it. Nick reached for the knife and caught Kit's wrist in mid-plunge. For the first time Kit spoke.

"'Yet who would have thought the old man to have had so much blood in him? What's done cannot be undone.'"

"Kit, I'm going to take the knife." Nick said as he pried it from Kit's grasp. He was stunned when Kit plunged a knife visible only to him, into the chopped chest of his father.

"'Yet who would have thought the old man to have had so much blood in him?' " he said again. "'What's done cannot be undone.'"

"Kit," cried Nick, seizing the blood-slippery hand. "Don't you know I'm here? For the love of God, look at me!"

"'Yet who would have thought the old man to have had so much blood in him? What's done cannot be undone.'" Kit fixed his glazed eyes on Nick. "He killed my brother," he whispered. "He killed Lizbet." His voice rose. "He killed my brother. He killed Lizbet. He..."

Kit's voice trailed off. He stared down at his bloody hands and at the body of Tom Rourke. Even as Nick watched, Kit's battered face changed. The living light left his eyes. He pitched forward into Nick's arms.

20

earst's *New York Journal* scooped Pulitzer's *New York World* and had the pictures and story on the front page in a special edition. Beneath the headline **M U R D E R   O N   B R O A D W A Y !** were stock photographs of the handsome actor as Angel Clare and Hamlet, and dire warnings.

Famed Actor Goes Berserk In Theatre
Murders Worker In Savage Attack

INSIDE SEE EXCLUSIVE
POLICE PHOTOGRAPHS
Unparalleled Scenes of Gore
Not For The Faint Of Heart
Ladies Strongly Cautioned

••

Noose or Asylum for St. Denys?
Police Commissioner Speaks Out

Kit was put in the New York City Lunatic Asylum on Blackwell's Island to await indictment. Not even the protests of influential friends, including Judge Wescott and Ava Astor, could prevent it. Nick tried to see him there, but was not granted admittance. Harrison Fiske contacted a muckraking reporter who had been looking for a hook on which to hang a series about Blackwell's Island. Now he had that hook, a name that had already seized the interest and imagination of the public. The reporter, through ways only he knew, gained access to the asylum and his series of articles blasted conditions there.

Actor Kit St. Denys, known and beloved by thousands of theatergoers, has been cast into a snake pit where twelve hundred or more men and women are crammed into a place built for three hundred.

Though not yet indicted, tried, or convicted of any crime, he and other pathetic creatures who inhabit this place are subjected to foul food, abuse, degradation, and other dreadful conditions unworthy of an enlightened society on the brink of a new century. Cholera, dysentery, and influenza sweep through regularly. Those who are condemned to exist (I cannot say _live_) within these walls die of starvation or mistreatment. Some are shackled to walls in filthy cells. Assault and violation by patients upon one another and by guards upon patients are common.

No human being, much less a gentleman such as St. Denys, should find himself in such a place. This a situation not to be borne by a civilized society.

Three weeks passed before Judge Wescott was able to call due a favor from the judge who had sent Kit to Blackwell. Kit was removed from the public asylum to Petrie Mental Sanitarium, a private institution on Long Island, which was the very best, according to its founder and director. "It is a sanctuary," Dr. Petrie said in an unctuous, soothing voice. "A place where the patients can be safe and sheltered."

"When may I see him?" Nick asked.

"Are you his brother or other blood kin?"

"No. Close friend."

"Then, I'm sorry. Until the Court decrees otherwise he can have no visitors other than family members. You understand. He is accused, poor creature, of a heinous crime."

"I'm his doctor, as well as his friend."

"Until the Court decrees otherwise, he will be seen only by our staff physicians." Petrie smiled loftily at Nick. "He will need no doctor but myself. I, after all, am a pioneer in the kind of treatment he requires. You, I assume, are a ... general practitioner."

Sick with disappointment, Nick wondered why he hadn't had the wit to claim kinship with Kit. Another long month passed before Nick saw Kit again, at his trial.

～҂｀

Kit shuffled into the courtroom between two armed guards who gripped his upper arms. His wrists were shackled, and every step brought the clank of the shackles on his ankles. His colorless face was gaunt, his eyes vacant. "My God," breathed Nick. Bronwyn, sitting beside Nick, took his hand. Throughout the trial Kit sat silent and unmoving, his head bowed as if he slept.

The defense attorney moved for dismissal of the charges, arguing that the defendant was not capable of taking part in his own defense. The motion was denied and the trial proceeded.

The medical examiner testified to the cause of Rourke's death: direct penetration of the heart muscle by a pointed object. Yes, People's Exhibit A, the jeweled dagger, crusted with blood, had the right shape and dimension to be the death weapon. He continued, "Immediately prior to death his left carotid artery had been severed, the result of a deep thrust with a pointed object. After death, the deceased was also stabbed in the chest fifty times at least, quite possibly many more. It was impossible to determine with any certainty, Your Honor. The chest of the deceased looked, if I may be allowed a non-legal, non-professional term, Your Honor, as if it had been put through a meat grinder."

Nick and Francis Mulholland were called as adverse witnesses to describe what they had found in the dressing room at the St. Denys Theatre. Police drawings and photographs of both the deceased and the blood-covered accused were introduced. The defense called for a mistrial because Hearst and Pulitzer had prejudiced the case by trying, convicting, and executing the defendant in their newspapers. The mistrial was denied.

The defense called a physician who testified to Kit's battered condition, which was obvious to anyone present in the courtroom when he stood Kit up in front of them. He pointed to the broken nose, the still-red scar on his brow bone and the one that made a vertical line through one side of his upper lip. He showed several photographs of Kit before the tragedy. Kit stood through it all in a stupor.

"He's drugged," Nick raged to Bronwyn that night. "They're keeping him drugged. How can he defend himself?"

"I thought so too, when I saw him. I suspect laudanum," she said.

"Laudanum, opium, morphine... I wish I knew. I just know he's drugged."

"Can't you complain to the judge?"

"I have no standing. I'm not his doctor anymore. I'm not anything."

"Yes, you are. You're his friend." Then she asked quietly, "Nicholas, did he kill that man?"

"Yes." It was a strangled whisper. "But he had good cause, Bronwyn. Good cause." He looked into her honest face, and pulled her to him, taking comfort in her warmth and compassion. "I can't tell you because I have to tell it on the witness stand. I couldn't bear to say it twice."

Testimony resumed. Francis Mulholland testified he had hired the man he had known as Smith. His voice broke as he said, "If I hadn't, this never would have happened." The prosecution could not shake him on cross-examination.

The Marlborough hotel clerk testified that a man identical to the deceased had forced him to tell him Mr. St. Denys' address. Kelly testified the deceased had used the name Smith and had asked many questions about Mr. St. Denys. Kelly, too, was unshakable on cross. A broken-down prostitute testified that a man answering Rourke's description had "hired me for my favors and was most awful cruel to me." The judge gaveled the tittering spectators to silence.

Nick was the last witness. The reporters scribbled as fast as their pencils could go as the defendant's doctor told the Court about the hell of Kit's childhood. His words fell into a hushed room as he told them about the nightmares. He told him of Kit's last words, that Rourke had killed his brother and his friend. The prosecution moved to strike his testimony as hearsay; the Court denied the motion.

As throughout the rest of the trial, Kit did not once lift his head. Without comment the defense attorney put into evidence photographs of the dozens of old scars on Kit's body, and the hand with the broken finger.

Heavy silence blanketed the courtroom as the defense and prosecution made their closing arguments. While the judge deliberated, newspapers continued to spew the story.

ST. DENYS VICTIM WAS HIS OWN FATHER
• •

PROSECUTION CALLS FOR GUILTY VERDICT
FIRST DEGREE MURDER CONVICTION = EXECUTION
• •

"A HEINOUS CRIME!" DECLARES POLICE COMMISSIONER

Three days later, Bronwyn, Nick, Rama, and Francis sat together on one high-backed, scarred bench, waiting the Judge's decision. Rama and Francis clutched one another's hand tightly. Still shackled, Kit sat oblivious beside his attorney.

"In the matter of the State of New York vs. Christopher St. Denys, born Jack Rourke, I find Christopher St. Denys, also known as Kit St. Denys, to be not guilty of first degree murder or criminal manslaughter."

Nick sagged in relief. Bronwyn squeezed his hand. Then he gasped in shock as the judge continued. "Deciding the guilt or innocence of the accused was not the difficult part of my deliberations. The defense has shown beyond a shadow of a doubt the defendant killed without premeditation, to save his own life. The issue that delayed the rendering of the decision was the question of public safety. The defendant was mentally deranged at the time of this unbelievably savage killing, and though the Court is disposed to pity, the Court has to also take into consideration whether public safety would be served by releasing him. It is the Court's decision that Christopher St. Denys is a menace to society. He is hereby returned to protective custody until such time as a competency hearing can be arranged."

Nick leaped to his feet. "No! You can't do that!" he shouted. "You can't! What's the matter with you? You're the one who's deranged!" The judge banged his gavel and ordered him to be silent. "I won't be silent! This is wrong! You're making a mistake!" A bailiff forced him back into his seat. He heard Rama crying.

❦❧

Nick stood at the barred window of the sanitarium and looked out over the grounds. Summer had come and gone; the leaves of the trees had turned. On the other side of the bars the world looked colorful and happy.

The plainness of the cell-like room was depressing; its walls were a muddy green. A narrow cot and a small dresser were bolted to the floor. There were no curtains. ("He might hang himself.") No pictures. ("He might shatter the glass and commit suicide.") No books. The director had looked at Nick as though he were simple-minded when he asked. There was nothing of the things Kit had loved, the things that made life civilized. Around the grounds, aesthetically disguised by shrubbery and trees, was a high brick wall with iron spikes atop it.

Nick leaned his forehead against the inside bars. Then he straightened and turned toward Kit, who lay curled up on the cot, his eyes open but unfocussed, his pupils mere pinpricks. Once, Nick jabbed the back of Kit's hand with a needle. No reaction. Nick's efforts to find out if he was being treated with narcotics came to naught.

"Kit, I wish I knew if you even heard me," Nick said. "Wescott is pulling strings to get a guardianship hearing before him as soon as possible. Then he'll name me as your guardian." Nick thought he saw a flicker of response to the word guardian. "I'll take you home. You'll recover there. How could you not? With the laughter of little Jamie, and Bronwyn's kindness, and my love, how could you not?" His voice cracked on the last word.

❦❧

Kit's hair hung in dull, greasy locks past his shoulders. He had not been shaved for many days. He smelled sour as if he had not been bathed for a long time; that one small detail was wrenching. Nick spent part of each visit giving him news of his world.

"Mrs. Fiske reopened the theatre and is keeping it going for you. She's paying rent to your account, and she's in rehearsal with *Doll's House*. She sends her love."

"Your friend Rama went back to the girls' school, but as soon as you're well, she's going to leave it for good to perform with you."

"You've had letters from home, many of them. From Miss Terry and Mr. Irving, and members of your Company, and the staff at the Hill. Wilde even wrote you from Paris. And Bernard Shaw. You surely remember Shaw. You and he didn't like one another. And yet he wishes you well and says he has a play for you to consider when you're well."

"That strange woman who thinks she's divine, Bernhardt, wrote you, Kit. The letter is in French and I can't read it. You'll have to tell me what it says, someday soon."

"I have a box full of letters for you, Kit. Most of them seem to be from ordinary people, theatregoers. They're just waiting for you to read them." Never was there even a small sign that Kit heard him.

～※～

Kit became wraith thin. Bloody lesions appeared at the corners of his mouth. When asked about the lesions, Petrie said, "When a patient won't eat, we have to force-feed him."

"And how is that done?"

The director fidgeted under Nick's questioning stare. "We pry the mouth open with a steel gag. Then we insert a tube and pour down liquefied food. When the patient starts vomiting we know it's time to stop." At Nick's angry expression he said, "Well, we can't let them starve, can we?"

"Maybe if you didn't drug him into insensibility, he'd eat."

"How dare you tell me how to treat a patient? You know nothing about it."

Nick's fingers clenched convulsively. "Give me some food. Now. If you give a bloody damn, at least let me try."

Reluctantly, Petrie ordered a small bowl of broth given him, and he returned to Kit's cell. He rolled up a blanket to make a pillow, and coaxed Kit into turning on his back. He knelt beside the bed, bowl and spoon in hand. "Kit, you must eat. Please, love. For me. For your Nico." He held the spoon close to the sore lips. After an eternity, just as he was ready to admit defeat, Kit's mouth opened a little. Nick spooned in the broth. Much of it ran down his chin, but he swallowed a little. Eventually he took another spoonful and another until the small bowl was empty.

When Nick left Kit's cell, he stormed into Petrie's office, showed him the empty bowl, and demanded an end to the forced feeding. He again put before him his own credentials as a doctor and said,

"I'll hire a private nurse if necessary to come here every day and see to this matter if you are unable to do so. But be assured, if that's the case it will become public record."

David willingly took over more hours at the clinic and in the surgery, freeing Nick to go every day to coax Kit into a few spoonfuls of broth or soup. It was not enough. Kit was starving before his eyes. He held Kit's unresponsive hand and vowed, "You'll get well. You'll act again. You'll be the greatest actor in the world again." Kit, as always, did not appear to realize anyone had spoken to him.

"I read the *Dramatic Mirror* every week," Nick said, stroking the lank hair. "so when you ask me I'll be able to tell you. Mrs. Fiske said to give you some good news: the Trust has competition from two brothers named Shubert. By the time you're well, the Trust will be only a bad memory."

❧❧

Thick snowflakes turned the air to lace the day Nick came to Petrie Sanitarium to take Kit home. He was now Kit's legal guardian, thanks to Judge Wescott's string-pulling and quick ruling. Kit's clothes hung on his bony frame and he neither assisted nor fought Nick as he put on boots and coat, hat and gloves. His hair had finally been raggedly cut, and his beard shaved. He was an unkempt, hollow-cheeked parody of himself.

Dr. Petrie strode into the room and bellowed, "Stuart, what do you think you're doing?"

"Taking him to my home."

"You're a fool. You're not trained to handle mentally deranged patients."

"But you are. And you've done nothing for him."

"What if he becomes violent? If you don't keep him heavily sedated, you're as mad as he is." The psychiatrist threw the release papers on the cot and stalked from the cell.

Nick hoped the trip out into the cold snowy air would arouse Kit's interest, but he moved through it like a tall, shadowy puppet, guided by Nick's hand on his arm.

Bronwyn paced the floor waiting for them to return. Nick had asked her if he could bring his friend home when he was well enough and she had agreed. She had even volunteered to provide the nursing care, but he had refused. He intended to do it himself. Back and forth she walked. Her sympathy was with the poor man, but she didn't want to give up even more of her husband's time. Dr. Galvin came into the parlor from the surgery.

"The last patient has left, Mrs. Stuart. Is something wrong?"

"My husband's bringing Mr. St. Denys here, today, to live until he's well."

"I didn't realize St. Denys was that far recovered."

Before she could answer, Nick was at the door. "David, I'm so glad you're still here. Help me with him, will you?" he said. David shrugged into his coat, and went with Nick into the snow. A few minutes later, they reappeared, supporting the stupefied patient between them.

Even seeing Mr. St. Denys in court had not prepared Bronwyn for what she saw. She looked into his uncomprehending eyes. He wasn't in there, she realized in horror. His mind was gone. Merciful God, what had she agreed to? She watched, pale-faced, as Nicholas and Dr. Galvin guided the sick man's stumbling steps up the stairs.

Kit lay down on the soft bed and curled up. Within seconds he was asleep. David looked questioningly at Nick. "I thought he was more fully recovered."

"If he stayed there he would be dead within a week. Look at him, David. He's starving. I finally got out of Petrie the information I need: they kept him drugged on morphine. Now I have to gradually get him off it. Maybe then... David, I'll be up here often throughout the day, so you'll have more of a burden to carry in the surgery. If you believe in prayer, he could use those too. "

"He has them. So do you." David squeezed Nick's shoulder and left.

Nick sat beside the bed, watching Kit sleep for several minutes, then tenderly kissed his temple. As he pulled the door shut, he hesitated. He could not completely discount Dr. Petrie's warning. He locked the door.

Days passed into a week, then two. Nick knew he couldn't continue the double burden of his practice and providing all the care for Kit. He took stock of their finances that evening and slumped in his chair. He couldn't afford to pay two nurses. He would simply have to do without one in the surgery.

When Ida Barr looked in to say she was leaving for the day, he invited her into the office. She stood waiting with her usual starched efficiency. "Miss Barr," he said reluctantly, "Dr. Galvin and I will have to do without an office nurse."

If she felt shock at being dismissed she did not show it. "You're letting me go?"

"I have a proposition. I must hire a private duty nurse to help me look after the patient upstairs. Would you like the position? I'd prefer to have someone I know."

"I've never cared for an asylum patient," she said.

"He's not an 'asylum' patient, Miss Barr. And I'll see to the difficult part of his care. What I need from you is more supervisory than anything else. If you choose not to, I'll find someone else. I need someone immediately." He was relieved when she agreed.

Every day before she left, Miss Barr reported to Nick, though she had little to report. Then Nick bolted his dinner while half-listening to his wife. He was unaware of the reproach in Bronwyn's eyes when, every day, he excused himself from table to prepare and carry a tray upstairs.

Each time he went into the bedroom he found Kit sitting on the bed, his knees drawn up, his spine wedged into a corner. Nick tried to find encouragement from that. At least he was no longer curled up like an unborn child.

Nick decreased the morphine little by little, uncertain if this was the correct procedure. He had consulted several other doctors, but there was not a consensus among them. He found some enthusiasm for the use of the newly discovered drug heroin, as a treatment for morphine addiction. He was tempted to try it. But in the end, he followed his instinct and prayed it was right. Kit slept less but other than that, little changed.

He never looked directly at Nick. He did as he was told, volunteering no motion of his own. Like a featherless nestling he opened his mouth for food.

Nick talked to him while feeding him. He spoke of their good times together. He talked of the plays. He often mentioned Rama, and Francis, and Mrs. Fiske and *Tess*. None of it passed beyond the lightless dark eyes.

Nick was giving Kit his breakfast one morning when Bronwyn knocked lightly at the door. "Nicholas, Miss Weisberg's come to visit Mr. St. Denys."

"Ask her to come upstairs," he said hopefully. "Perhaps seeing her will help."

Rama entered slowly, her stricken gaze fixed upon Kit. "I had to see him," she said. "I couldn't bear not knowing how he was."

Nick withdrew across the room so that Rama could sit down on the bed. She put her hand on Kit's. "Don't you think you've played this role long enough, Kit? You're awfully good at it, but it's time to change the bill. Francis misses you, too. Let's do *Taming of the Shrew* again. You're wonderful as Petruchio, and you know I'm a marvelous Kate. Remember the line at the end? 'Why, there's a wench! Come on and kiss me, Kate.'" Her voice quivered. "And the audience always loves it when you end the scene by giving that big kiss and I liked it too. Say you remember. Say the line, won't you? 'Kiss me, Kate,'" For several more minutes she talked. Then, with an expression of hopeless despair, walked to the door.

Suddenly Kit made a sound. Harsh, abrupt, a dead tone. Nick gasped and hurried to the bed, Rama on his heels. "You spoke!" Nick said. The sound came again, but neither Rama nor Nick could understand it. "Kit, talk to me. Talk to Miss Weisberg. Tell us what you're thinking just now. Please, Kit. Talk to one of us."

Kit made the sound once more. Nick and Rama exchanged puzzled, distraught glances. "Talk to me, Kit," Rama pleaded. "I don't know what you're saying. What do you mean?"

For the smallest fraction of a moment Kit looked puzzled but alert, as if he were seeking an answer to her question. Then he withdrew again into his hidden world. Nick pleaded with him for several more minutes to speak again, but Kit sat in the corner with his arms locked around his drawn-up legs, his forehead on his knees, his face hidden. At last, with a sigh of defeat, Nick left the room with Rama, locking the door behind him. Nothing was said until they were downstairs in his office.

Then Rama burst out, "Why do you keep him caged like an animal!" When he did not answer, she seized his sleeve. "What was it he said?"

"I don't know."

"Was it even a word? Please tell me it was a word and not just a sound."

"I don't know. I think it was a word. No. I'm certain of it."

"But what?"

"I don't know, Miss Weisberg." His voice was sharp. "I didn't know ten seconds ago, how could I know now?"

"You're supposed to be able to heal people, aren't you? Do it!"

"Don't you think I want to? Don't you think I would give anything I own to see him be himself again?"

"Would you? At least this way you can control him. You never could before!"

Nick paled. "Miss Weisberg, leave before I forget you're a woman and strike you." With a final scathing glare, Rama left and Nick was alone.

Nick had maintained the journal begun when he'd come to America. In the past months the journal had become a disheartening story of an odyssey to nowhere. Most entries read simply: No change today.

In the quiet of the house that night, he wrote the date at the top of the clean journal page.

> Kit spoke today. But was it intelligible speech? Or was
> it just a guttural protest against my constant badgering?
> Might it not even have been wishful thinking on my part?
> No, I know it was real. Miss Weisberg heard it too. I wish
> I could see into his mind. If the mind is even there.

He put the journal in the secret drawer, and took out the book of sonnets. The verses Kit had written in the front cried out to him. With his fingertips he traced Kit's handwriting. "Without the sanction of Society," he whispered, "Without the sanction of the Church, Without the sanction of God..." Above the words "I love you" he interlined his own wistful words. 'Without the sanction even of yourself.'

Nick had to escape the oppressive room. He put on his coat and went to the widow's walk, turning up his collar against the cold wind. A faint sliver of moon rode high in the overcast heavens.

"I haven't prayed for a long time," he said to God, "and I have no right to do it now. But if what's happened to him is punishment for what we did together, I beg You to punish me instead. He's not the one who betrayed Your trust. Make him well. I'll promise anything, do anything, just heal his mind. Do with me what You will; the sin was mine." As a boy he had believed God spoke to him. He waited now in the frigid silence. God did not speak.

᠅

Buds appeared on the trees. Jonquils pushed their way upward toward the sun. In the beginning, Rama and Francis and Judge

Wescott had made regular visits, but the visits became fewer and finally stopped. Francis awkwardly tried to explain. "It's just so difficult to see him like that." Faced with the stern question in Nick's eyes, Francis had to look away.

Bronwyn went into the office late one evening; anger and worry warred in her mind. He had not come to dinner. Again. He was completely engrossed in a book. He didn't look up when she said his name. She said it again.

With an absent smile, he said, "I'll come to dinner in a moment, darling."

"Dinner was over long ago. Jamie's in bed. He'd like to see his father once in a while. And I'd like to see my husband." She left, pulling the door shut with a bang.

Taken aback by her vehemence, he glanced at the clock and was surprised by the late hour. Regretfully, he closed the new book, *Principles of Psychology,* and placed it on his desk along with the notes he had made. It was such a new science, and some of what he read was beyond his ken. "But I have to try," he muttered. "I can't do anything for him with what I already know. I have to reach beyond." He rubbed his eyes and went to Bronwyn's sitting room.

"I'm sorry," he said, from the doorway. "I know I'm distracted these days."

"Yes. You are." She looked up at him, pleading in her eyes. "Nicholas, your friend isn't getting any better. He can't do anything, he can't even talk to you and yet you spend every spare minute waiting hand and foot on him. I know I'm being petty, but sometimes it seems you care more for him than you do for me and your son."

"That's not true! I love you and Jamie. You know I do."

"I know!" she said with a gesture of frustration. "But that's not how it seems. Nicholas, if he were not here, we would be happy." She drew a deep breath and said, "I want him to leave here. He's rich, isn't he? Can't he return to the Petrie Asylum?"

"He'd die there. And you're wrong to think he's not getting better. I see improvement every day. It's just a matter of time."

"And if he doesn't get well?"

"He will. I just told you. He's better already."

Bronwyn got up. "Prove it," she said. "Let him take his meals with the family. If I must share you with him at least I'll be able to see you."

Nick flinched. That silent, pathetic figure at the dinner table? "He's not ready. When he is, he'll join us."

"And then he'll be well and he can go home?"

"I hope so. Oh, I hope so," he said fervently.

After she was asleep that night, Nick let himself into Kit's room. In the flickering light of his candle, Nick could see that Kit's eyes were open and his pupils were wide, no longer abnormally constricted. He lay on his side with his left arm under his cheek. Nick pulled the chair over to the bed. "I've got a book, Kit. I hope it will tell me what to do. It's a new science, psychology, which may be able to unlock minds. That's all I need, isn't it? The proper key. Talk to me, Kit. If you remember what we were to each other, say my name."

Kit's lips moved and he made again that guttural sound that had mystified Nick and Rama. He had not said it since. Three times he croaked out the word, if it was a word. And then turned his head away and became silent once more.

pril. May. June.

"Talk to me, Kit," Nick begged. "Just say my name. Say anything. Who am I?"

Kit shook his head, whimpered, drew up his knees and hid his face against them.

July.

"Who are you? Do you know who you are? Can you say your name?" A flicker in Kit's eyes. The grunt that might be a word. "Say your name. You're my Kit. Kit St. Denys."

Nick wrote in his journal that night:

> I think Kit spoke again, that same sound of several months past. If only I knew what he is trying to tell me. It sounds like it might be a word. But what? Is he trying to say a word but can't remember how? I refuse to believe it is only meaningless babble. I am so tired. So frightened. Sometimes I fear I will join him in his madness. And what of Bronwyn in all this? I neglect her, but I don't mean to. I will make it up to her and Jamie as soon as Kit is well.

He stared bleakly at the page. And what if Kit were never well? He dared neither answer nor acknowledge the question.

The next morning he was conscious of having awakened in the night with the answer to something important and then had fallen asleep again. But what was the answer and what was the question?

A day or so later, he was writing out a prescription for a tonic for Mrs. Allen and only half listening to her as she chattered on about her Scottish terrier.

"He just hasn't been himself, poor thing, since the neighbor's mongrel got loose and chased him under the porch. Why, he just shakes all the time. I wish you were a veterinarian, Dr. Stuart. I'd bring in my poor Jack for you to examine."

He chuckled and handed her the prescription. "My days of treating cats and dogs are over, I'm afraid. But you, I can help. Take this to the chemist." He put his hands on her plump shoulders. "Mrs. Allen, what did you say your dog's name is?"

"Jackson Rob Roy MacDuff McTavish the Third, but we call him Jack. He's a purebred Scottie. Good heavens, Dr. Stuart!" she exclaimed, turning red when he planted a kiss on her cheek.

Jack. Jack Rourke. Short, abrupt names. Formed by vocal cords that had forgotten how to speak. " Thank you, Mrs. Allen. Thank you more than you know. And if you want to bring dear old Jack in to see me after hours, you're more than welcome."

Nick's patients were surprised at the sparkle in his eye. "You don't seen as tired today, Dr. Stuart," ventured the last patient of the day.

He laughed as he placed his stethoscope against her abdomen to listen for her baby's heartbeat. "I'm not, Mrs. Zorns. I think I found a piece to a puzzle I've been trying to put together." He listened then straightened, smiling. "And, dear lady, your child has the heartbeat of a lion."

Nick locked the surgery door and bolted upstairs without cleaning or sterilizing anything. When he burst in, Kit was asleep and Ida was reading. "Is something wrong, Dr. Stuart?" she asked in alarm. Nick did not realize he had a wide, almost manic grin.

"No, Miss Barr, something is right. I hope. Please. Take the rest of the day off."

She got up uncertainly, frowning. "Are you sure?"

"Yes. Enjoy your time to yourself."

Puzzled, she met Bronwyn coming up the stairs. "Ida, have you seen my husband? The surgery's locked but he's nowhere in sight."

Ida looked in the direction of Kit's room. "Yes. He's in there."
"Oh." She sighed. "I wanted him to have tea with me. Jamie's asleep and everything's so peaceful. Well, I can't interrupt him while he's with his patient." She said the last word as if it contained acid. The two women walked down together. "Have tea with me, Ida. I get so lonely these days. Jamie isn't much of a conversationalist." She sighed again. "I want to go back to work. I miss the patients. And at least then I'd get to see my husband. But he won't hear of it until Jamie's older."

Nick sat beside the bed until Kit's eyes opened slowly. Seeing Nick, he quickly sat up, pulled as far back into the corner as he could, and huddled into himself like a frightened deer. "Jack," he said again, and now the word was clear to Nick. But the pleading tone left Nick more mystified than before.
"I don't understand!" Nick cried. "I don't understand. Why are you afraid of me? Kit St. Denys is afraid of nothing."

❧ ❧

Michael Rourke stared at the man who sat beside the bed. He was scared. He had been scared for a very long time. Where was he? Who was that man? Who was that woman who came here every day? Where was Jack? Jack would know. Jack would take him away from there. They had money. Where was it? Where was Jack? Why didn't he come? He covered his face with his arms. "Jack," he moaned.
Big dark coat. Brass buttons. Black beard. Mum gone. Something on the bed. Hurt boy not moving
Michael fell on his knees beside the bed where the hurt boy lay. Michael. He was not Michael. He was Jack. The old man had hurt Michael. He pulled his brother into his arms and rocked him, stroking the blond hair so like his own, and promised to take care of him. Michael did not answer. He was dead. The old man had killed him.

❧ ❧

His joy fading, Nick said, "If only I knew what to do for you." He rested his hand for a moment on Kit's shoulder. "Jack...?" he said tentatively.

Kit's head snapped up and he leaped to his feet. Before Nick knew what was happening Kit had shoved him backward against the door. "You killed my brother!" he screamed. He had the strength of madness and his eyes blazed with hatred, his teeth were bared. "Damn you! God damn you!"

Nick felt oddly calm as Kit's hands closed around his throat as they had once before. He seized Kit's wrists. "Wait," he managed to gasp. "I'm not the old man. Michael's away somewhere. Kill me and you'll never find him."

Kit froze. "What?" He loosened his hold on Nick just enough so that Nick was able to bring his arms up and break away, almost falling into the hallway. He quickly shut and locked the door and leaned against it, breathing harshly. "Is there no end to it? God, God, he finally speaks and it is to threaten my life! I don't know how much longer I can bear it." But he had to bear it. The alternative was Kit in the madhouse forever.

Kit threw himself against the other side of the door and screamed threats and obscenities. After several long minutes, the room fell quiet. Nick risked opening the door. Kit was again huddled on the bed. Unmoving and silent once more.

Jack burrowed his face deeper into his arms. The explosion of fury had burned him out. That wasn't the old man, of course he wasn't. But who was he? And that on the bed wasn't Michael, it was a blanket. "Michael, help me," he whimpered. "I'm alone and I'm scared. I don't know where I am. I don't know where you are. I know you ain't dead because you can't be." He rocked back and forth and moaned.

July heat bore down upon the yellow house and turned the bright colors in the garden to brittle dun. Everyone and everything was listless. Except Kit. His lethargy had without warning become feverish energy. He paced the small room, glaring at Ida, who watched him warily.

"I'm going out," he said.

She had been taken by surprise when he abruptly started moving about. Now he had actually spoken. She was tempted to leave him long enough to tell Dr. Stuart of the change, but if she did he'd think she couldn't deal with it on her own. When her patient strode past her toward the door, she said, "Wait. You can't do that."

"I can so."

"No. Not yet. Doctor must make certain you're well enough first. Come along now. Be a good boy and sit down." She gasped in surprise and pain as he seized her upper arms.

"Hands off!" he barked, shoving her backward. He released her and turned again to the door. Locked. He swiveled toward her. "You got the key?"

Hastily she threw it at him. He fumbled with it, then rushed out into the hallway and looked frantically about. He didn't know how to get to the outside he saw from the window. He ran down the stairs, paused, and darted through the unoccupied dining room, then through the kitchen. Cook and the daygirl screamed. A heavy pot of potatoes slipped from Cook's hands and clattered at their feet.

Outside Kit stood still, spread out his arms to the sky, and gave an inarticulate cry of jubilation as he turned in a circle, his closed eyes and ecstatic face turned to the sun. Bronwyn, sitting in the sunshine with Jamie, gasped. She snatched up Jamie and held him tight, edging toward the safety of the house, away from the madman.

Ida pounded on the examination room door. "Doctor! Doctor!" When he opened the door a little bit, she said, "He made me give him the key and he went outside."

"Out? Outside? What in the world are you talking about? You gave him the key?" Full realization of her words hit him. "My God, he's come out of it!" He wanted to seize her around the waist and dance her about the room. "Miss Barr, see to Mr. Nash. Simple hand wound, needs bandaging." Without waiting for a reply he pressed his stethoscope into her hand. The nightmare was over! They could get their lives back again.

Kit ran, awkwardly, his body strange and unwieldy. He ran past the house and into a strange wood. His first joy faded into fear. He didn't see nothin' familiar. Shouldn't be no bloody trees. Where was the river and the houses and the alleyways? Where was the bony cats, and the trash of every kind? Toad and Spitter? Where was they? Where was the Royal Lion and where was Lizbet? Where was Michael? He fell against a tree, gasping. He'd dreamed Michael was dead. It was a dream because it could not be true.

He ran a little farther, confused, seeking his way. Branches slapped his face. Roots tripped him. He fell to the ground and lay there on a carpet of leaves so sheltered from the sun that they were still damp. He was lost and did not know how to get back to where he should be. Hearing footsteps on the leaves, he sat up, seized a fallen branch and started to get up. His foot slipped on the wet leaves and he fell heavily to the ground.

Nick knelt beside him. "Kit. Are you all right?"

The frightened brown eyes searched his face. "Stop calling me that. I'm Jack. Jack Rourke. Why do you keep calling me that? Who are you? Where's this place?"

Nick said softly, "Ki— Jack, I'm your friend. I'm a doctor. I'm taking care of you here, at my house."

"If the old man finds me here he'll kill me."

"He can't. He's gone away. He can't ever bother you or anyone ever again."

"Liar. Where's me brother?"

"He can't be with us just now."

Kit put his hands to his head. "I don't understand. Where's Lizbet?"

"Lizbet is away, also. Are you hurt?"

"What d'you care?"

Nick stood and started to help him. He jerked his arm from Nick's touch. "Get your hands off me." He clambered to his feet unaided.

"Come along then," Nick said, and walked away. He was happy that Kit was walking and talking again. But why was he insisting he was Jack? Maybe he should take him home, sit him down, explain everything. Maybe with it all laid out like playing cards in front of him, he would become Kit again. Behind him he heard the sound of stumbling feet.

Kit fell into step with him. "Don't you lock me up again."

"I can promise only if you give me your word you won't bolt. I can't make you well if you won't stay put and cooperate."

The silence was broken by the sounds of their steps. Then Kit muttered, "I won't bolt."

"Do you promise?"

"Yeah."

"I'll let you eat downstairs with the family if you like."

"Not if that bitch what locked me up will be there."

Nick stopped. "She'll be at our table sometimes, a guest just like you. You will respect her. Is that understood? You will not use that kind of language around my wife or any woman of my house. Is that also understood?" Kit mumbled rebellious assent.

Nick wondered what Bronwyn would think of the arrangement. When they arrived at the house, Nick said, "Go upstairs, Jack. Clean yourself for luncheon. Clean hands, clean face, and fresh clothes. I'll send Miss Barr to help you."

"Don't need no help. I ain't a baby. And I don't want her." Kit stomped loudly upstairs.

Nick found Bronwyn in the parlor, looking frightened. He told her the news. She took it quietly and then nodded. "I didn't know what to think. He looked like a wild man. But it must mean he's recovering."

Nick nodded. "I think he's living his early years over. He's confused, looking for something, anything he knows and there's nothing. Eventually, his memory will come back entirely and he'll be himself."

As he said it, he realized he could never tell the half-frightened, half-defiant thirty-year-old child what had happened. Not even if it meant he would never have Kit back again. If he were to know, it would have to come from inside himself.

"And if that doesn't happen? Nicholas, you have to face that possibility. If he doesn't get better, there will have to be another place for him." She tried to say it gently, trying to hide the panic she felt.

With a certainty he didn't feel, Nick said, "He's close to recovery. Very close." He took a deep breath and said, "I promised him I wouldn't lock his door after today."

Bronwyn's fear showed in her eyes. "Are sure that's a good idea?" He nodded, and prayed he was right.

Ida Barr came into the room without knocking. "Dr. Stuart, you don't pay me enough to allow myself to be manhandled. I quit."

"Oh, Ida!" Bronwyn protested. "Don't do that."

Nick said, "Miss Barr, he's not himself. He wasn't responsible."

"Nonetheless. You're a fool to keep a lunatic in the same house as your family. I don't know how you can endanger your wife and baby like that. You'll be lucky if he doesn't murder you all in your beds."

Nick was red-faced with anger as she walked out. Bronwyn hesitated and then followed her. "Ida, wait—Please reconsider. What will I do without you here? Nicholas is so caught up in treating him he has no time for anything else. Without you to talk to..." She blinked back tears.

Ida hugged her and said softly, "Even without me, Bronnie, you have a good friend in the house. Don't you realize Dr. Galvin still cares for you?"

Bronwyn stared at her. "No," she said uncertainly. "No, he doesn't. Not in that way." And yet, she realized for the first time, she had come to consider David Galvin a friend. She shut the door behind Ida and returned to Nick.

He said, "Darling, you know if there was any real danger to my family, Mr. St. Denys wouldn't be here. You believe me, don't you?"

She gave him a searching look, then said without conviction, "I suppose."

At the luncheon table, Kit's eyes darted from person to person. He used his fingers as much as he used his fork. When he spilled his water, he muttered obscenities. Bronwyn pretended he was not there. David watched him as if expecting him to become violent. Nick told himself it was a start. Perhaps not a good one, but they had to start somewhere.

❦

Cook came to him one day with a list of mysteriously missing food. The following day, money was missing from his cash box. That same evening Bronwyn came to him, tears glimmering in her eyes.

"My mother's little gold cross is missing, Nicholas," she said. "The clasp broke and I put it on the table last night, intending to take it for repair. It's gone."

"I'm sorry, sweetheart, but I don't know what you want me to do about it."

"I think Mr. St. Denys stole it. I'm sure he did. I must have it back."

"Perhaps you mislaid it," Nick said. "Perhaps it was the day girl."

"Mislaid it? I could as easily mislay my heart. And I trust Mary completely." She put her hand on his arm. "Please, Nicholas. It's all I have of my mother."

Nick's steps were heavy as he ascended the stairway, sick at the thought of confronting Kit over the missing things. Later it would have been easier, but how could he do it now?

Kit sat on the bed and refused to move when Nick said he wanted to check the bed. He folded his arms and glared. Nick folded his arms and glared back. Finally with a curse, Kit got up and lifted the pillow. It was all there: the locket, the money, even the pilfered food, which was moldy and all of it looking the worse for the passage of several days.

"Why, Jack?" he asked.

"Because."

"That's not an answer. You have everything you need here. Why did you think you had to steal?" He picked up a moldy scone. "And why steal food?"

"I wanted to put it away for if I go hungry."

"You won't go hungry here."

"Says you. Anyway, if Michael comes he'll need something to eat. We always save for each other."

"If Michael comes, we'll set another place at table and he can have all he wants. You needn't steal from us. You needn't steal anything."

Uncertainty clouded Kit's eyes. Slowly he picked up the money and the locket and put it all in Nick's hands. More reluctantly, he scooped up the food and put it into the little basket under the window. "You promise I ain't going to go hungry?" he asked.

"Yes," Nick said, smiling. "I promise." When he pulled the door shut behind him, Kit was standing at the window. Something inside Nick lurched; he didn't want to examine his feelings just then. Bronwyn was in the parlor. David had just arrived, and she was talking somberly to him. Nick greeted David, and then put the locket and chain into Bronwyn's hand.

Bronwyn looked at it, then into his eyes. Her eyes questioned him. He knew he would never admit where he found it. In his journal that night, he wrote:

> I want to weep, though whether from joy or sorrow, I don't really know. He stole, like the common thief he once was. But he returned everything. I have to believe my Kit lives in that darkened mind. I have to. Because if he does not, what shall I do? What shall I do?

22

K it's awareness increased little by little. Questions swarmed in his mind the way gnats swarmed in the sunshine.

He was at Old Stuart's house but that didn't tell him nothing, since he didn't know where it was. Old Stuart was a doctor. But he didn't need a doctor. Michael was away somewhere and the old man was gone forever, but Old Stuart wouldn't tell him where either one of them was. He hoped the old man was shark shit. But where was his friends? Where was Lizbet? Where was the theatre?

The strangest and most puzzling thing of all was himself. Everything was too big. His face. His feet. Even his willie. His arms and legs were a mile long. And Old Stuart was a little shorter than he was. It's like he was melted and poured in a bottle that didn't fit.

He spent long minutes staring into the mirror. His face was all wrong. Why was it rough in the morning? Why'd Old Stuart shave him? Men shaved. Kids didn't. What was them little lines on his forehead? And he saw some by his eyes. Where'd they come from? His nose was crooked, like Spitter's. Didn't remember getting it broke. He touched the scar over his eyebrow and the one that bisected one side of his upper lip. Must've been in a bloody bad fight. But when? And why couldn't he remember?

Sometimes his terror of these unknown things overwhelmed him and he would pass two or three days as withdrawn as he had been before.

※ ※

Kit sat cross-legged on the grass, elbows on his knees, his chin in his hands. With the spraddled, knees-up gait of a toddler, Little Jamie ran at him, shoved him, and ran away giggling. Kit smiled quizzically. He wasn't sure what fun it was for the little boy, but he patiently endured it. The little boy's mum wasn't never far away. Did him and Michael ever play like that while Mum watched? If they did, he couldn't remember it. A ripple of memory. "Look after your brother." And it was gone.

Jamie dove at him again. Kit grabbed him that time and tickled him into howls of giggles, laughing with him. Bronwyn took Jamie out of Kit's reach. "I think that's enough play for today for Master Jamie. He needs to take a nap." She bore the protesting child into the house. Kit watched, hurt, knowing from the way her mouth had tightened that he had done something wrong.

Before Kit had joined them, Bronwyn had been reading from a small book to Jamie. Kit looked for a long time toward the book that lay on the grass. Lizbet was teachin' him to read, but where was she? Old Stuart wouldn't tell him, but he knew the answer, Kit was sure of that. He glanced around to make sure no one saw him, and then slipped the book into his shirt and returned to his room. He sat on his bed, his back against the wall, the book propped on his lap, and opened it.

He read it cover to cover in five minutes and then he read it again. He felt a grin spread. Whatever was wrong with him, at least he could read! Maybe Old Stuart would let him try some of his books. Maybe there was books someplace that belonged to him.

Kit stuck the book partway under his pillow just as Old Stuart came in. "Hello. One of my patients canceled, so I thought I'd see how you are. I looked outside first and didn't see you."

"Thought I'd nipped out of here, didn't you," Kit said with a scowl.

"It crossed my mind."

"Told you I wouldn't."

"I know."

"You think I'm a bloody liar, don't you."

"No. But I know you don't like being confined."

"You don't know nothin' about me."

"I know more about you than you do." Kit looked surprised but let it pass. "Isn't that Jamie's book?" Nick asked.

"So what?" Kit's chin lifted in defiance. "I can read the stupid thing." Kit rattled off the entire text of the book word for word, even, unconsciously, adding dramatic and humorous touches with his voice.

Nick could not stop the soft cry, "My God."

"It's just a stupid story about rag dolls," Kit said, secretly pleased at Old Stuart's reaction. Then with his sharp gaze on Nick's face he asked the question Nick had prayed to hear and yet dreaded. "Whatcha mean, you know more about me than me."

"A terrible thing happened to you, Jack. It made you sick for a long time and it made you forget most of your life. Your name isn't Jack, really."

Kit jumped to his feet and shouted, "I don't want t'hear about it!"

"When you're ready, I'll tell you everything."

Kit looked at Nick, his eyes dark with confusion. "You used t'call me somethin' else. What was it?"

"Kit. Your name is Christopher. But those who love you call you Kit."

"No. No. It's Jack. Ain't nobody loves me. Just Michael."

Nick got up to leave. "Someday you'll ask me, and I'll tell you the truth." As he started toward the door, Kit's voice stopped him.

"Where's the theatre?"

Hope! If he remembered his theatre... Cautiously Nick asked, "What theatre?"

"The Royal Lion. Where's Lizbet? I want to see her. She teaches me stuff. 'Speak proper,' she says, 'and folks'll think you're a gentleman born.' She says that's important."

"She's right." Nick felt a surge of hope at the small opening of another door. Then he had an idea, one that might even be dangerous for Kit's recovery, but something told him he had to try it. "Jack," he said, "you can't go to the Royal Lion and Lizbet is not here. You're not in London anymore."

"Not in London? Then where the bloody hell am I?"

"Away from the City. But I can take you to a theatre."

Kit's eyes brightened. "Would you do that? Soon? And do you have books maybe I could try t'read?"

"Of course. I'll bring some up if you like."

"Lizbet says to always say please and thank you. So please if you would bring 'em and thank you for 'em. Just don't bring no stupid books about dolls."

Nick laughed, his first genuine laugh in a long, long time. "I promise. No dolls."

Nick took him some of Jamie's little rhyme books and Kit read them all in little over an hour and asked for something harder. The following day Nick borrowed short books from the lending library. Kit read, barely stopping to eat. Nick took him poetry. Then plays. Kit read them all avidly, asking Nick the meaning of words and phrases. Whenever Nick saw him the next two weeks he had a book open, reading as if the words were food and he was starving.

One night Nick wrote in his journal:

How wonderful it is to see him reading. Especially the plays. He makes no comment about any of them, but he asks for more. I've not given him Shakespeare because it would break my heart for him to reject them. Today I asked him if he remembered what he had read, some play by Sheridan, and he recited a great chunk of it. I don't know the play so I can't attest to the accuracy of his memory. He looked so pleased with himself, he almost looked like my old Kit. Tomorrow I am to see Mrs. Fiske and Miss Weisberg and Mr. Mulholland.

As for me, I wish I could say certain of my feelings have vanished. They have not. And as he grows more and more like the Kit I knew those feelings become more insistent. If he continues to follow, as he seems to be doing, a path that is leading him from his childhood forward through his life, he will soon reach the early maturity of his adolescence and what will happen then? He'll in his mind be a hot-blooded boy with physical needs unattached to emotion. And if my plan works, Mulholland will be there. And Mulholland was his lover before I was

He threw down the pen, appalled at what he had written. Then he picked up the pen and marked heavily through the entire unfinished paragraph. After he had locked the journal away, he climbed to the widow's walk. It had once been a place of peace, but now it was the place where he wrestled with his demons.

"My God," he said aloud. "Am I mad? What difference does it make to whom he turns as long as he recovers? I've promised God time and time again—'just make him well and I'll be a monk the rest of my life.' Well, it's almost time to keep that promise." He raised one hand to his eyes and cried in agony, "But I still love him and I still want to be with him. I wish to God I did not, but I do."

❧❧

Rama dried her eyes. Francis cleared his throat. Mrs. Fiske looked from Nick to Rama to Francis and back at Nick. "I can't speak for the others, Dr. Stuart, but it would be a privilege to help in any way I can."

"Yes," Rama said in a husky voice. "Kit. In the theatre again!"

"But not as himself," Nick reminded her. "As Jack Rourke. And it might not work. It might even make things worse."

"How much worse could they be?" Rama said.

"It's worth trying," Francis said. "Anything is worth trying."

"When will you bring him?" Mrs. Fiske asked.

"I'll bring him in the morning, and I'll stay. After that, we'll see. Mr. Mulholland, you would have to supervise him and show him what to do. I know it wouldn't be easy for you."

"A stagehand," Francis said sadly. "The most brilliant actor I've ever seen. A stagehand."

"He will act again," Rama said, her expression daring anyone to say otherwise. "Soon." Turning to Nick she said, "I never thought I'd say this, but I'm glad you're around."

He smiled. "Miss Weisberg, I could say the same."

❧❧

Kit walked out into the sunshine. After several gloomy rainy days it felt good; he stretched like a lazy cat. The lady and the little boy were gone. He'd seen them drive off in a buggy. The pleasure of being outdoors faded into restlessness. The teasing pictures were back in his head, buzzing, buzzing. He wished he could swat them, make them go away.

And then they were crystal clear images. *A huge stone house with many windows. Acres of emerald grass and trees. Enormous gardens of flowers. Many faceless people. Another house. Smaller. A naked man with dark hair.* They merged and vanished.

"No!" he cried aloud. Desperately, he tried in vain to bring them back. He turned slowly around in Bronwyn's garden and looked at the yellow house. Wherever he was, that wasn't the big stone house he had seen in his head.

He left the fenced garden behind and walked through the windbreak of poplars. In a few minutes he came upon a stable, not nearly as fine as the one at St. Denys Hill. Kit stumbled. *St. Denys Hill.* What was that? He had to remember. It was terribly important. But in the next moment the large stable was gone, and like the stone house, the smaller house, and the naked man, it would not return.

While he stood, shaken, a young groom led a black filly from the stable into the sunlight. "Hey, lass," the groom soothed, picking up the brush, unaware he was being watched. "I'll make you the belle of the ball." His sleeves were rolled up and muscles played in his forearm as he stroked the horse's ebony coat.

Kit's gaze traveled over the man's body as his torso, arse, and slightly bowed legs swayed in rhythm with the movement of his arm. A sweet fire flared deep inside Kit. His breath quickened. He moved closer, unseen. Slowly his hand moved forward and descended upon the groom's bare forearm. Beneath his palm the muscular flesh was sun-warm and damp. He was surprised and pleased by the hard stirring between his legs.

The young groom jumped, dropping the brush. "Mr. St. Denys, you gave me a bit of a start. I guess I was daydreamin'." He smiled shyly.

St. Denys. St. Denys Hill. The name burst once more into his brain. "Why do you call me that?" Kit asked, dropping his hand.

"Well, Dr. Stuart told me that you was coming to stay because you was sick and he wanted my help if he needed it. A crying shame what happened to you."

A knot tightened in Kit's chest. "So you know who I am?"

"Everybody knows who you are. I seen your picture on a theatre sign in the city once. 'Kit St. Denys,' it said in big black letters." He picked up the brush and resumed grooming the filly.

The name ran around in Kit's brain like a crazed squirrel. *Kit St. Denys. Kit. St. Denys. KitStDenys, KitStDenys. Kit.* That was what Nick had called him. Nick? Who was Nick? He was aware the groom had spoken. "Are you all right, sir? You look like you seen a ghost."

"Maybe I have," he whispered. "I'm dizzy. I need to sit down." The boy nodded and took him into his own quarters in the stable. Kit sat down on the cot and took a tin cup of water from the groom. "Do you know what Dr. Stuart's first name is?" Kit's mouth was dry. His tongue felt as if it were glued to the roof of his mouth as he waited for the answer, somehow knowing what it would be.

"It's Nicholas, I think."

Nick. Nico. St. Denys Hill. Other names hammered at his mind. *Rawdon. Xavier. Hamlet. Romeo. Rama. Francis.* He returned the cup to the groom and went outside. Dazed, he wondered why the name Nico seemed as natural as breathing. He broke into a run as he neared the house. Stuart had said when he wanted to know the answers he would be told. Stuart better make good on his promise or else.

✣

Nick's emotions were a maelstrom of hope, fear, uncertainty, and desperation. Would God be kind and restore Kit's memory tonight? Would he recognize his own theatre, and his friends? He wondered how Kit would react when he told him about tomorrow. And then he arrived home to an empty house. Bronwyn had left him a note telling him she and Jamie were visiting friends. But where was Kit?

Then Kit burst into the house. Sweat streaked his face; his hair was disheveled and his eyes were wild. "Stuart!" he cried. "Stuart, you said you'd tell me everything. Tell me. Tell me now."

Nick was certain he was dreaming; the voice, inflection and clear pronunciation were Kit's, not Jack's. Nick willed himself to be calm, detached. "Sit down," he said.

"No."

"As you wish."

Kit prowled continually as Nick talked. Nick told him about Rourke's abuse, about Lizbet and the theatre. When he told of Michael's death, Kit dropped onto a chair, his face as colorless as it had been at his trial. "I dreamed it. I dreamed it. But it wasn't a dream? It really happened?"

"Yes. I'm so sorry."

Kit leaned forward, his head in his hands. "Why can't I remember any of this?"

"Shall I go on?"

Kit nodded. Nick told him of the adoption by St. Denys and the work in the theatre, and of Michael's body being moved to St. Denys Hill. He told him of the night they met, when Kit injured his arm. He went no further, afraid Kit's hold on reality was too fragile to hear the rest.

"Is the old man in prison? I hope to God he rots there." Kit said in a trembling voice, as he blotted his wet face with his sleeve.

"He was punished as he deserved," Nick said quietly. There would be time later to tell him everything else. Lizbet's death, Tom Rourke's fate, and his own trial. He was taken by surprise when Kit looked fixedly at him as if to draw secrets from his soul.

"What were you to me?" Kit asked.

Nick was not prepared for the question. He stammered, "A good friend."

"Just a friend?"

"Of course. What else?"

"I don't know. But in my head this afternoon I kept hearing the name Nico. And somehow I know it was you. Something trying to be remembered. Nico. Why would I call you that?"

"It was... we were close friends. It was just a nickname."

"You said something made me lose my memory. What happened? What was it?"

"I'm your doctor as well as your friend, Kit. We've gone far enough for one night." He was afraid Kit would demand to know everything, but to Nick's relief he put it aside.

"Kit." He said his own name aloud, trying it as he would a new suit of clothing. "Kit. Not Jack Rourke. Kit St. Denys." He leaned back and closed his eyes. "You're right. I've heard about all I can take in today. New name. New everything. My brother..." He blinked. "How will I get used to it all?"

Nick hesitated, and then said, "I have an idea that may help." He told him then of his visit that afternoon to the theatre. He did not tell him the theatre belonged to him, but only that people who had known him before were going to do everything they could to bring him back to normal.

"So then I will find out who I really am." Kit frowned. "I'm afraid to find out. What if I'm a criminal or something of the sort?"

"You needn't be afraid. You're a well-respected man, a consummate professional of incredible talent."

Kit's expression said without words, 'I don't believe you.' Aloud he said, "Those people you just told me about Rama, Francis. I thought those names this afternoon. They are real people, not just my imagination?"

"Very real. They're your good friends and they love you very much. Mrs. Fiske, is also your friend, a great lady."

"And I'm to work in that theatre?"

"Yes, behind the scenes, learning it all over again. Maybe hearing the sounds and smelling the smells and watching the actors will open the door for you all the way."

"And I will remember everything?"

"It's my earnest prayer."

"I saw other things in my head today. A grand house. And a smaller house. And a black-haired man, but not you. I saw them, but for just an instant." Kit rubbed his temples. "I'm so confused! And you're one of the biggest mysteries in all this."

"Hardly. There are no mysteries to me at all." Kit clearly did not believe him.

Nick thought crossing the river by ferry would be less stressful than crossing the bridge. "You've made this journey several times," Nick said, as they stood at the rail. "But you don't remember."

Kit said nothing. He gnawed his thumbnail, his anxious gaze fixed on the city beyond. Maybe he would be better off never to know the secrets in the city. He gazed a moment at Stuart's clean profile and the dark hair sifting over his forehead in the breeze. Nico. The name seemed so right. Why?

As they approached the tidy red brick theatre, Kit's steps slowed. His apprehension darkened. Nick took hold of his arm and said, "Don't be afraid. I'm not going to leave you."

Kit resumed walking, still slowly, and halted beside a playbill advertising the final week of Mrs. Fiske's production. He stared hard at the red-haired woman pictured there. He had never seen her before.

"Her name is Minnie Fiske," Nick said. "She's your good friend."

As they entered the theatre, Kit balked again. The hair on the back of his neck stiffened; his scalp prickled. The small but ornate lobby was unlit. The pale walls were ghostly. The black marble on the floors was a bottomless pit into which he might fall. The brass fittings on the doors and the gold leaf on the picture frames gleamed like teeth in a dark beard. He was in an alleyway, and foul things reached out to snatch at him.

Nick pulled open one of the tall doors to the auditorium and waited. After a while, Kit went past him into the dark cave beyond, where only the seats near the stage were outlined and everything else was sensed but unseen. The only lights were on stage, where a rehearsal was under way. Halfway down the aisle, Nick guided him to a center row seat.

Kit sat rigid, his fists clenched upon his knees. He saw the red-haired woman. She and a man were on the stage. She exited, shutting a door. Several seconds after the door was shut there came a loud bang. Invisible people laughed somewhere behind the stage. The red-haired woman came back out on the stage, laughing. "Richard, if you do that tonight your head will roll." One of the invisible voices said, "Well, that slam is so important I just wanted to give it all the drama it deserved." The red-haired woman retorted, "As I said, Richard dear, your head will roll. Let me try it again. I wasn't happy with that last scene the way I did it last night."

Uneasily, Nick watched Kit, who fidgeted, shifted in his seat, looked up, looked around, looked everywhere but the stage, crossed and uncrossed his legs. Suddenly he stood up. "I want to go."

"But why? Don't you want to meet your old friends?"

"I want to go!" He gripped Nick's arm. Nick nodded and followed him from the auditorium to the street. Out in the sunlight he saw that Kit's face was ashen; a patina of sweat gleamed on his skin.

"Kit, what's wrong?"

"I don't know, I don't know. Something bad. It was so cold in there. Something bad happened in that place. I can feel it. I want to go back to the house."

Nick was unnerved. He hadn't made the slightest hint about Rourke's death. If he told Kit the truth now, would it do more harm than good? He had no way of knowing or even guessing with any degree of intelligence, but he had to do something. If he did the wrong thing, Kit might retreat into his shell and never come out. But if he did not face the theatre now he might never face it. "Kit, listen to me."

"I want to leave. Now. If I knew where to go, I'd leave without you."

"You were right. Something bad did happen there. Something terrible. And what happened is what made you sick."

Kit made a wild gesture. "Get me away from here now or I'm going to puke all over the sidewalk."

'Let this be the right thing to do,' Nick prayed and hoped God heard him. "I didn't want to tell you so soon, but I think you have to face it now. Kit, your father, Tom Rourke, died in this place."

Black beard, brutal hands, hateful voice, knife, blood. "Drink it like a man. Didn't lose much when he croaked." Kit's eyes were glazed as he took a step backward and then another. For one instant, like a frightened cat, he froze and then, like the cat, he shot into movement and was gone.

"Kit!" Nick ran after him, shoving people aside. He lost him in the crowd. Cursing himself for a fool, he searched as long as he dared and saw no sign of him. He questioned people. A baker had seen a tall, fair-haired man run by his window. A woman with a baby in a pram had been almost knocked to the ground by such a man. As he searched, Nick prayed for God to keep him safe until he was found.

He continued looking until twilight and then, footsore and sick with worry, he went to the nearest police station to report Kit's disappearance. Yawning, the desk officer said indifferently, "He ain't been missing long enough to be worried about it," he said.

"He's been ill. I'm his doctor. He was in a sanitarium for several months and has since been under my care. He doesn't know how to live in the outside world yet and something frightened him."

The officer's eyes narrowed. "A lunatic? There's a lunatic loose in this city?"

"He's not dangerous. I just want him found and returned to my care. Please. He hasn't committed any crime."

"Yet." The officer read off the description Nick had given to him. Then he frowned. "Sounds familiar." He glanced again at the name and his eyebrows shot up. "St. Denys! The actor who murdered his old man?"

Nick flinched. "It was self-defense."

"Some self-defense," the policeman snorted. "He cut his throat and stabbed him a hundred times. Got sent to the loony bin, didn't he? You call that not dangerous?"

"Just find him," Nick snapped. He wrote out his address. "Please send me a telegram at once, to this address. I'll pay a reward." With a sardonic smile the officer took the slip of paper.

※ ※

Kit ran until his legs would barely hold him up and his breath seared his lungs. Gulping air, he sagged against a tavern wall.

People flowed by in a blur. Some stared and passed by. Most did not bother staring. Drunks leaning against buildings were a common sight here. And he didn't look as if he had anything worth stealing.

Words, pictures, words, faces, voices beat at his mind until he wanted to dig his fingers into his head and pull them out. *Small stone house. Naked dark-haired man. Rawdon. Pain and pleasure. Romeo Romeo, wherefore art thou Romeo?*

"Buddy, are you sick?" The barman from the tavern had come out, wiping his hands on his apron.

"I don't know," Kit said, wagging his lowered head in despair. "I think so."

"Well, can't have you out here like this. Bad for business. Come in and sit down. Maybe you'll perk up." He guided Kit's unsteady steps into the dark interior, to a table far in the back. "I think you've had a few too many already. This'll help sober you up." He placed a cup of strong, black coffee in front of him. "It's on the house," he said.

Kit managed to thank the man as the memories hammered at him. *Blood, a lot of blood. 'Justifiable homicide, homicide, homicide, disordered mind, confined, confined, homicide.' Thud of a gavel.*

After a while, when the maddening images stopped, he left the sanctuary of the tavern. He had no place to go and no one to turn to. He was hungry, but his pockets yielded no money. He paused at a bakery and when the baker's attention was elsewhere, he stole two hot buns. He remembered stealing. He could still do it. As night fell he broke a rusty lock on an old shed filled with sacks of meal. There he spent the night, kicking at rats that came near. He fell asleep at some point, and woke to sunlight through the one tiny window.

Stiff and cramped, he wandered for hours without direction. Then he realized he was once again at the theatre where Stuart had taken him the day before. And again, as if they held the answers to his mysteries, he studied the playbills. They had a picture of the red-haired woman he had seen on stage when he was there with Stuart.

MRS. FISKE

in

A DOLL'S HOUSE

"Kit!" The red-haired woman appeared beside him, her delicate, ordinary-looking face transfigured by a beautiful smile. "Kit! We've all been worried sick about you!" She put her small hand on his arm. "We expected you yesterday."

"Ex-expected me?" he stammered.

"Dear boy, what's wrong? You don't look well."

"Nothing's wrong. Nothing." *Blood. Justifiable homicide. Disordered mind. Confined. Danger to society. Confined until—*

"You do remember me, don't you?" she asked.

"Stuart said you're one of my friends."

"He spoke the truth. Come in." Then she smiled. "What a silly woman I am! Inviting you into your own theatre."

He stared at her. "My theatre?"

"Of course, dear. Didn't he tell you that? Look." She drew him back a few steps and pointed to the elegant words on a carved golden sign over the marquee:

ST. DENYS THEATRE

His jaw dropped; he blinked. *"My* theatre? Mine?"

"Come along, dear." She unlocked the door and walked ahead of him, sensing his need for space and silence. When she turned to him, she said, "I have a few things to see to in my dressing room. If you need me, I'll be there."

"I don't know where the dressing rooms are."

"Then I'll show you."

He followed her down the stairs to the narrow corridor onto which the dressing rooms opened. Nauseating dizziness swept him; he stumbled. He was only half-aware of her face turned toward him, her mouth open and moving. The corridor stank like blood. Sweat soaked his shirt. His eyes were riveted on one door out of the many. One door. He reached for the door handle.

"No, Kit, you don't want to go in there," she said, restraining him with a gentle but firm hand on his arm.

His hand shook so violently he could hardly grip the cold metal. Whatever happened, had happened there. Stuart had said something about the old man. The old man had died. In the theatre. In this room? Couldn't be true. He'd killed the old man when he was a kid. He freed his arm from Minnie's grasp and opened the door. The woman's voice came from a far distance; he could not understand what she said.

For an eternity, he stood rooted to the threshold, staring at the floor. A large brownish stain marred the wood. He took a step into the room and reeled from the shock, reaching out to steady himself against the wall. He knelt and touched his palsied fingers to the brown stain. Slowly he stood up, unable to wrench his tortured gaze from it. He choked, watching the stain change from brown to red. It moved, spread, oozed across the floor until it lapped at the corners of the room and touched his shoes.

Minnie planted herself in front of him and made him look at her. "Kit, please come back to my suite. Harrison and I would love to have you stay with us for a few days."

"Leave me alone!" he shouted. "You, Stuart, everyone! Leave me alone!" He walked away from her, feeling he could not get away fast enough.

"Kit!" she called imploringly. He quickened his pace. She did not know what to do. Her instinct was to notify Dr. Stuart at once. Yet maybe Kit was right. Maybe what he needed most was to be left alone. She decided to compromise: if Kit did not return in twenty-four hours, she would send a telegram to his doctor.

❧

Two days passed. Kit was still missing. Nick enlisted his patients and friends in the Bowery, as well as the police. More and more he turned his practice over to David in order to comb the streets of New York. He cursed himself for telling Kit the terrible truth and cursed God for allowing him to do it.

He did not see the resentment in Bronwyn's face, or the tight way her lips clamped these days. David Galvin saw it. He tried to convince himself it was none of his business but eventually he felt he had to speak.

On this day Nick had to see two patients who refused to be examined by anyone else. Young Mrs. Webster was suffering false labor with her first pregnancy. He sent her home with assurances that Dr. Galvin was more than capable of delivering her baby. Mrs. Murdock, whose heart was "doing funny things," was sent home with a stern warning to stop doctoring herself with high-proof Danish Female Regulator. He entered the visits on their charts and prepared to leave for another day of searching.

David rapped on the doorframe. "Nick, are you busy?"

Nick smiled briefly. "Not now. I'm getting ready to leave. I'm sorry about those last two patients. You could have treated them as well as I."

"Didn't hurt my pride at all," David said. He shifted uncomfortably. "Nick, I'm going to risk our friendship by putting my nose in your business."

"Sounds ominous. I think our friendship can withstand whatever it is."

"It's Mrs. Stuart."

"What about Mrs. Stuart? If she were ill, I'd know it."

"Would you? Nick, I don't think you know how miserable she is."

Nick paused. A slight frown appeared. "And you do?"

"She's not said anything; she never will. I see it in her eyes when we have tea."

"You have tea with my wife?" The moment he said it, he realized how ridiculous it sounded. "I know I've neglected her lately. And my practice as well. But David, this missing patient is important." He didn't add 'to me.' "I'll do something about the situation. Thank you. I appreciate the concern."

"You two are the best friends I have," David said. "I don't want either of you to be unhappy."

After David left, Nick went to the nursery, where Bronwyn was rocking Jamie and reading to him. When he spoke her name, she looked over Jamie's head. Nick saw the bleakness in her eyes.

"Bronwyn, I was thinking today. Do you still want to return to nursing? I need you there. *We* need you there. Desperately."

Her face brightened. "Oh, yes! Remember how well we worked together before? I've missed it so. But what about Jamie?"

The little boy lifted his head and grinned at his father. "Whaboo Jamie?" he parroted.

Nick picked him up and kissed him. "What about Jamie? We'll just see about Jamie!" He tickled him and Jamie dissolved in giggles. Bronwyn laughed. Nick laughed, too. How long, he wondered with a pang, had it been since that had happened?

23

Bewildered, frightened, dizzy from nearly two days without food, Kit wandered the busy streets. Mothers held their children's hands tighter at the sight of the wild-eyed, desperate-looking stranger. He stumbled hastily backward and fell, barely escaping death beneath the wheels of an ale wagon and its iron-shod team of dray horses.

Beside him in the gutter, a bright curved shape shone in the sunlight. He scrabbled through the half-dried mud and found two coins which bought him two thick pretzels and a glass of beer at a nearby tavern. The pump behind the tavern helped him wash at least some of the dirt from his hands.

No longer hungry, he walked for a while, and then joined a knot of boys watching a man with a stack of posters at his feet, a small apron around his waist, and a hammer in his hand.

The man spit a large-headed tack at the hammer and in a smooth motion tacked one corner of a poster to the side of a building. Into his mouth went another tack. Spit. Hammer. One of the boys asked a question. The man paused long enough to demonstrate that the hammer was magnetic. He saw Kit, and looked him up and down.

"Hey, Bo," he said, "you lookin' to make a nickel?"

"Yes," Kit said eagerly. "Tell me what to do."

The man's eyebrows lifted at the cultured speech. "Pick up them signs. I been carrying them all over town and they're gettin' heavy. Carry the hammer, too."

Kit looked at one of the posters he picked up. It was gaudy yellow with bright red and black letters and dazzling pictures. Dozens of beautiful girls in spangled costumes rode horses and elephants with tassels and plumes. Clowns somersaulted. Other beautiful girls flew through the air, contorted into strange positions. A man balanced on a chair on a high wire. Lions bared their fangs. A man in white floated in midair above a black horse. Curling letters at the top declared NELLIS BROS. THRILLING THREE RING CIRCUS!

"Don't stand there lookin' at it all day," the man said. "I gotta get these all out in my section by sundown. I kinda got delayed with a dolly last night, if ya know what I mean. Come on, Bo, we gotta move! Damn, wish I had another hammer. My name's Buster. What's yours?"

"'Bo' will do," Kit said.

Relieved of his burden, Buster moved much faster up and down the streets, and had it down to a science. Tack in mouth, take poster, spit, hammer. Mouth, poster, spit, hammer. When he didn't have a tack in his mouth, he talked. He'd been a coal miner, hated it, joined a fireball show and was a shortchange artist with it until he got nailed by the law, joined another fireball show, did a shell game and sometimes the spiel for the freak show. The fireball show got burned out by a bunch of townies so he joined Nellis Bros., which was a real honest-to-God Sunday School show. "Was a Twenty-four Hour Man until I got drunk last month. Then I was demoted to bein' a Tack Spitter."

It was like listening to a rapid foreign language. Kit understood hardly any of the unfamiliar words but it sounded exciting. Finally the signs were all up. Buster fished a nickel from his pocket and gave it to him. "I need work," Kit said. "Do they need men at the circus?"

"They always need workers. We're here for three weeks at that damned Garden. When the parade comes through tomorrow, just fall in at the rear."

Kit's face fell. "I don't have anywhere to stay tonight. I was hoping for a job today."

"Oh, what th' hell. Come on back with me. They'll put you right to work, I'm sure."

Kit went with Buster to Madison Square Garden where, from the dome, a gilt Diana watched over bustling streets. Inside, the circus was being set up, and what looked like hundreds of people milled about. The experienced workingmen yelled and swore blistering curses as they set the performance rings, musician's platform, and rigs in place. Horses whinnied. Majestic elephants, called bulls even if they were female, pulled rigging into place. In the distance was a counterpoint of growls and phlegmy snarls of the big cats.

Kit stared, fascinated, until the boss handed him a shovel and a bucket of sawdust. "You ain't bein' paid to gawk, boy. Get that sawdust down."

"What's it for?" he asked.

"Shit, mostly. The bulls put out a mountain of it. Now swing that shovel."

As Kit soon learned, no one milled about, appearances to the contrary. The speed with which the show was prepared was amazing. All that evening the acts practiced their entrances, exits, and routines in the new set-ups, and he heard endless cursing and complaining about the Garden. It didn't take long to learn the reason. Used to practicing with acres of open space around a tent, both the performers and the animals hated the closed-in quarters. All of the animals were edgy, especially the horses. On a ramp waiting his turn was a good-looking man soothing a jittery black stallion.

Kit paused to admire both the man and the horse. "Beautiful animal," he said. The performer did not answer, but smiled briefly. Then the performer moved with his horse toward the ring, and Kit answered a shouted summons from the roustabout boss.

Early in the morning as the parade assembled, Kit and a few other "presentable" workers were given top hats and ill-fitting tail coats and pressed into service at the tail end of the line of wagons and animals that wound through the city streets. A brass band in the lead, another brass band in the middle, and a calliope at the end produced deafening music. The top-hatted "Nellis Bros. Gentlemen" threw paper-wrapped candy and passed out free tickets at random.

That night's performance enthralled Kit. Clowns. Ten Liberty Horses, which performed precision routines without riders or reins. Elephants swayed in wrinkled majesty, with girl riders in harem costumes. Lions and tigers leapt and snarled from their pedestals. Trapeze flyers and high wire walkers defied death. Wild West Cowboys vanquished Savage Feathered Indians. Thirty trained birds climbed ladders, waved flags and performed amazing stunts. And through it all the two combined brass bands performed musical gyrations. Kit had as much fun as the children in the audience.

The announcer bawled, "Ladies and Gentleman, appearing for the first time with Nellis Brothers, the only performer in America of *voltige Tcherkesse*, The Great Cossack Rider, Andrei Balakirev!"

With galvanic energy the performer Kit had seen the night before, now costumed in white, seemed to catapult into the center ring on the back of the black stallion. The stallion had no saddle, bridle, or reins. With only a surcingle to grip, the rider threw himself on and off the horse a dozen times, sometimes racing alongside or turning somersaults before leaping upon its back again. While the horse never slowed its pace, the rider faced front, faced rear, and front again. As the finale he hooked one foot in the loop on the surcingle and leaned backwards across the horse, his body stretched and bent like a bowstring, his neck arched, as he snatched up a bright red flower from the sawdust. Upright again, he rode with blood-curdling cries around the circle one more time, flung the flower into the audience, leaped a fence, and galloped out of sight.

The audience went wild. Moments later, he came back in, breathing hard and leading the black horse. He was handsome, his white shirt and tight white pants were soaked with sweat, as was his dark hair. A core of heat burst to life inside Kit. He wanted a man. He wanted *that* man. He wondered if he had once known how to make it happen, how to arrange a meeting.

Then the performance ended, the crowd left. As Kit worked cleaning up the mess the crowd had left behind, his boss called to him, "Hey, you. I just had a workingman quit and I gotta replace him. I been watchin' you. You're a good worker. Wanna stay on till the end of the date? Help us tear down and then travel with us during the season? If you work out, you could be hired for winter quarters. Ain't just summer work, you know. Them animals got to be fed and cleaned up after, things got to be fixed. How about it?"

"I'd like that," Kit said, holding an inexplicable stray man's shoe found beneath the seats. Steady work. Steady money. A chance—

slim but a chance nonetheless—to meet the Russian. What more could he ask?

The boss, a rough-voiced, rough-faced man several inches shorter than Kit, threw back his head and looked up at him. "Before I take you on, though, I got to know one thing. What's your story? You ain't American, that's for sure. And you talk like a gent. So what sent you down the garden path? Liquor, women, cards or the ponies?"

"It wasn't women," Kit said, remembering the stirring in his blood and between his legs as he watched Andrei Balakirev stretch his lean supple body backward and reach for the rose.

"Good. 'Cause if you'd said it was, I was gonna change my mind. Don't mind gambling. Lose all you want of your own money. Get drunk as a skunk on your own time, just report for work sober. Women? Hell, get all the tail you got time and energy for, long as you don't mess around with the girls in the acts. But I by-God won't have woman trouble with my crew. Get two fools fightin' over a broad and next thing you know y'got heads busted and men who can't work. Seen it happen. Ain't gonna happen with my crew. That's my policy. Take it or leave it."

"I give you my word," Kit said. "The girls in the acts are quite safe from me."

"Okay. Report to the paymaster. Tell him Doolin hired you permanent."

Kit gave his name to the paymaster as Jack Stuart. No one would look for Jack Stuart and in the unlikely event they did, they wouldn't look in a circus. He could go away, forget that red stain on the dressing room floor. He could forget the way Nick Stuart's dark hair looked in the sunlight and forget the beauty of his healing hands. And he could forget the dozens of other half-remembered things that beat insistently at him. This time when he forgot, it would be because he wanted to. Because he had to.

At one performance, he saw Stuart and his wife in the audience, laughing at the clowns. After a brief, wistful glance at Stuart's face, he hurried out of sight before he was seen. The circus couldn't leave the city too soon for him.

He thought it would take two or three days to get the circus loaded, but only a few hours later the last of the animals, the last of the equipment and costumes, the last of the crew and performers were on their way out of the hated New York City with its despised Garden and putrid drinking water. On their way to open air tent shows. Buster remarked to Kit, "We might have tents blow away and we might have mud to our knees or we might bake in the heat and have skeeters the size of bulls, but by God, we'll have fresh air and no mildew."

Kit settled down in a boxcar with the other roustabouts for a few hours of rest, sleeping on the floor with his head on his duffle bag. "Ain't no Pullman car," Buster said. "But it beats some of the other shows I been on." To an outsider the air of the boxcars would have been overpowering with the smells of sweaty men, and the creature smells that clung to the clothing of the animal handlers and cage hands. The men didn't notice.

Kit was well liked by the other men, who roared with laughter at some of his British pronunciations. Over the following weeks he came to have great respect for the men who could set up a circus and knock it down every twelve hours. When they were traveling, he sometimes joined in the drinking and gambling, or sprawled out and read some tattered Wild West adventures he'd bought for a penny. The amusing lurid prose kept his thoughts from going where he didn't want them to go.

❧❧

No word had come from or about Kit since the day of Mrs. Fiske's telegram, and he had been missing a full day before she sent it. Nick tried to occupy his mind with work and tried to make up for months of neglect of his family. He hired a nanny, and Bronwyn returned as office nurse. The patients were pleased; Bronwyn was happy. And if only he had known Kit's whereabouts, he would have been almost happy.

When she said she wanted to go to the circus, he had taken her, though he was in no mood for such silliness. To his surprise he enjoyed it. She was also going to hold him to his promise to take her to Coney Island. Nanny would go too, so she and Nick would be free to ride the more daring rides such as the Ferris wheel.

Saturday morning arrived clear and bright. The brooding clouds of the past few days were just a memory. He wished he had not promised Bronwyn the picnic and trip to the amusement park. He wanted to go back to the city and search again. But a promise is a promise even if one's heart is not in it.

He was in his room changing into old tweeds suitable for roller-coaster riding when Bronwyn came in. She looked fetching in a casual dress with few ruffles and frills, and a flat sailor hat on her piled-up hair. "This just came," she said, and handed him a telegram. Curious, she stood there waiting as he opened it. "Is it bad news?" she asked.

"Thank God, oh, thank God. He's been found." The relief was tempered by distress, though. ST DENYS IN CUSTODY. COME GET HIM BEFORE HE IS CHARGED. SGT MALONE NYPD. "I have to go," he said quickly. "I'll return as soon as I can." Charged? Charged with what?

"Where are you going?" she asked, her voice strained.

"The city," he said, avoiding her eyes.

"Now?" demanded Bronwyn. "Why?"

"He's in trouble. I don't know what to expect." Nick dropped a quick kiss on her cheek. "We'll go tomorrow. Or the next day. But we'll go. Soon." He was already halfway out the door.

For a full minute Bronwyn stared at the empty doorway. Nanny appeared carrying Jamie, ready for his outing. Bronwyn took her boy and smothered him with kisses. "We'll not be going today, Nanny," she said. "Doctor had an emergency." Behind the calm face that Nanny saw, Bronwyn was sick with anger.

❧

The police sergeant looked Nick over as if suspecting him of some crime. "You here to collect your friend, I reckon."

"Yes. But your wire said something about charges. I don't understand. What kind of charges?"

The sergeant snorted. "Public intoxication. Fighting. Assault upon a police officer. He fought all the way to the station. One of my men's got a black eye and another one's got a split lip. They had to bust a baton on his head to subdue him."

"He's sick," Nick protested.

"He's lucky he ain't dead. Sign here." He shoved a paper across the desk. "You said something about a reward," he added under his breath after making sure no one was near enough to hear. Nick nodded and counted out several bills. The sergeant gave orders for St. Denys to be released. An officer brought him out with a firm grip on his arm.

Nick stared. And snatched back the reward money. The only slight resemblances between Kit and the man with the bruised face were his height and his more-or-less blond hair. "That's not Kit St. Denys," he said.

"Fits the description," said the sergeant.

"No, he doesn't. This chap's much older. And his hair's bleached."

The sergeant glared at the prisoner. "What'd you say your name was St. Denys for, you dago nancy?"

"I didn't," the prisoner retorted. "You said I was and I agreed with you. Ain't givin' you my real name, you mick turd." He yelped in pain as he was hit with a baton, and as they dragged him back to his cell, Nick heard him screaming curses.

"Kit, where are you?" Nick whispered. "I'm so afraid for you. You could be hurt or lying dead somewhere."

❧❦

Kit reveled in the strenuous labor that left him no time or energy to brood. Soon his body was lean and hard, with no trace left of the invalid he had been. And every day he was more aware that he wanted to be with a man. More and more often, Andrei Balakirev appeared in his dreams. Kit also liked the affectionate mastery the Russian had over his two Arabians, the black stallion and a bay gelding. In his spare time, he liked to watch the performer work with them.

One afternoon, as Kit sipped a cup of steaming coffee outside the enclosure, the Russian slid from the back of the bay, and called out, "Do you like horses?"

Kit stared, and then laughed. "Is that a Russian accent?"

"Russia, Kentucky. A dimple in the road. My name's really Leon Wharton. You didn't answer my question. Do you like horses?"

"Yes. We had thoroughbreds." *The large house with many windows. The stables. The fine horses. St. Denys Hill.* He gave his head a little shake, but the images persisted for a moment. He concentrated on Leon Wharton from Russia, Kentucky. He was a little older up close, perhaps in his late thirties, but still attractive.

"Do horses like you?" Wharton asked.

"Yes."

"What's your name?"

"Jack."

"You're one of the roustabouts. I noticed you in New York. And I've seen you watching me."

"I watch a lot of people."

"Would you like to work with me? If the horses trust you, that is. They're hard to please and so am I." He motioned Kit into the enclosure. "See if Asad likes you. Shunnar, the black, is easy to please. Asad is not above kicking your head off." Within moments Asad was nuzzling Kit's hand and letting him stroke the warm, silken neck. Kit talked softly to him and Asad whuffed softly. Kit's eyes locked onto Wharton's. A slight smile touched each face.

"Stay here," Wharton said, and strode away, returning in a few minutes with the boss.

"He wants you to help with the horses the rest of the tour," the boss said. "It's up to you. I need you, but we gotta keep the stars happy."

Kit shrugged. "It doesn't matter to me." He was glad neither man could see how his pulse raced.

"I've been looking for a partner," said Wharton one morning in the horse tent, as Kit scratched between the eyes of the black stallion. "If you can ride as good as you look, I could incorporate you into the act." He was standing very close to Kit and his voice was low.

"I'm happy just being a horse handler," Kit said off-handedly. Wharton closed the space between then until his hip and thigh lightly leaned against Kit's.

"I think," said Wharton in an even lower voice, "you want more than that." He rested his hand against the small of Kit's back and ever so lightly drew it across the tight curve of his backside.

The contact was erotic and familiar. Kit half-remembered others... *Dark-haired man in the small stone house... Rawdon. Big man with big hands and a kind face...Francis. Slender man with dark hair and vivid blue eyes and innocent body...Nico.* A deep shudder of anticipation ran through Kit's body.

"There's a hotel in town, English," Wharton whispered. "The Wynchell. Seedy as hell. But they don't ask questions. Meet me there tonight."

The Dower House at midnight. Kit nodded.

In the run-down hotel that night his body remembered things his brain had forgotten. There was no talk of love and no tenderness. The couplings with Wharton had a savage aspect that left them both aching and bruised.

Wharton lay back, panting. "Never knew an Englishman could fuck like that," he said. "You've got to stay on now. I'm serious about making a change in my act. Include you." He laughed as he dressed to return to the circus. "Now that I know you can do some pretty amazing trick riding... If it works out, eventually I'll give you second billing."

"Kit St. Denys played a supporting role only once." Kit was as surprised by his own words as was the circus star. Another of those swift-appearing images flashed into his brain: a playbill.

MINNIE MADDERN FISKE
starring in
TESS OF THE D'URBERVILLES
Featuring
KIT ST. DENYS as ANGEL CLARE

"Who did you say?" Wharton asked, pausing at the door.

"It wasn't important." Kit knew he'd never see Wharton again. His real name had been said aloud and he had to leave before Wharton became curious. Early in the morning, Kit collected his wages, and disappeared from the circus.

He caught rides when he could and walked when he couldn't. He changed names at will, and did odd jobs in exchange for food and a place to sleep. His unkempt beard grew long and thick. He had few expenses, and when he earned a little money he tucked it away in a canvas bag sewn into his pocket. As he wandered from town to town, he gravitated to theatres the way drunkards gravitated to hard liquor. Sometimes he found work in a theatre for a few days, but he made no effort to see the production.

In Cincinnati, on the marquee of a small theatre he saw the proud announcement that the local amateur thespians were making their "First Foray Into Shakespeare" by presenting *Macbeth*. He was seized by a need to see it. He had enough money for a meal, admittance to the theatre, and a night's stay at a flophouse.

In his dank room, he saw himself in a mirror for the first time in months. "Merciful God," he said aloud. "Robinson Crusoe!" A barber shaved away his ragged beard and directed him to a public bathhouse. The hot water and soap felt so good! How had he lived without them for such a long time? The bath's attendant disdainfully brushed the worst of the grime from his clothes and did his best to polish the run-over shoes. The flophouse mirror then reflected someone Kit vaguely recognized.

That night, not long after the play began, a late-season thunderstorm provided atmospheric drama outside. Lightning and torrential rain beat at the little theatre as the amateur actors performed. As the second Witch intoned, "By the sticking of my thumbs, Something wicked this way comes," hailstones attacked the roof.

All through the performance Kit wordlessly repeated the lines of every character. Often he had an unaccountable urge to shout, "No, that's the wrong word" or "Do it this way" or "That's not authentic. Say it like this." He had to grip the arms of his seat to keep from taking the stage himself and showing how it should be done or said.

Act V, scene I, enter a sleepwalking Lady Macbeth. The actress entered, holding limp hands in front of her, bewailing in a nasal attempt at a British accent the imaginary blood upon them. "Yet who would have thought the old man to have had so much blood in him?" Kit gasped.

He was on his knees in a pool of blood on the dressing room floor, costumed as Angel Clare. "Yet who would have thought the old man to have had so much blood in him?" In his bloody hand he had an Italian stiletto from St. Denys Hill. A stiletto with jewels on the hilt. His hand plummeted downward to bury itself in Tom Rourke's chest. The dying devil's eyes begged him for mercy he could not give, would not give, did not give.

He leaped from his seat and ran outside to the alley behind the church. There, buffeted by wind and cold rain, illuminated by blinding flashes of lighting, he was violently sick until only bile burned his throat. Weak and shivering, he staggered back to the flophouse, hanging on to hitching rails, steadying himself on buildings and parked vehicles. He knew now he had been on his way to New York ever since he'd left the circus.

Impatient to face the demon in the dressing room and get it over with, he left town on a midnight train. The nearer he came to New York, the more his mind focused on the mysterious hell that waited for him there. What if it destroyed him? Terrifying images screamed inside his brain.

Gray sky. Claws of bare tree tops. Barred window. Fear. Faces. Struggle. Fighting. Tied down. Pain slashed his mouth. Vomiting, choking.

He squeezed his eyes shut. Another memory vanquished the first. *Gentle hands. A soft voice. "They'll never do this to you again."* Stuart. Stuart had saved him. If he went mad again, if bars again fenced him in, if the steel gag again tore into his mouth, if his brain were again smothered by nothingness, Stuart would not be there. This time it might be forever.

"I don't care," he said. "If it will be, it will simply have to be."

New York.

He stood for a long time looking at the façade. St. Denys Theatre. The words were still there. It hadn't been a dream. One sign was on the door, and it said simply: **IN REHEARSAL: "BECKY SHARP."** It must be that woman. What was her name? Minnie. Minnie Fiske. Another memory stirred: he and Mrs. Fiske saying lines from *Tess* into a recording bell.

The front door was locked, but the back door swung open. *An epidemic of unlocked doors.* When his eyes had accustomed themselves to the dimness of the unlit area, he lit the lantern that was kept on the wall near the door in the event of electrical failure. Holding the lantern high he descended the stairs and stood at the foot of the stairway for a moment. Two doors were visible within the circle of lantern light, but he sensed the door he sought was out there in the darkness.

He gave a start as, from nowhere, a group of chattering people appeared and went up the stairs. They were insubstantial as shadows and went past him without seeming to see him. A red-haired woman, taller and younger than Mrs. Fiske, brushed against him without noticing. As suddenly as they had appeared, they were gone.

He gathered his courage and walked slowly down the corridor, preceded by the small bright circle of light. He stopped at a door with a star painted upon it, and as he grasped the door handle, sickness rose in his throat. He forced it back, and leaned his forehead against the star.

"I can't," he whispered. "I can't do this. But if I don't, the old man will win." He flung open the door and with the push of a remembered button on the wall, light flooded the room. Images blasted into his head.

Himself at the makeup table. Someone behind him. The old man. Not dead. A dream, just a dream. Can't move. The old man pushes him backward. Chokes him. "Pay or else." "Didn't lose much when he croaked." Killed Michael. Killed Lizbet. Burned her. Stiletto. Shove it deep. Deeper. To the hilt under the heavy beard. Hot rain of blood. Make sure the devil stays dead. Drive the knife down again and again. Who would have thought the old man to have so much blood in him?

For a long time Kit stood in the doorway of the empty room. The ghosts were gone. No dying devil. No blood. Nothing but a makeup table with no makeup pots. Dust. Silence. A stain on the floor.

Gradually calm passed into him. He could not remember a moment in his life when he felt calm. Closing the door to the dressing room, he went to the flat above, letting himself in with the key over the door. Gradually the strange room took on an air of familiarity. In the corner was a guitar. His guitar.

He sat down with it and tentatively played a few notes. The strings hurt his fingers but it was a wonderful kind of hurt. Nick had always liked to hear him play. And Nick had liked to hear the Sonnets. Nick sang like an untalented frog. Nick. Nico.

He and Nick. Together. Friends. Companions. Lovers. Separated by a stupid quarrel. Brought back together by fate. Ripped apart again by tragedy. That was done. Finished. They had the rest of their lives to recapture what they'd lost. He had to see Nick immediately. But first he had to sleep. He did not dream.

When he awoke it was morning. To his surprise, the telephone in the flat still worked and a woman's voice said, "This is the surgery of Nicholas Stuart, Physician. Mrs. Stuart speaking." Kit sucked in his breath. He had not remembered about Nick's wife. He heard her say again, "Hello? Did you wish to speak to Doctor?"

He made himself speak. "Mrs. Stuart?" How difficult that was to say! "This is Kit St. Denys."

"I know who you are," she said. "I recognize your voice."

"May I speak to your husband? It's urgent."

"No." Her voice was frigid. "I hope you've recovered, sir. But my husband has said emphatically he doesn't want to speak to you. Ever. Don't call here again." The telephone went dead.

"Hello? Mrs. Stuart? Hello?" He replaced the receiver on the hook, his fingers lingering on it. "I remembered it all for naught." The telephone blurred.

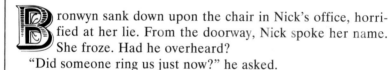

24

Bronwyn sank down upon the chair in Nick's office, horrified at her lie. From the doorway, Nick spoke her name.
She froze. Had he overheard?

"Did someone ring us just now?" he asked.

"No." She forced a smile. "You're hearing things."

She looked uneasily at him. His face was drawn and he looked
ready to drop. Since that accursed friend of his had disappeared,
he'd taken on extra hours in the Bowery, more hours at the hospital,
more hours in his home surgery. The only time she saw happiness
in his eyes these days was when he looked at the baby. And it was
all the fault of that man. The Beast. She would do whatever she
had to do to make sure Nicholas never found out he had returned.

She went to her husband and put her arms around him. "Nicholas,
you work too hard. Please take a holiday before you become ill."

Holiday. He remembered the holiday at St. Denys Hill a lifetime ago. At least it had started out to be a holiday. "I expect
you're right," he said. "I still owe you a trip to the amusement
park, if you'll ever forgive me enough to go."

"Oh, Nicholas, I already have. I was disappointed, yes. But I know you'll keep your promise even if it's late."

"Then we'll go tomorrow." He wished he could go to bed and sleep for a week instead, but somehow he would find the strength to go and at least give the appearance of having fun.

꿈 ☙

Backstage, amidst the ropes and pulleys, Kit stood unnoticed by the two people on stage, Minnie Fisk and a man with a full beard, spectacles, and Falstaffian girth. Taking a deep breath, Kit walked from the wings. "Good morning," he said. "I'd like to audition for any small role you may have."

Minnie spun at the sound of his voice. "Kit?" She looked afraid to believe what her eyes told her. She ran to him and seized his hands. "Oh my dear, dear friend!"

"Kit." The man came toward him, smiling, his eyes glistening. "You don't know me."

Kit laughed. "I didn't until you spoke. Frank."

Francis laughed huskily as he enveloped Kit in a huge hug. "Are you recovered now? Are you with us again?"

"Do you mean you missed me? I didn't think you'd even know I was gone. Where's Rama?" His voice was as rough as Frank's.

"Teaching at the girls' school. She still hates it."

Minnie said, "If you're ready to return to work I'll vacate your theatre at once. The Shubert brothers have said I could perform in one of theirs. I just wanted to keep it going for you."

His smile was a little crooked. "I don't yet know what I'm going to do. Or even what I'm capable of doing. Don't change your plans. Let me come to rehearsals and observe."

Her eyes brightened with excitement. "I've an idea! Are you up to directing? I fired my director yesterday. You're the answer to a prayer. Many prayers. Please say you will."

"I don't know." He hesitated and voiced his greatest fear. "I may have forgotten all I ever knew about theatre."

"Nonsense. The sun could as easily forget how to come up."

"I hope you're right. I'll try directing under one condition."

"Anything."

"If I can't do it well, don't keep me on out of pity. Have Francis throw me out."

"Agreed," she said. "It's so wonderful to have you back." She glanced at the little gold watch fastened to the bodice of her dress.

"Oh, dear. I promised my husband I would meet him and I should have been there several minutes ago. He'll be so thrilled at my news!"

"Minnie, ask him not to print anything about me for a while. If he feels he must, then he must. But I would appreciate a little time."

"Of course. Anything."

Then Kit and Francis were alone. Kit smiled gently and said, "Say it, Frank. You know you're wondering."

Francis made a face. "Of all your annoying habits, reading minds is the most annoying. Very well. What of Stuart?"

"What of him?" Kit said in a hard, off-hand way that did not reveal his turmoil. "He was a friend who helped me. I don't remember everything, but I remember enough to know I owe him my life." And that meant he owed Nick his life with his wife and his son. Nick had them. He had his work, and Francis, and his friends. 'God be with ye, Nico,' he thought in silent, wistful benediction.

⚜

The weather had turned unseasonably warm. The sky was a cloudless, aching blue that declared autumn and winter had decided not to come that year. People put away their light coats and capes for a last fling at summer fun. On Coney Island summer hats made a whimsical reappearance on some heads, and parasols shaded delicate faces.

Towering over everything else and visible from every part of the park was The Elephant. It amazed all who saw it for the first time. It was one hundred twenty-two feet tall, with shops in its enormous legs and a howdah on top that was an observation tower with telescopes. Rumor had it that the Elephant also had bedrooms for rent by sports and girls who weren't any better than they ought to be.

The merry-go-round cranked out tinny, happy-go-lucky tunes. The noise of the barkers and the rides, the screams of young people on the rides, the voices of the families and an occasional crying child created a thick fabric of sound that smothered any unshouted conversation. Bronwyn wheedled Nick into going on the merry-go-round with her and Jamie, who sat between them in a seat shaped like a swan crowned with roses. Jamie crowed, showing pearly teeth in open-mouthed delight. And then Nick saw them: Kit and Rama, arm in arm. An instant later they were lost to sight as the swan swept him along.

"My God," he said, shocked. "My God, he's back! He's safe. He's here. And he didn't let me know. My God." Bronwyn did not hear him over the music and Jamie's laughter.

Rama had seen Nick at the same moment he saw them. "Did you see Stuart on the merry-go-round?" She shifted a small parcel from one arm to the other. "Merry-go-round, for heaven's sake."

"I did." Kit heard the wistfulness in his voice and cut it off with a laugh. "Come on. Ferris wheel. Tallest one in America, so they say."

Stuart went in circles in one direction and Kit went in circles in another, thought Rama. Never the twain would meet, if there was a God. The Ferris wheel quit working when she and Kit were at the top. Rama cursed under her breath.

Kit laughed and poked her with his elbow. "Enjoy the view and stop saying rude things. I wonder which of those specks are Nick and his family."

"I really don't give a bloody fig," she said, clutching the bar of the swaying seat. "I want down! I hate this. If I don't get down, I shall be sick all over you."

"Sissy."

"I'm a lady, not a sissy."

"Ladies don't say bloody fig. There. That looks like them."

"Must we talk about them? If Miss Dragonface Squires finds out I came to this den of iniquity, she'll put my head on a pikestaff. So kindly don't ruin my last day on earth." She caught her breath as the Ferris wheel began its descent. On solid ground once more, she said, "I want to give you your gift now. Come on. Let's get some ices and then you can see it."

At a table in the shade of an awning, they ate the refreshing ice, and when the last sweet, sticky drop was gone she licked her fingers and opened the parcel. She held up the pieces of a daring bathing dress in spring-apple green—the top that would bare her elbows and forearms, as well as a shameful portion of her shoulders and throat, and the ruffled green bloomers and dark stockings that would show off her long, shapely legs.

"I do hope you're not expecting me to wear that!" Kit said in alarm.

Rama giggled and handed him his suit. "No, no. Yours is very manly."

"If you say so," he said, eyeing the blue and gray horizontal stripes.

"This will be our last chance to run in the sand and frolic in the sea. Everyone will be looking at us," she wheedled.

"I'm sure they will."

"And later," she said, with a mysterious smile, "I have another surprise. A special one to celebrate your coming home." She crossed her fingers and prayed to St. Jude that the room in the Elephant and the French lingerie in her reticule would make her dream come true.

Nick threw balls at a bobbing line of clowns and won a huge lady-doll in a satin gown. Perplexed, he said, "Now what in the world am I going to do with that?"

"You're going to give it to your loving wife, silly. I've wanted one like this all my life. The only doll I ever had was one my mother made for me, and somehow it was lost. How did you get so good at throwing?"

"I was a country boy, remember? I can even skip stones on water."

They rode the mechanical horses at Steeplechase. They swooped up and down on the Ferris wheel. And finally, with Nanny and Jamie, rested at one of the tables near the band shell at one end of the boardwalk. Bronwyn talked him into trying the new rage, hot dogs. They were quite as nasty as he expected. While they ate, the German band oom-pahed brassy tunes and the tide of people eddied and flowed about them.

"I want to go to the observation tower on the Elephant," Bronwyn said.

Nick looked upward. The observation tower was far, far from the ground. Nanny had the perfect excuse not to go: Jamie was asleep on her lap. Bronwyn clutched Nick's hand and pulled him to the spiral staircase inside the hind leg of the elephant. He gamely dragged himself up the stairs behind her.

Through the telescopes they could see the entire park. Bronwyn laughed and made fun of those who were shameless enough and foolish enough to brave the cold water. Then she tensed in alarm. Emerging from the water onto the beach, his bathing costume plastered to him in a most disgusting manner, was Mr. St. Denys. She darted a quick glance at Nicholas. He was frozen, his glass fixed. He had seen.

Nick saw Kit, but not at a crowded public beach. He closed his eyes for a moment, lost in a sweet memory: the two of them splashing in the stream at St. Denys Hill, then falling wet, cold, and naked upon the rough bank, slippery in each others arms as they laughed and wrestled, watched only by ancient trees. He willed the memory away. Before him was only the crowded beach with Kit turning to help Rama Weisberg from the water. Rama looked like a damned witch.

Why in the name of God didn't Kit let him know he was safe, recovered and back in the city? Well, what did it matter after all? It was the bargain he'd made with God. He had a life without Kit now because that's the way both God and Kit wanted it.

He wanted to go somewhere alone where he could curse and smash his hands against things. Instead, he smiled, smiled, smiled until his face hurt as he shepherded his family around Coney Island the rest of the day. When Bronwyn squeezed his hand on the ride home, he knew he had carried off the charade as well as any man alive could have.

҂Ⰻ Ⰻ҂

Long after the sun had gone down and the day's happiness was only a memory, Rama lay in Kit's arms feeling more alone than she had ever felt. The exotic bedroom was no longer a place of promise but the graveyard of her hope. "Kit," she stammered into the darkness, "I'm ... I'm so sorry about..." She could go no farther without crying. She pressed her lips together to still their quivering.

"You've nothing to be sorry for."

"I shouldn't have ... I mean, you've told me so often in so many ways but I guess I just didn't want to admit the truth of it. I just ... I'm so sorry."

"My dear girl, you didn't hit me on the head with a club and drag me into bed. I'm here because I'm a man. And men are egotistical brutes who believe they can always rise to the occasion, so to speak." He stroked her hair and kissed her forehead. "Rama, this changes nothing between us. You know that, don't you?"

"Yes," she whispered, but knew it changed everything.

When he tried to see her the following day at the school, Miss Squires herself coldly informed him that Miss Weisberg was no longer in their employ. The Squires nostrils flared as she told him, in capital letters and indignant exclamations, "Miss Weisberg Was Seen Cavorting Nearly Nude On a Coney Island Beach! With You!

Her Own Cousin! Have You No Shame? Either of You?" She spread her fingers upon her outraged bosom. "She was Quite Impertinent with me when I questioned her. Quite Impertinent. Your Cousin has a Thing or Two to Learn About Being a Lady! And You, sir, Have Even More to Learn About Decency and Being a Gentleman!"

"Do you know where she is?"

"No, I do not. And I don't care where That Woman has gone."

For several minutes after the door slammed, he stood irresolute. "Damn," he said softly. "Damn." What would he do without her?

※※

Kit was amazed by the three boxes of letters Harry and Minnie Fiske had saved for him, every letter a wish for his recovery. And it always surprised him when strangers recognized him in public and stopped to wish him well and express hope he would soon be acting again.

A few days after seeing Nick at the amusement park, he met a handsome older gentleman who greeted him with the warmth of a long-lost friend. "Kit, do you remember me at all? Philip Wescott."

Kit seized the man's hand. "Judge Wescott? I was told you were a good friend to me while I was ill but to my regret, I don't remember." Though they stood on a busy street corner with dozens of people passing them by, Kit had the oddest feeling they were alone.

"I was so happy when I heard you were home. Dine with me tonight, Kit. I'll have pheasant, I know you like that. And the best wine in my cellar."

That evening, while they were talking of the theatre, Kit interrupted Philip's conversation by saying, "I remember now. I bought the theatre from you. And I visited you at your country home."

"Be with me there again, Kit. Will you?"

Kit was determined that Philip would be the perfect replacement for Nick Stuart. *Better* than Nick. What had he and Nick ever had in common? He and Philip enjoyed good books and plays and music. Philip was knowledgeable about things that mattered. Philip, though cautious in public, was not a Puritan in the bedroom. Why shouldn't Philip be his new Nick? But before long he had to face the truth. Philip could no more take Nick's place than the moon could take the place of the sun.

He had his work, directing Minnie in *Becky Sharp*. It was not a great play, but then, he knew ruefully, he was not a great director. He wondered if he ever had been. But directing the play was doing what Minnie had prayed it would: he felt the itch to perform again.

⊰ ⊱

Nick almost groaned with tiredness, as he put the medicines into his black bag. The Bowery surgery had been burglarized and his precious stores of morphine, ether, and digitalis had been stolen the previous month. Now he carried them back and forth, with Kelly and two tough friends as bodyguards. He hated the need for it.

He yawned until his ears popped. The front door was a mile away. Then he had to endure the cab ride home. He glanced longingly at the uncomfortable cot in the corner, but knew he must go home.

Later, in the cab he was too tired to fight the memories of Kit. But he didn't need memories after all. Kit was right there beside him and in a few minutes they would be at the flat…

"Doc. Wake up."

Nick jerked awake as the driver shook his shoulder. "You're here, Doc. Are you all right? You was sawing logs. Can you make it to your house?"

"I'm fine. That little catnap was all I needed to rejuvenate."

"Well, you're the doctor. But you look like hell. Maybe you need to take some time off."

"You sound like my wife. But you're not nearly as pretty."

He had not eaten since morning. As he rummaged in the kitchen for something, Bronwyn spoke behind him. "I was getting worried," she said. She stood in the doorway, her long black hair in a single plait, her feet bare beneath the red dressing gown.

"Where are your slippers?" he scolded. "You ought not go about on these cold floors with nothing on your feet."

"Your son hid them. Well, if I get sick I know two fine doctors. Sit down. I'll fix you something to eat."

"Not at this hour, you won't. Go back to bed."

"Sit, if you value your life."

He dropped into a chair at the kitchen table, too exhausted to argue.

"Nicholas, I've been thinking…"

He smiled. "That means I'm in trouble."

"Not yet. As long as we have Nanny, why don't I start going with you to the surgery on Wednesdays? You'd get home much sooner and not be as tired. I could take care of the minor aches and pains while you tend to the really sick patients."

"No!"

"Why not?" she demanded, her voice rising.

"It's no place for you."

"You didn't mind letting me help in London. That wasn't exactly Mayfair!"

"I said no and there's an end to it."

"Really! And I have nothing to say about it."

"No, you don't."

"I don't understand why it was all right in London but not here."

"You weren't my wife then, that's why." They glared stubbornly at each other. She clattered a plate of cold beef and cheese in front of him and crossed her arms. He ignored her by picking up *The Post*.

On the front page was a new scandal involving horse racing at Brighton Beach on Coney Island. The only words in the story that meant anything were "Coney Island." Where he had seen Kit. Recovered. With Rama Weisberg. He laid the paper aside.

He ate a few bites, drank a little coffee and pushed the plate away. Then he looked up at her, still standing with her arms crossed, waiting for him to say something. "I'm sorry," he said. "I shouldn't have snapped at you. But I mean what I say." Then with a sigh, he added, "I don't believe I can eat anything more. But thank you for fixing it."

She picked up the dishes and the cup and when she turned again, he was leaving the kitchen, walking with a shambling gait quite unlike his normally erect carriage. She stepped to the kitchen doorway as he started up the stairs, holding to the banister like an old, old man.

"Nicholas..." Regretting their argument, she followed him from the kitchen and heard him mumble, "Why didn't he come to me? I must see him. I must know why." She stopped, her hands clasped together and rigid.

In answer to the knock, Kit opened the door of the flat. A telegraph boy gave him a message, one that stopped him in his tracks. NICHOLAS ASKS TO SEE YOU MRS. NS

The first flash of happiness died. Fear rose in its place. She had told him Nick never wanted to see him again. Nick must be ill. Perhaps very ill. He left immediately. Night was falling as Kit approached the yellow house. The last few small missing pieces of his past with Nick fell into place. Their life together, his and Nick's. The love, the laughter, the disagreements, the vicious quarrel at St. Denys Hill. *Life* together. That was what it had been and that was why no one else could take Nick's place.

When Nick's wife answered his knock, he said, "I came as soon as I could, Mrs. Stuart. Is something wrong?"

She spoke no word of greeting, but nodded curtly. "I would say welcome, but you're not."

Her hostility took him off guard. "I'm sorry you feel that way. Why do you?"

"You're the cause of all my trouble. I sent for you because I will never be rid of you until my husband knows his pet patient is alive and well. Reassure him. Then never come here again."

"You haven't told me what's wrong."

"Exhaustion. Because of you. He worked himself almost to death taking care of you, and has worried ever since you were ungrateful enough to disappear without so much as a by-your-leave."

"Did you tell him I telephoned the day I returned?"

"Yes!" She almost spat the word.

"And what did he say when you told him?" He wondered why she was lying.

"He repeated what he had said before: he said he hoped he never set eyes on you again. He said there were many doctors in the city and you would just have to find one to take care of you."

"Then why did he ask for me?"

Her mouth opened in retort, then slowly closed. Her shoulders slumped a little. "I suppose he changed his mind."

Kit let it go. No point in belaboring her lie. Nick was sprawled on the floor of the parlor, laughing, as his small boy crawled over him from one side to the other.

"Nicholas," Bronwyn said in a brittle voice, "you have a visitor."

Nick looked up; the smile froze on his face. "You!" he said. Over Jamie's protests, he got to his feet. Jamie pulled at his trousers and cried for attention. Nick picked him up. "Wait here," he said to Kit, and carried his son upstairs.

Bronwyn directed one withering look at Kit before leaving the room. "Reassure him," she said. "Then get out of our lives."

As Kit watched her leave, a poignant memory came back: she held the infant in her arms and smiled like an angel as he sang a lullaby. That woman had been nothing like the cold, thin-lipped woman he had just seen. She hated him now; that would never change. He didn't wait for Nick to return.

Coming down the stairs, Nick saw the door close and he hurried outside just as Kit turned his horse's head to ride away. "Wait!" Nick cried. "Don't go." Clouds had slid in front of the full moon and they could see one another's face only indistinctly. Nick approached slowly. "Why didn't you write or call? I was almost out of my mind with worry."

Kit opened his mouth to say, 'I did. She didn't tell you.' The words died unspoken. "I thought it would be better not to," he said.

Covered by darkness, Nick dared to put his hand on Kit's bent leg. Kit shuddered a little and trapped Nick's hand between his thigh and the horse.

"Kit, come with me to the widow's walk. We could talk there."

"What if your wife saw us?"

"We're only going to talk. How could she object? She'd understand that two old friends have much to catch up on after so long a time."

Kit marveled at Nick's naiveté. Did he really know his wife so little? "It's late," Kit said. "The breeze is cold. She'd think we were mad."

"Not at all. I go to the widow's walk to think in all kinds of weather. And I'm sure she's already gone to bed. She was tired today."

"Then by all means, let's go to the widow's walk. And think."

Kit dismounted and followed Nick around the house into the kitchen. Nick left him there and returned a few minutes later with a candle in a holder. A narrow door off the kitchen opened onto a circular staircase with wedge-shaped steps barely the width of a man's foot, and the only light was from the candle.

"Step carefully," Nick cautioned. The twisting ascent ended at another door. Nick took a heavy old key from a nail and unlocked the door, letting a blast of fresh air into the stuffy stairwell.

Below, in the gazebo, wrapped in a hooded woolen cloak, Bronwyn was startled by movement on the widow's walk. She saw them, dimly at first, then more clearly as the clouds drifted from the face of the moon. Nicholas and the Beast. Curious, she leaned forward, wondering why they had gone up there instead of staying in the comfort of the parlor.

"Somewhere out there," Kit said, sweeping his arm in the general direction of New York City, "is Broadway. I wish I could see it from here. All the electrical lights would make it look like a necklace. My theatre, of course, would be sitting there alone in the dark. No necklace of lights for that street yet. Soon there will be. Soon they'll be everywhere." They spoke of safe, mundane things for a while, unaware of the silent watcher. Gradually they ran out of things to say about the weather, medicine, the theatre.

Finally Nick said, "Where were you all those months?"

"Shoveling shit," Kit said with a laugh.

Nick scowled. "Very well. Don't tell me."

"It's true. I traveled with a circus." He told Nick some of his life as a roustabout, not mentioning the Cossack from Russia, Kentucky.

Leaning against the white balustrade, Nick laughed. "The greatest actor of the English speaking world—cleaning up after horses."

"And elephants, and trained goats. Big cats. Even birds. Amazing how much of it there is in a circus."

Nick's smile faded. "How could you not have come to see me as soon as you came back? When I saw you at Coney Island with Miss Weisberg I didn't know whether to thank God you were home and all right, or curse you for making me suffer."

"I didn't mean to make you suffer." Without even realizing it, they had moved closer to each other. "Nico. I still love you." He put his hand on the back of Nick's head, and gave a sigh that was nearly a groan as their open mouths met in a deep kiss. Body met body, each hard and needful. With a gasp, Nick pulled away. He looked long at Kit, then without a word turned and locked the door leading from the stairwell onto the widow's walk.

Bronwyn stared, her lips parted in disbelief. The figures on the widow's walk merged into one. It looked like an embrace. But it could not be. The silhouettes broke apart only to merge again. Soft laughter floated on the night air. Terrible fear filled her—

but fear of what? Her nails dug into her palms as she whispered, "I don't understand." Unable to watch any more, she hurried inside. The door slammed behind her.

At the sharp crack of the closing door, Nick froze, and hastily broke free of the embrace. "My God, what are we doing?"

The only sounds were those of their ragged breathing and the call of an owl. Kit raked his fingers through his hair. "Come to the flat, Nico. Tomorrow night. Please. I need you. We need each other."

"Yes..." Unaccountably, Nick's eyes were drawn to the gazebo. The back of his neck prickled as if he had looked into the eyes of someone unseen. "Yes," he said again. "Tomorrow. It will be safe there."

25

Bronwyn knelt in her fallow garden and violently dug a trowel into the hard earth. Clods of dirt, many of them bearing roots of hibernating perennials, were thrown helter-skelter around her. From time to time she brushed her gloved hand across her eyes. She did not know anyone was beside her until she heard a male voice.

"Mrs. Stuart, is something wrong?"

She looked up for an instant into David Galvin's concerned face. She made no answer, but instead gouged the ragged hole deeper.

He crouched beside her. "What are you digging?" he asked.

When she looked up again, her face was disfigured by a savage grin. "A grave," she said.

"A grave?"

"Yes. A grave. And as God is my witness I wish I could put him in it!"

David stared at her. This wild-eyed woman bore little resemblance to the warm, efficient woman he admired. "Who?" he asked, bewildered.

Her answer was a bitter laugh. "Mr. St. Denys."

"But why? I know you dislike him, but…" He put out his hand and after a moment she took it, and let him help her to her feet.

"I don't dislike him, Dr. Galvin. I hate him. He's returned. And he's infested my husband's mind and heart like a canker worm. He's eaten away at my marriage for years. Now he has—he has—" She threw the trowel aside and ran toward the gazebo, where she sat bent over, crying, hitting at her knee with a clenched fist.

He followed her and sat down beside her. "What is it? What is it? What's he done to upset you so?"

She shook her head. "I don't know what he's done or how he's done it. But last night I saw him and Nicholas up there… on the widow's walk. They were together. Close together." She turned bewildered, tear-filled eyes upon him. "They—they kissed, David! I tried to make myself believe that wasn't what I saw. But it was. It was. Why? What does it mean? Oh, God, I want him dead. I want him out of our lives!"

"Mrs. Stuart," he whispered, looking sick. "Surely you are mistaken. The shadows, the moonlight— they played tricks on you. You have to believe that."

She brushed away tears and looked long at him. She made herself believe. She knew her heart would break if she didn't.

❧ ❧

Harry Fiske greeted Kit with a wide, happy grin and his Gatling-gun delivery. "Kit! Come in, come in. Whiskey? Old and smooth? I know, it's a little early in the day, but a wee drop in a strong cup of coffee does wonders. Gets me awake and relaxes me at the same time. It's so good to see you! I'm sure you have a purpose in coming here. What is it? Business or pleasure?"

Kit laughed, and took the whiskey-laced coffee, which contained more than a 'wee drop.' "Both, but mostly business. I want to place a casting call." He didn't tell Harry that the decision to perform had been a sudden one, arrived at the night before, on the widow's walk. He glanced at the clock on the wall behind Harry and smiled. Twelve hours until Nick would arrive.

"You're going to act again," Harry observed with pleasure.

"Directing Minnie has proven to me that I'm a better actor than director."

"Bunner will hate to lose you, but I know she'll be as happy as I am that you're going back on stage. This calls for a celebration. You and your young lady will have to join us for dinner, very soon."

Rama... Kit wished he knew where she was. Then he realized Harry was asking him what play he would be doing, and Kit wondered if he had asked more than once. "Hamlet. Apparently people want to see it."

"Of course. There could be no other choice for your return. And I want to write the casting call myself."

"I yield to your literary skills. There is another advert I need you to put in as prominent a place as you can."

❦

Nick did not come to the flat. As the hours passed, Kit went over every word of the brief time on the widow's walk and saw nothing amiss. Finally, hurt and disappointed, he went to bed alone near dawn.

Across the river, Nick stood again on the widow's walk in the cold wind and looked in the direction of the city, imagining he could see Kit in the flat, in bed. How much he wanted to be there! But he and God had a bargain: his loneliness for Kit's sanity. If he went back on the bargain he or someone he loved would pay dearly for it. In his mind he molded himself and Kit together the way they had been, so briefly, last night. If only the wind, or God, had not slammed that door shut...

❦

The casting call was unlike any ever before placed in the *Dramatic Mirror*:

ST. DENYS CASTING CALL
Actors Actresses
St. Denys is Back
Loaded For Bear
NOW CASTING HAMLET

And in the same issue Kit's advertisement appeared in bold print.

DANISH PRINCE SEEKING MOTHER
RAMA CONTACT KSD AT ONCE

That afternoon the door of the flat burst open without benefit of a knock. A red-haired whirlwind flung herself into his arms. "Kit!" Rama screamed, half-laughing, half-crying, "Kit! Kit! Kit!" She hugged him, smothered his face with kisses, and hugged him again.

"Madam," he said, "If you think this unseemly behavior will get you a small part in my production..."

Hamlet was cast in record time. Wardrobe frantically fitted and sewed. Properties frantically searched and created. Francis no longer wanted to act, and was hired as stage manager. The cast was made up of veterans. Rehearsals began immediately.

Kit didn't like the changes he saw in Frank and Rama. Frank loved someone else now, the mousy little man who was Minnie's prompter. And Rama encouraged the courtship of a well-dressed man with an impressive Roosevelt mustache. Ruefully, Kit admitted he missed his friends' unabashed worship. As for himself, he slept alone and waited for Nick.

❦

Day after day Nick was tormented by his need to go to Kit. But always, always, he knew God was watching, poised to punish them in some horrible way if he violated the bargain.

On a Wednesday, a heavy London-like fog moved in and blanketed the city and river with a chilling mist. Nick decided to stay at the surgery. He blessed Kelly's foresight in making sure he had a plentiful supply of firewood at the surgery. He was warm, sitting wrapped in blankets beside the fire, lost in thought, when someone came in. He gave a start. He thought he had locked the door. The surgery was unlit except for the fireplace.

"Hello?" he said, getting up and laying the blanket aside. "Wait, I'll get the light."

Kit's voice came from the darkness around the door. "No need."

"Kit? How did you know where I was?"

"It's Wednesday. The weather is bad so I didn't think you'd go home. And you weren't with me. Why, Nico? I thought things were good for us again. But you never came to me." Kit stayed where he was. So did Nick.

"I wanted to. I intended to. I can't explain it, Kit. But I have to stay away to protect you, to protect all of us."

"From what?"

"From God. He doesn't like broken promises, you know. I told you I can't explain." He hesitated, then said wistfully, "Won't you come closer to the fire?"

"If I came closer to the fire, your God might throw me in it." He sighed. "This isn't the last act I had in mind, Nico, but if it's the one you've written I suppose I must live with it. I came intending to give you two things. Myself and this." He held out a flat parcel. "Will you take this, at least?"

Nick opened it and when he looked up, Kit was gone. If he had not held in his hand a new photograph of Kit in costume as Hamlet, he would have thought it was all his imagination. He sat down beside the fire once more, and leaned forward with the photograph in his hands. Nick remembered the other photograph, the one given him in London long ago, when Kit had been young and his face perfect. In this picture the face was older, scarred, and oddly ravaged though still handsome. The brooding dark eyes challenged him.

When Nick returned home the next day, he hid the picture in the secret locked drawer in his desk along with the Sonnets and his journal.

※ ※

Three weeks passed. Bronwyn could no longer sustain the belief she had forced on herself while with David. There had been no trick of moonlight and shadow. She had seen what she had seen, though it was beyond the realm of meaning. She saw it waking. She saw it when she slept. And she saw something else: the horrified expression on David Galvin's face when she told him. He knew something, but she couldn't bring herself to ask him. There had to be someone who could tell her. She went to Ida, and tremulously told Ida what she had seen.

Ida's answer was hasty. "You need to talk to your pastor, Bronnie," she said. "I can't help you with this."

Bronwyn had to wait two more days, until she knew Nicholas would be late returning from the city, before she went to Reverend Lanston. He greeted her with a warm smile. "Mrs. Stuart. What brings one of my favorite parishioners to see me? Would you like some tea?"

She nervously nodded her head, though tea was not what she wanted from him. Her cup rattled against the saucer and she put them on the desk.

"I have a friend," she said, forcing the words out. "She needs help. She's too shy to ask you herself, so I'm her go-between." She hoped he believed her. "She has reason to believe her husband has ... been drawn into ... into ... sin." Bronwyn could feel her cheeks burn. "She doesn't know what to do."

The minister frowned slightly. "There are many sins, my dear. What nature of sin? Carnal?"

"S-she doesn't really know. She has no proof that there is an actual sin. And it certainly *couldn't* be—carnal! No. But there is someone in his life who ... who has a pernicious influence on him. She loves her husband. How can she save him?"

He tented his fingers and peered over them at her. "No proof of his sin? Perhaps there is none. Perhaps your friend is making an assumption. Assumptions are often wrong."

"But if she finds proof...?" she asked in a distraught whisper.

"She should ask God for guidance. It is not up to her to judge anyone else, for she, too, has sinned and fallen short of the glory of God, as have we all. She promised before God to cherish her husband in sickness and health, for better or worse, until death. She promised to obey him, just as he promised to cherish her, and cleave only unto her, until death. If her husband has turned to another woman, perhaps your friend has fallen short as a wife. She needs to look inward and examine her own mind and soul."

Platitudes! she thought bitterly. *I need help to fight a demon and he gives me a sermon.*

A week after her visit to the church Bronwyn and Nanny took Jamie across to the city to buy a new pair of shoes. As they left the shoe shop, a tall young woman entered. She had flaming red hair beneath a wide, elaborate hat. Bronwyn said in an undertone to Nanny, "Take Mr. Wiggly for ice cream, will you? And then take him home. I'll be along in just a little while. I need to speak to this lady."

Nervously, she loitered beside the door while the tall young woman finished her business and started to leave. Bronwyn blocked her way. "Miss Weisberg?" she asked. "The actress?"

The young woman paused and smiled. "I am."

"You came to my house to see Mr. St. Denys when he was a patient there."

"Ah. Mrs. Stuart." When Bronwyn did not move, Rama asked with a touch of impatience, "Is there some way I may help you?"

"I—I don't know. " Then the unplanned words came out in a rush. "You're a friend of Mr. St. Denys. You've known him for a long time, haven't you?"

"Yes."

"How can you be his friend? Don't you know what a bad man he is? He's evil, Miss Weisberg! Evil in a way that is beyond comprehension." She cut off the lava flow of anger. "Forgive me. Please. But I... I have to know about him. There's something I—need to understand. I thought perhaps you would help me."

Rama's eyes narrowed. The silly little chit! Her Kit—*evil?* She should leave the woman standing there like the fool she was. Instead she said, "Let's have tea and a chat. Almost anything is better taken with tea."

Later, Bronwyn huddled in the cab as it clattered over the great bridge. She could not wrap her understanding around what the actress had told her. Nicholas and The Beast: lovers. "I tried, believe me I tried," the woman had said, "to rid Kit of your husband's influence. I tried to convince Kit he loved me instead. I tried for years. Give it up, Mrs. Stuart. It won't work. I don't understand how two men can feel that way about one another, but they do. They need each other the way we need air and nothing you or I can do will change them."

Bronwyn had the dizzying sensation of being pushed slowly toward a precipice. Feverishly, she knew she had to find something that would prove either her husband's innocence or his guilt. There was one place that might hold what she needed.

Nick would not be home until late. David, Nanny, and the household help were gone for the day. Jamie was asleep. Bronwyn stood for a long time in front of the roll top desk. She saw nothing but familiar papers and records, neatly stacked or pigeonholed.

Her hands were icy as she unlocked the secret drawer that had so delighted Nick, and laid out the contents in front of her. A photograph of the Beast. A small, very old book with *Sonnets by William Shakespeare* stamped in faded gold on a soft, leather cover.

A larger book stamped "Journal". She had never seen these things before.

She wanted to tear the photograph into bits and watch them burn.

She made herself put it back in the drawer. The old book was lovely to look at and to touch. On the fragile first page were words written in a firm hand she did not recognize:

> Without the Sanction of Society
> Without the Sanction of the Church
> Without the Sanction of God
> Without the sanction even of yourself
> I love you."

Even then she could have convinced herself it meant nothing. But the fourth line was written in her husband's clear script, which was as familiar to her as his smile. Nausea swept her.

She returned the picture and book to the drawer and opened the third object: the Journal . She read the day-by-day account of her husband's months of caring for the Beast. Every entry showed his extreme distress. One page had a scratched-out paragraph; she held it to the light. A few words could still be deciphered. Damning words. ~~And Mulholland was his lover before I was~~

"No," she whimpered. "No. No. No." She turned pages and read on, and from another page other damning words jeered at her: 'I have to believe my Kit lives.'

"'My Kit,'" she choked. "'*My Kit!*'" She ripped the page from the book, and watched it burn, just as she wanted the Beast to burn in Hell for what he'd done and for whatever sick and insane thing he was doing.

The next day, a hand-written invitation to Dr. and Mrs. Nicholas Stuart arrived by messenger, accompanied by two front-row-center tickets for the opening night of *Hamlet.* The handwriting on the envelope was the same as that in the old book.

Nick escorted his wife to opening night. Despite a light snow a long queue had formed outside the theatre. Throughout the play, Bronwyn watched her husband, not the stage. She hated the pride she saw in his face. The Beast was winning. Somehow she had to find a way to confront her husband. She prayed to God to show her how.

🦅🦅

As Kit examined Yorick's skull and said the words appropriate to the scene, he knew something wasn't right. None of it had felt right, not during rehearsals and not now. The play seemed endless. *Something isn't right,* he thought again with growing desperation as he recited the familiar words, phrases, and sentences. *What am I doing wrong?*

The applause was enthusiastic. The cast was ecstatic. The reviews the next day both from local critics and critics from as far away as Chicago were full of praise. Kit's private evaluation of his performance, stated only to his reflection in the mirror, was brutal. "You stunk like a three-day-dead fish."

Performance after performance, he felt the same way. It puzzled him. How could everyone else be so impressed with the power and quality of his performance when he did not find it even adequate?

When the initial run of *Hamlet* ended, Kit shocked the theatre world by not renewing contracts. The playbills were removed from the outside of the theatre. He paid the cast and crew more than they had contracted for. Further shocks awaited his friends and the theatre world: another sign appeared. FOR SALE.

Rama stormed into the flat and demanded to know what had happened. "Are you ill again?" she asked.

"Not at all. It came to me during the last performance."

"What did?"

"That I don't want to do this anymore."

"Kit, you can't mean that! What will we do without you?"

He kissed her cheek. "My sweet, you have followed me from country to country, suffered with me, loved me, been my friend...for how many years?"

"What has that to do with anything?"

"It's time to cut the apron strings. You're a good actress, my girl. You may even be a great actress. Without me to distract you and hold you back, you can be what you have the talent to be." He saw her protest coming and stopped it with his finger against her lips. "You've got to make your own life because I won't be here anymore."

"But why?"

"Just because."

Nick did not believe the rumors until he went to the theatre and saw the sign for himself. Kit was not in the flat, and cold fear struck Nick deep inside. He hurried downstairs to the dressing room. Kit was not there, either, and the room was tidy, as if the owner did not expect to come back. He found him at last in the auditorium, alone on the stage.

The darkness was relieved only by barred shadows cast by the moonlight. Kit had taken off his coat and held it hooked over his shoulder as he slowly paced the stage, his head lowered. Several times he paused and looked up, where lines and sandbags and the catwalk were hidden in the blackness. Once he gently laid his hand on one side of the proscenium arch. Another time he stopped and gazed without moving at the scenery, still set up for the last scene of *Hamlet*.

Nick went up the side stairs to the stage, unnoticed. When he was near, he said softly, "Kit, what are you doing in the dark? All alone?"

At the sound of his voice, Kit looked up. "I'm not alone," he said. "You're here."

"What has happened? You closed the play. Now you're selling the theatre. Are you buying a larger one? This one really is too small now."

"Nico, I'm going home. To the Hill."

Nick could not breathe for an instant. "What! My God, why?"

"This…" He made a gesture that encompassed the theatre and his life in it. "This means nothing to me anymore. I was terrible as Hamlet and I didn't even care."

"Terrible? But the reviews were wonderful."

"I've never trusted any critic but myself," Kit said with a shrug.

"You can't go."

"Nico, what if one day you woke up and found that being a doctor meant no more to you than an unimportant way to spend your time? What if it didn't matter anymore whether your patients lived or died? What if you didn't want to practice medicine anymore?"

"But that's not the same."

"Of course it is. Acting was my passion, as medicine is yours. And if I can't feel the passion in me for what I do, I don't want to do it. The world doesn't need one more mediocre actor." He was silent a moment. "I don't know if Kit St. Denys exists anymore, if he ever did. I'm Michael and Romeo and Hamlet and Angel Claire and Cyrano, even Tom Rourke and Xavier St. Denys. I have to go home. I have to find out if I'm substance or shadow."

"Kit…"

"I envy you, you know. You never had to be ashamed or hide where you came from. Your father was strict, but he was a father and you knew he loved you. Your mother held you when you were a baby, the way your wife holds your son. You and your wife dream dreams for that little boy. No one dreamed a dream for me until Lizbet. You've made a good life here. You've passed on your name to your son. My name is not even my own. And regardless of the reason I did it, I murdered my own father."

"And paid dearly for it."

"I'm sure the old man is laughing at me in Hell. Which changes nothing. I'm going home."

"You can't go."

"I already have passage on the *Clarise*."

Nick cried, "I sacrificed two years of my life and my family's life to save you, and this is the thanks I get. Desertion."

"My dear Nico, I have waited for you night after night. I have sought no one else out. Very well. You made your choice, and for you it was the right one. You need a nest to settle down in. You have that with her. I have nothing to give you."

"Yourself. I'll find a way to—"

"What self do you want?" Kit asked with a despairing gesture. "The lunatic? The clown in costume? The inconstant lover who's been with every man but the 'ugly, the insane and the dead?'"

"That's low!"

"Yes. It was. I'm sorry. Nico, I want you to stay away from the dock when I leave. I love you. I'm giving you the last and best gift I can. Now go away. Please."

Nick swallowed the painful lump in his throat. "When do you leave?"

"Tomorrow"

"I have until then to change your mind."

Kit said, "Go home, Nico. I don't want to see you again."

That night a stormy wind scratched at the walls of the yellow house, but the small parlor was as cozy as any Christmas scene from Dickens. A fire lived within the hearth. Bronwyn sat beside an electric light, mending one of Jamie's dresses. Nick lay on the floor near the fire, and lifted Jamie high in the air as Jamie shouted,

"Bood! Bood!" Bronwyn glanced up from her mending. When she returned to it, she was back in her dark thoughts.

Nick's thoughts, too, were only half with the high-flying eagle he held kicking and wiggling over his head. Finally, he lowered the child. "My arms are wearing down, Jamie." To which Jamie replied, "Bood! Mo' bood!" Nick hoisted him once more. Then, getting up, he said, "Enough bird, my fine-feathered son. I think it's bedtime."

"I'll take him," Bronwyn said, laying aside her mending. She did not look at Nick.

"No, I want to."

She settled back and picked up the dress. Nick looked down upon her lowered head. How had it come to this? Silent people in a silent house. Not meeting each other's eyes. Professional in front of the patients and David, but polite strangers after hours. They went to church Sunday mornings, and then separated by unspoken agreement when they came home. They were brought together only at meals and nights such as this, with Jamie. He didn't know the reason for Bronwyn's coldness, and he had been too enervated by his soul's battle to ask her. He sighed and carried Jamie upstairs.

He took a long time getting Jamie ready for bed, then sat with him in the rocking chair and sang to him in the tuneless voice that only Jamie could love. He thought his heart would burst with love for this small child in his arms. He kissed Jamie's ear as he laid him down and drew the coverlet over him. Jamie's eyes opened halfway. Then the dewy lids slid shut; he was still smiling. His father put a gentle hand against the mop of dark hair. "My son," he whispered. "My heart."

※ ※

The morning at the hospital had been uneventful. Nick was consoling a little girl whose scalp wound he had just sutured, when he became aware of excited voices and hurrying feet. Nick gave the girl a lollipop, sent her on her way, and stepped into the hall-way to see what was causing the disturbance. A fellow doctor grabbed his arm. "There's been a terrible accident, Dr. Stuart. They're calling in all available doctors and nurses."

"What kind of accident?"

"An explosion on a ship about six miles out to sea. The Coast Guard says it's in flames and sinking. We're waiting for survivors."

There was a roaring in Nick's ears. "What ship?" he managed to ask. "Do you know?"

"The *Clarise*."

Had it not been for the voices of the people waiting for word, many of them weeping, the hospital would have been strangely quiet. Hours had passed, and still the doctors and nurses waited for the hoped-for flood of survivors from the *Clarise*. Since noon the rescue boats had brought back only corpses for safekeeping in the hospital morgue. The ship had sunk, and it was believed that all hands and most passengers went down with it.

Nick tried not to think. Francis Mulholland reeled through the door, saw Nick, and clutched his arm. Nick steadied him.

"I just heard," Francis said. His lips trembled as if he had palsy. "Has he been found?"

"We're still waiting."

Francis covered his face with his hands. "Oh, oh, my God, my God." He sagged against the wall, crying.

The clanging bells of ambulances sharpened the afternoon into a thousand knives. Four men and two women were rushed in, all suffering from hypothermia and severe burns. One by one they died. The most severely injured lingered the longest, his face burned beyond recognition. There was no way to administer morphine to ease the pain. Even after he died, his screams seemed to echo through the halls.

Numbed by horror beyond belief, Nick dragged himself into the crowded waiting room. Francis was still there; Rama was with him now, clutching his hand. Before they could ask, Nick said in a toneless voice, "I don't know. There was a man. A tall man. No identification. His face … body … no way to recognize for certain … I don't know. It could have been. It could have been. But I do not accept it." He walked away, leaving them to comfort each other.

Nick steadfastly refused to believe the thick black headlines that declared there to be no survivors. No one would know for certain who the victims were until the list of passengers and crew was verified. There were ways someone could have survived, because there had to be.

He moved mechanically through the nightmare. He treated patients. He ate and slept. Played with Jamie. Paid creditors. Did all the things that a man did every day. And hardly was aware of any of it.

And then the passenger list was published. The nightmare was now reality. Harry Fiske put out a special edition. The black-bordered front page bore the new picture of Kit as Hamlet. Its headline:

KIT ST. DENYS LOST IN CLARISE TRAGEDY
THEATRE WORLD MOURNS

Harry wrote a poignant biography of his friend. Minnie wrote a heartbroken tribute, as did other friends and colleagues. Maude Adams contributed, and Joe Jefferson and Steele MacKaye. From England had come other tributes from Henry Irving and Ellen Terry, and from Paris a poem from the disgraced and exiled Oscar Wilde. Even Charles Frohman wrote in praise of Kit, as did the Shubert brothers.

Bronwyn found the passenger list on the office floor where Nick had dropped it. Nick was not there. She braved the darkness of the twisting, narrow stairs and the heights of the widow's walk, and found him sitting with his back against the wall, Fiske's special edition in his hand. She knelt beside him. "Nicholas ... I'm sorry. Truly."

He looked long at her. "You hated him. I could see it in your eyes, though I never admitted it even to myself."

"Yes," she said. "I did. But you have lost a friend in a horrid way. I'm sorry for your loss and your grief." She gently stroked his hair and drew his head to her shoulder. "Come down from here. It's cold. Come now." Standing up, she tugged at his hand until he stood and went with her.

That night, in bed, she felt Nick shudder repeatedly, as if suppressing sobs. She turned to him. "Nicholas, I'm here, my darling. I understand. Oh, my dearest, I understand..."

As she whispered, she kissed him. He clutched her to him. Bronwyn gasped in surprise as he smothered her with ungentle kisses. When he took her it was with a roughness he had never used before. Afterward, she thought with joy, "He's mine! He's all mine now!"

Beside her, Nick wondered how a man could have physical release with someone and at the same time feel nothing but raw grief. In the darkness of the room, he saw Kit's face, with his eyebrows, eyelids, nose, and lips blackened and partially burnt away. He knew he would see it as long as he lived.

"Bronwyn," he said, his voice hollow, "you must divorce me."

Her life stopped for a moment. "What did you say?" she whispered when she could speak.

"I want you to divorce me."

"Y-you're distraught." She got out of bed and pulled on a warm robe. "I'll fix us some hot chocolate." Her robe billowed behind her as she hurried from the room, trying to outdistance the thing he had said. In the kitchen, she stood in the middle of the floor, trying desperately to remember what to do next.

Nick came into the kitchen and enveloped her in his arms. "Bronwyn, hush. Listen to me, not with your ears but with your heart. You must divorce me." She struggled, but he held her tightly. "Listen to me! I betrayed you. With him. Not once, but many times. I didn't mean to hurt you. But I have. Terribly. I was a fool to think I could have him without hurting you."

Bronwyn struggled harder. "I don't want to know any of this. He's gone now. We can start over."

"Gone? Yes. But I'll never forget him."

Her resistance flagged and she leaned against him. "I thought you loved us. I thought you loved Jamie even if you didn't love me."

"I do love you. Both of you. I always will."

"I don't understand!" She pushed herself free of him. "You're not making sense. "

"Yes, I am, for the first time in many years. I love you, my dear girl, with all my heart. But I was in love with him, with all my soul. And there's a huge difference."

"That's impossible! He was a man! A man! It's sick and twisted and evil."

"Perhaps it is. I don't know anymore. I know only that when he died, so did part of me. You need a husband who can give you his whole heart. "

"I don't care about that." Her face was distorted with grief. "I've loved you from the day I walked into the surgery in London. Whatever you can give me is enough."

"No," he said. "It isn't." He reached out to touch her and she stepped back. His hand dropped to his side.

A strand of hair fell across her face; her breathing was ragged. "And if I refuse to do what you want? Will you abandon me?"

"No. We'll stay together. And we'll live out our lives like prisoners chained to each other." After a moment he said, "Bronwyn, I can't make you understand how it is with me; I don't understand it myself. I told him once that he was my private devil.

He said I was wrong, that he was my one true love. I didn't see the truth of it—" His voice broke. "—until I saw him die."

With all the strength of her arm, she slapped him. "Your 'one true love!' How can you say that? It's vile. It's filthy. If it's true, then you have broken every law of nature and spit in the face of God."

"Bron—"

She slapped him again. The print of her hand was a clear brand on his cheek. "You will never see your son again."

"You can't mean that," he said. He reached out toward her and she took another step backward. Her fists were clenched at her sides.

Her face was cold and pinched as she said in a controlled, hard voice, "Pray that God can forgive you, for I never will. And when Jamie is old enough, he will be told what manner of creature you are. He will hate you. I'll see to that."

※ ※

The passenger train jolted its passengers awake as it groaned to a stop in Chicago in the small hours of the morning. Kit apologized to the lady against whose shoulder he had been thrown. After a leisurely cup of coffee in the station, he bought a ticket on the next train to "anywhere between here and California." He was given a ticket to Kansas City, Missouri. St. Denys Hill beckoned with a siren's song, but it was too safe a harbor. He had questions that needed answering before he went home.

As stubbled brown cornfields flew by the windows of the train, he thought about the young man who was steaming across the Atlantic aboard the *Clarise*. Kit didn't even remember his name. He'd been a walk-on in *Hamlet,* and Francis had told him the boy pined to go home to his sweetheart but had not the money to do so. Kit had met him by accident the morning of departure. He looked so woebegone that Kit had impulsively given the astonished boy his ticket with a cheerful, "My best to you and your girl." By the time the *Clarise* sailed, Kit was well on his way to Chicago, carrying with him only a carpetbag and his guitar. *The phoenix*, he thought, *about to give birth to myself again.*

He looked forward to working with his hands and his back, as he had done with the circus. He wanted to wear himself out physically, and sleep like a corpse so there would be no time to think about Nick for a long, long time. Maybe he'd find the Nellis Bros.

Circus and that "Great Cossack Rider, Andrei Balakirev" again and start a new career as a circus performer. Why not?

Inevitably, his thoughts turned to Nick. Kit's lawyer was to notify Nick in a fortnight that Kit had secretly set up a trust fund for his use. Now Nick could set up a dozen poverty surgeries if he wanted, and never have to worry about money. *I did a good deed*, Kit thought. That was more amusing than being a circus star. A sleepy smile touched his lips as he drifted to sleep listening to the rhythm of the train's wheels. *Goodbye, Nico, Nico, Nico.*

In Kansas City he learned of the fate of the *Clarise*. Horrified, he hurried to the telegraph office and wrote a message: **NICO. DID NOT SAIL ON THE CLARISE. I AM SAFE AND WILL BE IN TOUCH SOON.** The telegraph agent waited impatiently for the message to be slid beneath the cage. Slowly Kit crumpled the message and threw it away. "I've changed my mind," he said. A clean amputation. This time he would do it right.

26
Los Angeles, California

Kit smiled down at the cheque in his hand. Five dollars.
"Thank you," he said to the magazine editor who had given
it to him.

The editor, John Pennypacker, grinned and settled his thick
glasses more firmly on his nose. "It was a pleasure, Mr. Rourke.
Do you have any more stories for us?"

"If you like." He had many stories on paper and many more in
his head, for during his travels he had discovered an unsuspected
gift for writing. When he had been in California as a boy, he had
not comprehended the hugeness of America, its savage beauty,
and its sometimes simple savagery. It was a dozen countries rolled
into one. His stories reflected these things.

They were tales that came out of his experiences during the time
he was with the circus, and the months he worked his way west
from Kansas City. Months of listening to strangers. Months of
backbreaking work stringing barbed wire and harvesting wheat
and picking oranges. Months of seeing the anger, resentment, and
sometimes violence between immigrant workers and bosses. Long
weeks delayed by snow, with only the stories in his head and the
soft music of the guitar to keep him company.

When he arrived in Los Angeles, he had, on a whim, taken one of the stories to the editor who sat across the desk from him. Pennypacker handed him a copy of the magazine. "Assume you want one for your portfolio."

"My... oh, yes." It looked odd to see the name Jack Rourke as author beneath the title, "Playing the Moon." He knew the story was not literature, but it had struck a chord with the editor. And, judging from the handful of letters Pennypacker gave him, it had also resonated with the readers.

"There's more to you than meets the eye, Rourke," said Pennypacker as he leaned back in his chair.

Kit laughed and folded the cheque. "Not at all. I'm just a chance visitor from your Mother Country, scribbling down impressions."

"Huh-uh. You've got a dramatic flair, like a playwright. And you look familiar. I could swear I've seen you before."

Kit smiled easily. He doubted that Pennypacker recognized him. He had maintained the short-cropped beard and could see little resemblance between his face in the mirror now and his face in the mirror as it had been months earlier. "Unless you're been to England, sir, it's unlikely we would have met."

The chair creaked as Pennypacker leaned forward again. "Ah, it doesn't matter anyway. The publisher wants more stories from you. And—" he pointed at the letters in Kit's hand. "—as you can see, so do the folks who read us. Y'know, young fella, your writing reminds me of a crackerjack writer named London. Energetic. A bit of a wild boy. Ever hear of Jack London?"

"I've read some of his work. I'm flattered if you see any comparison."

"Yup. We missed out on London because my publisher's a skinfl—" He coughed to cover up. "I wanted to buy some of London's stories last year but the publisher wouldn't hear of it. Didn't like the man. Now he's gotten pretty well-known and we'd have to pay him too much. But we got you. You give me a series of stories and we'll bill you as the new Jack London."

"I don't think so," Kit said with a laugh. "The only thing we have in common is a first name. His work is far beyond anything I'll ever do."

"Just get us the stories and let us be the judge of that."

"I'll see." He left the newspaper office and stepped into the noisy, bustling world of Los Angeles. He stood bathed in the bright California sunshine and wanted to be home again. He wanted to see the mist rising around the walls of the Hill. He wanted to hear Big Ben again, and get excited at the possibility of seeing the new King. The Queen was dead; long live the King. Home. And home was nowhere in this country.

He began buying every British newspaper he could find, feeding his homesickness. Only one thing held him back from going home: he had to contact Nick one more time, ask his forgiveness for the cruel charade of the past year. He wired a simple message to Nick at the yellow house. "I AM ALIVE. IF YOU WISH TO CONTACT ME..."

When a telegraph boy put the answer into his hand, he read it in disbelief, and then read it again. HE HAS DESERTED US. I WISH YOU BOTH THE JOY OF SERVING SATAN YOUR MASTER. B. STUART

"Deserted?" Kit said aloud, in disbelief. What madness was this? Nick would never have left her. He would never have left his son. And if he wasn't in New York with them, where was he?

And then on a sunny day on which he was thoroughly tired of California with its abundance of overly sweet flowers, and palm trees that looked like upended chambermaids' mops, he opened the *Times* to a story and a picture that made him sit up straighter, with an explosive "I'll be bloody damned."

A group of placard-carrying men and women had demonstrated outside Parliament while the King was making his Opening Day speech. Their chants and signs demanded safeguards for child factory workers, demanded limits to the hours the children could work, demanded schools for them. A dozen demonstrators had been manhandled by the police and thrown into gaol. There they went on a hunger strike. Among the names listed was Nicholas M. Stuart, Physician.

Most of the protestors in gaol, such as Emmaline Pankhurst and W. T. Stead, were well known to the public. There was nothing new about them. So the story concentrated upon Stuart, the new name in the rogue's gallery. A grainy picture showed him scuffling with a police officer. Mr. Stuart had returned from America and established the St. Denys Surgery For Women and Children, a charity institution that provided health care for the indigent. It was rumored that Mr. Stuart and Mr. W. T. Stead were communists.

"Nico—a communist?" Kit spluttered. "He's as political as a potato! He wouldn't know a communist if one bit him. And the

St. Denys Surgery—!" Kit was overcome with tenderness. "I must go home and save him from himself. And I can't let him get away with putting my name on a place of good works. It will ruin my reputation." He drew a deep breath. "My God. My dear God. I must go home."

⚜

Nick bent over and peered into the mouth and throat of the pale girl. "Much better," he said. "All you needed was rest and good food and someone to coddle you for a day or so." She adored him with lackluster eyes sunken in a gaunt face. As with so many of the London girls he saw, her arms and legs were thin, all out of proportion with the burgeoning belly of her pregnancy.

He had been stunned when the New York attorney notified him of the trust fund Kit had set up just before he sailed to his death. At first he had not wanted to touch the money. But when it became too painful to live in New York forbidden to see Jamie, he decided to return home and put Kit's money to good use.

Nick was quietly proud of this surgery he had opened in a once-nice home on the edge of the city's decay, within walking distance for his patients. When he first saw it, the brick house had the air of a raddled old whore and he was able to buy it for almost nothing. For the first time he understood Kit's satisfaction in restoring his theatre.

Nick put a great deal of the Foundation funds into turning the old whore into a smiling lassie, dressing her in cheerful colors. Upstairs were three lying-in rooms and three bedrooms, and each room had two cots with bright coverlets, white starched curtains at the windows, and pictures on the walls. The patients seldom wanted to go home. Downstairs were two examination rooms, and one immaculate room where he delivered babies and did minor surgeries. A small office and an even smaller bedroom served his simple needs.

Outside, behind the wrought iron fence that hugged the property, was a white sign with black letters:

St. Denys
Women's & Children's
Free Surgery
N. M. Stuart
Physician & Surgeon

Below the words was a silhouette of a woman's head superimposed over a caduceus. Since most of his patients could not read, he had pondered what to use for a symbol. The housekeeper suggested, "Use the snakes and pole." Mystified, Nick had asked, "Snakes and pole? I don't know what you mean." She pointed to the caduceus on the cover of the medical periodical on his desk and said, "That. It'll be like a pub sign. Everyone will recognize it."

Since the day he returned from America he had worked without ceasing. Healing the pain of others was the only way he could ignore his own. Along the way he found something completely unexpected: notoriety. It had begun innocently enough with a visit by W. T. Stead, a crusader lauded by some as a hero and reviled by others as a communist and anarchist. "Though," Stead remarked, "I'm not quite certain how one can be both. Join us," he urged Nick. "We've done much to stop the exploitation of women and children, but we've barely scratched the surface of what needs to be done."

The tragedy of the Rourke brothers was still vivid in Nick's mind, as it would always be. "I'll do what I can," he said. "Though I don't know how much help I can be."

Stead beamed. "Good man! Those of us who have been involved in reform for many years are getting tired. We need new blood. Young men like you, who see wrongs and try to make them right. We won't see true reform in our lifetime, but we can't let that stop us."

Against Nick's will, Stead had pressed him into service as a speaker. Many of the women's groups to whom he spoke, were Suffragists, more interested in getting women the vote than in other forms of social reform. To his own surprise, Nick had an ability to persuade, and drew some of those outspoken women to embrace his cause, too.

"Ladies adore you," Stead chortled. "Every time you speak, we have a capacity attendance. And we are getting some influential supporters thanks to you." He grinned at Nick. "According to my wife, it's your eyes."

"That's ridiculous," Nick said, blushing.

He found an untapped well of anger deep inside, anger that led to writing letters to newspapers and politicians, carrying signs and getting arrested. And after his first experience in gaol, he grimly decided that prison reform needed to be looked into as well.

It all helped him forget the pain of losing Kit, and the more recent pain of learning from Bronwyn's attorney that the divorce had been granted, that she had married David Galvin, and that the court had allowed Dr. David Galvin to adopt the child. He was also, the letter coldly informed him, forbidden by the court to contact Jamie before he was twenty-one, and could do so then only if his son initiated the contact. With that letter, all ties with America were severed.

※ ※

Mrs. Lowell, the surgery's five-foot-tall head housekeeper, had a bulldog jaw and a bulldog devotion to the surgery and its founder. Her official job was to supervise everything but the medical care at the London surgery, and terrorize tradesmen who tried to cheat them out of a bob or two. She was also the self-anointed protector of the doctor's time and person. No one got past her.

One morning she paused at the window and watched as a tall, foreign-looking stranger approached the surgery. He stopped, looked at the sign, and appeared to laugh. A moment afterward the doorknocker sounded. She answered the summons and stared up at him.

His skin was an unEnglish golden brown but his neat, short beard and his hair were so blonde as to be almost white. A livid scar stood out over his left eyebrow. His eyes were dark. An A-rab, she decided, no matter that he *sounded* English when he asked to see the doctor. After all, a person could *sound* like anything. And for all she knew some A-rabs had blond hair. When she did not answer his request to speak with the doctor, he repeated it.

"This is a surgery for women and children," she snapped, folding her arms over her ample chest. "*Poor* women and children. You don't look poor. And you ain't a woman." She looked him up and down. "And you ain't a child, that's certain."

He gave a courtly bow. "Right on all counts, Horatia. You would obviously guard this bridge until death. But I'm harmless. Just tell him an old friend has come to call."

Her eyes narrowed. Bridges? Death? He was completely daft. She was tempted to tell him Mr. Stuart was not in. It would almost be the truth, since the doctor was readying to leave for a rare fortnight of rest. "I'll tell him," she grumbled, and then firmly shut the door in his face.

Nick was in the office, making a few last-minute notes for the doctor who was going to take his place for a fortnight. It was a Spartan room, with no decorations except four photographs. On the wall directly over the desk, was a faded photograph of the late Queen and beside it was a fresh photograph of King Edward VII.

On the desk were two photographs he looked at every day, many times. The only photograph he had of Bronwyn and Jamie, as he had last seen them. In it Jamie was healthy, his blue eyes merry with devilment. The other photograph was the last one he had of Kit, costumed as Hamlet.

When he was finished with his notes, he leaned back, absorbed in the photographs. How much he had once had! Now all was lost but his work. He gave a start when Mrs. Lowell came in, frowning. "Is the dairyman trying to cheat us on butter again?" he asked her, smiling.

"There's a A-rab at the door. Says he's an old friend."

"I don't know any Arabs," Nick said. "But perhaps I met him and don't rememb—"

"She means me," said the man who suddenly loomed behind her. "I may not be an Arab, but I am most certainly a gypsy."

The voice—it could not be! As if in a dream, Nick slowly got to his feet. "Yes, Mrs. Lowell. I—I think I know the gentleman. He's a friend from long ago. Please see that we're not disturbed."

"But sir, you don't know what them A-rabs will do. I hear tell they cut off people's heads for the fun of it!"

"With you as his guardian, I wouldn't dare," Kit said. He stepped around her to enter the office and firmly shut the door.

For a lifetime they looked at each other in silence, unmoving, not knowing what to say. Kit saw the photograph on the desk and said with wonder, "You still have the picture."

Then Nick touched the tips of his fingers to the soft, short blond beard. "I saw you die screaming in pain. How is it possible you're here?"

Kit held Nick's palm against his lips for a moment and looked into his eyes. He saw deep sorrow there, and Kit sensed it had nothing to do with him. "Your God made a mistake," he said softly. "He took some poor homesick lad instead." He released Nick's hand. "We're older, Nico. Are we wiser?"

"I very much doubt it," Nick said in an unsteady voice. "And I don't even care anymore. You're here. Nothing else matters."

"Can you forgive me for letting you think—"

"Plague take the past. It's over and done with. Look at you." Nick managed a shaky laugh. "You truly are burnt as dark as an Arab."

"That's what the California sun does to English skin." Kit's smile was whimsical. "Do you realize the absurdity of all this? We've been apart more than we've been together and yet... Oh, Nico, I'm bloody sick of playing hide-and-go-seek with you. Let's put an end to it."

Nick stared at Kit for an instant, and then seized him in a fierce embrace. "Never again," he said. "Never again."

The End